GUILT BY ASSOCIATION

a novel

MICHAEL FARRIS

BROADMAN
& HOLMAN
PUBLISHERS

Nashville, Tennessee

GUILT BY ASSOCIATION

a novel

© 1997 by Michael Farris
Printed in the United States of America
Published by Broadman & Holman Publishers, Nashville, Tennessee

0-8054-0155-5

Dewey Decimal Classification: F
Subject Heading: PRO-LIFE MOVEMENT—FICTION
Library of Congress Card Catalog Number: 97-19126

Library of Congress Cataloging-in-Publication Data
Farris, Michael P., 1951–
    Guilt by association / by Michael Farris.
        p.   cm.
    ISBN 0-8054-0155-5
    I. Title.
    PS3556.A7774G85   1997
    813'.54—dc21

97-19126
CIP

1 2 3 4 5   01 00 99 98 97

To Vickie

who has loved me faithfully
as I have struggled to balance my family
and my responsibilities in the courtroom.

1

Colonel Hank Danners turned the corner at Magnolia and Garden Streets in his Jeep Cherokee and bumped the curb as he parked, analyzing the spectacle half a block ahead of him. Bellingham's famous drizzle had turned into a brief, steady rain, but even so he could see Ginny quietly pleading with a coed as a young man angrily motioned toward the door of the Whatcom Women's Center for Choice. Sobbing and drenched, the young woman looked alternately at Ginny and the man, as he held the door to the clinic open. Several other men and women, holding picket signs, paused their march in front of the clinic and looked on as the man released the door and stormed toward Ginny and the young woman.

In an instant Danners was outside the Cherokee, yanking his umbrella open as he stepped gingerly toward the scene. Though still several yards away, he could hear their dispute.

"Jason, I can't do it," she blurted out between sobs. "Drive me back to the dorm, please!"

Ginny touched the woman's sleeve, keeping her eye on Jason.

Glancing at Ginny, he grabbed his girlfriend's arm. "Sarah, we've discussed this. Now let's get it over with!"

"I can't, I just can't," Sarah said weakly.

"You don't have to," said Ginny, holding her hand out to the young woman. "There are alternatives—"

"You keep out of this!" the young man snapped at Ginny.

By this time Danners was standing only a few feet away from the trio, but he held his tongue. Things weren't out of control, yet.

In a more soothing voice, the man coaxed, "Sarah, the clinic is going to close soon. We already missed one appointment. Come on, it'll be over with real quick and we can go home, huh?"

Staring at Ginny through red, glassy eyes, the woman unconsciously rubbed her abdomen and slowly followed her boyfriend's lead inside the clinic.

Ginny Kettner was somber as she and Lisa Edgar, one of her closest friends from church, lugged the protest signs down Garden Street to where Colonel Danners had parked his car.

"How many did we lose today?" Ginny asked, more of herself than her two companions.

"We saved five babies," Lisa replied in her usual optimistic tone. "And that's just the number we know of. Who knows how many just drove by without stopping."

"Yeah, but lots more got through. All those little lives."

Ginny's voice trailed off. After years of testing and careful planning, she and Jim had been unsuccessful in their efforts to have a baby. She never made it through a sidewalk counseling episode without some emotions bursting through to the surface.

The colonel gently put his hand on Ginny's shoulder. She reminded him of his oldest daughter, who was only two years younger. "Ginny, look on the bright side. We saved five babies today—five that we know about. You helped five little ones. Focus on that for now, OK?"

Though this was Danners's first foray into social activism after twenty-eight years of active duty in the air force, his organizational ability and experience as a father both made him invaluable to his new calling.

Ginny quickly regained control of her emotions and silently walked to her car, parked not far away from the colonel's. "Where's Shirley?" she asked, pointing to the empty Toyota behind her own car.

"She stayed behind with Suzie and the other three girls, waiting for the doctor and staff to leave so they can try to give them tracts again," Lisa replied.

"They have more guts than me," Ginny replied.

"And more faith than me," Danners answered. "I have a hard time believing that people so dedicated to abortion would ever soften their hearts toward God."

"Yeah, Suzie and her crew are great. See you on Tuesday night, Colonel," Lisa said.

"I'll drive by and make sure the tract team is OK," Danners said. "See ya. And remember, it really was a good day."

An hour after Danners left the clinic, Dr. Rhonda Marsano's cellular phone rang just as she got into her Volvo sedan. "Hello?" she said, knowing full well who was calling her.

"Rhonda, it's Jane. I just wanted to know how we did today. I tried the clinic number, but you were gone."

"I'm leaving the parking lot right now. We did twelve; all of them went well."

"How many were scheduled?"

Rhonda wanted to lie, but she knew it would do little good since Jane Hayward, or her partner, Karen Ballentine, would be checking the books. "We had six no-shows. The guards think that four, maybe five of them, made it to the parking lot, but the protesters were out in full force today."

"Six!" the Los Angeles woman screamed. "That's $2,100 down the drain. You've lost over $8,000 so far this month, and it's not over yet!"

"Jane, I know you're disappointed with the profitability of the clinic, but we're doing the best we can." Rhonda shifted the Volvo into reverse and backed out of the parking stall. "But it's these protesters. In fact, they're trying to hand me some kind of leaflet right now. You know, med school didn't offer a how-to-handle-demonstrators class. I'm doing what I was hired to do."

"And we pay you well—very well—to do it. I'll bet no one else in your class is making $100,000 a year just eight months after completing her residency."

"Yeah, but no one else in my class faces protesters coming and going to work every day, either. Can't your legal team do something?"

"They're working on it. At least that's what they tell me. I just wish these blasted protesters weren't so careful. It would be a whole lot easier if they would step off the sidewalk onto the property. Just a little tres-pass or two. Then we could nail their hides in court."

"They're a careful, well-organized bunch, that's for sure. I think it's that colonel who keeps them in line."

"I think we'll have to bring Vince in to see if he can work his magic with them," Jane concluded just before her voice began to break up. The steep hillsides often blocked the cellular connection as Interstate 5 wound its way toward South Lake Samish.

Before Rhonda could respond, her cell phone went dead. "Vince. Magic. Right," she mimicked, placing the phone in its cradle.

Rhonda knew Vince and the kind of magic Jane had in mind. But she had also experienced another side of Vince Davis that Jane knew nothing about. The thought of seeing him again sent a silent panic through her emotions.

She wanted to call Jane back and ask if there wasn't some other way, but she knew better than to argue with her. Jane Hayward was not a sympathetic person and would not look compassionately on Rhonda's perennial problems with Vince Davis.

Rhonda exited the freeway in silence. The drizzle stopped, and the clouds parted long enough to allow a red reflection of the sunset to play on the crystal waters of Lake Samish. Whenever it rained, which was often, Rhonda wondered why anyone would choose to live in this dreary place. But as the clouds parted and the lake glistened against the moun-tain backdrop, she knew there was no place on earth more beautiful.

"I wonder how Vince is going to like beautiful Bellingham," she said under her breath as she pulled into the driveway of her rented, glass-and-cedar waterfront home. She tried to put the idea out of her mind but knew she would sleep very little that night.

2

Colonel Danners and his crew of protesters had been demonstrating at the Whatcom Women's Center for Choice ever since it opened in August, but public outcry had begun well before that. The first facility ever to offer abortions in Bellingham, Washington—a college town of seventy-five thousand situated ninety miles north of Seattle—the clinic had been the target of prayer and discussion since its inception.

A meeting at Immanuel Bible Church of Bellingham introduced Danners and others to the proposed clinic. A strong pro-life advocate with many leadership qualities, Danners soon found himself the chairman of the "Whatcom Life Coalition." From then on, all subsequent WLC meetings were held in his spacious home on the southern shore of Lake Whatcom.

Danners's first order of business was the formation of a five-person leadership council for WLC. Pastor Randy Wallace of Immanuel Bible, one of the largest churches in town, was a natural choice, as was Shirley Alper, a grandmother in her mid-sixties who had been a pro-life activist for over two decades. Ginny Kettner, the thirty-year-old wife of Pastor Jim Kettner, was chosen because of her background as a television reporter in Moses Lake, Washington. While Danners pretty much let the selection of the leadership council take its own course, he surprised everyone when he insisted on the inclusion of Suzie O'Dell as the fifth member. The clinic's main "marketing target" was college girls, he argued; therefore the council should include a college student who could relate.

Suzie was a nineteen-year-old sophomore from Spokane who was actively involved in Campus Christian Fellowship at Western Washington University. Every weekday morning at 8:30, Suzie led a group of forty brave believers as they stood in a circle next to the fountain at the campus's "Red Square" to sing and pray. Although there had been fluctuations in numbers over the years, the group had an unbroken twenty-five-year history of providing a visible Christian witness to all twelve thousand students on the secular, left-leaning campus.

After her appointment to the council, Suzie quickly proved the value of the colonel's choice. She organized her Christian friends to do a monthly "lit drop" in every dorm on campus and in many of the student-intensive apartment complexes in the Fairhaven district. Most students wouldn't admit to reading the "pro-life propaganda," but many did read the material; and it had a great effect in cutting down the profitability of the clinic. Suzie was well liked by the adult leaders and respected for her commitment.

By the time the Whatcom Women's Center for Choice opened, Danners had organized enough peoplepower to cover the clinic every Saturday—its busiest day—while he frequently cruised the sidewalks during the weekdays. Armed with picket signs, pro-life leaflets, and lots of energy, his band of protesters were drawing the attention of the community, its leaders, and the media. But not the police—Danners's group stayed strictly within the bounds of the laws regarding demonstrations in the city.

Despite their early hope that it would quickly close, the clinic persisted. Yet Danners was pleased with their progress. He knew anything worthwhile would take time to accomplish.

Rhonda Marsano had suffered from both weather and culture shock when she first arrived in Bellingham several months ago. But now, as she rambled across her kitchen with her Sunday morning coffee and plopped down on the leather couch facing the lake, she knew that today she would be able to appreciate all that Bellingham had to offer—gorgeous clear skies, majestic scenery, and peaceful living.

Rhonda had grown up in Piscataway, New Jersey, about an hour south of New York City. Her father had worked as an accountant for NBC in the City. Her mother was a part-time librarian for Rutgers University, just over the Raritan River from her neighborhood. A big Italian family, her grandparents were serious Catholics, her parents considerably less serious. Rhonda knew she had turned her back on any claim to even nominal Catholicism when she agreed to work in an abortion clinic.

As a chemistry major she had been sailing along near the top of her class at Arizona State University, in an obvious path toward medical school, when her father died during the last part of her senior year. It was all her mother could do to help her finish that last year in college.

A pre-med adviser at Arizona State told Rhonda about the Women's Choice Clinic's recruitment program. The program would finance her medical training in exchange for a four-year commitment in one of the clinics after residency was over. Her grandmother was furious when Rhonda told her she had accepted the organization's offer; her mother only commented that someone would do the abortions anyway. It was her only chance of becoming a doctor. So Rhonda went to UCLA Medical School and then served an internship and residency in two different Southern California hospitals.

A little over three more years with the clinic in Bellingham and Rhonda would be free to truly practice medicine—her lifelong dream— in any part of the country she chose. Bellingham was smaller than any places she had ever lived, and wetter, but when the sun came out, as it had this morning, Rhonda was spellbound by the mountains, the water, and the towering evergreens.

Since she worked every Saturday, she frequently took off on Sunday morning and headed south to Seattle or north to Vancouver, British Columbia. Both locations offered the profound beauty she loved as well as the urban cultural atmosphere of a large port city. Walking through Vancouver's massive Stanley Park seemed to restore a bit of personal dignity that she subconsciously felt slipping away with her grisly job. She tried to believe she was helping people, but it was draining.

She toyed with the idea of staying in the area after fulfilling her commitment to the clinic, but because of the nature of her present practice, she knew she would have to move a considerable distance to have any real chance of changing her image from an abortionist to a doctor who wanted to save lives.

Rhonda drained the last sip of coffee from her mug and glanced at her watch. Seeing the time, she snapped back to reality and scrambled to her feet. Professor David Gleason would arrive in twenty minutes to take her on yet another outing to Seattle.

She had met Gleason, a sociology professor at Western Washington University, at a coffee shop in the Fairhaven district, a liberal neighborhood that used to be a separate town a hundred years ago. Like many college communities, Fairhaven was "hippy heaven" during the sixties. But unlike most, it retained its counterculture flavor—replete with coffeehouses, long hair, and Volkswagen buses smeared with psychedelic art—long after the flower child era had passed. Here, Rhonda's job made her a hero of "the movement." Environmentalists were held in great esteem, but they were a dime a dozen. Bellingham's first abortionist was a rare commodity and a veritable hero in this politically correct community.

David had been delighted to find Rhonda. She was beautiful, and her "feminist" practice enhanced his standing among his liberal peers. Inwardly, however, Rhonda's views were more traditional, and she was far from enthralled with David's all-consuming commitment to the movement.

As she finished touching up her minimal makeup, her thoughts wandered to a comparison between David and Vince. As much as she had been hurt by Vince, it still wasn't much of a contest.

A knock at the door jolted the subject from her mind. She grabbed her purse, Eddie Bauer jacket, and the obligatory umbrella—just in case—and headed out for a day in the city. The subject of Vince would have to wait.

4

Suzie O'Dell waited for just a moment on Lakeway Drive before completing her left-hand turn in her roommate's car onto the short, dead-end street where Colonel Danners and his wife, Evie, lived. Their house was a light blue, two-story colonial with grey trim and shutters and a beautiful lawn that sloped down to the waterfront of Lake Whatcom. Suzie always showed up early for their pro-life meetings; she enjoyed being in a real home—a welcome escape from the charged atmosphere of her coed dorm.

"Suzie, come on in. I knew it would be you," Evie said with a broad smile as she greeted her at the front door. "Nice and early as usual."

"Hope I'm not too early," Suzie replied, timidly stepping inside.

"Not at all. You know my husband, there's no such thing as too early."

"I've noticed," Suzie said with a laugh.

"Can I get you something?" Evie asked as they walked down the hallway to the living room.

"I don't want to be a bother," Suzie replied. Evie knew Suzie's polite routine. She would accept a cup of tea and some fresh cookies, then walk around the periphery of the living room, looking once more at the staggering collection of family and military photographs that graced its walls. This family had truly lived all over the globe. The pictures simply fascinated this nineteen-year-old, who was now as far away from home as she had ever been. Spokane was only 360 miles away, but it seemed like half a continent to Suzie. At times the distance felt liberating, but most of the time it just felt lonely.

"You do love those old photos, don't you Suzie?" the colonel said, suddenly walking into the room. Suzie was a little startled.

"Colonel, you scared me" she said, turning and smiling just a bit self-consciously. "Looking at your family pictures is . . . well, it reminds me of home."

"Don't you like the college?"

"I like school fine. But I'm not crazy about the dorm. It's coed, and the atmosphere is not very good. I'm hoping that a few girls from our fellowship group can find an apartment next quarter. I think I'd like that a lot better."

The doorbell interrupted their conversation. "I'd better get that," Danners said. "Evie's busy with the refreshments in the kitchen."

He returned with Randy Wallace and Shirley Alper, who had driven to the meeting together. Shirley was a long-time member of Wallace's church, and she didn't especially like driving at night.

At the appointed hour for the leadership council meeting to begin, Ginny was still missing. The colonel handed each person an agenda, fresh off his home printer, and drummed his fingers on the armrest of his chair. Military meetings had been so much more predictable.

Evie brought in a variety of drinks and cookies. Just as she finished handing the last cup of coffee to her husband, the doorbell rang again. "See, she's not too late," Evie volunteered before her husband could say anything. "Just five minutes. That's right on time in the real world."

The colonel rolled his eyes. "It's seven minutes, but that's a little better than usual" he said, trying his best not to sound disgusted. He genuinely liked all of the members of his leadership team—especially Ginny—despite her habit of late arrivals.

After Ginny was settled and Randy opened the meeting in prayer, the colonel began the agenda.

"Our main purpose tonight is to talk about how to handle this summer. Most of the college students will be out of town, which means fewer girls will be coming to the clinic. Unfortunately, Suzie will also be heading home for the summer, as will most of her team, who are so vital to our work."

"I hate to be the one to bring up more problems," Shirley said, "but I'm afraid we might see a big influx of high school girls going to the clinic in the early part of the summer. High school prom season is just around the corner—a lot of pregnancies begin on that night."

"Well, you certainly have more experience than me in this whole issue," the colonel said somberly.

"We'll just have to recruit more people to man the lines," Randy said. "I'll bring it up again at the pastor's meeting next week."

"Lot of good that'll do," Ginny replied. "Both you and my husband, Jim, have been beating that issue for months, and only a handful of churches have ever really done anything about it."

"We'll have to try again," Randy answered. "Having enough people is key to our success. The more we have on the sidewalk, the fewer who decide to go into the clinic."

Shirley set her cup of tea down on the coaster Evie had provided. "What about recruiting some high school kids? Suzie's group has certainly proven valuable when college students are the primary target. If we're going to see a lot of high school girls coming to the clinic, let's try to get as many of their peers to be on the line as possible."

"That's a great idea," Suzie replied. "Peer pressure. Positive peer pressure for a change."

"But we'll need someone to organize and train a bunch of high schoolers," Danners responded. "And all of us are stretched pretty thin already."

"Maybe my friend Lisa Edgar could help out. She's single and may have a little more time," Ginny suggested.

"Well, she's certainly been faithful on Saturdays," Randy said. "If Lisa's willing, I think we ought to use her."

"Sounds good to me," Danners said with a voice he had used hundreds of times to wrap up military meetings. "Just a couple more things. . . ."

The clinic phone rang. Rhonda Marsano glanced at her watch. Quitting time. It would be either Jane or Karen calling from Los Angeles to check on the numbers. She quickly glanced at the schedule for "no shows." Seven of the eighteen names remained unchecked. "They won't like it," Rhonda said to herself as she answered the phone.

"Whatcom Women's Center for Choice," Rhonda intoned, holding her breath.

"Boy, do you sound professional," a male voice said. "I guess you really are a doctor."

Rhonda said nothing as she was attempting to retain her composure.

"Hello . . . hello? Rhonda, are you there?"

"I'm . . . I'm here. Vince, I wasn't expecting to hear from you so soon."

"You heard I was coming?"

"Jane told me last week. 'I'm sending Vince to work his magic.' I believe those were her exact words."

He laughed, sending Rhonda's mind racing back in time. Vince's laugh made something inside her dance. Suddenly she remembered why she had fallen so hard for him.

"Do you believe in magic?" he sang the words of the 1960s hit by the Luvin' Spoonful. If he felt any reservations about bringing up the past, he certainly wasn't showing it. And his charm was working; his singing transported Rhonda back to the best months of their relationship.

"Well," she finally said, "did you have something specific in mind for this call, or are you simply letting me know that your life still consists of nothing more than oldies, fried foods, and sequential relationships?"

"Whew . . . where did that come from?"

"Oh, nowhere. Maybe Syracuse. Wasn't it a redhead in Syracuse? Or was the redhead from Austin? I forget. It's so hard to keep track."

"Hey, Bellingham isn't nearly as bad as Jane and Karen let on," Vince said, changing the subject. "It's kind of pretty here. Do you like it, Rhonda?"

"I like Bellingham. I don't like all the pressure Jane and Karen put me under because of these cancelled appointments. The clinic is still quite profitable, but that simply doesn't satisfy them. I'm tired of their pressure, Vince. I would be grateful if you . . . if you could get them off my back."

Vince brightened. "Well, that's what I'm here for, Angel. I guarantee you that in a few weeks, Jane and Karen will be singing our collective praises. We can work well together, remember?" he said with silver-lined laughter.

"Well . . . OK. But on a professional level only," she said, punching each of the last three words.

"So you won't accept the offer of an old friend to take you to a nice steak dinner? I drove past a great looking place down by the harbor. The Chart House, I think?"

"Vince, let's get three facts straight. One, it *is* a great restaurant. Two, they call it the bay, not the harbor. And three, I have plans for the evening. A date with a man I'm very serious about, a professor from the university. So I'm NOT interested in having steak with you, today or ever. Clear?"

"Well, excuse me," Vince rejoined. "I'm sorry to have troubled you, Dr. Marsano. I'll schedule an appointment for a professional consultation in a few days. If we can't be friends, can we at least be cordial?"

"I'm sorry . . . but . . . I still . . . oh, never mind," Rhonda blurted out. "I'll be cordial in our *professional* interaction only; otherwise, give me space."

"Fair enough," he said with smooth softness. "I really am sorry about the past. Cordial is OK with me. Talk to you soon."

Vince hung up the phone before Rhonda could say anything else. She hated lying about her relationship with David, but she had to find some excuse to keep Vince away from her.

An overcast sky shed little natural light through the colored glass window of Pacific Street Baptist Church as the ushers prepared for the

Sunday morning worship service. At five minutes before eleven, about half of the 150 plastic molded chairs were filled with regular attenders, with a few dozen more expected to come from the Sunday school rooms.

"Good morning, sir, welcome to our church," an elderly gentlemen at the door said as he shook hands with a handsome young man in his thirties. "Is this your first Sunday here with us at Pacific Baptist?"

"It is," the young man replied. "I'm new to town and just starting to look for a church home. First things first when you move."

"Well, we sure hope you like our church. We're still small enough to be friendly, but we're alive and growing. By the way, the name's Charlie Britt."

"I'm Stephen Gray."

"Can I give you a visitor's card and packet about our church?"

"Why, yes, that'd be fine."

"Here you are." The silver-haired man offered Gray a large blue folder. "Bibles and hymnals are in the pew racks; the Bibles are black."

"Thanks, but I have my own." The younger man lifted up a large brown Bible for the usher to inspect. The name "Stephen Gray" was printed on the front in gold script.

Gray sat in an aisle seat three rows from the back. An elderly couple sat on the other end of the row. The lady smiled warmly and handed Gray a hymnal already opened to the first song. The song leader strode to the podium, wishing everyone a good morning. "Good morning," the audience weakly responded in unison.

"Well, I hope you do better as we sing our first song! Please turn to number 113, "Nothing but the Blood," and we'll sing all four verses," the leader announced in a peppy voice.

The elderly lady in Gray's row noted that the new visitor barely glanced at the hymnal as he sang out with a strong voice.

A thirtyish, well-dressed, dark-haired man took the podium. "Good morning!" he called out.

The congregation echoed the greeting back, this time with enthusiasm.

"Doug, they obviously love their pastor more than they love you," he said, turning to the song leader with a grin and a wink.

"Just don't try to sing. Your voice will kill the enthusiasm for weeks," Doug said, returning the banter.

The audience laughed and nodded knowingly.

"Well, let's get right to our announcements," the pastor said. After listing several typical items, the pastor said, "And now, my lovely wife would like to make a special announcement about our participation in the pro-life ministry."

Gray took one look at Ginny Kettner and agreed with the pastor's description. Reaching inside his jacket for an expensive gold pen, he sat up in his chair and jotted some notes on his bulletin as she urged the congregation to become more active in the sidewalk counseling at the abortion clinic.

"We've got to stand up for life," she concluded. "Please see me after the service if you would like to help."

Gray put his pen away for the rest of the service. But, as the lady at the end of the row noted, he skillfully turned his Bible to every passage in the pastor's sermon and robustly sang each of the hymns throughout the service.

After the benediction, the elderly couple quickly moved down the row to Gray and greeted him.

"We're so glad you visited with us this morning," the lady began. "You obviously come from a good church background. I couldn't help but notice you knew all the hymns. And you have such a nice voice."

"Thank you," Gray said, flashing a row of nearly perfect teeth. "I have sung them a time or two."

"Are you visiting us from out of town?" the man asked.

"No, I just moved to Bellingham earlier this week from Cedarville, Ohio."

"Well, I hope you enjoyed the service. Oh! Here's our new pastor and his wife now," the man said as Jim and Ginny Kettner walked up.

"I was impressed with your sermon," Gray said, shaking hands with the pastor.

"Jim Kettner," the pastor responded. "Thanks for the compliment."

"I'm Stephen Gray," the young man said, smiling warmly again. "You're welcome. But to tell you the truth, the strongest draw to your church was your wife's announcement. I'm so tired of churches who talk about God's principles but never do anything practical to stand up for them." Suddenly Gray's face became quite serious. Lowering his voice to almost a whisper, he added, "I lost a cousin three years ago after having an abortion. She bled to death. What happened to my cousin—and the baby—shouldn't happen to anyone."

Ginny spoke first after a moment of awkward silence. "Stephen, you're welcome to be a part of our pro-life ministry team, if you think you'd like to join us. Why don't you call me at home some night this week and I can give you more details."

"Or better yet," the pastor interjected, "why don't you join us for lunch? About a dozen of us from the church go over to the Royal Fork every Sunday after church for the buffet. It's not gourmet dining, but it's pretty good. Unless you have a family to get back to?"

"No, I'm not married. And my family is back east."

"That'll be great," the pastor said. Twisting around, he saw Lisa walking up behind him. "Oh, speaking of the pro-life team, here's Lisa Edgar, my wife's right-hand woman and friend. And she's single, too!"

Lisa blushed and shoved the pastor in the ribs. "There he goes again," she said in obvious embarrassment. "I apologize for our extremely ill-mannered pastor."

"No apologies necessary," Gray said. "Lisa, I'm Stephen Gray. I'm happy to make your acquaintance." He extended his hand and bowed his head slightly in a gentlemanly fashion. Lisa took his hand and shook it softly. Her blush deepened. She glanced askance at Ginny, then back at Gray.

"Well, let's go eat," Ginny said. "Stephen, why don't you follow Lisa and me? I'm driving the dingy yellow Pontiac out back."

"I'm ready," Gray said, tucking his Bible under his arm.

Ginny and Lisa talked and giggled like high schoolers all the way to the Royal Fork Restaurant. In his car, Gray made sure he had the right wallet in his pocket. Driver's license, Visa Gold card, and other identification all in the name of Stephen Gray from Cedarville, Ohio. The wallet including a driver's license belonging to Vince Davis from Santa Monica, California, was safely locked in the glove compartment.

| **5** |

Dr. Marsano was masked, gloved, and ready to go forward with the procedure when her patient—a twenty-year-old redhead, a junior from Walla Walla—got up on her elbows from her supine position on the examination table.

"Doctor, is it . . . is it killing?" the woman asked with eyes that pleaded for the truth.

In the months she had been working at the clinic, no one had ever approached Rhonda with such straightforward apprehension before. Usually those with doubts were expertly handled by the clinic's staff of trained counselors, and if a rare client was still not convinced of her course of action, then she was sent home. Either way, by the time a woman was prepped and on the table, she was usually more focused on the methodology than the morality of the surgery.

Rhonda struggled to find appropriate words to satisfy her client's distress, but found none. Even though her Catholic upbringing had been only mediocre, she still held onto the belief that life was sacred. Yet the need to pay for her medical training had overruled her weak convictions. And medical school had hardened her. Once, in a sexuality and women's issues class, another student had asked the professor this woman's same question. The professor replied with practiced nonchalance, "Is removing an inflamed gall bladder, killing?"

But Rhonda knew she couldn't give that crass reply to this searching client. Instead, she patted her on the shoulder gently. "If you feel uncomfortable with this, we can still stop."

For a moment the woman deliberated, but finally she laid back down on the table. "No, go ahead, I guess."

Looking at the clock, Rhonda knew she had to hurry up to keep on schedule. She looked at her assistant and nodded.

"OK, Ms. McKenna, relax now, I'll be right here the whole time," the assistant assured her charge.

Rhonda quickly began pressing on the woman's abdomen, checking the term of the pregnancy. "Hmmm, about twelve weeks, I figure. Does that sound about right?" she inquired of the patient.

"Yes, that sounds about right."

"Good. Ms. McKenna, we are going to do a simple vacuum aspiration procedure on you. I am going to give you a shot of xylocaine to reduce the pain of the procedure, but you will still feel some pressure and cramping. That's normal. Do you understand? Are you ready?"

The redhead nodded hesitantly.

"Syringe, please," Rhonda said.

"Dr. Marsano." The receptionist poked her head into the room. "I left a message on your desk, someone with some post-procedure questions. Should I ask one of the counselors to take the call?"

Rhonda nodded, not wanting to break her concentration on the xylocaine injection. That done, she turned to the patient. "We'll give that a few minutes to work. You just lay still and relax."

Rhonda moved around the room by rote, moving instruments from here to there and putting several supplies away while she waited for the medication to take effect. She wondered what the call was about, hoping it was not an incomplete procedure or another perforation of the uterus, as happened her first month of performing abortions. She could not handle having another screaming, hemorrhaging patient pass out in her arms.

"I think we're through," she said in relief, more to herself than her assistant. "You OK, Ms. McKenna?"

"Yes . . . it felt kind of strange, but I guess I'm OK."

"All done," the assistant said to the patient. "In a couple of minutes I'm going to take you to our recovery room, where you can relax for awhile. We have some crackers and juice if you like."

Suddenly the receptionist peeked into the room again. "Doctor, your two o'clock appears to be a no show. Sorry."

Rhonda shook her head over the news of another lost client, then gave some final instructions to the redhead.

After finishing, Rhonda left the room and climbed the stairs to her office. She scanned the several messages that cluttered her desk top, then went to the window to look for protesters. She pulled the blinds apart and scanned the sidewalk. Nothing. She opened the window a crack, allowing a cold breeze to enter the room, and listened for signs of demonstrators. All she could hear were the songs of birds singing in some nearby trees. *Opposition's unusually light for a Saturday,* she thought.

Beneath one of the trees, however, Colonel Danners and Ginny Kettner conversed quietly. Rhonda knew their names from pictures she'd seen in the local newspaper but couldn't hear their voices.

Then another woman, Lisa Edgar, came around the corner into Rhonda's view. The doctor recognized Lisa as a regular protester but didn't know her name. Rhonda's vision was riveted on Lisa—not because of any intrinsic interest in her, but because of the man walking beside her, someone she knew all too well. "So that's Vince's angle," she said aloud. "Hitting on the chicks to get into the inner circle."

Rhonda judged Vince's target—a petite woman with jet black hair—to be in her late twenties. She was reasonably attractive but not over-powering, Rhonda thought. "That Kettner woman is certainly better looking," the doctor said to herself.

She knew better than to feel jealous but couldn't help it. Her thoughts were becoming emersed in an ebb and flow of bitter-sweet memories when a burst of chilled air came through the open window. She closed it and sat at her desk.

After returning a few phone calls, Rhonda returned to the recovery room to check on the redhead, who was lying on her side on a bench, moaning. "You'll feel better in just a few hours," the doctor told her. "It's just a little cramping." Deep inside she wished the timetable for relief from her own emotional pain would be "just a few hours" as well.

Later that evening, Rhonda sat curled up before the television, sip-ping hot chocolate. She had begged off from yet another one of David Gleason's Fairhaven parties and picked up a Clark Gable video on the

way home from the clinic. The movie was over and she was half-asleep
when the sound of a car pulling into her driveway woke her up. It was
half past ten. Her heart began to pound—no one except Gleason ever
came to see her at night, and he never came unannounced. Before she
had time to imagine unknown intruders, she heard a familiar tune being
whistled as footsteps crunched briskly toward the front door. It was
Vince.

Rhonda pulled the belt of her robe tighter around her waist, walked
to the door, and leaned her ear to the wood to listen. Soon the whistling
stopped and there was a knock at the door.

"Yes?" she said in a shaky voice.

"Rhonda, it's me."

"I told you I don't want to see you."

Vince spoke in a barely audible voice. "Listen, Rhonda, I can't afford
for your neighbors to see me here. This is business, just let me in."

She hesitated for a brief second, then opened the door quickly, keeping her head down and motioning him in without looking at him.

Vince closed the door behind him, while Rhonda stared blankly at
the floor. "Make it fast," she said weakly. He slid quietly up to her, saying nothing. Finally, she looked up into his eyes. He reached out his left
hand, touched her right arm with feather-like softness, and rubbed his
two fingers gently up and down her arm.

"Rhonda, relax. I'm not going to bite you, and I promised I would
remain cordial and business-like, remember?"

She moved her arm slightly away from his hand, an audible sigh
coming from deep within. "This is going to be a lot harder than I
thought," she said to herself.

Waving toward a nearby chair, she said, "Tell me your business." She
walked back to the couch and sat down, keeping her eyes away from

Vince's. He sat down quietly on the leather arm chair and waited. After what seemed like a minute of awkward silence, Rhonda finally looked up, trying to determine what he was waiting for. Gazing at her, Vince seized the moment.

"Ronnie," he said, "this is hard for me, too. Please don't make it harder than it has to be. I've got to be able to talk to you at least a little. I'm your only hope to satisfy Jane and Karen, right?"

Rhonda smiled slightly in spite of herself. She had come to detest Jane and Karen. Having an ally to gain some relief from the pressure of the situation was worth almost any price. "OK," she sighed. "Tell me your plan."

"Well, to tell you the truth, I don't have a real plan, yet. But I can tell you the basic objective. I'm trying to get inside your little nest of protesters to help our legal team find the best tactical angle to win an injunction. The quicker I can do that, the quicker I can get these protesters —and a major source of irritation—out of your life, all at the same time."

"Have you talked with the lawyers yet?" Rhonda asked.

"For three hours before leaving L.A., and then a couple times since I arrived. They have some really good ideas."

"Can't they just file something immediately?"

"Yeah, they could. But in every case they've won, they were able to juice up the record with some kind of obnoxious behavior from the protesters. Something to put the judge on edge, like a few harassing phone calls to you, a protest in your neighborhood, a couple threatening letters, stuff like that. If we can prove the protesters are acting over the edge, most judges are inclined to simply ignore their First Amendment arguments."

"You think you can get them to do that? I've heard that colonel on TV. He seems excruciatingly ethical."

"Excuse me, Rhonda, but you of all people should know just how obnoxious I can be, and how I can provoke others to do likewise. Mr. Obnoxious. That's me. Your ol' buddy, Vince."

Before Rhonda could catch herself, she was laughing. She couldn't help it. "Well, you're right about one thing—I have never met anyone more obnoxious and smooth in my life. If anyone can do it, you can."

"So now that we've established my job in this, let's talk about you. You've got a role in this little drama as well."

"Me? I already have my hands full; I can't handle any sneaking around."

"Don't worry, I'm not asking you to do anything dishonest. I like working with the truth whenever possible. All I want you to do is keep track of every single thing these protesters say to you. Any mail they send you, I want to see it. Any comments they make, record them in writing and then tell me. From now on, you are a victim of their oppression, and keeping good records will help our legal team prove that."

"But they haven't said or done anything to me."

"Not yet. Just give me a few weeks, five or six, max. Then my job'll be done, and this obnoxious jerk will fly out of your life."

"Again," she added.

"Yeah," he said self-consciously. "Again." He paused for a minute. "Rhonda, I don't expect you to buy this, but I really am sorry about before. I wasn't planning for either of us to fall so hard. I just wanted to have a little fun; remember I told you that at the beginning?"

"Yeah, but then you changed the ground rules. You started acting so serious."

"I wasn't acting. I was serious."

"I can't believe that," Rhonda said, staring at the hardwood floor.

"Listen. This isn't a snow job—it's my best self-analysis, and it's taken me four years to figure it out." Vince paused, bending over to catch and hold Rhonda's gaze. "I was getting serious about you, real serious. But I hadn't grown up yet. Inside I was still a kid, so I started behaving more like a hormonal teenager than a grown man falling in love with a real woman."

"Your smoke screen has improved, Vince. Those lines sound almost believable."

"Rhonda, I don't expect you to believe me, but I'm speaking from my heart. Just do me one favor: Keep the tiniest window open in your mind, and watch."

"I was watching you today with that protester. She's probably cross-stitching your name to hang on her wall already."

"You don't miss a thing, do you?"

"I'm paid to be detail oriented," she said, allowing her gaze to drift toward the window facing the black outdoors.

"But nobody ever paid me to fall in love with you. I did that on my own." Vince stood up after a couple of minutes of awkward silence. "I'm sorry, I didn't mean to get this deep into all this personal stuff. I was just trying to convince you I was sorry so we could get on with our jobs. Just one last thing and I'll leave."

She looked up at Vince's six-foot-one-inch frame and for the first time that evening, stared hard.

"If you see me in public, you don't know me. My name is Stephen Gray, but you don't know that unless someone else tells you. I won't come here anymore. When we talk from now on, it's either on secure land phones—no car phones, no multiple extensions with other people—or it's someplace thirty or more miles from Bellingham." He turned to leave.

"Oh, I don't want anyone else in the clinic to know anything about me. You haven't said anything, have you?"

"No. Nothing."

"Good. Well, goodnight, Rhonda."

She walked Vince to the door and listened as he started his car and drove down her narrow driveway toward the interstate. She turned the dead bolt and then sank back into the couch.

She played his flowery words over and over again in her mind. The old Vince would never have just up and walked out without trying to lure her back with smooth talk and a soft touch. At least that much was different.

The next morning Stephen Gray walked through the front door of Pacific Street Baptist Church at 9:25. Jim Kettner greeted him warmly as he locked his office door, located on one side of the church foyer. He was heading toward the Young Adult Sunday school class and invited Gray to come with him.

The two men chatted as they walked the short distance down a narrow hallway, then turned left into the designated room. About fifteen people were seated in a double semicircle of forty or so chairs. As the men entered the room, Lisa Edgar looked around expectantly from her seat, the second chair in the back row. The aisle chair was conveniently empty.

"Saving this for someone special?" Gray asked with his trademark smile.

"Only you, stranger."

"Well, I am stranger than most," Gray replied with a wink.

Lisa removed her purse from the floor between the two chairs and hung it over her seat. She didn't want anything coming between her and her handsome new friend.

"So how was the rest of your evening?" Gray whispered quietly as Jim wheeled the overhead projector into place.

"Just my typical Saturday night routine. But I sure enjoyed our dinner, and the walk along the bay was lovely."

"You're entirely welcome. I had a great time, too. We'll have to try a Friday night outing next time—won't have to get back quite so early."

"Well, I go to the clinic early on Saturday mornings, remember?"

"Oh, yeah. Well, we're both adults; I guess we can handle staying up late and still get up early the next morning, huh?"

"I think I can find time in my busy—" Lisa cut herself short and placed an index finger over her mouth with a feigned "shush." The pastor was about to start.

Gray joined in the class discussion several times over the course of the hour. Enough to be noticed, but not dominate. Occasionally he—with his arms crossed above the open Bible on his lap—would reach sideways with his partially hidden right hand and gently stroke Lisa's arm. Lisa clearly enjoyed these small gestures of affection. And she couldn't help planning a wedding in her mind as she vacantly stared out a window as low white clouds whisked by. Several times she had to consciously drag herself back to reality. But even there, Stephen Gray was beside her, and she basked in the presence of the most handsome man to ever shower her with attention in her entire life.

Derrick Walker pulled his guitar out of its case and leaned it up against the wide ledge of the circular fountain that was the morning gathering spot for Western Washington's Campus Christian Fellowship. Derrick, a junior from Bonners Ferry, Idaho, had been active in the group ever since his arrival at Western; this year he took over as song leader. He and several girls stood quietly chatting as Stephen Gray strode toward them across the red bricks of the square.

Gray stopped a few feet from the group and looked around, bewildered.

"Morning," Derrick said eyeing Gray, who was dressed in jeans, a Bugle Boy white shirt and a tan plaid sports jacket. *Too sharply dressed for a student, and too young for a professor,* Derrick thought.

"Uh . . . good morning," Gray replied, glancing at his watch. "I'm supposed to meet Suzie O'Dell in Red Square at 8:00. Am I at the right place?"

"Yup. Suzie's usually here by now, must be running a few minutes late. You here for the prayer time?"

Gray didn't answer him. "I thought there were supposed to be forty or fifty of you students here every morning."

"The rest of the group shows up at 8:30, but a few of us come early to prepare. You know, pray and stuff."

Gray nodded and smiled.

"You a friend of Suzie's?" Derrick probed.

"Yeah, we met down at the abortion clinic on Saturday. I go to Pacific Street Baptist, and we're trying to recruit for the pro-life effort. I've come to make an announcement to your group—to see how many of you will be available to help out during the summer."

"You're welcome to make the announcement," Derrick said warily, "but Suzie is pretty good about reminding us about the effort."

"Well, Suzie thought if a fresh face came and announced the need for summer recruits, it might help generate a little more interest."

"Can't hurt, I guess. Can you stick around for the singing and prayer?"

"I do okay with a hymnal in my hands, but these praise choruses are all new to me. I'm afraid I won't be able to contribute much."

"Don't worry, we'll teach you!" a young blonde chimed in.

"Thanks, I'll give it a try."

Gray spotted Suzie and two other girls walking across the Square from the direction of the library. He waved vigorously to her; she shyly waved back. Immediately the two girls flanking Suzie's side pounced on her for an explanation of the handsome newcomer. Suzie quickly assured them that Stephen Gray was taken; he and her friend, Lisa, were seeing each other regularly. Suzie liked Lisa, and was glad she had found someone who seemed to share her interests.

Gray's announcement met with better-than-anticipated success. Initially six coeds, who had not heard Suzie's "he's taken" speech, volunteered, followed by three guys who were interested in whatever the girls were doing. By the end of the meeting, Gray had a cluster of students surrounding him who agreed to meet at Viking Union for a quick strategy session. Cappuccino—a craze indigenous to the Pacific Northwest—was on him.

A few minutes later, twelve new volunteers and six regulars lounged comfortably in the far corner of Viking Union's food court.

"Suzie's a great leader," Gray began after everyone seemed settled with their cappuccinos. "There's really not a lot that I can say that she can't say a lot better."

Suzie smiled. A murmur of support ran through her friends.

"I realize I'm the Johnny-come-lately in this whole effort, but being a night manager at a pizza place up in Ferndale, I'm the only one—other than Suzie, of course—who's available to meet with you guys for your morning meetings on a regular basis. So I got elected to help head up the college effort."

"Pizza?" Derrick said hopefully. "How 'bout we hold our meetings at your restaurant?"

"Not a bad idea," Gray replied. "First time it'll be on me."

The smiles all around told Gray he was clearly fitting in.

"I just want to say a couple more things, then we're finished. When I was at student at Ohio State about ten years ago, the only thing I cared about was pizza and beer. Oh yeah, and girls. So you guys really inspire me, the way you take a stand for the Lord on this campus."

His words were inspirational, and true in the abstract. Even the deadened conscience of Vince Davis was impressed by these kids' dedication to serve their God.

"And now you're willing to go a step further and fight on the front lines, where lives are literally saved or lost. Our efforts at the clinic have been OK up to this point, but we're still losing at least fifteen each Saturday. And that doesn't count the ones who come during the week, when only the colonel shows up. We gotta step it up. We gotta do better."

There were nods all around.

"I'm hoping we can get coverage three, maybe four afternoons a week. Hey, why not all five? Even if it's just a couple hours a day."

Gray concluded by giving several scriptural illustrations regarding God's love for children. For someone who cared only for himself, his "Christian talk" was very convincing. All those years in the home of the Reverend Warren Davis had not been without some effect. His head was as full of biblical knowledge as his calloused heart was empty.

Twenty-five minutes went by quickly. Gray suddenly sprang to his feet, looking as if he had an appointment. In reality, he couldn't stand continuing the charade any longer and wanted to get away.

He walked with Derrick across campus toward the visitor parking lot behind the Political Science building. Firing up his newly acquired, aging Ford Taurus, his thoughts raced to Santa Monica, where his white BMW convertible sat unused in his garage. For now, he had to look like a pizza manager.

Driving home to a rented double-wide trailer, he cranked up the loudest, most obnoxious rock music he could find as an antidote to the past hour and a half. His real work done for the day, he looked forward to an afternoon of TV and a couple beers, before having to get up and go make pizzas for a few hours that night.

The pizza parlor was owned by one of Jane and Karen's acquaintances. Gray was given a job—fifteen hours a week, low pay, flexible evening hours—as a front during his stay in Bellingham. The $3,500 a week the clinic chain paid him more than made up for the inconvenience of living away from home.

At the trailer, Vince slammed the front door behind him, collapsed on the couch, and dialed the clinic's number on his portable phone. "Hello, this is Dr. Winston in the Albuquerque Clinic. Is Dr. Marsano there?"

"Hello?"

"Rhonda? Vince. I need to see you tonight. Meet me at the Blue Lantern tavern in Blaine. Ten thirty."

"Mr. Gray," a perky brunette waitress said, sticking her head in the kitchen, "there's a bunch of college kids out here saying that you offered to buy them a free pizza."

"What?" Gray said, momentarily taken back. *I just met them this morning; these kids move fast,* he thought. "I'll talk to them in a minute, Stephanie. Just take their order."

He wiped his hands on a towel and looked at his watch. 9:15 P.M. The restaurant closed at 10—after all, it was in Ferndale—and he had to leave immediately afterward. Feed 'em quick and chat fast.

Gray walked, all smiles, out into the dining room. He remembered the students' faces—three guys, three girls—but only four of their names.

"Derrick, what a surprise. I thought we'd decided to meet next week?"

"We weren't planning it either," Derrick replied. "But then we learned they were serving Salisbury steak for dinner!" All six of them made a face at the thought.

"Well, I wanted to treat you guys some night when I wasn't on duty, so I could really sit and talk with you."

One of the girls poked Derrick hard in the ribs.

"Hey, we just came on our own. Don't worry, we'll pay. It was just kind of fun to get out of Bellingham," Derrick said.

"Ferndale's not much of an escape, especially in the evening," Gray laughed.

"We know you have to get back to work," Derrick volunteered. "Maybe we can talk for a few minutes after you close."

"I'm sorry, but I have to leave immediately after closing. I'm meeting an old friend."

"Oh, sounds great. Is the friend visiting from Ohio?"

"No, the person is not really visiting me, it's just someone I know." Gray felt himself sinking deeper into his attempt to be truthful and regretted not inventing some flat-out lie. He was usually much more convincing with a total fabrication. "Well," he added quickly, "I really am needed in the kitchen. Next Tuesday I'll treat you all, OK?"

Derrick and his friends stayed until closing, then lingered in the parking lot for a few minutes. Gray helped wash the dishes and pizza pans, then scrubbed tables until they were gone. Driving north toward Blaine, he realized he would have to be very careful anytime he met with Rhonda—Whatcom County was a lot smaller than most places he'd been, and the chances of running into someone from the church were fairly high.

Fifteen minutes later he looked into the dimly lit bar searching for Rhonda's familiar face. Finally he spotted her in a booth along the middle of the back wall.

"Sorry I'm late," he said, slipping into the seat across from her. Suddenly the urge to kiss her cheek, as he'd done so many times before, swept over him. He stared at her, then looked away.

"You OK? The Vince Davis I knew was always on time."

"Well, I hit a snag, nothing major."

"Did you have to leave your new love interest to fly up here to meet me?" she said with icy overtones.

"No, no. I was working at a pizza place, can you believe that? I own a home with a view in Santa Monica, and here I am, working in a pizza joint in Ferndale, Washington, living in a double-wide trailer!"

"Sounds like fair punishment to me," Rhonda said, smiling at him for the first time since he had arrived.

"I'll pass on that for now. Anyhow, some college students I'm recruiting showed up unexpectedly and hung around in the parking lot, wanting to talk."

"So you're playing with coeds as well as Ms. Protester?"

Vince shot her a glance of genuine irritation. "Will you knock it off? I am not playing with coeds, and I'm not romancing Lisa, either. I want her to think I'm falling for her, but I'm not. But even if I were, I don't owe you an explanation!"

Vince glared at Rhonda. She stared at the table as an awkward silence hung between them. Finally she whispered, "Sorry. I guess you're right."

Vince reached out both of his hands and gently grasped hers, which had been clutching the edge of the table. "Listen, Ronnie. I told you I'm sorry. And you told me that you wanted a cordial, professional relationship between us. I'm trying to do that, but every conversation we have comes back to the same old thing. You still haven't let this go."

He paused in his intense delivery as he saw a tear trickle down her cheek. In a much gentler tone he proceeded, "Just as I haven't been able to let you go. Let's face it, Ronnie, you're bitter because you still care. I think you love me. And . . . I have finally grown up enough to know that I love you—and you alone."

Tears flowed freely down her face as a smile took complete possession of her entire being. *He can still read me like a book,* she thought, glad to finally have her feelings out in the open. Vince stood and offered his hand to Rhonda. She took it and they started toward her car. In the parking lot she turned, clutching him desperately with both arms as her body vibrated from the silent sobs of release. He held her for a long time, then whispered and nuzzled her ear as he had done in happier times.

After the bar closed and all the employees had left, a single car—a black Volvo—sat all night in the parking lot.

"Yeah, it's drizzling," Vince said the next morning. "You ain't in L.A. anymore, Ronnie."

Rhonda's voice came from the bathroom. "I sure didn't plan this little overnighter very well. My mouth feels icky. You don't have a new toothbrush in some drawer, do you?"

"Just use mine."

"Are you crazy? Think of the germs."

"You don't think we shared some last night? What's the difference?"

"Men are so uncouth," she replied. "Is there a grocery or something around here?"

"Well, there's a little corner market just a couple blocks away. Why don't I go get you one?"

"How 'bout if I ride along?"

"All right, but I'll go in, OK?"

Vince parked his Taurus in front of the gas pumps and quickly ran inside. The door jangled to alert the single clerk there was someone in the store. Grabbing a toothbrush, he was heading for the counter when he heard the door jingle again. He turned to see Rhonda stick her head inside. "Get some mouthwash, too."

Vince jerked around to see if the clerk had seen Rhonda. A large man in his fifties busied himself sorting videos out of the night bin. Vince could not be sure if he'd seen her or not.

"Ronnie," he said, after shutting the car door behind him, "that was really stupid."

"What was stupid?" she said testily.

"That clerk knows me. I can't be seen with you in there. I don't think he saw you, but blast it, you had better be more careful. You said you were going to just wait in the car."

"Maybe we shouldn't be doing this at all . . . maybe last night was a mistake," she replied.

"Oh, don't be silly, Ronnie," Vince said softly, shifting the car into gear. "Let's just be more careful in the future."

Rhonda bit her lip and stared out her rain-splattered window.

Derrick Walters shifted the protest sign into his right hand to get a look at his watch. 2:15 P.M. He could stay for twenty more minutes before he had to leave for his three o'clock international relations class.

Jim O'Rourke, a sophomore from Edmonds, caught up with Derrick as he turned the corner of Magnolia and marched the hundred feet along Garden Street that fronted the abortion clinic property. Together they turned and began the circuit all over again. Approaching Magnolia Street again, they could see Stephen Gray advancing toward them with a bag of Herfy's hamburgers in one hand and a tray of Cokes in the other.

A stark, yellow-colored building on the corner of Garden and Magnolia, the clinic was just four blocks from the heart of downtown Bellingham. Across from it, the historic Garden Street Methodist Church lay silent. The church had not been involved in any of the picketing although its associate pastor, Linda Fleming-Nance, had participated in a pro-life press conference when the dispute about the clinic first sprang into the media spotlight. Another corner of the intersection was occupied by a large, faded Victorian home that had long been converted into a maze of five apartments. On the fourth corner was a small Pontiac dealership.

Colonel Danners had laid down very strict rules. No one was to park anywhere near the intersection or in the parking lots of the adjacent buildings. He didn't even want anyone to cut through the parking lot of the car lot. He absolutely insisted that no reproach fall on the protest effort other than that directly arising from the fact that the protesters were trying to save unborn babies.

The one business that hadn't been ruled off-limits was the Herfy's fast-food restaurant, a block south on Magnolia. Gray walked toward the two students from that direction. "Hey, guys, I got the food," he yelled in a moderate voice as his foot stepped off the curb onto Garden Street.

Derrick's left hand shot to his mouth signaling, "Sshhhh. The colonel said no yelling, remember?"

"Oops," Gray said in a much more subdued voice.

The trio ate burgers and talked as they continued to pace the sidewalk. A bright yellow Volkswagen Rabbit with a college-aged couple appeared around the corner and slowed to turn into the clinic parking lot. "Potential customers," Jim said, picking up the pace to meet them.

The driver paused in the middle of his turn as Derrick and Jim waved him down.

"Hey, man, can we talk to you for just a second?" Derrick asked in a polite tone.

"Whadaya want?" the driver said brusquely.

"We just want to talk about your baby."

Jim looked at the young woman in the car. Dark sunglasses, on such a cloudy day. Without responding, the driver thrust the Volkswagen into gear. It lurched forward and pulled into the parking stall closest to the clinic's side door.

"Can't we please talk?" Derrick pleaded from the sidewalk.

Rounding the back of the car to open the passenger door for his girlfriend, the man flashed him an obscene gesture.

"We've got to save this baby," Gray whispered to the two students who were about to give up. In a moment, Gray began chanting, slowly but deliberately, "Let this baby live. . . . Let this baby live. . . ." Jim and

Derrick looked at him in surprise, then picked up the lament. Gray stepped back several feet but continued the chant, allowing it to grow louder with each line.

As the couple neared the clinic entrance, Jim implored, "Please let us talk to you, only for a minute!"

"We just want to ask you about the baby," Derrick added.

While the two students pleaded with the couple from the sidewalk, Gray crossed the street and continued the dirge more loudly. Suddenly, fire flashed in the eyes of the boyfriend as he herded the woman toward the clinic door. He spun around and strode toward the two protesters, shoving Derrick to the ground. Derrick steadied himself, then lunged toward the man. If it hadn't been for Jim, who caught him and held his arms fast, he would have hit the man.

"Let him go, Derrick! This isn't what it's all about!" Jim hissed, trying not to make a further scene.

Meanwhile, Stephen Gray stood on the corner across the street with his head bowed in mock prayer, safely out of range of the rented video camera he had strategically placed in a window of the second story office two weeks before.

The Danners' living room was brimming with young people the following Tuesday evening. Fourteen college students and twenty high schoolers squeezed together on the furniture and the floor, singing and clapping to music led by Derrick and Suzie. Stephen Gray sat on the other side of Derrick. Once, during a praise chorus, he took the opportunity to pat Derrick on the shoulder in encouragement. He knew the colonel would be addressing the incident at the clinic the week before. Lisa Edgar watched him admiringly from a couch on the side of the room.

Gray leaned his head toward Derrick after the last song and whispered in his ear, then pulled a Bible out from under his folding chair.

Placing his guitar inside its case, Derrick announced, "Stephen would like to share a few verses with us before the colonel speaks."

The colonel fidgeted in his chair at the entrance to the kitchen. This was unplanned, but surely there couldn't be any harm in reading from Scripture, he reasoned.

"The first verse I'd like to read is Proverbs 24, verse 11," Gray began. "It really makes it clear that our mission to save unborn babies is commanded by God. The verse says: 'Rescue those being led away to death, hold back those staggering toward slaughter.' I think we need to be willing to do anything we can, anything at all, to obey that command. Like God's army, we need to fight for truth."

Eager young heads nodded in agreement as Gray scanned the audience like a practiced speaker.

The colonel stood up and began to walk slowly toward the front of the room. Pretending not to see, Gray quickly continued, "I have just one last passage. It is from the Gospel of Mark chapter 3, the first five verses. 'Another time He went into the synagogue, and a man with a shriveled hand was there. Some of them were looking for a reason to accuse Jesus, so they watched Him closely to see if He would heal him on the Sabbath. Jesus said to the man with the shriveled hand, "Stand up in front of everyone." Then Jesus asked them, "Which is lawful on the Sabbath: to do good or to do evil, to save life or to kill?" But they remained silent. He looked around at them in anger and, deeply distressed at their stubborn hearts, said to the man, "Stretch out your hand." He stretched it out, and his hand was completely restored.' You know, sometimes we are like the Pharisees. We get all concerned about man's laws and traditions when we should be worried about people's lives. We need to keep our sights high and be committed to God's law, not man's."

Danners, who by now was at Gray's side, was on the verge of anger; nevertheless, he forced a smile. "Well, fortunately this is one time when we don't have to choose between obeying man's laws and God's. With the escalation of manpower, we have been able to rescue about a third of the babies scheduled to die each Saturday; and the numbers are climbing during the week, as well. All with methods that are perfectly legal. If we switch to unethical methods, we might rescue a few more, but sooner or later we would be forced to cease our activities altogether. Then, no babies would be saved at all."

"Colonel," Gray said from his new seat against Lisa's legs, "I didn't mean to imply that we should do something illegal. I was just trying to encourage the young people not to give way to peer pressure among their friends and things like that. I probably didn't say it very well, but that's what I meant."

"No problem, Stephen," the colonel said coolly, "I understand, and we do appreciate your hard work and leadership on this issue."

Gray smiled, leaned back, and began to gently rub Lisa's ankle with his right hand.

The colonel spoke about a variety of issues, went over the next month's protesting schedule, then briefly admonished Derrick for his actions the preceding Saturday. Finally, he encouraged everyone to keep a light-hearted attitude. "We all see what's happening in the clinic as murder, but we've got to keep our heads on and spirits up."

At the end of the meeting, Lisa, Suzie, and two of her college friends, Rachel and Kim, waited patiently near the front door for Stephen. The colonel had invited him "down the hall" immediately after the meeting concluded. The four of them could hear the colonel's voice, and Gray's, coming from within the study, but the words were indistinct. After about ten minutes, the study door opened slowly. Gray was half out the door when Danners's voice called out, "One more thing, Stephen. Lisa's with you when you meet with these college kids, isn't she?"

"Yes, sir. She's my constant companion on these things. I promise you'll be happy."

"Fair enough," the colonel said as Gray fully emerged from the room and saw Lisa staring at him. Immediately his face reddened, and he looked away.

No one said a thing for about a mile as Stephen guided his car down Lakeway Drive toward the university to drop off the three girls. Finally, Lisa spoke. "Was the colonel yelling at you about something?"

"Not exactly," Gray answered. "But he did want to make himself clear."

"What about?" Lisa asked, glancing over her shoulder at the three silent riders in the back seat.

"He didn't like the verses I read," Gray replied.

"Why not?" Suzie asked.

"He thought they were off the point."

"Oh, I don't know," Suzie replied. "After thinking about it, the second passage especially, it made sense to me."

"Yeah?" Gray replied.

"Yeah," Suzie said. "I've been wondering why we don't do more. I mean, the Bible speaks clearly about the sanctity of life. And I think we are God's army, like you were saying. So why shouldn't we do more to try to save the babies?"

"What do the rest of you think?" Gray asked, glancing quickly into the rear view mirror at the girls in the back seat.

"I'm not sure. I guess we could do more. But I would be afraid to," Kim replied.

"What about you, Rachel?" Gray asked.

"This is all new for me. I'm really unsure."

"Well, it really doesn't matter what any of us think. The colonel has a plan and we are going to stick to it." Gray's voice was perky and bright, without the slightest hint of bitterness. Still, he thought that his words, dripping with just a hint of mutinous poison, had at least pulled Suzie in his direction. This is just the beginning, he thought, smiling to himself. Gray pulled up before the college dorms and let the three girls out of the car. A few minutes later Lisa bent over and gave him a quick kiss on the cheek as she got out in front of her house. He snickered as he drove off. Lisa had let his lie pass about her always accompanying him when he was with the college kids. She wouldn't stand in his way—she was hooked.

Two and a half weeks later, Rhonda's phone rang early on a Saturday morning.

After struggling to first find consciousness, and then the phone, she was finally able to answer it on the fifth ring.

"Hullo," she groaned.

"Whoa. You're sleeping in this morning."

"Oh, Vince, you kept me out so late. Didn't I tell you Vancouver is beautiful?"

"Yeah, and I want to go there again tonight. But this time I want you to pack a bag for a couple days."

"Do you think we should? Won't Ms. Protester miss you at church?"

"I've got her covered. Told her I'm going to a men's retreat up in the mountains that I read a flyer about at the Christian bookstore."

"Hmmm, sounds good," Rhonda sighed sleepily.

"Bring your warm weather outfits, OK?"

"Are we going to the hot springs?"

"Just do as I ask—clothing for a warm climate. Vancouver might not be our final destination."

"Sure, love. A mystery sounds fun."

At nine o'clock that evening, Vince and Rhonda were seated side by side in the first class cabin of an Air Canada flight from Vancouver to Los Angeles. The plane landed at LAX at 11:30. They walked briskly in the night air—warm by Washington standards—to the parking area where Vince's BMW convertible sat waiting. "A friend brought it over earlier," Vince explained. They got in and headed toward the Santa Monica Freeway.

"You sure know how to impress a girl," Rhonda said happily, remembering the ocean view out Vince's back porch. "You sure you can afford this little trip on a pizza manager's salary?"

Vince looked over at Rhonda as her long hair blew around, glistening in the passing lights. "I didn't pay for this at all," he replied. "This is entirely on Jane and Karen's tab. We've got a meeting with their legal team on Monday morning, and they wanted us both down here."

"Really? Are we ready for that? Have you got enough recorded?"

"Don't you worry your pretty little head about that. Let's just say that I know how to edit tape to maximize its effect. But until Monday morning, let's forget all about Bellingham and concentrate on us."

Rhonda leaned back in her seat and closed her eyes. It seemed like her troubles with the protesters were about to vanish like the warm California night breeze.

Rhonda's hand was noticeably shaking as she punched the button for the thirty-fourth floor.

"Ronnie, relax. Jane and Karen are on our side. I'll handle them, OK?"

She gulped impulsively and nodded.

The elevator doors opened to the polished marble floor of the entrance to the law firm of Doss, Stroshchein, Weiser, and Penner. A thick Persian carpet lay in the center of the lobby area, which was decorated with pieces of modern art and three black leather couches. A stunning redhead sat behind a marble counter and addressed them as they approached. Rhonda watched Vince intently as he asked her to announce their presence to Barry Penner, but she detected nothing in his voice to confirm the jealous anxiety she felt whenever they were in the presence of one so young and attractive. The secretary talked briefly on the phone, then disappeared through a doorway behind her desk. Immediately Rhonda heard the click-clack of high heels as the secretary opened the internal glass door and invited them inside. "Mr. Penner will be with you in just a moment, in conference room D. I'll take you there now."

Vince clutched Rhonda's hand as they walked down the marble corridor. Modern mahogany modular furniture, grouped in clusters for legal secretaries and other assistants, lined the right-hand side of the hall. A string of massive mahogany doors extended down the left-hand side. Two or three doors were open as Vince and Rhonda passed by, revealing a stunning view of downtown Los Angeles.

Near the end of the hallway, the secretary paused at a door on the left. "Here you are; you'll find some refreshments and coffee on the counter. I understand you'll be using our video equipment. Will you need any assistance?"

"No, I can handle it," Vince said cheerfully. "Thanks a lot."

"Mr. Penner will be here momentarily," she said again, closing the door behind her.

Rhonda wasn't really hungry but went over to examine the spread along the burnished mahogany counter. Bagels, cream cheese, lox, and a variety of croissants and muffins lay elegantly atop two silver trays. The coffee selections were latté, cappuccino, and regular coffee, all in a massive unit of stainless steel.

"You want anything, Vince?" Rhonda asked.

"Just a couple more days here with you."

"We have to go back tonight. I've got patients scheduled in the morning. Karen and Linda would kill me if I—"

She suddenly stopped speaking as the door swung open, revealing Jane Hayward and Karen Ballentine, followed by Barry Penner, Esq., one of the name partners in this 250-lawyer firm.

"Keep talking, dear," Jane said in a overly friendly voice. "I can't wait to hear the end of that sentence."

"Hello, Jane. Why I . . . I was just, uh . . . saying to Vince that the office girls would be upset if I missed a whole day of appointments, so we need to be sure and catch our flight—the last one out of LAX tonight."

"That she was," Vince said warmly, springing to his feet to shake hands all around. "Why don't we all sit down? I think the three of you are going to be very pleased with the work Rhonda and I have accomplished together. We've got an exciting tape to show you this morning. Bellingham goes Hollywood. Are you ready for the debut?"

"I see you haven't lost your touch, Vincent," Karen said, eying Rhonda and dropping her 190-pound, 5-foot 4-inch frame into one of the oversized conference chairs. Jane took the corner seat beside Karen, while Penner stood at the end chair. Vince and Rhonda sat opposite their bosses.

"It's always tough to know who's in charge when Vince Davis is in the room," Penner added. "But first things, first. I don't believe I've had the pleasure of meeting our charming victim. Dr. Rhonda Marsano, I presume? I'm Barry Penner, and I'll be representing you in court—that is, if the video from Mr. Davis here meets the criteria I have established for him."

Rhonda shook his hand, smiling faintly. Her fingers felt a slight crunch from the massive gold and diamond ring Penner wore on his right hand. Penner was impeccably dressed in a gray pin-striped suit and a Hermes silk tie, with matching handkerchief in his breast pocket.

"Well, Mr. Davis, if it is all right with my chief clients—Ms. Ballentine, Ms. Hayward—I believe you may start your presentation."

Vince popped open his briefcase, withdrew a cassette, and walked over to the video cassette recorder. With the remote control device in hand, he said, "Let the show begin."

"Baby killer, baby killer," came the chant. Four people with picket signs were visible. "Baby killer, baby killer," the chant continued. A young, male protester suddenly darted from the sidewalk across the lawn area toward the front door of the clinic. The subject disappeared from the scene, apparently out of range of the fixed position camera, then suddenly reappeared walking slowly back across the grass toward the sidewalk.

Next, a car with two young women inside paused in the driveway and rolled down the window as two protesters walked up. A brief exchange of words, then, "Let this baby live . . . Let this baby live!" the two protesters implored over and over again, as an entire group of sign-carrying chanters blocked the car's entrance into the parking lot.

For eighteen minutes the tape rolled, finally culminating in the scene where Derrick Walker tried to punch a client as he approached the clinic. Vince snapped off the video and rocked back in the swivel chair with an air of triumph. Rhonda reached under the table and squeezed his hand. Her eyes asked the question that Karen asked aloud, "How'd you do that? I thought these were the most disciplined protesters ever."

"A lot of Hollywood magic and a few lucky breaks," Vince replied. "The guy running across the lawn was chasing his baseball cap. The wind did us a real favor and blew it right by the clinic door."

"So how'd you get the 'baby killer' chant?" Rhonda asked. "I never heard any of that."

"That was recorded in my little ol' Ford Taurus. Some of the college kids were blowin' off steam on the way back from treating them to pizza. The visual was taken from another harmless sequence. But the block-ade of the car was my favorite," Vince continued. "The chants were dubbed in and the car sequence was edited in later. The two women in the car were plants. They actually called the two protesters over to ask them some questions."

"Was the near-punch a result of editing magic, as well?" inquired Mr. Penner.

"No. Luckily, that really happened, with a little provocation I had a hand in." Vince smiled. "And, Rhonda has a small stack of letters she received at home, threatening her if she continued working at the clinic. She also has an audio tape of harassing messages that she saved from her office voice mail. You brought it all with you, didn't you?" Vince asked, nodding toward Rhonda.

Rhonda nodded in response. Vince looked at Karen, Jane, and the lawyer, obviously pleased with himself. He knew this was his best work ever.

"Well, done, Vince, well done. We've got those blasted protesters right where we want them, haven't we, Barry?" Karen asked.

"Absolutely no problem, ladies. I'll have the papers filed by Friday, and we should have an injunction within a couple of weeks."

Rhonda squeezed Vince's hand once again. "Thank you," she whispered in the general direction of his ear.

"Anything for you, honey," he said softly in her ear while the others stood to leave. "Anything."

6

Suzie had never seen the colonel mad before that Saturday morning. He stalked the periphery of the living room. He slammed the legal papers down on the table, followed by his fist on the polished surface.

Suzie sat at the end of the dining room table quivering, too afraid to say a word. She was being sued in federal court—one million dollars, plus attorney fees. Suzie O'Dell, college sophomore and mobster.

"I will have this lawyer's license. He has to know all of this is a wicked sham. These people have no shame, no shame!" The colonel's voice echoed down the hallway. "How can these people say these things?"

"People who kill babies for a living will say anything." The voice was Shirley Alper's. She stood in the hallway, along with Pastor Randy Wallace, who had once again given her a ride to the colonel's house. Both were upset but in control.

"No matter what they say in these papers, we know the truth," Randy added. "And truth is a powerful weapon in God's arsenal."

The colonel said nothing but turned his back to the table and glared out the window onto the choppy waters of Lake Whatcom. Early morning showers had given way to gusting winds, and the evergreens surrounding the lake dipped and bowed before the invisible force. At that moment, the colonel felt like one of those trees, being shoved by something he could not touch or see.

While the colonel stared vacantly at the trees and the lake, Ginny Kettner slipped quietly in and sat on an empty seat at the dining room table. No one said a thing as the colonel leaned against the window frame, one hand up high supporting his weight, the other massaging his forehead with his fingertips.

An awkward minute passed. "I do wish just this once that our dear little Ginny would get here on time," the colonel said.

"Uh, Colonel, I'm here," Ginny replied sheepishly.

Spinning around, the colonel's eyes met Ginny's, his face turning bright red. "Ohhh," he moaned. "I'm so sorry, it's just . . ."

"Colonel, it's OK. I deserve it. I—"

Suddenly Randy Wallace's voice overpowered the others.

"Listen friends, our enemy is counting on division among us at this moment. Let's not satisfy him." He could see the puzzled looks on their faces. "No, not the lawyer, not the abortion clinic. The enemy of our souls." He let the words sink in for just a little bit. "There are two things that are vital right now. First, we cannot let anything come between us, no matter what anyone accuses us of. We know the truth. And second, we've got to turn this legal battle over to someone who can do some good . . . Him," he said, pointing heavenward. "Before we do anything else, let's get on our knees and beg God for His intervention."

One by one they slipped off their dining room chairs and onto their knees. Danners was the last to join them, but almost as soon as his knees touched the ground, he began to pray. Not a prayer of fear, nor of desperation. But the fervent prayer of a man who had flown time and again into the face of mortal danger, knew the risk, but undertook the mission anyway because he knew it was right.

After forty-five minutes of sometimes tearful, always intense pleas to the Almighty, the group of five stood and instinctively held hands. Softly, Ginny began singing, "Blest be the tie that binds . . ." In a moment, the others joined her. As the last note ended, Randy said, "Normally after I sing that song, I dismiss the church. This time I feel like we're just beginning—there's a lot of work to do."

"Yeah," Shirley agreed.

"Well," the colonel said, taking a seat and motioning for the others to do the same. "Anybody know a good lawyer?"

"I do," Suzie said meekly.

"You do?" Shirley laughed a little incredulously. "When have you needed a lawyer?"

"Oh, it's not like that. I used to babysit for this lawyer in Spokane. He and his wife have the cutest little girl. I know them from my home church."

"Suzie, I'm sure he's very nice, but this is a very special case, and we need someone who is used to complex suits. Lots of experience, that sort of thing," the colonel said with a tone that meant it was time to move on. "Anyone else know an experienced lawyer?"

"We have a man in our church," Randy said, "but I think he only does wills and corporations."

"Well, maybe he could refer us to someone who would be appropriate."

"Good idea," Shirley said. "Let's call him at home. Do you know his number, Pastor?"

"No, I'll have to look it up," he called over his shoulder as he walked to the kitchen. After a minute he returned to the dining room. "Not home," he said. "Just got his answering machine. I wish we could find someone today, even if it was just to give us a reference."

"Me, too," Danners replied. "The way I read these papers, there's some kind of hearing in Seattle next Friday. Federal court. We really need someone with some experience in federal litigation."

Suzie hadn't stirred since she had been cut off by the colonel. Feeling the urge to speak up again, she almost bit her tongue to keep quiet, but something inside said, "Go ahead."

"Colonel, I don't want to be rude, but my lawyer friend in Spokane does have experience. I used to read about this big case he did in the newspapers and I even saw him on TV. We prayed about it in church a lot, something involving the Supreme Court in Washington. He won a lot of money."

"Suzie," the colonel began gently, "the Supreme Court of Washington is a state court. We need someone with federal court experience. And besides, he's all the way in Spokane."

"No," Suzie said suddenly. "I don't mean the Supreme Court in Washington state, I mean Washington, D.C. He won over a million dollars from the state."

"OK, I give," Danners said. "Why don't we call him?"

"Yeah, he actually sounds pretty good," Randy chimed in. "What's his name, Suzie?"

"Peter Barron," she replied. "And I'll go call him right now. I have his home number memorized from baby-sitting," she announced triumphantly as she stood to head for the phone in the colonel's den.

Gwen Barron was in Casey's bedroom when she heard the phone ring. "Oh brother," she said, as she was in the middle of changing the sheets on her seven-year-old daughter's bed. She walked across the hallway and down a few steps to her bedroom and grabbed the phone just in time to avoid the answering machine.

"Good morning."

"Hi, Gwen—I mean Mrs. Barron—this is Suzie O'Dell."

"Oh, hi, Suzie," Gwen said enthusiastically. "It's OK to call me Gwen. But I thought you were away at school. Aren't you supposed to be in Bellingham?"

"Yes, I am in Bellingham. I'm sorry to call on Saturday, but it's kind of important. I'm being sued."

"You? What happened? Were you in a traffic accident or something?"

"No, I'm being sued for a million dollars."

"Suzie, is this a joke?"

"No, I wish it was. Why won't anyone believe me this morning?"

Gwen detected the sound of frayed nerves starting to turn to tears in Suzie's voice.

"Suzie, I believe you, and I know you need help. Let me get Peter; he's outside mowing the lawn."

"Oh, I don't want to interrupt him if he's outside."

"No, really. This sounds very important. Let me go get him right now."

Suzie heard Gwen place the receiver on a table. "His wife has gone to get him," she said to Danners and Randy, who were standing anxiously in the kitchen. "He's mowing the yard."

"Suzie O'Dell, my favorite baby-sitter," the voice of Peter Barron boomed over the telephone a minute or so later. "What's all this about a million-dollar lawsuit?"

"Yes, Mr. Barron, it's about a pro-life protest I'm involved in over here. The abortion clinic is suing us in federal court. I don't understand it all."

"Us? Are there more of you?"

"Yes, there are five of us. We're the leaders of the Whatcom Life Coalition. Mr. Barron, maybe it would be better if you could talk to Colonel Danners. He's our chairman, and I'm calling from his house."

"OK, Suzie, put him on the phone."

After twenty minutes of conversation, Danners and Wallace walked back into the dining room where the three women had been waiting expectantly.

"Has Suzie found our man?" Shirley asked in an obvious move to reinforce Suzie's confidence.

"Indeed she has," the colonel said with a broad smile. "This man sounds absolutely great. His name's Peter Barron; he's a solid Christian and totally pro-life. And he did win an important constitutional case in the Supreme Court in Washington, D.C. It went all the way through the federal system. And he's willing to do our case for free if we will just pay his expenses."

"How much will that be?" Ginny asked.

"He said perhaps two or three thousand, initially. Depending on how things go, it could be more, but not like hundreds of thousands or anything. And he said that some pro-life groups from D.C. might help us out with money down the road."

Ginny looked worried. "We don't have anything close to that in our treasury. And Jim and I sure can't afford that kind of money."

"Don't worry about the money," the colonel said. "I'll make good on the first two thousand dollars if I have to. Any other lawyer would cost us ten times that amount."

"I'll talk to our elders tomorrow," Randy volunteered. "Perhaps there's something our church can do."

"So, where do we start?" Shirley asked.

"Peter wants all the paperwork sent to him immediately," Danners said. "I'll head down to Kinko's and get it copied and then fax it from there. Peter's going to drive down to his office this afternoon to look it over so he can get going on it right away." Danners headed for the door to say goodbye as everyone left.

"Why don't we close in prayer?" Suzie suggested.

Danners stopped and leaned against the wall. "Suzie, aren't you tired of being right?" the colonel said, turning toward her. Afraid she might have taken the comment as an angry remark, he walked over to her side and gave her a strong hug. "I appreciate your persistence, Suzie. Thank you."

Suzie smiled, beaming confidently in the colonel's acceptance.

In Spokane, Casey Barron jumped into the back seat of her dad's white Explorer and began buckling her seat belt. Peter checked it to be sure it was fastened properly and gently slammed the rear door shut. "And now for my other favorite lady," Peter said with a bow, as he opened the front door for his wife. After Gwen got in, he stood looking at her for a moment as she stretched the seat and shoulder belt around her body, smoothing out the fabric of her blouse as best she could.

"What are you looking at?" she finally said with a puzzled look on her face.

"I'm just seeing if it's true," he replied.

"What?"

"I'm just seeing if pregnant women really do glow in the sunshine."

"Oh you . . ." Gwen said with a half-hearted swipe at Peter's arm.

Peter leaned over and kissed her quickly, then patted her still-flat abdomen. "Ride safe, baby."

"Can I ride on the carousel, Mommy?" Casey asked from the back seat as the car headed north on Liberty Lake Drive toward the interstate.

"Sure, Casey doll," Gwen replied. "We'll have lots of fun in the park. Daddy will be in his office for a little while and we can ride the carousel and go on the big slide and feed the ducks."

"And I'll get there real quick, Casey," Peter said, looking at his daughter in the rearview mirror. "I'll just grab some papers and meet you and Mommy in just a little bit. It's our day in Riverfront Park, just like I promised."

Casey hummed, contentedly kicking her dangling feet back and forth as she stared out the windows at the mix of houses and small commercial developments that lay along Interstate 90 in the eastern part of the Spokane Valley. Casey's occasional kicks on the back of her seat caused Gwen to focus on the baby she was carrying, due in late November. It wouldn't be that much longer until the gentle little thumps would start from the inside.

Gwen stroked her stomach. She often wondered whether Peter could love this child—the first from their marriage—as much as he loved Casey, her daughter from a previous marriage. The two seemed inseparable.

"Well, here we are. Jump out ladies," Peter said after a twenty-five-minute ride. "I'll go over to the office and be back quick as a wink."

"Now don't you start researching things, Mr. Attorney," Gwen said with a grin. "Just get the papers and get back here. You promised."

Peter raised his right hand and straightened his back. "I solemnly swear, I shall return."

"On time," Gwen said with a slight edge of seriousness in her voice.

"Yes, ma'am. Promptly."

Peter's dedication to his work was one thing that attracted Gwen to him when he represented her three years earlier. Now as his wife, his busy schedule created conflicts in their marriage. She was increasingly concerned about how much time he would spend with the family once the new baby arrived.

Peter turned the Explorer south for two blocks and then headed east on Riverside, parking in front of the Paulsen Building. He jumped out, fed the meter, bounded into the foyer, and punched the button for the twelfth floor. Three minutes later he was at the fax machine, pouring over the forty-five-page document that had arrived from the Bellingham Kinko's an hour earlier.

The name of the Los Angeles firm was the first thing that caught Peter's attention. "Big time outfit," he said to himself. Glancing through the complaint, motion, affidavit, and especially the supporting brief, he immediately recognized that this case had not been filed by amateurs— these people had done this before.

Peter's instincts told him to sit down and read through everything, then head to the law library. But as he turned the corner from the receptionist's station into his office, he saw Riverfront Park looming four blocks away and remembered his wife and daughter, waiting for him by the carousel.

He threw the papers and a fresh legal pad into his briefcase. He would make just one quick stop in the law library, just two floors below. A quick stop on the tenth floor yielded a three-page photocopy of 18 U.S.C. § 248, the Freedom of Access to Clinic Entrances Act—the FACE Act, as it was called when President Clinton signed it in 1994.

As experienced as he was with the federal system, he had never had occasion to read this particular statute before. He scanned it briefly, then took a second look at the legal papers and verified that Suzie's lawsuit was, indeed, grounded on the FACE Act. Peter tossed the photocopied statute into his briefcase, but continued reading the pleading as he descended the ten flights back to the main lobby. Twenty minutes later he arrived at the carousel and could see Casey vainly trying to grab the brass ring that would yield a ticket for a free ride.

Peter snuck up behind his wife, seated on a nearby bench, and began gently massaging her neck below the large, hinged hair clip that kept her blond hair held neatly back. The carousel continued to spin before their eyes, and both he and Gwen waved at Casey each time she flew by on her winged horse.

"I'll give you thirty minutes to cut that out, stranger," Gwen said, rotating her head from side to side.

Peter laughed, came around the bench, and plopped down close beside her. "I bet you talk to all the guys that way."

"Only the ones that take forty-five minutes to 'just pick up a fax.'"

"It was thirty minutes for the fax and fifteen minutes to find a parking spot here at the park."

"You should have just walked from your office. That wouldn't have taken nearly as long."

"Well, I didn't want the pregnant mother of our child to have to walk too far."

"Your concern is noted and logged, sir," she said, pulling him toward her as the carousel spun in front of them. Leaning her head on Peter's shoulder, Gwen continued, "So what did you learn? Are Suzie and her friends in real trouble?"

Pulling back, Peter's face drew up into a concerned frown. "They're in the midst of a real lawsuit, that's for sure. The abortion clinic is represented by a huge firm from L.A., plus a group of lawyers in Seattle called McGar and Leonard."

"Two big firms from big cities?" she asked.

"Yeah."

"Is that fair?"

Peter looked at her quizzically.

"I mean, how can only two big city firms expect to have a chance against Peter Barron & Associates? You'll cream 'em, Peter."

Peter smiled and hugged his wife, grateful for her humor and confidence. But as the carousel slowed to a stop, Peter's gut suddenly told him that he was running up against a level of legal talent and power unknown to his Spokane practice.

"I hope so, honey, I hope so," Peter said as they walked to the point where Casey came bounding from the carousel.

"Can I ride it again, Mommy, please?" Casey pleaded.

"Not right now, honey. Let's go over to the slide and maybe we can feed the ducks along the river."

"Daddy, please, can I ride one more time?" Casey appealed.

Peter grabbed his auburn-haired little bundle and flipped her up on his shoulders. "Let's go do some other things first, and when we are ready to leave, you and I can ride the carousel once more together. And I'll grab the brass ring—guaranteed."

Casey giggled and settled in on Peter's shoulders as they headed toward the slide made to look like a Paul Bunyan-sized Radio Flyer wagon. Peter guarded the bottom of the slide for Casey's first three trips down, then settled in on the bench beside Gwen, where they could watch their daughter and a dozen or so other kids take turns on the popular contraption.

"Peter, are you worried about Suzie's case? You seem distant."

"I'm concerned—that's all."

"That bad, huh? Have they really done something wrong?"

"Morally wrong, no. But legally, I can't tell. The head of their coalition, a Colonel Danners, told me that some of the things they're accused of are flat-out lies while others are gross exaggerations. I'll just have to see how the evidence comes together."

"Sounds complicated; are you sure you should take the case? I mean, if you have to spend a lot of time there; Bellingham is a long way away."

"Yeah, but the case will be tried in federal court in Seattle, a forty-five-minute plane ride away."

"But how often will you need to go?"

"If you mean, *exactly* how much time will I be away from home, I don't know," Peter responded with an air of irritation, sensing the direction the conversation was heading. Gwen, who had been leaning against his side, pulled away suddenly and glared at him.

"I was merely thinking of your other commitments, and yes, come to think of it, how much time you'll be away as the time for the baby's delivery approaches. Peter, I want you home when our baby comes!"

"Honey, this is a really important case, not only because it's Suzie, but because of the work they're doing. These people are saving dozens of lives each month. I think I should help them. Don't you?"

"Of course I do," Gwen agreed, relaxing a bit.

"I don't think I'll be gone for more than five or six days total over the next six months. And I really doubt this case will ever go to a full trial. The judge will probably decide it on motions. If it is tried, it won't last more than two or three days. Seven days max—that's all I foresee over six or eight months. That's not that bad."

"But you know how optimistic you can be about time. It seems like things always take twice as long as you expect."

Peter looked away, scanning the playground for Casey. She was immersed in play with two other little girls and oblivious to her parents. He realized that as Gwen grew in size with the pregnancy, she would be less able to handle Casey's seemingly unlimited energy alone. Turning back to Gwen, he said, "Honey, if you don't want me to take this case, just say so. I don't want this to cause a problem between us."

Gwen smiled. "No, Peter, I want you to take it. I like it when you're fighting for things like this. I just want you close by as much as possible."

Peter wrapped his arms around Gwen. "This close enough? Or can we get even closer?"

"Peter Barron, we are in public," Gwen whispered forcibly. "Behave yourself!"

"You want to go over and let Casey ride the airplanes?"

"Well, actually I was hoping we could go eat something somewhere."

"But it's only a quarter to four."

Gwen patted her abdomen. "Tell that to this little guy!"

Peter quickly bent down and faced Gwen's stomach. "Hey, you in there. It's only a quarter to four; it's not dinner time yet!"

Gwen blushed and wheeled away, her green eyes laughing. "Just get Casey and let's go, Mr. Smart-mouth."

Peter wanted desperately to spend some time that evening pouring over the legal papers, but his wife's pleas in the park kept him by her side all evening. At five o'clock the next morning, however, his mind was fully awake. He crept carefully out of bed, made some coffee, and sat in his study until seven, reading and analyzing the situation until it was time to get ready for church.

At five minutes to three that afternoon, Peter entered his study again and arranged some papers on the desk. He walked over and opened the blinds of the window overlooking the backyard, which sloped very gently downward to Liberty Lake. Gwen was on the lower patio in a recliner, dressed in sweatpants and an oversized T-shirt. Casey was in a log fort, built on stilts, with a neighbor girl.

The phone rang. "Peter Barron here," he said.

"Mr. Barron, thank you for being willing to talk to us on a Sunday afternoon," Randy Wallace said. "All five of us are here in my church study. Can you hear us OK on this speaker phone?"

"I can hear you fine."

"So how bad is it?" Danners's voice broke in.

"Well, that's hard to say exactly. It depends a lot on what in their papers is fact, and how much we can prove is fiction. But I can say this: You are not up against amateurs. The lawyers representing the clinic appear to be very experienced in this sort of case. They were thorough to the last detail. And, although numbers don't necessarily mean anything, both firms are huge. They have a lot of manpower to draw from."

"Exactly how many are there in your firm?" Ginny Kettner asked. "If you don't mind me asking," she quickly added.

"No, not at all," Peter said with a laugh. "There are three. My partner Joe and I, and a new associate, Cooper Stone. He's just out of law school."

"How many in their firms?" Ginny asked.

"The Seattle firm has about 300 lawyers, according to my legal directory. And the L.A. firm has 625 scattered over five offices around the country—250 in L.A. alone."

For several moments, there was total silence. "Please, don't let that worry you too much," Peter said as cheerfully as he could. "Only one lawyer can talk at a time in court, and there are page limits for the briefs they write. It'll be OK."

"I'm sure it will," the colonel said with an enthusiastic voice, but with a growing pit in his stomach.

"Well, let me begin by telling you this much," Peter began. "There are two important parts to this lawsuit: a RICO cause of action and a FACE cause of action."

Shirley Alper and the colonel both began to take notes.

"The RICO charge," Peter continued, "stands for Racketeer Influenced and Corrupt Organizations Act. It was really designed by Congress to go after organized crime, but the abortion industry appears to have twisted it into something they like to use against pro-life protesters."

"Can they do that?" Shirley Alper asked.

"Well, several courts have said they can, but it is not a slam-dunk case. They have to be able to prove that you were engaged in some underlying illegal activity and had a desire to harm their business."

"Well, we certainly didn't do anything illegal; the colonel was insistent on that," Shirley said.

"That's right, Peter," Randy said. "We were very careful—never went on the clinic property; always stayed on the sidewalk. No excessive chanting. And certainly no name calling or threats."

"Well, I'm glad to hear that, although they have filed some affidavits to the contrary."

"But did we desire to harm their business?" Shirley broke in. "We wanted the abortions to stop—I guess that would mean shutting down the clinic completely, since that's all they handle."

"Well, in any event, if we can prove that you behaved yourselves, then hopefully that'll take care of the RICO part of the case. And that's good because that's where they are seeking the most money."

"OK," the colonel said, sounding exhausted. "What's this FACE complaint about?"

"That's a little more problematic," Peter replied. "They don't have to prove actual criminal activity to win under the FACE complaint."

"What does FACE mean anyway?" Shirley asked.

"It stands for Freedom of Access to Clinic Entrances. It was passed in response to groups like Operation Rescue, which were blocking clinic entrances."

"But we weren't doing anything like that," Ginny interjected.

"Well, they're claiming you used threat of force or physical obstruction by blocking their driveways to stop people from getting an abortion."

"That's just not true, so I don't think that should be a problem, Peter," the colonel said. "We were very careful. I don't think anyone who actually watched our operation could possibly claim that we used threat of force or physical obstruction."

"That all sounds good, but the U.S. Justice Department and the abortion industry's lawyers have been very good at creatively interpreting very peaceful protests in ways that have caused real problems. It will not be easy to convince a judge to simply dismiss this part of the case—especially since there is apparently a big dispute over the facts. You are saying one thing, and their affidavits say something quite different. Factual disputes are what juries are all about."

"Will there be a jury on Friday?" Wallace asked.

"No," Peter replied, "just a judge ruling on this motion to stop the demonstrations. But it will be very important—it will set the tone for the whole case. We will have to fight hard and be prepared."

"What do we need to do?" the colonel asked.

"Well, I'd like to come see you all tomorrow. I'm going to have my secretary clear my calendar. I'll fly over to Seattle early in the morning, rent a car, and be up there by mid-morning."

"Can't you fly into Bellingham?" the colonel asked. "We do have commuter lines that land here from Seattle."

"I don't care for those little commuter flights. They scare me to death."

"Well," the colonel said, clearing his throat. "There will be no need to rent a car. I'll pick you up at Sea-Tac."

By the sound of his voice, Peter could tell that the colonel was not used to being challenged, and the trip would give him extra time to quiz the colonel about the background facts.

"Fine. The flight arrives at 7:00 A.M., Alaskan Airlines Flight 107. I'll see you then."

"Great. How can we prepare?"

"I need your best recollections of everything that occurred at the clinic. Take some time to think about it beforehand, and put your thoughts on paper."

"Should I skip my classes and come too?" Suzie asked.

"Suzie, is that you? I wasn't sure you were there, you've been so quiet."

"I have classes tomorrow morning. Should I go to them?"

"Sorry, but I think you'd better come to our meeting. The more heads we have on this, the better."

"We'll be ready," the colonel said. "See you in the morning."

7

By now Rhonda had analyzed hundreds of pregnancy tests. They were almost always positive; few came to the clinic without confirming the pregnancy in some manner beforehand. But the clinic test—a blood test—was by far the most reliable of all methods.

Rhonda glanced nervously at her watch as she waited for the test to finish processing. The clinic would open in fifteen minutes. Pacing the length of the hallway connecting the various rooms in the clinic, she walked over to the window at the end of the hall and stared blankly outside. She turned and headed back toward the reception area, where a wall clock indicated three more minutes until the test was complete.

She walked over to her desk and started flipping through the mail— bills and other business mail. One plain envelope with no outside markings caught her attention. She opened it quickly, glancing at her watch. Inside she found a colorful pamphlet with a yellow Post-It note on the front. "We love you, Dr. Marsano. We pray for you every day. And for the babies," the note read.

Normally she would have crumpled the note and the "How to Have Peace with God" pamphlet and thrown them in the trash. But checking her watch, she just let them drop gently onto the desk and paced quickly back to check the test. She read the result, then sat down on a nearby chair. Feeling faint, she put her head between her legs for a few moments. There was no mistake—she was pregnant.

She still had a couple of minutes until the clinic opened. Walking back to her office, she swept the pamphlet and the rest of the mail into the top drawer of her desk and picked up the phone. She dialed his number. No answer. She dialed the number for his cellular phone.

"Hello," Vince's voice said with mild crackling discernible in the background.

"Vince, it's me."

"Rhonda?"

"Yes, of course."

"This is my cell phone. We aren't supposed—"

"I know. I know. Listen. We have to talk. Tonight."

"OK."

"Meet me at Boulevard Park. Over by Fairhaven, 9:30."

"Fine."

She pressed down the button disconnecting the call but froze in thought with the receiver still held to her ear. For a brief moment she stared out the window beside her desk, then started to dial her mother's number. Halfway through dialing she hung the receiver back on its cradle. Brushing away a few tears from her eyes, she went to the front door and unlocked it. The doctor must have a confident face on when the patients arrive, she thought.

Patients who—like her—were facing an unplanned pregnancy.

The colonel's Jeep skimmed north on Interstate 5, away from Sea-Tac Airport, with the two men locked in intense conversation. The colonel barely noticed the lush scenery as they traversed along the Skagit Valley and entered the range of high hills that separate the valley from Bellingham. But being from the much-dryer climate of Spokane, Peter spoke up. "Sure is beautiful up here," he said. "I've never really spent any time in this part of the state. I think I've only driven through Bellingham once, on my way to a bar association convention in Vancouver."

"Well, you'll have to return with your wife under different circumstances. I'm sure you'd both enjoy it. Do you have any children?"

"My wife, Gwen, is pregnant with our first child. We also have a seven-year-old girl, Casey, from my wife's previous marriage. I adopted Casey about a year after her father died."

"Oh, that's right, Suzie told us about baby-sitting your little girl," Danners said with a big smile. "One thing I have come to appreciate while working on this pro-life project is that children really are a blessing from the Lord. My wife and I both wish we'd had more children, but the military made that difficult."

"Hmmm," Peter replied. "Were you away from home a lot?"

"Yes, and my wife didn't want the stress of raising a large family on her own."

"I hear you there," Peter said.

"We're almost there now." The colonel exited the freeway, passed a conglomeration of strip malls, and proceeded quickly into the residential area along Lakeway Drive.

Within minutes Peter was shaking hands with Ginny Kettner, Shirley Alper, and Randy Wallace. He gave Suzie a quick hug. "Glad to see you again," he said, nudging Suzie in the ribs.

After two and a half hours of shooting questions, reviewing documents, and making notes, Peter looked up from his yellow pad and said, "Well, I suppose I should give you all a little feedback and a chance to ask me some questions for a change. Let me begin with what you can expect on Friday."

Five heads nodded in eager affirmation.

"This first hearing is a request for a preliminary injunction. That means that the clinic owners are asking the court to stop you from picketing while any further action is being decided. The order couldn't stop you from picketing forever, but it could stop your efforts for a year or more, until the case comes to trial."

"Do you think the judge will do that?" Shirley asked.

"I can't really say, Shirley. That depends on what kind of immediate evidence the other attorneys have to back up their claims. But I'll give you my best, educated guess: I think he'll grant them some kind of order."

"But most of their claims are false," the colonel said with a flash of anger.

"That's right," Peter replied. "But even though the technical rules of evidence are otherwise, because you are pro-life, the burden of proof will fall on you; and so far all you have is your word. Presumably they will have some kind of hard evidence, which we don't know about yet. And, the federal courts are so biased in favor of abortion, I'd be surprised if this judge—Judge Tyler—didn't rule in favor of the clinic on that fact alone. So yes, I predict an order against you on Friday. Our job, then, will be to keep you from being completely shut down. If we can accomplish that, we ought to consider Friday a victory."

"I'm not used to that definition of a victory," the colonel responded dejectedly.

Peter shrugged and stared at the table for a moment. Looking up, he fixed his eyes firmly on the colonel and said, "Well, Colonel, I wish I could guarantee you greater hope. But only God can do that. We'll just have to depend on Him for the outcome."

"Of course," Danners said, "you're absolutely right. I don't mean to appear pessimistic or ungrateful; it's just that I'm used to a different kind of warfare."

"Warfare. That's not a bad analogy," Peter replied.

Wallace added, "I'm sure the angels have their hands full with this one."

"Well, the front line can't fight on an empty stomach," the colonel interjected, standing up. "It's lunchtime, and I'll bet my wife has something waiting for us on the back deck."

With the lake glistening in the noonday sun, the five-member coalition, Danners's wife, and Peter joined hands and prayed over the food, and for the hearing on Friday.

Vince had no trouble finding Rhonda's Volvo, which sat empty in the park's dimly-lit parking lot. But finding Rhonda was considerably more difficult. He finally saw her sitting on a boulder on the water's edge. She was wearing a light-colored windbreaker and had her hair tucked up inside a baseball cap.

The moon briefly broke through a hole in the cloud cover as Vince scuffed across a spot of gravel about ten yards behind Rhonda. She turned to see who was coming and gasped seeing a shadowy figure approaching in the moonlight.

"It's OK, Rhonda. It's just me."

Relaxing, Rhonda turned her gaze away from Vince and back onto the dark waters of Puget Sound. A few boats lay offshore in the distance. The lights of a huge Japanese freighter waiting for a load of Pacific Northwest timber lay a half mile off to their left. Otherwise, no signs of activity appeared anywhere within her range of vision.

"I had a hard time finding you over here in the dark," Vince said.

She did not respond. Vince thought she seemed hypnotized by the gently rocking swells on the water.

"Rhonda," he said after another uncomfortable silence. "What's wrong? Something's obviously up, but I can't read your mind. You have to talk to me."

Vince could not see the tears flowing down her cheeks, but he could hear her soft sobs as she tried to regain her composure. He reached out and put his arm around her. She collapsed immediately into his arms and began to sob without restraint. "Oh, Vince," were the only words she could say.

After a minute of gentle rocking in Vince's embrace, Rhonda finally continued. "Oh, Vince, I'm so sorry."

"Sorry about what?" he asked softly.

"I'm . . . I'm pregnant," she stammered.

"You're what?" he said with a slight laugh. He pushed her gently back so he could look into her eyes. "What did you say?"

"You heard me," she replied, turning her eyes away.

"Yeah, I heard you, but I don't believe you."

"Well, believe it. It's definitely true. I ran the test at the clinic myself. There is no mistake."

"Well, OK," Vince replied with a smile, pulling her into his arms again. "How big a problem can this be? You solve this same problem for dozens of women every week. You know what to do."

"I can't perform an abortion on myself."

"Of course not, I didn't mean that. Take a couple days off and go to the sister clinic in Eugene."

Rhonda freed herself of Vince's embrace. "I don't want to go to Eugene." She sat staring once again at the dark waters of the bay.

"OK, so go someplace else."

"Vince, I don't want to go anywhere for an abortion."

"What are you talking about? Is it the travel? Do you want Jane and Karen to fly in another doctor and take care of it here in Bellingham? They'd probably do it, you know. And I'll cover the expense."

"You still don't get it. I don't want to have an abortion, period. You know I was raised Catholic. Performing abortions on others is one thing, but with my own baby everything changes. I want to have this baby. I want to have *your* baby."

"You what?" Vince said incredulously. "You're out of your mind. You can't work at an abortion clinic and be pregnant!"

"I thought we were about choice—not just abortions."

"Choice is for politics. Abortion is a business. You're in the abortion business, not the choice business."

"Well, no matter what anyone says, I *choose* to have this baby."

"Rhonda, be reasonable," he said with a softer voice. "No matter what I think, Jane and Karen will not allow a pregnant woman to do abortions. It would freak out too many customers."

"So, let them fire me. If they fire me, I'm not bound to repay the loan."

"Rhonda, you signed their contract. It's not that simple."

"No court would uphold such a contract, would it?"

"You don't get to go to court. You'd go to an arbiter, chosen from a list of independent arbiters maintained by their law firm."

"And just how do you know all this?"

"I've been working for Jane and Karen for years, remember?"

"Well, we can eventually pay them off. After all, I am a doctor, and you can find a different job—you're a very talented guy."

"What's this 'we' bit? These aren't my medical school loans."

"No, but it is your baby."

"Rhonda, I'm not ready to be a father yet."

"And I suppose you're not ready to be a husband yet, either?"

"Is that what this is all about? You want to have this baby so I will *marry* you? You gotta be kidding."

Rhonda sprang to her feet and headed toward the parking lot. Vince grabbed her, gently but firmly, by the arm.

"Take your hands off of me!" Rhonda beat on Vince's chest until he released his grasp. She quickly darted up the rocks and across the grass, then jumped into her car and drove away. Vince stood and stared as she drove away. Shaking his head, he dusted off the backside of his pants and slowly walked across the park, just as the moon made a brief cameo appearance in the northwest sky.

Peter knew his Los Angeles opponent by his suit as he came down the hall outside the clerk's office. Barry Penner's silvery grey, double-breasted jacket and pants were stylishly loose, in the Italian fashion. The tie was a geometric pattern of silver, charcoal, black, and white, lightly accented with red streaks. Few Seattle lawyers would wear such a flashy suit to federal court.

"Mr. Penner?" Peter said, extending his hand. "I'm Peter Barron. I'm representing the defendants in your case today."

"Oh, Mr. Barron," Penner said warmly. "I was hoping to meet you before court today. How did you know who I was?"

"Lucky guess," Peter replied.

"This is my associate, Dana Storino," Penner said, gesturing to a thirtyish woman by his side. She wore a tailored red wool suit, and her short auburn hair was moussed stylishly but rigidly in place.

"Ms. Storino, happy to meet you," Peter replied.

"Hello, Mr. Barron," she said, holding tightly to the black leather litigation case she was pulling along behind her.

"See you in just a few minutes," Penner said with a friendly smile.

Peter was struck by Penner's pleasant manner and willingness to engage in amiable conversation. From what he'd been able to gather about Judge Tyler, he wished he were facing Dana Storino in the courtroom instead of Penner. Judge Tyler disdained arrogant lawyers, especially those from out of state.

Penner and Storino turned a corner of the hallway and disappeared. Peter had not yet looked at the directory to see which courtroom he was in but guessed if he followed Penner he'd find out. Turning the same corner as Penner and Storino, he peered through a small glass window built into one of two massive mahogany courtroom doors. Empty. The room was much larger than the ones in the Spokane courthouse and was paneled in the same red wood as the massive doors. Peter looked into the other courtroom. A group of seventy people, mostly college students, crowded together, filling a good portion of the room. Penner and Storino and a handful of others, huddled together like a football team, stood whispering in the front of the courtroom. Together with two other grey-suited associates—from the Seattle firm, Peter guessed—they took their seats at the counsel table to the judge's left.

Suzie saw Peter stride through the courtroom door, stood, and then made her way to the aisle to wait for him. "Mr. Barron, I'm so glad to see you! Let me introduce you to the others," she said, feeling as if she were introducing a celebrity. Three of the coalition defendants were seated in the front row on the judge's right: Randy Wallace, Shirley Alper, and Ginny Kettner, who had the seat next to Suzie's. Lisa Edgar sat on the other side of Ginny, with her steady boyfriend, Stephen Gray, by her side. The colonel sat by himself at the counsel table in front of the other defendants. Seeing Peter, he got up from his seat and shook his hand. Peter went to counsel table, unloaded his files and notes, chatting with the colonel in the process.

As they sat talking, the bailiff, who had been looking half asleep along a side wall, came alive and called, "All rise!" as Judge Tyler strode into the courtroom from his chambers. Everyone in the entire court-room sprang to their feet. Unlike most state courtrooms, there were four chairs around each of the counsel tables. Consequently, the tables were turned facing the opposite counsel table rather than the judge. Peter kept his chair at a forty-five-degree angle, so he could keep his focus directly on the judge.

Tyler had been raised in a tiny logging town on the Olympic Peninsula. Overweight with reddish hair and a ruddy face, he struck many as a country bumpkin. As a lawyer, he wrestled for many years with the legacy of his "backward" upbringing and education. In fact, however, he'd finished first in his class at the University of Washington and in the top 10 percent at Yale Law School. Now that he was a federal judge with high-paid lawyers bowing daily to his merest whim, Tyler took great pleasure in appearing to be a somewhat simple thinking, gullible judge, then skewering pompous, big-city lawyers with his superior intellect.

The law clerk placed a stack of files next to Tyler. He opened the top one and examined its contents, stroking the remaining wisps of red hair across the top of his head. Satisfied, he said, "All right, counsel, let us begin. How about identifying all of yourselves for the court reporter here? She just loves people who talk slowly and leave a copy of their business cards with her after the hearing so she can spell their names correctly."

"Your Honor, my name is Burton Welch, from McGuire and Parr, appearing as local counsel for the plaintiffs," the first grey-suited man at the plaintiffs' table said.

"Bruce Gentry, also from McGuire and Parr, Your Honor," the second man said.

"Glad to see that McGuire and Parr gets to bill for two of you boys today. Gotta keep our local economy strong," the judge remarked with a wry grin. "And you are . . . ?" Tyler said, looking straight at Barry Penner.

"Barry Penner, Your Honor, from Doss, Stroshchein, Weiser, and Penner in Los Angeles. And this is Dana Storino, also from our office. If the court please, I think the first order of business might be to act on our motion for admission *pro hac vice,* since Ms. Storino and I are not members of this bar."

"Well, I had in mind to find out who these nice lookin' fellows are over here at this other table, Mr. Penner, and after that, why, I'll get right back to that motion of yours," the judge replied.

"Good morning, Your Honor," Peter said with a broad smile. "I'm Peter Barron from Spokane, and I represent all five defendants in this case. And this gentleman on my right is one of my clients, Colonel Hank

Danners. The other four are seated in the front row," Peter said, pointing in the direction of the other members of the board.

Shirley Alper started to stand up, but Peter quickly shook his head
and she collapsed back in her seat without drawing the attention of the
judge. Suzie smiled at Shirley, whose face reddened slightly.

"Welcome, Mr. Barron. I'll try to keep the fight fair this mornin',
with it being four against one and all. What I'll do is allow only one of
'em to talk at a time. OK, Mr. Barron?"

"Fine by me, Your Honor," Peter replied.

The judge quickly scanned the courtroom and noted with approval
that both Peter Barron and Barry Penner were smiling at his banter. The
other lawyers in the room appeared to be vying for the hardest stare at
the yellow pads in front of them.

"All right, Mr. Penner, your motion for admission is granted," the
judge said rocking back in his chair. "Now, why don't you tell me about
your motion-in-chief."

"Thank you, Your Honor," Penner said as he walked to the lectern
positioned in front of both tables in the dead center of the courtroom.
"This case involves both the Freedom of Access to Clinics Act and RICO,
coming from a series of illegal anti-abortion protests in Bellingham.
We are here today seeking a temporary injunction to stop this illegal
behavior, so that my clients' clinic may offer unhindered, constitutionally protected medical services at their facility."

"Counsel," the judge interrupted, "looks to me, from your papers,
like you're trying to shut down *all* of the defendants' activities—not just
those that are arguably illegal. These people have a right to walk peace-
ably up and down the sidewalk in an unobstructive manner, don't they?"

"Your Honor, it is our position that their illegal and threatening
behavior has become so intertwined with their constitutionally protected

activities that the only way to assure our patients of their rights is to curtail all their activities within two hundred feet of the clinic. They could still protest; it would just have to be down the street."

"What would the people with houses and businesses 'down the street' say to that? And what about the young girls visiting the clinic, and their rights to hear the defendants' message? How can they carry on a real protest if the people they want to reach can't see or hear them? These laws are meant to protect everyone, Mr. Penner, both the clinic and the demonstrators."

Shirley squeezed Suzie's hand. "This is great, don't you think?" she whispered softly. Suzie nodded and smiled.

"I understand your point, Your Honor," Penner replied. "It's tough to balance competing constitutional rights. In the abstract, it would be nice to protect both sets of rights in this case—our patients' right to a legal medical procedure, and the protesters' right to peacefully communicate a message. But in this particular case, while our clinic and our patients have fully obeyed the law and respected the rights of others, these defendants have not obeyed the law; and they have certainly not respected the rights of our patients. All I can say in answer to your question, sir, is when you have to balance competing constitutional rights, you should tip the scale in favor of those who have been law-abiding and minded their own business."

"Hmmm," the judge replied, jotting some notes down on his pad. The colonel caught Peter's eye, their faces acknowledging that Penner's last response had scored real points with the judge.

"All right, Mr. Penner, that leaves me with just one question for you. Assuming I agree with your legal argument about balancing constitutional rights, how am I to know which side to tip the scale toward in this dispute? Your affidavits claim that all the defendants have engaged in undeniably illegal activity, yet the affidavits Mr. Barron has filed says these claims aren't true—that his clients have scrupulously obeyed every law governing public demonstrations. Who am I to believe, and why?"

"Your Honor, I would respectfully request that you review this videotape and make up your own mind about that." Penner took a videocassette from Dana Storino, who had been holding it in her lap during the entire argument.

Peter turned sharply toward Danners with brows scrunched together over flashing eyes, indicating surprise and anger. "He's bluffing," the colonel whispered. "It simply is not true."

"Let's hope not," Peter replied.

"Your Honor, I would asked the court's permission to call Dr. Rhonda Marsano for the purpose of laying a foundation to introduce this videotape into evidence," Penner continued.

"This is a bit unusual, Counsel," the judge replied. "I normally don't take evidence in a motion hearing, but I'll at least let you lay the foundation."

"Dr. Marsano," Penner said, "could you please come forward and be sworn in?"

Rhonda pushed through the swinging mahogany gate, came down the aisle between both counsel tables, and stopped less than five feet from Peter. She nervously raised her right hand and repeated the words the clerk intoned, asking her to promise to tell the truth.

She straightened the skirt of her navy and white suit as she settled in the witness stand beside the judge.

"Please state your name and business address for the record," Penner said, loosely gripping the lectern.

"Rhonda Marsano. My business address is 300 Garden Street, Bellingham, Washington."

"And you are Dr. Marsano, right?"

"Yes, sir."

"What is your position at that address, Dr. Marsano?"

"I am the medical director at the Whatcom Women's Center for Choice."

"And that is in Bellingham?"

"Yes, sir. At the address I just gave."

"I would like to hand you a videotape, Dr. Marsano, and ask if you've seen it before."

"Well, I think so. It has the same label on it as the one I've seen. I would know for sure if I saw it played."

"Your Honor, I would like to have the exhibit marked for identification," Penner said looking up at the judge.

"Go ahead."

"Mark the tape plaintiff's number 1," Penner instructed the clerk.

"Dr. Marsano, do you know who made this tape?" Penner asked.

"Well, I directed a member of my staff to install a video camera in a spot on our second floor, where we had a good view of the demonstrators."

"And why did you do that?" Penner asked.

"To document some of the problems we were having."

"What kind of problems?"

"Objection," Peter called out. "He's going way beyond simply laying a foundation for the exhibit. Her version of the problems has already been submitted in her affidavit. I see no need for a repetition of what is contained there."

"Objection sustained," the judge replied, rocking back in his chair and staring hard at the tense witness.

"Am I supposed to—" Marsano began.

"No, Doctor," the judge said kindly. "When I say 'objection sustained' that means don't answer the question, and your lawyer should ask you a different question."

"Dr. Marsano," Penner began again, "has this videotape been kept as a part of the records of your business and in your custody until you gave it to me?"

"It has been either in my custody or the custody of one of my employees, yes."

"Does the video accurately represent events at the clinic?"

"Yes, it does," Marsano replied, her ears burning under her dark hair. She didn't like to deliberately lie, but Vince and Penner had convinced her that her answer was "essentially correct."

"Your Honor, I move to admit the tape as plaintiffs' exhibit 1 and have it played to demonstrate that the defendants did not behave as scrupulously as they would have you believe in their affidavits."

"Mr. Barron?" the judge asked, giving Peter an opportunity to argue against the video's admission.

Rising from his chair and tapping his silver and gold pen in the palm of his left hand, Peter said, "Your Honor, I have a few questions on voir dire before I can argue on the tape's admission."

"Fine," the judge replied. "I'll hold you to a few questions."

Standing beside his chair, Peter squared his shoulders to face the doctor. "Dr. Marsano, can you tell me how long this video runs?"

"I don't know exactly."

"Approximately?"

"About fifteen minutes."

"Does that fifteen minutes show continuous footage of one single event, or are there a number of different events?"

"There are a number of different events," Marsano replied, gripping the arm rests of her leather-bound chair.

"I take it, then, that you shot a lot of footage over time, then selected certain segments to edit together to show the court, is that right?"

"Yes, more or less."

"Did you edit the tape personally?"

"No."

"Who did edit the tape?"

Marsano had been briefed. This time she knew she had to tell an outright lie. "My bookkeeper did it. She has two VCRs and occasionally edits commercials out of soap operas, that sort of thing. She said she knew how to do it."

"Did you watch her do the editing?" Peter asked, pacing a few steps to his left.

"No, not directly."

"Not directly?"

"I guess I mean just no. I'm nervous, Mr. Barron, I've never testified before."

"Are the events on this video accurate after editing?"

"Yes, they are."

"Well, Your Honor, I would object to the admission of this tape unless all the original footage is submitted to the court, as well. That's the only way the edited version can be tested for accuracy."

"If this were a full-blown trial, Mr. Barron, I would agree with you," the judge replied. "But for the purposes of this motion, I am inclined to let it in so that I can watch it."

"Your Honor," Peter began, "may I reserve the right to renew my objection, once we have watched this edited tape?"

"Certainly, Mr. Barron," Tyler replied, swiveling his chair toward the monitor being placed into position by the bailiff.

"Watch closely and make notes of anything that looks suspicious," Peter whispered to the colonel. "I'm going to tell the others the same thing."

As the video was being readied, Peter walked to the bar of the courtroom, motioned to his four clients into the first row to lean over, and gave them the same message. Hearing the message, Gray's neck and face reddened slightly, but otherwise he gave no indication that Peter's comment was of any special interest.

The VCR blinked on to a line of protesters marching along the sidewalk in front of the clinic. Penner adjusted the volume. "Baby killer . . . baby killer . . . baby killer!" pierced the silence within the courtroom, followed by gasps from the dozens of spectators in the audience. The defendants merely shook their heads in disbelief of what they were seeing, until the scene depicting a car unable to pass through the protest line.

The colonel sat in silence, watching the video and then scribbling furiously on his note pad as the scenes unfolded.

The tape ended, and Peter looked grimly at Danners. Red in the face, the colonel whispered, "I don't know how they did it, Peter, but that tape has been doctored something fierce."

"If you're sure, then I'll take a chance."

Rising to his feet, Peter cleared his throat, "Your Honor, I would like to ask the court for a thirty-minute recess. In addition, I would like permission to take my clients into a jury room, or some other location, and review that tape with them."

"Well, Mr. Barron, we're behind schedule as is; there's no time for a recess. Whatever it is, I'm afraid you'll have to get it out right now."

"All right, Your Honor," Peter replied. "I'd like to ask Dr. Marsano just a couple follow-up questions?"

"Fine, Mr. Barron, you may proceed," the judge said.

Peter walked over to the remote and hit rewind. "While I'm rewinding the tape, Dr. Marsano, will you please tell us from what location these images were taken?"

"They were shot from a second-story window."

"Was there an operator at the camera?"

"No. It was just in one fixed position, shooting continuously throughout the day."

"How did you get the audio?"

"We kept the window open a crack and used an external microphone."

"OK, I think it's finished rewinding," Peter said, turning his back to the witness stand. He hit the play button and let the "baby killer" scene play before hitting the stop button.

"All right, Dr. Marsano, can you tell us please where these voices are coming from? I watched very closely this time, and I can't see anyone in the picket line who appears to be chanting or shouting. Can you?"

Marsano started to look at Vince for help but quickly caught herself. "I . . . I'm not sure. I mean, I guess the voices are coming from people just out of the camera's range. Like I said, it was in a fixed position."

"Outside the camera's range, huh?" Peter hit the fast forward button. "OK, let's take this scene where a young man suddenly runs across the grass to your front door. Is it possible, doctor, that he was innocently just chasing his hat that had blown away as the colonel tells me?"

The video played. Marsano watched nervously, digging her fingernails into the leather armrests.

"Well, Doctor," Peter said when the scene had ended. "Don't you think the colonel's explanation could be right if this tape hadn't been edited?"

"Objection," Penner cried out. "The colonel hasn't testified, and he's asking the witness to blatantly speculate."

"That's why we need to have the complete set of tapes, Your Honor!"

"That's enough arguing, gentlemen." Judge Tyler said wryly. "Let's do our objections and responses a bit more orderly."

"I'm sorry, Your Honor, I withdraw the question," Peter replied, confident he had made his point with the judge.

"All right," the judge replied. "You may take a seat," he said, nodding to the doctor. "Gentlemen, you've both made your positions clear. Mr. Penner, is there anything else you would like to add to the record at this point?"

"No," Penner replied. "The tape speaks for itself and demonstrates that our affidavits are accurate."

The judge turned and looked at Peter without saying a word.

"Your Honor, as you said, normally witnesses are not allowed at a motion hearing; but in light of the surprise production of this videotape, I would also like to have the opportunity to call one witness. I promise, it will be brief."

"OK. Mr. Barron, I'll let you call one, and only one."

"I'd like to call Colonel Hank Danners to the stand."

The colonel rose confidently from his chair, walked briskly toward the witness stand, and took his oath.

"Please state your name and address for the court," Peter began.

"Henry Danners. 3775 Fairlake Court, Bellingham, Washington."

"You retired from the air force with what rank, sir?"

"I retired two years ago, as a colonel."

"In the interest of time," Peter said, "I will not ask you to recite your outstanding military record since we covered your accomplishments in your affidavit."

"Objection, Your Honor," Penner called out. "Mr. Barron appears to be testifying on the colonel's behalf. The colonel's record need not be characterized as 'outstanding.'"

"Are you saying his record isn't outstanding?" the judge demanded, looking sternly at Penner with his eyebrows pressed together.

"No, Your Honor—"

"Well, then, Mr. Penner, your objection is overruled. You will do well in my courtroom, Counsel, not to object to preliminary questions unless you have something more than a technicality to bring to my attention."

Penner pressed his lips together and silently nodded at the judge.

"Continue, Mr. Barron," the judge said, turning away from the Los Angeles lawyer.

"Colonel Danners, do you have an explanation for any of the incidents we have seen on this video?"

"Yes, I do. At least in one scene."

"Which is that?"

"Well, as you mentioned a minute or two ago, the video shows an incident of a young man running toward the front door of the clinic, and then shows him a minute later walking slowly back across the lawn. I remember that incident from about three months ago. The wind had blown the young man's baseball cap off his head, and he merely was chasing his hat."

"Did he in any way threaten the clinic?" Peter asked.

"Absolutely not," Danners replied. "There were no patients around, nor any clinic employees."

"Did you say anything to him afterwards?"

"Yes, I reminded him of our rule against going on the clinic's property. I told him I understood he meant no harm, but that in the future he should abandon his hat and not run after it."

"What did the young man say to you?"

"He was very apologetic."

"Are there any other scenes that you believe were different in real life than they appeared on the video?" Peter asked, pacing back and forth in front of the counsel table.

"Well, let me say that I think the entire video is different from my personal experience at the clinic and the experiences related to me by others. We have never shouted or chanted loudly, and we certainly never blockaded any cars."

"OK, Colonel. But specifically, are there any other scenes you can explain to the court?"

"No, not right now. But I believe if we had a chance to review the video in detail, we would be able to explain many, if not all of these incidents."

"All right, Colonel, I have no further questions."

"Any questions, Mr. Penner?" the judge asked.

"Two, Your Honor," Penner replied. "Colonel, can you tell me why this young man, whom you claim was chasing his hat, was not seen with a hat either in his hand or on his head when he was walking back to the picket line?"

"No, Mr. Penner, I can't. I think he might have stuffed the hat inside his jacket, but I don't really recall."

"What about the scene in which one of the protesters had to be held back from punching a patron of the clinic—do you expect this court to believe that incident was just manufactured?"

"I can't say what happened. I don't think I was there that day," the colonel replied looking angrily in the direction of Stephen Gray.

"No more questions, Your Honor," Penner said. He turned and looked at his clients, Jane Hayward and Karen Ballentine, with an air of victory.

Ginny Kettner squeezed Lisa's arm and whispered in her ear, "Well, we tried." Lisa passed the squeeze on to Stephen Gray's hand.

"Colonel, you may step down. Anything else Mr. Barron?" the judge asked.

"Could I have one more moment to confer with the other defendants, Your Honor? They may remember something that the colonel wasn't aware of."

"No, Mr. Barron, I'm afraid not. We're well over our time limit, and I'm ready to rule."

Peter returned to his seat as the room hushed. All eyes turned to Judge Tyler.

The judge sighed deeply. "I am not afraid to tell either of you that I am uncertain as to what actually happened up there in Bellingham. Your tape left a lot of unanswered questions, Mr. Penner. But I have no doubt about one thing. Outbursts such as the one by the young man who was ready to fight one of the clinic's patrons must never happen again. To insure that, I am going to grant a preliminary injunction."

Tears began to well up in the eyes of a number of the pro-life supporters. Ginny Kettner swallowed hard to hold back sobs.

"But," the judge continued, "the injunction I am granting is considerably different from the one requested by the plaintiffs. The defendants claim they are under strict orders from the colonel concerning their behavior at the clinic. I have read the colonel's rules—and agree that a protest held within the bounds of these guidelines is acceptable. My injunction is to prohibit any kind of protest that violates these rules. If you are really serious about your own standards of behavior that you have submitted to this court in writing, then you will have no problem."

"If there is *any* credible evidence of a single violation of my order, I will not hesitate to expand this injunction, and somebody will probably be headed to jail for contempt of court. Is that clear?"

"Yes, sir!" Peter nodded, trying hard to contain his joy.

"And Mr. Penner," the judge continued. "Just so you understand also, when I say credible evidence, I don't mean edited videotapes. Do you understand?"

"Certainly, Your Honor," Penner replied with overstated enthusiasm.

"Fine. And let me just say one more thing to both sides. I am going to direct the U.S. Marshalls to make regular visits to the clinic—especially on Saturdays, when it appears that most of the protests occur. I am going to have them keep an eye on all of you, and I expect absolute compliance with my orders. Does everyone understand?" Judge Tyler glared at the plaintiffs and defendants to be sure they comprehended his potential wrath.

Satisfied with their somber demeanor, the judge continued, "All right. Mr. Barron, assuming I don't see you again, I would encourage you to file a motion to dismiss this case based on your people's good behavior after a year. And Mr. Penner, if you have solid evidence of violations of my order, not only do I expect you to file contempt citations, but you would be well-advised to file a motion for summary judgment as to liability. Do both of you understand my point?"

Both Peter and Penner stood and nodded affirmatively.

"Fine, then this hearing is adjourned."

"All rise," the bailiff cried out. In a heartbeat, the judge was gone.

Peter slowly sat down and sighed heavily as all five defendants gathered around the table. "Whew, that was something else," he said. "But the end result is better than I dared hope for! So, as long as everyone obeys the rules, you're OK. But if there is the slightest problem, one of you will go to jail, and the rest of you will be in very serious trouble. You'd better explain that very carefully to everyone, Colonel."

"Well, almost the entire team is here. Can you explain to them the seriousness of the injunction?" Danners asked.

"Sure," Peter replied. "But I think we'd better go outside. The judge has people for another hearing waiting in the hall."

Ten minutes later, a smiling, chattering group was gathered on the plaza in front of the federal courthouse. It was drizzling slightly, but no one bothered to even raise an umbrella. Peter walked to the front of the group.

"Well, we can thank the Lord that the judge has allowed all of you to be able to continue your protests. And there is no question that the colonel's fastidious insistence on discipline and obedience to the rules is the reason things turned out as well as they did. So it's imperative that you continue to obey his rules. No deviations, no little errors, no mistakes."

"What did he mean by coming back in a year?" Stephen Gray asked.

"Essentially what he has done is to put the five defendants on probation for one year. But the injunction covers everyone. If any of you messes up, the judge is going to throw the book at the defendants."

"Are we taking a great risk—" Shirley Alper began.

Just then the judge's clerk burst out the door of the courthouse, yelling, "Mr. Barron!"

"Yes," Peter replied.

"Am I glad I found you," he said, out of breath from running down the stairs. "You have an emergency phone call from Spokane. Please come with me."

Peter handed his briefcase to the colonel. "Hold this," he said quickly. He dashed off behind the clerk and disappeared into the granite building.

8

The wooden door burst open into the outer compartment of the judge's chambers. Two secretaries immediately looked up from their computer screens as the law clerk and Peter crashed into their normally sedate environment, still breathing heavily from their dash up the stairs. The secretary closest to the door said, "Mr. Barron, your secretary is on line two. You can use my phone."

"Thank you," Peter panted, his face growing paler with each heartbeat. He lifted the receiver.

"Hello?" Peter said, still struggling for a normal breath.

"Peter, it's Sally."

"Yes, Sally, what's wrong?"

"It's Gwen. She's been taken by ambulance to the hospital."

"Ambulance? Is she OK?"

"Yeah, she's out of danger, but . . ." She couldn't finish her sentence without breaking down into tears.

"What is it then?" Peter demanded impatiently.

"It's the baby," Sally said softly. "Gwen started bleeding badly about an hour and a half ago."

"She's lost the baby?" Peter said softly.

"That's what they think has happened."

"When did you find out?"

"About five or six minutes ago. Lynn called me from the hospital."

"Lynn Roberts?"

"Yeah, Gwen called her when the bleeding started, and she went over to the house right away. She left her oldest son with Casey for a few minutes until your pastor's wife could come, then followed the ambulance. I had Joe call over there and check on them while I was waiting for you to come to the phone. Everything is fine there. I knew you'd want to know."

"Thanks, Sally. Which hospital is Gwen in?"

"Sacred Heart. Lynn said that's where she insisted on going."

"Can I call her? Do you have her room number?"

"She's still in the emergency room, I think. But I'm sure they'll connect you to her, or at least to Lynn. You want the number?"

Peter felt his eyes brimming as he caught a look of puzzlement and sorrow on the secretary's face. She looked away quickly when she noticed Peter catch her eye; still, her expression unleashed a torrent of grief within Peter that he'd been trying to keep under control. A few uncontrollable tears began to trickle silently down his cheeks.

"Thanks, Sally," Peter said, trying to read the numbers he was jotting down on the back of one of his business cards. "I'll call right now."

"Peter?" Sally asked. "Just one more thing. When can you get to the airport? Gwen wants you here just as soon as possible."

"I'm through here. I'll go there immediately and catch the next flight out."

"I've already checked," Sally said. "Northwest has a plane at two. Can you make that?"

"Isn't there anything before two? It's barely after eleven."

"Well, United Express has a flight at twelve fifteen, but it's a commuter."

"I'll make an exception this time. Get me on that flight."

"Sure."

"Thanks, Sally." Peter hung up the phone and looked sheepishly at the secretary, brushing tears from his cheeks.

"Mr. Barron, I hope there's nothing too seriously wrong," she said softly.

"Well, looks like my wife's going to be OK, but I think she lost the baby she was carrying."

"Oh, I'm so sorry to hear that," she replied.

"Thank you," Peter said in a subdued voice. "Can I borrow the phone for one last call?"

"Go ahead. Just dial nine first."

"Thanks," Peter replied.

Three internal transfers later, Peter was finally connected by the hospital operator to Lynn Roberts, wife of his long-time friend, Aaron. She and Gwen had also become close since Gwen and Peter started dating.

"Peter, I am so glad you called. Gwen keeps asking how soon you'll get here," Lynn said.

"Tell me about her condition," Peter said anxiously.

"They say the bleeding has slowed down to within normal ranges for a miscarriage. She was hemorrhaging badly at first. Both doctors say everything should be fine, but they want her to stay here overnight, just to keep an eye on her."

"Can I talk to her?"

"Right now they've got her down the hall doing a sonogram. They're ninety-nine percent sure she's miscarried, but they want to make sure. When can you get here, Peter? She really needs you right now."

"I'm catching a plane at 12:15. It's a commuter, so it doesn't arrive until nearly two. I'll try to get there by 2:30. Tell her I love her and I'll be there soon."

"I'll tell her."

"Thanks for stepping in for me, Lynn."

"No one can step in for you, Peter."

"Well, thanks for being there, then," Peter said, glancing nervously at his watch and then at the judge's secretary. "I gotta run for the airport."

"Thanks, again," Peter said to the secretary. "I appreciate your letting me use the phone."

"Good luck, Mr. Barron," she said, as Peter disappeared out the door.

"Stephen, isn't that weird about Mr. Barron's wife losing her baby on the very day he was in court arguing to save the lives of other people's babies?" Lisa said, wrapping her arm around her boyfriend's as they headed north on the interstate toward Bellingham.

Gray drove along silently for a moment, watching the rain fall on the hood of his Ford Taurus. He'd stopped believing in God a long time ago, so to him this was just a quirky case of coincidence. He wondered how Barron was handling his faith right now.

"Yeah, it's really strange," he finally said, remembering he needed to stay in character.

"I wonder why God allows things like this to happen? I mean, especially when Mr. Barron was fighting to protect innocent lives."

Gray sat motionless with his eyes fixed dead ahead on the freeway.

Lisa cuddled a little closer and continued to prattle. "Life can be so ironic," she said lackadaisically. "I mean, Peter's wife loses the baby, and people in the clinic get pregnant and nobody wants these babies."

Gray started and jerked the wheel momentarily to the left.

"Wha—what's wrong?" Lisa said, suddenly sitting erect.

"I'm sorry," Gray said, trying to sound reassuring. "I think I must've nodded off for a split second."

"You fell asleep? Am I that boring, Stephen?"

"No, Lisa. I was thinking about what you said. It was really profound. I guess I'm just tired."

"So what *did* I say?" she demanded, not yet sure whether to be offended.

"You were talking about the irony of Peter Barron losing his baby when he was fighting to save babies," he replied, flashing his perfect smile. "See?"

"I guess so," Lisa said, leaning against the door.

"What's wrong now?"

"Oh, nothing."

"Right," he said with a laugh. "Come on, tell me what's wrong."

Lisa sighed heavily and stared blankly out the window as acre after acre of commercial tulip farms, blanketing the upper portion of the Skagit Valley, passed by her window. "It was your words, 'paying attention.' You seem so distant lately. I mean, you say all the right things, and you're the perfect gentlemen. But you don't seem to be paying attention to the real me. I can't put my finger on it exactly, but everything seems so superficial."

"Lisa, honey, that's not true. We talk about a lot of important subjects."

"Yeah, sort of," she said, letting the words roll slowly off her tongue. "But we never talk about our dreams . . . where you see your life heading, and . . ."

"And what?" Gray asked after a half-minute's silence.

Lisa turned and looked Gray squarely in the eye. He could see big tears welling up, fighting to stay put in her large brown eyes.

"You never, ever talk of your dreams for us. If you love me like you keep saying, you should have some thoughts about us and where we're heading. And I deserve to hear them."

"So that's it," Gray said, reaching across the seat to lay his hand gently on her knee. "You want to know about the future. Our future," he added after a moment's pause.

"Lisa, I'm not the type of guy who can talk about those dreams until I'm certain. I told God I would diligently seek His guidance about this for two months. I'm almost there. I've got a month to go. I think you know where *my* heart and *my* desires are. But I have to be sure what God wants, too."

Lisa brightened a bit, but after a few minutes of thought, the turmoil inside intensified again. "Well, I wish you would have made sure of God's direction before expressing your love for me and telling me I was perfect for you. A girl interprets those words pretty seriously."

"You're probably right," Gray responded. "But I couldn't help it. I do love you. You're absolutely gorgeous, and I think you're perfect for me. Just give me a little more time, then I think we can start dreaming out loud together, OK? Trust me."

Gray spoke the words she'd been wanting to hear with such conviction that it was difficult to keep pouting for too long. Lisa scooted slowly away from the door and leaned her head back on his shoulder. While she hummed softly for the remaining thirty-five minutes of the trip, Vince Davis tried to sort out his real life problems with Dr. Rhonda Marsano. Stephen Gray would tell Lisa whatever was necessary in a week or so.

Peter prayed harder than usual as the fifty-passenger turbo prop rocked violently over the crest of the Cascade Range. At least, that's where the captain said they were—to him it was simply a mass of swirling gray clouds. A couple of years earlier, a small plane he'd been in dropped several hundred feet in a thunderstorm. Now, as this little plane jerked and twitched in its effort toward eastern Washington, he simply couldn't shake the flashbacks that invaded his mind of those thirty terrible seconds years before.

An older woman seated immediately across the aisle seemed perfectly calm as Peter glanced her way. She was a heavy-set woman, dressed in a light blue business suit and carrying a briefcase. "Lots of turbulence, huh?" she said in a cheery voice.

"Yeah, you said it," Peter said, still tightly clutching the armrests.

"When I was little my dad was in the military, so we flew all over the place. I thought turbulence was fun, then, like a ride at Disneyland."

Peter laughed, thankful for her friendliness. "Do you have business in Spokane?"

"Yes; you?" the woman said.

"No, I'm returning home from business, a little earlier than expected, actually. My wife's having problems in the hospital."

"Oh, I'm sorry to hear that. Nothing serious, I hope?"

"Well, she had a miscarriage this morning. I don't know what happens next."

"Oh dear, I am terribly sorry. My daughter suffered a miscarriage several months ago. It was traumatic because they knew the baby was a boy, and they already had the nursery set up. But within a few weeks, Theresa—that's my daughter—was fine, and now they're expecting again. Your wife will be just fine, I'm sure."

For the remainder of the trip, Peter prayed, thought about Gwen and the woman's words, and stared out the window. Around Ellensburg, the clouds broke up as the dry, sunnier side of Washington came into view. Soon the arid wheat fields, punctuated by acres of sage brush and stubble, filled the small window, a sign that they were approaching Spokane. When the plane finally landed, Peter ran through the airport, found his Explorer on the third floor of the parking garage, and exited the cashier's lane with just a hint of a squeal from his tires.

Twenty minutes later he was exiting Sacred Heart's sixth-floor elevator and jogging down the corridor toward Gwen's room. The door was half open. Lynn was seated in a blue vinyl chair in front of a massive picture window that looked over the South Hill and parts of downtown Spokane. Gwen was turned slightly on her hip, looking at Lynn.

He stepped into the room. "Gwen, honey, I'm here."

Shifting her weight uneasily to the opposite hip, Gwen saw Peter enter the room and smiled. "Oh Peter. Finally," she said, with tension evident in her voice.

Peter closed the distance between them and embraced her firmly. Lynn stood, picking up her purse. "I think I'll go down to the cafeteria for a few minutes." Peter responded with a nod.

"I am so, so sorry, lover. I am so sorry," he said tenderly as Gwen's body shook in his arms. He rocked her gently back and forth repeating, "I'm so sorry."

As her crying gradually subsided, Gwen spoke again. "I don't ever want you to leave me alone like this again." Her voice had a fierce edge to it, yet Peter detected a vulnerability as well.

"Honey, I won't. I'll stay right here with you." He held her silently for several minutes until he felt it was OK to talk again. "Don't worry. I think the case in Seattle is wrapped up, so I won't have to leave Spokane again."

"It's a little late now," she replied bitterly.

"Now wait a minute, you don't think my leaving had anything to do with the baby, do you?"

"No," Gwen said, breaking down again. "It's just that, oh I don't know. It would've been easier if you'd been here. Why did God allow this to happen, anyway?"

"Gwen, we serve a sovereign God. For whatever reason, He felt this was best. But we must remember that He always loves us."

"I can't feel that love right now."

"But you know it's real, don't you? And you know I love you, and I'm here."

"Yeah," she replied, pausing. "But this morning it felt like both of you had abandoned me. And now my baby, my baby . . ."

Silent sobs again shook her body. Peter held his wife and said nothing.

After a few minutes, Gwen pushed away from his embrace and collapsed back on the bed. "I need to lay back for a while."

"Sure," Peter replied, standing slowly. He walked softly around the bed and sat down in the chair Lynn had vacated. He noticed a whiteness in her face that made her seem even more vulnerable as she lay on the hospital bed staring vacantly in the direction of the window.

"Gwen, are you up to telling me what happened?" Peter asked softly.

She exhaled loudly. "I guess so." For a moment she lay absolutely still, then shifted the pillows to better support her shoulders and head. "I was just putting a load of laundry into the dryer when I felt a sharp pain in my abdomen. I'd felt this heaviness in my hips all morning, but thought it was normal. It obviously wasn't." Her voice trembled as she searched for each word. "I collapsed on the floor and screamed at Casey to bring me the portable phone. I called 9-1-1 for an ambulance, and then Lynn to come help me with Casey."

"Did the doctor tell you what he thought had happened?"

"No. He just said it was one of life's mysteries."

"Hmmm. One of life's mysteries," Peter repeated, rubbing his hands over his temples slowly.

"Peter, I just don't understand it. I was so happy."

"So was I. I really wanted to have this baby."

Gwen lay silently on the bed, staring vacantly at the ceiling.

"How long did you hemorrhage?" Peter asked after a bit.

"I guess for about forty-five minutes. They stopped it pretty quickly once we arrived at the emergency room. The nurse says things look pretty normal now. That is, normal for having a miscarriage."

"Was it Dr. Bobosky who saw you?"

"Yeah, he rushed down from his office."

"Did he say what's going to happen next?"

"I'll have some mild symptoms for about a week—cramping, I guess. And I'm supposed to take it easy for another three weeks or so."

"Casey and I will wait on you hand and foot," Peter said with a smile.

Gwen lay back against the pillow and smiled warmly for the first time that day. "I'm so glad you're here, Peter."

"Me too. I'm real sorry I was gone."

"So what happened in Seattle?" she asked. "You said you won't have to go back again?"

"Well, I shouldn't say definitely, but probably not. The judge granted a one-year injunction. As long as Suzie and her friends behave themselves for a year, he'll probably dismiss the case."

"So you may have to go back again."

"Well, maybe for just one short hearing. And that'll be a year from now."

"I don't think I can handle even that. What if something bad happens again while you are gone?"

"Nothing bad is going to happen. Gwen, we lead such blessed lives normally. This is bad, but it's an isolated incident."

"I just . . . I have a strange feeling about this whole thing. Peter, I want you to quit this case."

She closed her eyes and rolled onto her hip, facing the door. Peter watched her intently. He could see the top sheet starting to vibrate with her silent sobs once again.

Peter quickly sprang to his feet and sat on the bed. Leaning toward Gwen, he began to gently stroke her uncovered shoulder and arm with his hand.

"Gwen, if that's what you really want, I'll do it. But let's wait awhile until things become a little clearer, OK? Right now our emotions are running pretty high. Then, if you still want me to quit the case, I'll quit."

"You know it's not just this case," Gwen said after a short pause.

Peter paused, then continued stroking her arm.

"I've been telling you a lot lately that I don't like you being gone so much. You work entirely too much."

"It's not just work, though. You know that. There are other things that keep me away at night, like the elder board."

"Sometimes I wish you hadn't been elected as an elder. You're gone far too much with meetings and all that stuff you do for other families."

"Gwen, I don't understand what you're saying. You *wanted* me to be an elder, remember? You seemed pleased at the time they asked me to join the board. And you wanted me to take this case, too. You said you wanted me to fight for Suzie and the unborn babies. Remember?"

"I know," she replied softly. "I did say those things. And I want you to use your talents for good causes and everything. It's just that Casey and I need you, too. We need to see more of you."

"I'll try to do better, Gwen. I really will," he replied.

Gwen slowly drew her arm out from under the sheets and grabbed Peter's hand, squeezing intensely. Peter embraced his wife from behind. "Everything will be OK," he whispered. "It really will."

Vince Davis's message light was blinking on his answering machine when he arrived home after the drive home from Seattle.

"Vince, it's me," Rhonda's voice said. "Karen wants you to meet her at ten. Lake Padden swim area. She'll be in a blue Regal."

"What does *she* want?" Vince said out loud.

He rambled around his trailer for an hour or so, ate some leftover pizza, then headed out for a walk to burn off some nervous energy. Meeting Karen in secret on the night of the court hearing did not mean good news. He was supposed to be able to quietly slip away from

Bellingham—a family emergency back in Ohio—in a week or two, and had been looking forward to getting away from the rain, and Rhonda . . . and that nuisance Lisa.

He walked east on Smith Road in the dark, taking care to get onto the grass when an occasional car came in his direction. After awhile he turned back, but instead of heading straight home, he walked a block past the lane his mobile home shared with two small houses to the small country store on the corner of Smith and Northwest.

The door jangled as Vince entered.

"Hey, Larry," Vince called out to the familiar clerk. "How's it going?"

"Same ol', same ol'," Larry grunted, sitting on a stool with his arms crossed over the Seattle Sonics logo on his gray T-shirt. Nothing could cover his massive stomach that bulged out under his arms.

Vince placed a six-pack of Miller Light on the counter.

"Say, Steve," the clerk said as he rang up the six pack, "haven't seen you lately with that good lookin' woman you was in here with a couple months back."

Vince's heart stopped. "What woman?" he replied, trying to sound nonchalant.

"That brunette—the one who told you to get some mouthwash."

"Oh, her. That was my cousin, visiting from Ohio. I guess she's good looking, I haven't really noticed. I just think of her as cousin Shelly."

"She'd be a good kissin' cousin, if you ask me."

"Well, if she ever comes back for another visit, I'll tell her you want a smooch," Vince said, laughing nervously.

"Yeah, right," Larry replied, his massive belly shaking up and down with the slightest laugh.

Later that night, Vince turned right off Samish Way into the first entrance to Lake Padden Park. He glided down and around a sharp hill, coming to a stop by the tennis courts. He swung immediately into the first parking spot in the abandoned lot, quickly switching off his lights. He opened his door slightly. The interior dome light allowed him to look once again at his watch: 9:40 P.M. He got slowly out of his car, hitting the door lock as he exited.

Looking down the darkened park road toward the swimming area, nothing but the dark shapes of sixty-foot firs and pines were visible. Turning right off the road, he headed down a steep wooded embankment, with the tennis courts immediately on his left. After a 150 yards of tromping through wet ferns, pine needles, and occasional fallen branches, the rocky shore was suddenly at his feet. It was a partly cloudy night, and for the moment the moon was hidden behind a huge, darkened cloud.

Vince headed toward the swimming area, carefully picking his way along the beach. In the dim light of a distant street lamp, he thought he could make out the shape of the offshore swimming dock about five hundred yards ahead and a bit to his right.

Just as Vince felt the crunch of the rocky shore turn into the soft wet sand of the man-made beach, car lights appeared about a half mile ahead. He watched the lights illuminate various portions of the woods and then the shoreline, as it navigated the curves from the middle entrance to the park, down toward the bathhouse used by the swimmers of this pristine lake.

The lights of the car shone directly across the beach as it pulled into a parking space. Vince hit the ground lest the lights shine on him, but he was a good twenty yards shy of their illumination. He brushed the sand off his chest and legs and quickly made his way around the bath house. Rounding the corner, he was surprised to see Rhonda's Volvo instead of the rented blue Regal he had expected.

He tapped twice on the passenger side window. Suddenly Karen Ballentine's face appeared in the window, looking pale and surprised in the moonlight. Hearing the automatic door locks click, Vince quickly opened the right rear door and darted into the Volvo's back seat.

"You scared us," Ballentine said, her husky smoker's voice sounding even more gravely than normal. "Where's your car, anyway?"

"In a darkened parking lot about a half mile away. I walked up the shoreline. I didn't want my car seen with yours."

"I guess that's smart," Ballentine growled.

"So what's this all about?" Vince demanded.

"We're changing your assignments," the clinic owner replied, shifting her weight so she could look more easily at the back seat.

"Assignments?" Vince replied, glancing at Rhonda in the driver's seat.

"Yeah, both of you," Ballentine answered. "After what happened today, Jane and I have concluded we need to take a different tack."

"You sound like you're blaming us. We delivered what you and Penner told us to; it's not our fault the judge didn't give you the kind of injunction you wanted. If you're looking for a scapegoat, blame Penner. He's the one who put it all together in court."

"Penner seems to think that if you had gotten these people to do a little real trespassing, then the local police could have been called in to write a few citations, and the judge would've ruled in our favor today," Ballentine replied.

"Now he tells me," Vince replied sarcastically.

"You're not exactly a beginner at this." Ballentine's voice was cold and deep.

"Well, there's still time for that. Seems to me the judge would crucify these turkeys if he caught them on the property after today."

"I am afraid that is impossible."

"Oh? Fine with me. It's time to split anyway, I can't stand this rainy, dreary place any longer."

Vince heard a muffled whimper from the driver's seat. It was the first noise he'd heard out of Rhonda.

"Not so fast, lover boy," Karen's gravely voice replied. "You've got some loose ends to clean up."

"What are you talking about?" Suddenly he turned his head in Rhonda's direction. "What have you told her?"

Rhonda turned her head toward the side window and stared out at the darkness.

"She told me everything, Vince." Ballentine replied, "although it took a little persuasion."

"Persuasion; what do you—Rhonda, did she hit you?" Vince demanded.

Another, louder whimper was all the answer he needed.

"You both amaze me," Ballentine said with a sarcastic laugh. "I can't believe you got her pregnant, Vincent, though it fits right in with the sloppy work you did editing the video. And *you,*" she cried, shoving her face right next to Rhonda's. "You think having this baby will save you from hell? Remember, you are an abortionist, little Miss Prissy. Nothing will save *you!*"

Vince collapsed back into his seat. He sighed heavily and ran his hand slowly backwards through his hair. Then, in a low, calm voice he said, "So what are our new assignments?"

Ballentine leaned over the seat and squared her body to face Vince. "We want you to start a little fire at the clinic."

Vince's eyes grew wide. "You want me to torch the clinic?" he said in horror.

"Penner seems to think this court decision will set a terrible precedent if today's decision is published. He wants the clinic in ashes before the time for appeal of this order has passed. He thinks our judge could retract today's order and not send it out for publication if there is a little clinic fire. An unpublished decision has no precedential power. That is, if you can pull off this little assignment without further complications."

"You're serious?"

"Of course, I'm serious," she said gruffly. She reached down on the floorboard, got her purse from under the seat and pulled out a pack of cigarettes. She put the cigarette in her mouth and positioned her lighter, then suddenly stopped. "One more thing. We want to make sure that Stephen Gray is readily identified as the arsonist."

"Are you crazy?" Vince exclaimed.

"Stephen Gray, you idiot. Not Vince Davis. Why do you think we went to all this trouble setting you up with a perfect second identity?"

"Hey, I never agreed to anything like this—" he began.

"Oh shut up and listen to me. If Stephen Gray is identified as the culprit, these anti-abortion extremists will get blamed for the fire. To satisfy your new philosophical side, Rhonda, it's really their fault anyway. If they would honor a woman's constitutional right to choose, none of this would be necessary, right? A little deception in the cause of women's liberty is more than justified."

"What am I supposed to do afterwards?" Vince asked. "I mean, I can't just show up in L.A. and resume life as usual."

"You'll go on a nice, all-expenses-paid vacation. Toronto first, then Europe if necessary. In six or eight months you should be free to go wherever you like. By then, the protesters will be well on their way to a conviction for conspiracy to commit arson."

"What's going to happen to Rhonda? Where's she going to work when the clinic is gone?" Vince demanded.

"Well, that depends on her. If she'll agree to a sensible course of action, we'll send her to any clinic she chooses to complete her term. . . ."

"I won't have an abortion," Rhonda said, looking straight at Vince for the first time. The side of her face that had been facing the window was visibly puffy and red.

"There, you see?" Ballentine laughed. "She simply won't listen to me. She even had the audacity to suggest that she would snitch to the officials about our little plan. I had to give her a little rebuke for that and a gentle reminder that she's already perjured herself in federal court."

Rhonda rubbed the side of her face and started to cry again.

"I see," Vince said softly. "I'll talk to her."

"That's the kind of response I like from my employees. See, Rhonda? Your lover boy knows how to give me a sensible response. You ought to follow his example and get with the program."

Rhonda sat silently, staring at Ballentine.

"Rhonda, we'll talk about this later," Vince soothed. "Karen, I'll take care of things. OK?"

"See that you do. I'll be out of town for a few days. But when I return, I'll expect everything to be in place for final action. Got it?"

"Yeah, I got it," Vince said tersely.

The following Wednesday, Lisa Edgar smiled broadly when she saw Stephen Gray enter the back of Immanuel Bible Church's youth group meeting room, which was filled almost to capacity with a couple hundred people. Lisa had told at least a dozen people she was saving the aisle seat next to her, expecting Gray to show up. Two of those who had tried to take the seat were newspaper reporters.

Television cameras were perched on tripods along the left side of the room, near the front. Promptly at 7:30 P.M., Colonel Danners gave a slight nod of the head to Pastor Wallace. This meeting would start on time, like all others the colonel conducted.

"Good evening," Wallace announced. Bright lights from the television cameras switched on. Wallace blinked furiously for a few seconds as his eyes adjusted to the lights. "Thanks for coming out tonight. We have much to be grateful for after the court hearing a couple weeks ago. We are here to worship God and to hear how the pro-life coalition plans to keep its efforts both effective and legal. In a minute I'm going to ask Colonel Danners to address you, as well as our able attorney, Peter Barron, who will be speaking via telephone from Spokane. But first, I would like to open our time in thanksgiving and prayer."

The Bellingham camera crew members switched off their equipment for the prayers, but the Seattle reporters kept on rolling, hoping to catch some provocative statement on film. After the prayer was concluded, Danners assumed the podium, and everyone in the room focused intently on him. About five minutes into Danner's talk, Gray leaned over to Lisa and whispered, "I need to make a call, I'll be right back."

She patted Gray's hand as he stood. "Hurry back," she whispered.

Gray slipped quietly out the back door, down the hall, and around the corner toward Randy Wallace's study. He tried the knob, looked around, and quietly entered the room. Crossing the room, he picked up the phone and pushed eleven buttons. "You have reached the Los Angeles Office of the Women's Center for Choice," the voice on the other end said. "Our office is closed for the day. Please call back, or you may leave a message at the beep."

"Your Bellingham clinic had better watch its back," Gray whispered softly into the receiver in a falsetto voice. He hung up the phone quickly, crossed the room, and closed the door, making his way back into the youth group facility.

"No answer," Gray whispered to Lisa as he sat back down. He listened intently as Danners completed his remarks, then to Peter Barron, who gave a message of encouragement over a speaker phone. As the meeting was about to end, Lisa pulled a bulletin from her Bible and wrote on it, "Can we talk afterwards?" She then held it out for Gray to see.

He took her pen and the bulletin. "Tomorrow morning for breakfast at Shari's by the mall?"

She nodded affirmatively. After the meeting Gray followed up the conversation. "So, eight o'clock at Shari's?"

"OK," she replied. "What's wrong with tonight?"

"I have to take some of the college kids home." It was a good excuse to duck out of a potentially serious conversation. He didn't have time for that tonight. Gray pecked Lisa lightly on the cheek, promising a long talk in the morning, then made his way to the back of the room. Watching Gray closely as he exited, the only student Lisa could see leaving with him was Suzie, but it was hard to say for sure in the press of the crowd.

Gray and Suzie chatted about her studies and Peter Barron as they drove through the center of town on the way back to her dorm.

"Suzie, I need to make a quick stop at Fred Meyer before it closes. Do you have a minute?"

"Sure, Stephen," she replied.

"I just need to pick up a couple things."

Gray parked his Taurus near the entrance of the huge store. Suzie accepted his offer to come in with him rather than remain in the car. He looked up at the directory hanging at the entrance to the store. "Hardware, aisles three through seven," he said aloud. The two walked to the hardware section of the massive building and found what he was looking for—rolls of copper wire. He picked up two. Around the corner he found the automotive section, where he picked up three two-gallon gasoline cans.

"Suzie, would you hold one of these cans for me? I should have gotten a basket."

"No problem," she replied, taking a container. "But Stephen, if you need to hold six gallons, why not buy one of those?" she said, pointing to several large containers sitting on a bottom shelf.

"Good question," Gray replied, nodding for them to head toward the cashier. "I'm using these for lawn equipment. I need regular gas for my lawn mower, a mixture of gas and oil for my weed trimmer, and a different mix of gas and oil for my small chain saw."

"Oh, that makes sense." She shrugged innocently.

Suzie led the way to the check stand, laying the gas can on the moving belt. Gray followed, placing the two remaining cans down on the belt. Reaching into his back pocket, he removed his wallet. He checked his cash, then pulled a Visa card in the name of Stephen Gray and waited for the checker to ring up the purchase.

Gray looked up to make sure the security camera he'd seen on an earlier trip was still in place. He noticed the red light blinking on the top of the unit. Satisfied, he completed the purchase.

Approaching Suzie's dorm, he thought about suggesting that they go for a walk in the park along the bay. But he stifled the thought, knowing that Stephen Gray would never behave in a way similar to Vince Davis. Gray was a one-woman man. A few more days and the charade would be over.

The next morning, Gray found Lisa waiting on a padded bench inside the front door of Shari's.

"You made it!" Lisa said, brightening.

"Sure, what did you expect, sweetie?" Gray replied, offering her his hand.

"Lately, I haven't been sure what to expect," she replied, clutching Gray's arm instead.

Gray winked at her and gave her a quick kiss as the waitress led them toward a table about a quarter way around the nearly circular restaurant. After ordering, Gray took the initiative. "I've got some news that I think will make you happy," he announced.

Lisa looked at him warily.

Squeezing her hands, Gray continued. "Well, after weeks of prayer, I feel quite certain that God is calling us to be a couple, a *permanent* couple."

"Really?" Lisa's eyes shone in the sunlight that permeated their booth.

"But there's still one more thing I want to do before making that final decision. Remember my pastor back in Ohio, the one who led me to the Lord years ago?"

"You've mentioned him before," Lisa replied.

"Well, he's been like a spiritual father to me. I promised him that before I got married, I would talk to him first. I think he just wants to make sure I find a girl who loves the Lord as much as she loves me."

Lisa smiled, but still looked a little unsure. "So?"

"So, I feel confident enough in his answer to ask if you have time to visit a few jewelry stores with me on Saturday morning," Gray said with a triumphant smile.

"Isn't that a bit premature?" Lisa wryly. "Isn't there something you need to ask me first?"

"Well, to be true to my pastor, let me ask you this: If he says yes and I ask you an important question afterwards, then do you think you might have time to go shopping on Saturday?"

"Oh, Stephen, you're driving me crazy! Why can't you just ask me straight out," she said in mock annoyance.

Gray looked suddenly very serious. "I have every intention of asking you —the love of my life—the most important question I have ever asked anyone, first thing Saturday morning. Can I pick you up at ten?"

Lisa's heart pounded as she listened to his cleverly chosen words. "Yes, Stephen, ten will be OK. I can't wait."

9

On Friday Vince Davis packed up his few belongings and threw them into the back of his Taurus. He made several trips throughout the day—the pizza parlor to pick up his paycheck, and then the bank. When he got home, he laid a red sports equipment bag out on the floor of his apartment and carefully placed the items he'd purchased with Suzie inside, along with a few tools. Then he fell asleep. He had a long night ahead of him.

Pulling his Taurus into the Herfy's Drive-in parking lot just down the street from the clinic, he glanced at his watch. 9:50 P.M. He hit the button in the glove compartment that popped the trunk open, then got out of the car and pulled the sports bag out of the trunk. He slung the bag's long black strap over his shoulder and headed in the direction of the clinic.

Walking past the front door of the clinic, he noticed it was padlocked from the outside, as usual. As he slowly cruised the sidewalk around the back of the building, he noticed a light burning in an upstairs window, which, like all the clinic's windows, had been covered with evenly spaced iron bars to prevent "anti-abortion vandalism." He walked past the back door, then around the building to the front again, this time scanning the parking lot for cars. Just one, a blue Regal.

Vince slowly approached the back door of the clinic again, this time noticing that the padlock was missing and the hinged clasp open. He set the sports bag on the ground in the alcove area, where he unzipped it and pulled out a gasoline can. He set the can down against the alcove wall, popping open both the regular lid and the small, yellow vent lid. Reaching into the bag again, he pulled out a large, square dry cell battery and a small, hand-wound alarm clock. He wired the clock to the battery's positive terminal, then ran a fine filament wire from the clock through the two openings in the gas can and back to the battery's negative terminal. He set the alarm for 10:40 P.M.

Vince reached back into the red bag once again and found a crowbar. *Seems silly to work so hard when I have a key,* he thought, prying the door open.

Once inside, he set the bag down on a desk. Reaching in with both hands, he drew out a second can of gasoline and set it by the foot of the stairs. Once again, he popped open the gas can lids and wired an identical battery device and timer.

Vince jogged up the stairs and opened the door to Rhonda's office. Karen Ballentine sat with a furrowed brow behind Rhonda's desk, tapping a pencil on the smooth surface. Rhonda sat dejectedly on one of her padded rolling chairs. Vince thought her eyes looked red from crying.

"Everything's all set," he said.

"It's about time," Ballentine retorted.

"Are you OK?" Vince asked, touching Rhonda on the shoulder. She shook her head up and down but said nothing.

"She still won't listen to reason. I guess I'm going to have to sue her for breach of contract when this situation settles down a bit," the clinic owner growled.

"So much for a woman's choice," Rhonda said bitterly.

"We'll settle that later," Vince replied. "Listen, these cans are set to ignite in about twenty-five minutes. I'm heading back to Herfy's. You two get out in ten minutes—don't follow right after me because I don't want anyone to think we're together, but don't leave any later, either. I don't want you to take any chances."

"Right," Ballentine replied.

"Rhonda, I'll call you as soon as I can," Vince said with his hand on the doorknob. "You'll be at your mother's in New Jersey?"

"Yeah, you've got her number," Rhonda replied.

"OK. Remember, ten minutes," Vince repeated.

Turning quickly, he jogged down the stairs, grabbed the bag, and headed out the back door, shutting it quietly behind him. He reached into his bag one last time and pulled out the third can of gasoline. He quickly poured it around the back door, making sure he splashed some on his hands and clothing. Tossing the third can into an open dumpster near the rear of the clinic parking lot, he jogged quickly back to Herfy's. A customer stood at the window, waiting for his order. When Vince walked up, he turned around and looked at him.

"Gas leak," Vince said, explaining the odor.

"Better get it fixed," the man grunted, then grabbed his food bag from the attendant and walked away. Vince stepped up to the window.

"Deluxe burger and a large Coke to go. Make it quick," he announced. He rolled a five-dollar bill around in his hand several times while the Herfy's window attendant filled a large Coke cup. The attendant handed Vince his order and took the bill, wrinkling his nose at the stench of gasoline. The odor was so strong, he laid the bill beside the register rather than contaminate the entire till.

Vince did his best to squeal the tires of the Taurus as he pulled out of the Herfy's lot, and around every corner on his way toward State Street. There he turned onto the I-5 on-ramp and headed north for the Canadian border.

About four minutes after Vince had left the clinic, Ballentine glanced at her gold and chrome-tone watch. "I'm going to go to the bathroom and then we'll leave."

Rhonda said nothing as the clinic owner brushed past her and out into the hall.

A minute later Rhonda heard the toilet flush. She expected to hear Ballentine's heavy footsteps coming back up the hall. Another minute passed, then she heard the back door open and close. Rhonda jumped to her feet and headed quickly down the stairs. Before she could reach the door, Ballentine had the clasp shut and the padlock snapped in place on the outside.

Ballentine lumbered to her car, which was parked near the telephone pole that serviced the clinic. Clamoring up onto the hood of the rental, she pulled a small pair of wire clippers out of her jacket pocket and quickly snipped the phone line that ran into the building.

Inside, Rhonda ran first to the back door, then to the front, trying the cross bar that normally opened the door. The bar depressed and the door opened a fraction of an inch, but then stopped against the pad-locked clasp. Her eyes dilated as a hot flash of terror swept over her body. "Karen, let me out of here! Karen . . . Karen!"

Rhonda heard the Regal's engine fire up and could see the headlights come on through the barred window behind the receptionist's desk. For a second the lights fell on the telephone beside the computer as the car swung around the parking lot. The phone! Without listening for a tone, Rhonda dialed 9-1-1 and waited. A cooling wave of hope spread across her back and arms, replaced by another surge of despair.

"Hello? Hello!"

Nothing. The phone was dead. Another swell of heat swept up her back, settling like burning nettles in her face and neck. Rhonda threw the receiver down and bounded up the stairs at top speed, hoping against hope that the phone in her office—a separate line—would work. Again nothing. She slammed the receiver against the desk.

Rhonda slowly walked toward the door of her office, grasped the sides of the door jam with her hands and suddenly began wheezing loudly. *Another panic attack,* she thought. She'd been having them spo-radically since a few weeks before the hearing. Gasping for air, she slid down to the floor. "Gotta . . . relax . . . relax." Her voice sputtered into a wail as tears of hopelessness overwhelmed her. Finally the tears sub-sided and her breathing eased. She glanced at her watch. 10:35 P.M. Five more minutes.

Seeing Vince's gas can contraption at the bottom of the stairs, she froze in place, reasoning within herself that it was not a bomb, just a fire waiting to happen. Gathering her composure, she hurried down the stairs and fell to her knees beside the can. Very slowly, she disconnected the wire from the battery terminal. For good measure, she carefully unhooked the wire clamped to the other terminal and kicked the alarm clock across the room.

Her head collapsed into her hands as she rocked back and forth on her knees. Tears of relief wetted her cheeks and hands. Thinking the real danger was past, she began to contemplate how to get out of the clinic before morning. The worst that could happen now, she told herself, was that she would have to wait for her staff to arrive to unlock the doors.

She looked at her watch again. A few seconds before 10:40. She kept her eyes fixed on the watch as the second hand swept toward the top of the dial, and then as another minute ticked passed: 10:41.

Suddenly a noise outside drew her focus away from the watch. At first she thought it was her imagination when she heard an alarm clock ringing outside. She stumbled to her feet and put her ear to the door. A deep, sickening horror gripped her stomach as she heard the unmistakable clang of an alarm clock just outside the door.

"Nooo! Nooo!" Rhonda wailed, her head spinning wildly. After several seconds, the sound of the alarm began to subside as the device ran out of power. *"Maybe it didn't work,"* she thought. She ran to the receptionist's window and pressed herself against the glass, staring hard to the left. A contraption similar to the one she'd disarmed near the stairs sat on the cement of the alcove. Suddenly she heard a pop, followed by the glow of flames as the gas ignited. Seconds later the entire alcove was engulfed in flames.

Rhonda turned and ran back up the stairs. Perhaps the fire would be spotted before it reached the second floor, and a fire truck would come in time to save her. She grabbed some towels from a second-floor examination room, soaked them in the sink, then darted into her office and slammed the door. She fell to her knees and crammed the towels tightly in the crack beneath the door, then rested her head on her forearms. Soon her body wrenched up and down in sobs. "Please, God. Please!" she cried aloud in a mournful wail. Something in her mind raced back several weeks. She crossed the room quickly and pulled from her desk drawer the letter and gospel tract she had received in the mail.

Glancing quickly at the tract, she squeezed it and the letter tight against her breast. "God, please. Please God, save me! I don't want to die, God. My baby, God. Please, save my baby!"

Rhonda felt a wave of nausea and dizziness grip her body. Using the doorknob, she pulled herself up off the floor and dropped onto her chair, catching only its front edge. The chair lunged backwards, toppling her against the corner of her desk. There was a loud crack as her head hit the desk, then a thunk as she landed unconscious on the carpeted floor.

Slowly at first, then rapidly, the flames worked their way up the side of the clinic. The glass window behind the receptionist's desk shattered with the force of the heat and flames, and the fire quickly spread indoors. Another blast—coming from the gas can at the foot of the stairs—erupted the lobby and stairwell in flames. Soon the roof was engulfed as flames marched relentlessly across the rafters, meeting the already inflamed interior walls.

The fire engines came within ten minutes. But it was far too late for Dr. Rhonda Marsano.

10

The sound of the phone ringing jolted Colonel Danners out of his sleep. He glanced at his bedside clock as he reached for the receiver. 6:10 A.M. He waited a moment before answering, rubbing his eyes with his extended fingers.

"Hello," he said, finally sounding fully alert.

"Colonel, it's Shirley Alper."

"Shirley, what are you doing calling this early on a Saturday morning?"

"Something terrible has happened." Her voice was quivering.

"What? What is it?"

"There's been a fire at the clinic."

"What? When?" he exclaimed.

"Late last night. But that's not the worst part."

"For crying out loud, Shirley—"

"Colonel," she interrupted. "The clinic's doctor—Dr. Rhonda Marsano—she died in the fire."

"Oh, Lord God, no, please no," Danners replied, collapsing back on his pillow.

Evie raised up in bed with a worried look on her face.

"I'm afraid it's true," Shirley replied, barely able to choke out the words.

"How did you hear about it?"

"A cousin of mine works as a dispatcher for the police department. When she got to work this morning, everyone was talking about it."

"Why did she call you?"

"She knows about our protests and the federal lawsuit and everything, and—"

"Yes . . . yes . . . and what?"

"The buzz in the department is that the fire was deliberately set and that our group might be responsible."

"Oh, that's utterly ridiculous!" the colonel shouted.

"I know we didn't do it, Colonel, but that's what they seem to think. And you can be guaranteed that the media will be quick to blame us, too."

"Oh, Shirley," he sighed heavily. "This is awful news. Who would have done such a thing? No, no, no, I just can't believe it. It's got to be an accident."

"I wish it were that simple," Shirley replied. "My cousin couldn't be real specific, but she did tell me that an amateur bomb started the blaze. And that both doors to the clinic were padlocked from the outside, trapping Dr. Marsano within. She said they're already talking about murder."

"Shirley, I've got to call Peter Barron immediately."

"Yeah, that's what I was thinking, too."

"I'll call him right now," Danners said. "You call the others. Tell them not to talk to anybody—I mean *anybody*—until I've talked to Peter."

"Okay," Shirley replied.

"Lord have mercy on us all," Danners said sadly.

"Call me back when you've talked with Mr. Barron."

"Sure thing. Bye."

Danners sunk into his pillow, closed his eyes, and moaned loudly.

"What happened?" his wife cried out. By now she was sitting upright in bed.

"The clinic's doctor was killed in a fire at the clinic last night. It looks suspicious, and the police suspect our group."

"Oh no. That can't be right," she replied, her voice on the edge of tears. "What are you going to do?"

"First thing is to call our lawyer," Danners said dejectedly.

He raised up in bed, shifted his weight to his right hip, and leaned over to punch the buttons on the phone.

Danners heard the receiver on the other end rattle after the third ring, then a loud clunk.

"Hold on, I dropped the phone." Peter's voice sounded distant. "Hello?"

"Peter, I'm terribly sorry to wake you. This is Hank Danners calling. We have an emergency here."

"Colonel, what's up?"

"Terrible news. There was a fire at the clinic late last night. I don't know yet what the damage was—"

"Ohhh . . ." Peter moaned. "You've got to be kidding!"

"I wish I were. Shirley Alper just called me. Her cousin works for the police and called her this morning after hearing about it in the station.

Evidently a homemade bomb is responsible for the fire, and our names top their list of suspects. What do we do?"

"I . . . I'm not sure. I've never handled this kind of thing before. For one thing, tell your people not to talk to *anyone.*"

"Peter, our problems don't stop there. Dr. Rhonda Marsano was trapped inside the building at the time of the fire. She's dead."

"Lord God, no," Peter cried, letting his head fall into his free hand in disbelief.

Gwen rolled over to face her husband and mouthed the words, "Who is it?"

"Bellingham," Peter whispered with the mouthpiece twisted away from his face.

"Peter?" Danners said.

"I'm here. Look, don't talk to the police, whatever you do."

"Won't that make them more suspicious of us?" Danners questioned.

"It's better than shooting yourselves in the foot," Peter replied.

"What do you mean? We're innocent!"

"I know that, but sometimes innocent people get caught in traps, and the police will be looking for someone to nail this on."

"I really think we should cooperate with the police," Danners said, with a bit of urgency in his voice.

"Cooperation and foolish statements are two different things, Hank. Now, don't call them—wait until they contact you. Then blame your refusal to talk on me—say something like, 'I have nothing to hide, but my lawyer wants me to wait until he gets here.'"

Gwen straightened up in bed and glared at Peter in astonishment.

"How soon can you get here?" Danners asked.

"It will probably take me at least until noon, maybe a little after. I'll get there as soon as I can."

"OK. Call me back when you know your schedule."

"I'll call you back soon; meanwhile, be sure to contact the rest of your team and tell them to keep quiet! And not just with the police, but with the media as well. They'll be crawling all over them."

"All right," Danners sighed.

"I'll be in touch soon. Goodbye." Peter let the phone drop from his hand and dangle from the bedside table as he collapsed back in bed with a loud moan. "This is awful," he said, laying back with his eyes closed.

Gwen cleared her throat. "Are you going to tell me what's going on, or do I have to guess?"

"I'm sorry, honey, I'm just so stunned. The clinic in Bellingham was burned last night, and the doctor was killed in the fire. There's sure to be trouble for Suzie and her friends."

"Do you think they did it?"

"I don't think any of the people in the leadership are responsible," he replied. "Beyond that, I really don't know."

"So what happens next?"

"The police will be swarming all over this—as well as the media. One stray word could get them in big trouble. I need to get over there immediately."

"But why do you have to go? Can't you call in one of your associates, or refer them to a criminal lawyer?"

"Gwen, these folk trust me. I'm the one most familiar with the case. I can't let them down."

"So much for never leaving me alone again," Gwen said dejectedly as she collapsed back onto her side of the bed.

Peter rolled over on his side and scooted close to his wife. "I know we talked about this, but things are far more serious now. My being there could mean the difference between any one of these people being arrested on suspicion of murder."

"I know," she said with a loud sigh. "And I would like you to help in these kinds of cases. But Bellingham—that's nearly four hundred miles away."

"Well, who says I have to leave you alone?" Peter said as he gently cuddled his wife.

"What?"

"You could come with me. Casey can spend a couple days with your parents. And when my business is done, we could go up to Vancouver for dinner, or maybe spend the night."

"I don't know."

"Gwen, it's very sad what happened over there, and the police investigation will only make things worse. The media will be all over this; undoubtedly it will be a national story. Everyone's going to be under a lot of stress. You'd be a great asset to help calm people down. And it'd do you good to have a change of scenery." Peter was becoming more animated with each word.

"You're getting a rush out of all this, aren't you?"

"I can't help it—this is the kind of situation I love. Kind of the emergency room of lawyering."

"Peter, you're impossible, impractical, and impertinent!"

"But I'm cute," he laughed.

"Not cute enough to get me up early on a Saturday morning to go chasing airplanes. No one is that cute."

"You are," he replied, tousling his wife's long blond hair.

Gwen looked deep into Peter's brilliant blue eyes. It wasn't his good looks that would make her agree to this journey, nor her desire not to be left alone. It was the fire that burned deep within him that changed her mind. For a moment, she saw Peter as he was when she first fell in love with him—in full battle.

The red-eye flight from Vancouver hit the run way in Toronto at 7:30 Saturday morning. Vince Davis jolted awake and peered out the window as the plane taxied toward the terminal. It was a bright spring day in Canada's largest city. He lumbered sleepily into the gate area looking for the nearest restroom. Around the huge room, four televisions tuned permanently to a news channel blared to no one in particular.

He saw a sign pointing him to a men's room on the right, when suddenly he thought he heard the words Bellingham abortion clinic coming from the nearest television. He paused to watch his handiwork. He was not completely surprised to see a picture of Rhonda Marsano on the screen— as the clinic's doctor, she would be a focal point of the media. Then a graphic streaked across the screen and stopped above the doctor's picture. Huge red letters, D-E-A-D, flashed above her head.

"No!" Vince gasped, then suddenly looked around him to see if anyone heard. The other passengers were far too interested in getting out of the airport to pay any attention to him. Vince felt his head swim as he stared at the screen in disbelief. As the story of the grisly fire that ended the doctor's life unfolded before him, Vince collapsed into the nearest chair. He suddenly felt dizzy and sick to his stomach. He grabbed both sides of his head with his hands and tried to steady his elbows on his knees. He moaned again and again.

"Are you all right?" a flight attendant's voice said out of nowhere.

Vince tried to stifle his groaning, but the impulse welled up from deep within and wouldn't be ignored. He moaned another time, then another.

"Sir, are you all right?" the voice repeated.

"I, uh, I think so," he groaned.

"You don't look too good. I think I should call for some help."

Vince opened his eyes. He could make out the image of a flight attendant, but the world was swirling about her. "I think I'll be OK," he managed to mutter.

"What happened? I recognize you from the plane—you didn't seem sick then."

"I guess the excitement from last night finally caught up with me . . . a going away party, you know."

"I understand," she replied. "Can I call you an electric cart?"

"No, I'll . . . I'll be OK," Vince sputtered.

"I insist. That's the least I can do."

"Oh, OK." Vince realized he could use the help and that he needed to do something to get rid of this woman. "I'll just wait here for the cart. You can go on, thanks."

"Sure you don't want me to wait with you?"

"Thanks anyway. Just send me a cart."

"OK," she replied.

"Better yet," Vince said, struggling to his feet, "just point me to the men's room. I think I just need some cold water on my face."

"OK," she replied, reaching out her hand and helping him stand up.

Vince staggered into the restroom and grabbed the sides of the first sink. He splashed cold water on his face until he was able to gather his wits, then looked up in the mirror. The image of Rhonda's face on the television screen flashed violently in his mind's eye. He grabbed the sink again as the world started to swirl around him again. His face flushed, and beads of sweat began pouring from his forehead. More cold water helped, but nothing could get rid of the grinding knot in his stomach.

Finally, he stood as straight as possible and shuffled out the door. The flight attendant was gone.

Within fifteen minutes, Vince was sitting slumped over in the back seat of a taxi. He would spend the day on his back in a hotel, he thought, and empty the contents of his room's mini-bar. Maybe then he could forget what he'd done.

11

Detective John Dunn paced back and forth behind the gray metal conference table, looking impatiently at his watch for the fourth time in five minutes. It was not often that he called his small investigative unit in on a Saturday morning, but when he did, he expected instant obedience. "When is MacMillan gonna get here?" he growled.

"He just radioed in, Captain," came the reply from a husky man in his twenties who was leaning back in his metal conference chair. "He's a block away."

Dunn, a thin man just over six feet and in his mid-fifties, pulled a pack of Winston's out of the pocket of his short-sleeved white shirt. His tie, which bore the grimy reminders of both coffee and Tabasco sauce, was askew and pulled away from his throat. He lit the cigarette, blew the smoke deliberately toward the ceiling, and glanced at his watch again.

"What are you so nervous about?" the younger detective asked, still leaning his chair against the wall.

"I'm not nervous," Dunn snapped. "I'm just in a hurry."

"Hey, the gal's dead, the building's a total loss. I don't think five minutes here or there is gonna make a big difference in this investigation."

"Just shows how much you know, Castille," Dunn replied. "You rookies think you're such hot stuff."

"Huh?"

"I want to be way down the road on this one before the feds land on it," Dunn said, taking a long drag on his cigarette.

"Feds?" Carl Castille asked.

"Come on, Carl, wake up! This is a suspicious fire at an abortion clinic—the feds'll be crawling all over this like ants on day-old meatloaf. I want our investigation to be thorough and a long way ahead by the time they get here."

"Why? We can't keep them out."

"Probably not. But I want to have as much information as possible before they come in with their know-it-all, button-down slickness. Maybe at least we'll get some respect for once."

Dunn saw the other detective out of the corner of his eye, pouring himself a cup of coffee in the next room. "MacMillan, over here and let's get going," he bellowed.

"Sure, Cap'n," MacMillan replied. "Sorry I'm a little late. I just thought you might want to see this." He pulled a large, plastic bag containing a red gasoline can from behind his back and sat it down on the table in front of the captain.

"Where'd you get that, Jamie?" Castille asked.

"I pulled it from the trash bin behind the clinic," MacMillan replied. "It's still got the Fred Meyer sticker on the top."

"Why were you over there?" Dunn demanded. "You were supposed to come here first and get your instructions."

"I always drive by the clinic on my way to work. After your call, I decided to stop and look around a little bit," MacMillan replied. "Say, Cap'n, can't you put out that cigarette? You know my allergies."

Dunn growled and smashed his cigarette forcefully into the glass ashtray sitting on the table. "All right, if we are all done showing off, Mr. MacMillan, can we get to work now?"

Castille's chair thunked down on the linoleum as the young detective assumed a more somber pose, with his forearms resting on the table's edge. MacMillan took a seat beside him.

Dunn ran the fingers of both hands through his full head of white hair, then held them against the back of his neck. His pale blue eyes looked vacantly out the window across the street toward the Whatcom County Courthouse as he paced the room. "I, uh, let's see . . . ah, heck, MacMillan," he finally said, swinging around to face the two young men and nabbing a fresh cigarette out of his shirt pocket. "I can't even think without smoking. Hold your breath for awhile."

Jamie MacMillan rolled his eyes in the direction of Castille, hoping Captain Dunn wouldn't see.

"Gentlemen," Dunn said, drawing in a deep smokey breath, "this is the most important case this department has handled in years. We've done other murder investigations, but never one that received national attention."

"Is this—" Castille began. A jerk of Dunn's head and a scowl told him to shut up.

"Because of the protests surrounding this clinic, within a couple hours, every big news agency in the country will be crowding into our little town, looking for the hottest angle on this case. If it turns out to involve one of these clinic protesters—and I suspect it well—why, Katie-bar-the-door we're going to have ourselves some center-stage coverage. With that in mind, gentlemen, we had better at least act like a team of professionals. And we gotta be absolutely tight lipped. With a chief of police and a county attorney both with egos up the kazoo, they'll eat us alive if we say one word to the media."

Dunn stopped for a second, leaned over the table, and gripped both hands firmly on the edge as he looked his two assistants directly in the eyes, shifting his unblinking gaze from one to the other. Both of the young detectives looked at each other to avoid their captain's glare.

"Men, we're going to do this case right," Dunn concluded. "We're going to keep our mouths shut. And maybe, just maybe, if we solve this murder and bring in a conviction, someone important will give us a pat on the back. I want this unit to be the pride of American police work, ya got that?"

Dunn waited to allow the seriousness of his words to soak in.

"Yeah, Jamie, no playing footsie with that cute little redhead from the *Bellingham Herald!*" Castille broke in.

"Shut up, Castille." MacMillan snickered.

Dunn sighed and shook his head. "OK, let's finish this up and then hit the field."

Dunn continued to pace and bark instructions for the next twenty minutes. MacMillan and Castille wrote furiously, daring to interrupt only occasionally for clarification. When Dunn latched onto a case with such passion, they knew they'd better pay attention.

"You both ready to go?" Dunn finally said. "Get over to the Fred Meyer store and see what you can find out about this gas can. I'm going down to meet the state fire marshall's arson team at the clinic. You can join me there when you're through at Fred Meyer. Then I'll pay a visit to Colonel Hank Danners."

"Yes, Cap'n," they both chimed cheerfully.

"Let's hit it then," Dunn said, his second nearly spent cigarette dangling from the corner of his mouth. As he opened the door of the smoke-filled room, he turned back toward MacMillan. "You can breath now," he said, his blue eyes dancing.

Peter swung the bright red Toyota into the Danners's driveway just before two. Two cars were already parked on the long, sloped concrete surface; another two were parked along the edge of the colonel's immaculately groomed yard. The sun peaked out from behind a bank of clouds as Gwen emerged from the car. She smiled as she saw every inch of Peter move with brisk determination—his mouth was fixed, his jaw taut, and his eyes were alive with intensity. She had often seen that expression two years earlier, when he had won both her case and her heart.

Peter reached his arm out for Gwen to take. Instead she grabbed him around the neck and kissed him lightly on the cheek. "Thanks for bringing me," she said softly. "I'm glad to be with you today."

Peter reached around her waist and lifted her lightly off her feet as he drew her close. "I wouldn't want it any other way." They both smiled broadly as they continued to the front door and rang the bell.

Evie Danners opened the door with her usual hospitality, but something in her eyes struck Gwen. A foreboding look, Gwen thought; Peter had told her of Colonel Danners's extensive experience as a military pilot. Evie Danners had sent her husband off to dangerous situations on numerous occasions, yet Gwen couldn't help but wonder if the current crisis was different from anything they'd yet faced. This time the enemy had no face and no name. As they walked down the hall to the living room where the others were waiting, Gwen let go of Peter's hand and put her arm around her hostess's shoulder. "It's really good to meet you, Mrs. Danners. I've heard so many wonderful things about you and your husband!"

Evie smiled at Gwen and then quickly excused herself as they came to the entrance of the living room.

"Mrs. Barron!" a familiar voice cried out. Suzie was on her feet and grabbed Gwen in an embrace that spoke more of gratitude than fondness. "I'm so glad you came, too," Suzie said.

Colonel Danners cleared his throat in a way that brought the room to attention. "Peter, seems to me the rest of us need an introduction to your lovely wife as soon as Suzie is through hugging her."

Peter chuckled softly as he introduced Gwen.

Jim Kettner was on the love seat, holding hands with his wife Ginny; Randy and Kristy Wallace were on a pair of dining room chairs; Shirley Alper sat with Suzie and the Danners on the couch.

Peter and Gwen settled into another pair of dining room chairs. By force of habit, Peter popped open his briefcase and drew out a yellow pad. "Before we get started, let me say a couple things." Peter paused, making eye contact with each person as he looked around the room. "First, although we disagreed with her practices, Dr. Rhonda Marsano was a person created in the image of God, and her death is a great tragedy. We need to be praying for her family during this difficult time." He paused again. Several heads nodded affirmatively.

"The second thing I want to say is that while we need to be wise and extraordinarily careful, we need not be locked into fear. I am absolutely confident that every person in this room is absolutely innocent of any wrongdoing, and we have to work on the assumption that truth and justice are going to prevail in the days ahead."

"But they lied in court in Seattle," Shirley Alper said. "Why do you think they'll be constrained to the truth this time?"

"Well, they may not. But that doesn't change our responsibility. But this time we'll be dealing with more than the clinic's attorneys—the police and the county prosecutor, even the FBI might be involved."

Ginny Kettner gasped, then slapped her hand over her mouth. Her husband slid closer on the love seat and tightened his embrace with his arm around her shoulder.

Peter continued. "With these new federal laws on abortion clinics, we have to assume that this matter will be investigated by the FBI."

"Peter," Randy interrupted, "we've been talking ourselves into a frenzy the past hour, speculating on who could've set the fire and what the consequences might be if we're blamed for it. Just how bad is our legal situation?"

Peter sighed, leaning forward with his forearms on his knees. "Well, you haven't been formally charged with anything yet, but you can bet the clinic owners will be pointing the finger publicly."

"We already figured that part out," Shirley said disgustedly.

"But what about the police?" Randy persisted.

The colonel looked up quickly in alarm when Peter sighed yet again in response to Randy's question.

"The police will want to question you all sooner or later, but they are the least of your worries," Peter answered. "It's the county prosecutor, and potentially the FBI and the U.S. Justice Department who'll probably come down hard. This is a very politically charged situation. By the way, anyone know the county prosecutor's name?"

"Max Franklin," Danners answered. "A Democrat."

"An extremely liberal one, with political aspirations," Alper added.

"How old is he?" Peter asked.

"About thirty-five," Alper replied.

"Hmmm," Peter said, sighing again. "None of this sounds too encouraging. There may be some political heavyweights trying to pull strings in this case, but even the most left-leaning prosecutor knows he has to have some hard evidence before filing a complaint. If he files a high profile case without evidence, it could end up backfiring on him politically. Surely your ambitious prosecutor is smart enough to figure that out."

"Are you saying people in political office are that smart?" Alper asked with a twinkle in her eye.

"Well, you got me there," Peter said with a soft chuckle. "Let's just hope he at least has some common sense. As things stand, it would be ridiculous to charge any of you with arson, or—" He stopped short of finishing the sentence.

"Murder," Danners said flatly.

"Yeah," Peter replied, nodding.

"Can I—can we really be charged with murder?" Suzie's voice was trembling.

"It's possible, Suzie," Peter replied, "although highly unlikely."

"But how?" The tears that had been brimming in Suzie's eyes all afternoon now spilled down her cheeks in earnest.

Gwen slipped off her chair and quietly sat on the floor beside Suzie, putting her arm around her favorite baby-sitter. "It's gonna be OK," she whispered softly.

"Their argument would go something like this: You all conspired to burn the clinic down, with someone in your group playing the lead. And even if you didn't know Dr. Marsano was in the building that night—

so there was no obvious intent to kill her—she died nonetheless as a result of arson, and that makes it a felony murder. Any felony that results in a death is considered murder, whether you intended to kill or not."

Suzie leaned her head against Gwen and began to sob out loud.

"Suzie," Peter said gently, "and all of you for that matter—I want you to know that I am going to do everything I can to keep you from being charged. But even if you are charged, I truly don't believe you could ever be convicted of anything."

"So you'll represent us in a criminal case?" Danners asked.

Peter's eyes met Gwen's. She bit her lower lip as Suzie continued to sob softly in her embrace. Gwen nodded affirmatively just once.

"Yes," he replied, smiling at his wife. "But if that happens, I'll need some help from my associates. I can't do it all myself. But we're getting ahead of ourselves here. Let's get down to business. First off, can anyone think who might have done this?"

Each member looked around the room, as if catching each other's eyes might help jog their memories.

"I can't think of anyone," Danners eventually said. The rest of the group muttered and shrugged in agreement.

"OK. Keep your eyes and your ears open. The very best defense we could possibly have is to find out who really did this and help them get convicted. Colonel, do you have a list of all the people who are part of your effort?"

Shirley laughed out loud. "Does Colonel Danners have a list? Does the word 'Pentagon' mean anything to you, Mr. Barron? He not only has a general list of each participant, he's got a record of the protests every person participated in, sorted by date."

"All except those times Stephen Gray took some students down there during the week without me," Danners replied sheepishly.

"Stephen Gray? Who's he?" Peter queried.

"He's one of our regulars," Danners explained. "Belongs to Pastor Kettner's church. He's been with us about three or four months."

"He doesn't officially belong to our church," Jim replied. "But he is a regular attendee."

"Do you think he has a list of the people who attended the sessions you're talking about?" Peter asked.

"It's hard to say," Danners replied. "I wasn't always aware of the protests he spearheaded. He got a little exuberant and just kind of did them on his own."

"Hmmm. Is he OK?"

"Well—" Danners began. From the beginning he'd never completely trusted Gray. Everyone knew it and accepted it as simply a personality conflict.

"He's dating one of my best friends, who also attends our church," Ginny replied.

"What's her name?"

"Lisa Edgar," Ginny responded.

Peter scribbled fast on his yellow tablet to keep up with everything being said.

"How long has she been with the group?"

"Since the very beginning," Ginny responded. "She's fine, and I think Gray is as well."

"Would both of their phone numbers be on the lists you have, Colonel?"

"Yes, sir."

"Great. Be sure to give them to me before I leave, OK?"

"I'll go print everything out right now," Danners said, rising.

"Fine, I'll need to use the computer in just a few minutes anyway. I want to hammer out a press release. We're going to have to officially say something to the press before long. In fact, I'm surprised they haven't called already."

"Well, we've had the ringer turned off the phone so we wouldn't be interrupted," Evie Danners replied as the colonel disappeared down the hall. "Any calls are going into our answering machine."

"It might be a good idea for you to check it for any messages," Peter said.

With the Danners out of the room, everyone took the opportunity to stand up and stretch. Randy was talking to Peter when Evie appeared, ashen-faced, at the hallway entrance. "Mr. Barron," she said. Peter twisted in his chair to look in her direction. "There is a message from a police detective. He wants to come over and interview my husband."

"Can you take me to the phone, Mrs. Danners? I would like to hear exactly what the detective said."

"Certainly," she replied. "There were also three calls from reporters." Peter and Evie disappeared down the hall. In a minute he returned to a silent room, with every eye fixed on him.

"OK, here's the deal," Peter said. "We're going to receive a visit from a Detective Dunn in about thirty minutes. I think the colonel and I ought to talk with him alone, so I would like to ask you all to leave for awhile. But don't go too far, and don't go home. The press is out for blood, and they're liable to be waiting on your doorstep."

"But we'll have to go home eventually," Shirley said.

"Give me a couple hours first, to let this detective know that I represent all of you. That way you won't have to go into a big explanation as to why you can't talk without my being present. That should take care of the police for awhile. I'm going to call the Associated Press in Seattle in a couple of minutes and tell them I will be holding a press conference I guess at . . . uh, six . . . so if you run into any media people, that's all you should tell them! OK?"

"And remember," Danners said, "no talking to anyone. No press, no friends, nobody. Ginny, that includes Lisa."

"What do we say if one of our supporters asks us what's going on? 'No comment,' is that it?" Ginny asked.

"I see your point." Peter began to pace. "How about, 'I'm terribly sorry about the fire and the death of Dr. Marsano. I have no idea how it all happened. But I cannot comment right now on the advice of our lawyer.'" Peter looked around the room. "That sound good?" Heads nodded in agreement.

"OK. Colonel, let's go type up that statement so you can all memorize it. The rest of you disappear for about ninety minutes, then give us a call before returning."

"Got it," Randy said, answering for the group.

Colonel Danners watched closely as a gray-haired man emerged from a full-sized Ford. The car was unmarked, but a special radio antenna on the rear quarter-panel gave it away as a police car. The man, who appeared to be a few years younger than the colonel, stepped deliberately across the driveway and rang the doorbell.

"Hello, you must be Detective Dunn," the colonel said, opening the door. "Come in. My attorney and I have been expecting you."

"Thank you, sir," Dunn said, wiping his feet on the brown bristle mat.

"I take it you're General Danners," the detective said, watching his host's eyes carefully.

"Colonel Danners, sir, only a colonel," he replied with a chuckle.

"That's right," Dunn said. He knew full well the correct rank, but wanted to hear at least a few uncoached words from Danners. He assumed the lawyer—with whom he had spoken on the phone—would tightly control the conversation, and he wanted to get a least some gut feeling for the colonel's personality.

"Air force was it?"

"Yes sir, twenty-eight years."

"I was in the army for a couple years, saw a little action in Viet Nam. Were you there?"

"Six tours. It was an interesting time."

"Yeah, you can say that again." Dunn liked what he was hearing. Danners was definitely an unusual suspect. Once in a while a witness of this caliber would come along—polite, professional, and unmistakably distinguished—but these kind of people were almost never suspects, at least not in Bellingham.

As the two men entered the living room from the hallway, Peter stood up in front of the love seat where he'd been sitting. The dining room chairs had been replaced around the table. Peter didn't want to broadcast the fact that the whole leadership committee had been meeting in this room just forty-five minutes earlier.

"Detective Dunn, I'm Peter Barron."

"Afternoon, sir, nice to meet you."

"Same here," Peter replied.

"Won't both of you be seated?" Danners motioned for the detective to take the couch while he assumed a place in one of the two stuffed chairs.

"Nice home you have here; beautiful view."

"Thanks," Danners replied. "My wife keeps the house beautifully decorated; I leave the view up to God."

"Humph." The detective grumbled. "I guess you know why I'm here," Dunn continued.

"Yes," Peter replied. "And I would like to explain why I'm here."

"That's not necessary," Dunn answered, even though he very much wanted to hear the explanation. "Everyone has a right to a lawyer. I don't have a problem with that."

"Well, in this situation, I'd still like to explain, if that's OK."

Dunn nodded affirmatively.

"The colonel here and a number of others are involved in an ongoing lawsuit with the clinic owners in federal court in Seattle. I represent all of them in that case. During the proceeding, the clinic alleged threats of violence, which we strongly disputed. In fact, not much more than a single trespasser chasing a runaway cap on a windy day was ever proven. But like I say, there were a number of allegations. And in light of last night's events, it seems logical that the pro-life coalition may be blamed.

"We have nothing to hide from your department, detective. We would like to cooperate as fully as possible. But I also need to try to protect my clients since the attorneys for the clinic may gain access to the information you uncover. So, while my clients are anxious to help you unravel the fire and Dr. Marsano's death, I'm here to try and insure that all this doesn't come back to haunt us in that federal case."

"Sounds fair enough," Dunn replied. "So can we proceed with some questions?"

"Fire away."

"All right," Dunn said, positioning himself to face the colonel. "First of all, let me just say that this interview is preliminary in our investigation.

We are here to talk with you because of the protest activities, but we have no evidence to suggest at this point that your group is involved in any crime. Clear?"

Danners nodded. "I understand." He very much liked hearing the part about no evidence but winced internally at the words, "at this point."

Dunn asked about a half dozen background questions, then jumped into the focus of the line of questioning. "All right, let me ask you point blank. Do have any idea how this clinic caught fire?"

"None whatsoever," the colonel replied instantaneously.

"Can I can assume from your answer that it is your position that you personally had nothing to do with it?"

"That is correct, I had nothing to do with it."

Peter cleared his throat and shifted his weight on the love seat to catch the colonel's attention. Danners had been instructed to catch Peter's eye before responding to any substantive questions. He had no problem with Danners's answer to these first two questions, but he didn't want a bad habit to develop.

"If I were to ask you," the detective began, "which member of your group you believed might be responsible for this fire, who would you suggest?"

"I'm afraid I'm going to have to instruct the colonel not to engage in pure speculation," Peter said.

"Do you have any factual evidence, Colonel, that would lead you to believe that a member of your group may be responsible for this fire?"

"No, no reason to suspect anyone," Danners replied.

It was not the answer the detective wanted, but because of Peter he decided not to try it again in a different form. "When was the last time you were at the clinic?"

"Last Saturday."

"Did you notice anything unusual?"

"No, nothing."

"Have you ever met Dr. Marsano?"

The colonel caught Peter's gaze, as he had done for the last several questions. Peter nodded slightly. It was the signal to proceed.

"No, I saw her drive into the clinic on a few occasions. And I saw her in court in Seattle. But I never actually met her."

"Did the two of you ever talk on the phone?"

"No."

"To your knowledge, did anyone in your group ever talk to her in person or on the phone?"

The colonel looked at Peter with questioning eyes. Interpreting his look, Peter said, "Mr. Dunn, the colonel and I need to talk for just a minute. We'll be right back."

Moving quickly down the hall, Peter whispered, "What is it?" as soon as they were safely out of range.

"It's just that Shirley and Ginny had been trying to witness to the doctor. They would say a few words to her when she would cross over our line in her car, if her window was rolled down."

"Did they yell or anything?"

"I don't think so. They told me they would say things like, 'Dr. Marsano, God really loves you and so do we.' That sort of thing."

"Do you think anyone else in the clinic knew about this?"

"I think there may have been other staffers in the car with her on a couple of occasions."

"We might as well tell him about it now. He's going to learn about it eventually."

Danners nodded, and both men turned and paced back into the living room.

"He'll answer your question now," Peter said, resuming his place on the love seat.

Dunn raised his eyebrows, hoping for an explanation for their discussion. Seeing that one wasn't coming, he shook his head and said, "OK, Colonel what do you know about other people in your group talking to Dr. Marsano?"

"It's just this—two of the ladies in our group used to talk to her in her car from time to time, as she drove past us on the way into the clinic parking lot."

"What did they say to her?"

"They were trying to tell the doctor that God loves her."

"What? God loves her?"

"Yeah, they were trying to plant some seeds in her mind that would maybe lead her to God. They were always very polite, and the conversations only lasted a few seconds on those occasions."

"Which ladies are you referring to?"

"Shirley Alper and Ginny Kettner."

"You want to save me the trouble of looking up their phone numbers?" the detective said, with his pen poised.

"I'll make it even easier for you," Peter interrupted. "Shirley and Ginny are both part of the leadership team that I represent. I'll be happy to supply you with their phone numbers, but if you want to talk with them, just call me and I'll arrange an appointment. In fact, I'll advise you right now that I represent all five members of the leadership group, so I will need to be present for any interviews."

"That's fine, Mr. Barron. Before I leave, let's schedule those appointments."

"Well, I'm afraid it'll have to wait for a couple weeks. I'll need to clear my calendar in Spokane before I can return—I obviously just jumped on a plane this morning and had no time to check my schedule."

"A couple weeks? You're going to have to do better than that." Dunn's face flushed slightly but otherwise made no indication of genuine anger. "This is a murder investigation, and we are gonna need to move forward promptly. You got that?"

Peter smiled ever so slightly as he glared silently in response to the detective's bullying. Rays of sunlight, eking through the cloud cover, shone through the large glass window and fell on the detective's hands as he clicked his ballpoint pen in and out, in and out. During the next twenty seconds of silence, an unmistakable scowl grew on his face. "So it's going to be that way, is it? Two can play at that game, Mr. Barron; and I guarantee you, I'll win."

"Listen here, Mr. Dunn," Peter said, letting the detective's name roll slowly off his lips. "You cannot intimidate me or my clients. These people are innocent, but clearly there are political forces that would like to charge my clients with responsibility for this tragedy. So you're just going to have to accept my presence in this process. You've had virtually free reign with the colonel here, so there's no reason for you to get your nose out of joint. I suggest we just finish this up quickly and keep moving forward."

A slow red burn crept up Dunn's neck. He knew Peter could rule out any interviews, but the detective wasn't ready to let this out-of-town lawyer interfere with his murder investigation.

"Do you have any further questions?" Peter asked.

"Not at the present time," Dunn growled, standing abruptly. "I'll show myself out."

"What was that all about?" Danners asked as soon as he heard the front door close with a slam. Peter shrugged. Danners continued, "I'm not sure being so abrupt was the best thing. He got pretty mad."

"I think it was OK," Peter replied. "He strikes me as the kind of guy who only gets mad on purpose. I think it was more a ploy to throw a little fear and confusion into our camp—trying to keep us off balance."

"I just hope we're doing the right thing," Danners replied.

"Yeah, me too," Peter said. "Well, that's one episode over with. Let's get ready to face the press."

12

Vince's head was throbbing when he woke up late Sunday afternoon after a day of drinking and passing in and out of consciousness. He struggled to his feet and staggered into the bathroom. Five minutes later he emerged and stared hard at the bed and then at the drawn shades. Hardly any light seeped in around the edges any more; earlier that afternoon he thought those stray rays of light would pierce his skull. He managed to make it over to the window, grasped the ledge, and hung on with one hand long enough to open the curtain about five inches.

The sun was just about down over Toronto. Vince tried to focus his eyes on the traffic, but it was mostly a blur.

He staggered back to the bed and sat down heavily on the edge. He picked up the phone and began to punch buttons.

"Your call cannot be completed as dialed. You must first dial an eight," the recording commanded.

He cleared the line and starting punching numbers again. "You have reached a number that is no longer in service or has been disconnected," another recording said a few seconds later.

"They can't have changed their number," Vince said out loud. He punched again, trying to be more careful.

Ring, ring, ring, ring, ring, ring. He was about to hang up when a woman's voice came on the line. "Hello?"

"Karen?"

"Who's this?"

"Vince Davis."

"Why are you calling here?"

"I wanna know what happened."

"What are you talking about?" Ballentine answered.

"You know what I mean. Rhonda's dead." He choked out the words.

"I know," Ballentine answered with manufactured sadness. "It's really awful what these clinic protesters have done."

"Save the charade for somebody else." Vince's words were slurred and slow. "Now tell me what happened!"

"All right, but this is the last conversation we're having for quite a while. Don't ever call me here again." She paused, waiting to hear his agreement. "After you left the clinic, I went downstairs to go to the bath-room. Just as I came out, your little device by the stairs went off early and a fireball raced up the stairs in an instant. I called Rhonda, but she couldn't come down the stairs because of the fire. I had to run outside to save myself. There was nothing I could do."

"Why didn't you call the fire department?"

"I jumped into my car and raced around trying to find a pay phone. I didn't have the cellular with me. About five minutes passed before I found a phone. It was just too late by the time they got there."

"Did you stick around to tell them what happened?"

"Are you crazy? Of course not. Rhonda was an accident, but I wasn't about to confess to the fire."

"What are we going to do?"

"What *you* are going to do is stay in Toronto until further notice. A Federal Express package will be delivered to your hotel under the name Austin Hall on Monday, containing a complete set of identity papers. Everything is going to go just like we planned. The only difference is that the protesters are now going to have to face murder charges as well as arson."

"How can you be so sure that they'll be charged with murder?"

"I've already talked with Amanda, my friend at the Justice Department in Washington, D.C. She assures me that the nature of the death dictates that a murder charge should be brought against whoever is charged with the arson."

"Ooohh," Vince groaned, his stomach reeling around inside. "It wasn't supposed to happen this way—"

"Look, Vince, I'm very sorry, but it was an accident. Now I've gotta go. And remember, don't call here again."

The line went dead and Vince fell back onto the bed in a stupor of drunkenness and sorrow.

The moon seemed twice its normal size as it rose over the jagged mountains that dominate Vancouver's western horizon. Peter leaned on the railing with both forearms bearing his weight as he gazed upon the skyline of British Columbia's largest city. Gwen rested her right hand gently on Peter's back as the gentle May breeze blew her hair away from her face.

They had debated the relative merits of many of Vancouver's fine restaurants, but had settled on room service from the Four Season's fabled chefs. The view from their fifteenth story room rivaled nearly all the restaurants in the guidebook they had found in the dresser drawer. And the atmosphere could not have been more intimate. It was quite an expensive hotel, but they were not billing the evening to Peter's pro-life clients. Even though Gwen's case from two years earlier had produced a significant award for both of them, they had kept their lifestyles pretty much as before. But once in a while they would simply splurge for something that they could clearly afford but did not necessarily need.

"Peter . . ." Gwen said, letting his name just hang in the air.

"Yes, honey," he replied after several seconds.

"Oh . . . I was just thinking. So many things are swirling in my head all at once."

"Sure, it's been that kind of day," he replied with a gentle laugh.

"Yeah, a very interesting day. I thought that one reporter from Seattle, you know, the tall brunette, was going to bite your head off when you wouldn't let the colonel answer any questions."

"She did look like a pit bull with lipstick, didn't she?"

"That's a new one. I thought I knew all your joke lines."

"I got it from Aaron at our Bible study yesterday morning."

"Oh my. When you say that I get a real feeling of how far removed we are from our normal world. It's only four hundred miles, but it seems like almost a different continent or something."

"We are in another country, you know."

"Of course, I know that, you . . . you . . ."

"Cutey?" Peter suggested playfully.

"It wasn't the word I had in mind," Gwen replied with a forced frown. "Anyway, it's not just here in Vancouver. Bellingham seems so far away from Spokane that it doesn't even seem part of the same state or anything."

"Washington is a pretty large state."

"You just don't get what I'm trying to say." She took her hand away and walked slowly to the other end of the balcony. "Peter, I'm trying to talk about something serious, so just be quiet and listen without answering so quickly."

"OK," he replied, standing up straight to watch his wife, as it was now her turn to lean on the railing and look out over the city.

"I was very proud of you today. And I can see that you are involved in a very important case for a cause I believe in. You know how I feel about abortion and babies."

Gwen paused for a while and then broke the silence with a soft laugh. "And it was really fun watching you deal with those press people. You have gotten really good with them. Better than most politicians. You come across so reasonable it drives them crazy. They want pro-lifers to be loud and angry, not nice and logical."

"Thanks, honey. I appreciate you saying that," Peter said softly.

"But all this stuff scares me so much when I think of how far it is from our world. When you are over here you are such a long, long way from our house, from Casey . . . and from me." She breathed heavily. The rush of cool night air in her lungs soothed her body and spirit. "I know I'm being selfish and a little irrational, but it is so hard for me to think of letting you go to come over here and to work on this."

"Gwen, it won't be that bad, even if it goes to a full blown trial."

"Peter, you can't fool me with that line. You must remember I was your client before I was your wife. I've seen you in an all-consuming case before. I know what you are like."

"But I was being consumed with you, not just with your case."

"It was both. And even after you had caught me, I could tell that when you got immersed in the lawsuit, your mind became so dominated thinking about it that I had flashes of jealousy about my own case taking you away from me. This one is going to consume you. And I know I told you at the colonel's that you should do it, but I just want you to know how hard it is for me."

Peter strode gently behind his wife, placed his arms around her waist, locked his fingers together, and pulled her back gently to his chest. He wisely said nothing.

"I want you to help Suzie and the others, but I'm afraid of losing you. Do you understand what I mean?"

"You don't mean losing me to another woman or anything? That's crazy if that's what you're thinking."

"I didn't mean that, but I'm glad to hear you say it anyway. What I mean is that I don't want to lose the focus and attention that Casey and I need from you. I want you to be an active dad and husband for us. I don't want leftovers. It's hard enough when you have just regular cases taking your time and attention. But when you get one like this, I know what you're going to be like, so don't try to bluff me by saying otherwise."

"But it may not become a real case. They may not charge our people with any crime. Maybe they'll catch the real culprit."

"Maybe. But I have a sick feeling in my spirit that says otherwise."

Peter knew the feeling she was describing. He felt it, too. But all he said at first was, "Hmmm."

"Gwen, I don't know what to say exactly. There's got to be an answer to all of this. I *think* God wants me to do this case—if it does go further. But I *know* that God wants me to be a good husband to you and a good father to Casey. If He really wants me to handle this lawsuit, then there has got to be a way for me to love you and Casey intensely while I'm doing it."

"I just wish I knew what the answer was now," Gwen replied.

"Me, too," Peter said, pulling his wife even more tightly against his chest. "The only thing I can think of is the verse that says that if we lack wisdom, we should ask God and He'll give it to us. I clearly need wisdom about how to find the balance between my job and my family. All I can promise is that I will really seek God in prayer about this."

"Every day?" Gwen asked, twisting in his arms so she was not locked in a face-to-face embrace.

"Every day," he replied tenderly.

He bent to kiss his wife with the passion that the moon and the moment called for, but just as their lips touched, a loud rapping was heard on the door. "Room service," a voice yelled.

On Monday morning, Jamie MacMillan glanced up at the shapely receptionist in the Fred Meyer corporate office building for the sixth or seventh time. Each time she caught him looking, she smiled in embarrassment. "Mr. Mannion should be here in just another minute," she said, shaking her long brown hair after one of MacMillan's once-overs. "In fact, here he comes now." As she spoke, a lanky man came down the corridor behind her and through the door.

"You gentlemen the police officers from Bellingham?" the man asked.

"Yes sir," Castille said, jumping to his feet. "Carl Castille," he said, extending his hand. "And this is Jamie MacMillan." Both detectives flashed their IDs long enough for Mannion to take a good look.

"Harold Mannion's the name. Come with me. We've got the tapes set up for you in a room down the hall."

MacMillan twisted around for one last look over his shoulder at the attractive receptionist as he followed Mannion down the hallway. "I'll be back," MacMillan whispered to her as he passed by.

He had to jog a step or two to catch up with his partner and their host, who had disappeared around a corner. He rounded the corner in time to see them enter a room on the right side of the hallway. A small round table with a Formica top sat in the middle of the room, with four metal and black vinyl chairs surrounding it. A television set, perched on a rolling stand in one corner, was on, its screen reflecting blue hues along the opposite side of the room. A VCR sat on a shelf under the TV. On the floor beside the stand were several boxes stacked in a neat pile.

"Based on the coding on the price sticker, we're certain the gasoline container you found came from our Bellingham store. These boxes contain the security videos for the two weeks immediately preceding the fire. The tapes in the top box are from three days before the fire, six tapes for each day, and they go back in order from top to bottom. I suggest you watch them in a fast scan mode until you see something you think is worth looking at."

"Oh boy," MacMillan sighed. "Two hundred twenty-four hours worth of tapes—what fun. Any way to get a second VCR and TV so we can each watch a different tape?"

"We can do that," Mannion replied. "I'll go get it. In the meantime, if you need anything, Ms. Turner will be glad to assist you."

"Very good," MacMillan said smiling.

"Can we start our job now, Romeo?" Castille asked as soon as Mannion left the room.

"Sure thing," MacMillan said as he walked over to the boxes. "Let's start with the top box and hope the culprit wasn't a plan-things-well-in-advance type of guy."

After about three minutes, Mannion wheeled in the second TV/VCR unit and set it up beside the first one.

"You keep going with the first tape in the box," Castille said. "I'll start with the last tape in the box, and we can work our way to the middle."

An hour later Castille called out. "Gas can on lane three!" MacMillan hit the pause button on his machine.

A man in his forties, dressed in slacks and a golf shirt, walked through the checkout stand holding both a gas can and a weed trimmer. The two detectives slowed the tape to normal speed to watch more carefully.

"I don't think this is our guy," Castille said as they watched the scene for a second time.

"You're probably right, but let's make a note of it anyway," MacMillan said as he returned to his own screen.

Both men struggled to stay awake as the tedium of watching purchase after purchase continued for several hours.

Checking his watch, Castille called out, "Hey, you wanna go to lunch? It's past one o'clock."

"Yeah, especially if they have an employee cafeteria," MacMillan replied.

"MacMillan, you have a one-track mind," Castille replied.

"You used to be just like me until that cute little wife of yours got you wrapped around her little finger," MacMillan replied, reaching for the stop button on the VCR. "Hey look," he called out suddenly, pointing at the screen. "Gas cans on lane seven. There's two . . . no, three cans."

"Yeah, and look what else they've got there. Is that a roll of wire?" Castille asked.

"Sure looks like it. And those things next to the wire look like dry-cell batteries if you ask me!"

"Yeah," Castille answered excitedly. "I think we've got our bombers. Play it again, will ya?"

"We definitely need a copy of this," his partner said, hitting the rewind button. Both men froze in concentration as the scene rolled before their eyes a second time.

"Are you sure they're together?" Castille asked, pointing to Stephen Gray and Suzie on the video screen.

"Hard to tell from the tape," MacMillan replied.

"I'd say he's about thirty; she looks like a high school girl, maybe a freshman in college, tops."

"Is that a credit card he's paying with?"

"Yeah, sure looks like it. This is too easy! I'll just run down to that cute little receptionist and find out how to get a copy of that credit card slip."

"Figures you'd volunteer for that," Castille replied. "I'll dub a copy between the two machines while you're gone. Where's that blank tape we brought?"

MacMillan reached in his sports jacket pocket and tossed a blank tape, still in the wrapper, to his partner. "Be back soon."

"Yeah, right," Castille replied, biting the shrink-wrap to open it up.

Fifteen minutes passed and Castille was beginning to steam. He was sure MacMillan was flirting with the secretary. He stuck the duplicate tape in his own jacket pocket and started to head toward the reception area when he saw MacMillan coming toward him down the hall, whistling loudly.

"I suppose this means you got a date," Castille said tersely.

"Yep. Friday night. But I also got us the name of the user on that credit card."

"You did?"

"She did it as a special favor to me. Cap'n always says, 'Be nice to people and they'll give you more information than you'll know what to do with.' Just following the captain's orders!"

"All right, wise guy. So what'd you find out?"

"Stephen Gray's our man. I've got his Visa account number here and his address and phone number. Seems he's been in the store before."

"Great. Now let's get out of here and get this tape to the captain."

Peter spent all day Wednesday in hearings, but was in his office early Thursday morning to review his notes from the weekend. When Sally arrived, he asked her not to disturb him unless it was an emergency.

Still emersed in thought at mid-afternoon, Sally's voice over the intercom was an unwelcome interruption.

"Peter?"

"What is it, Sally?" Peter asked.

"Detective Dunn on line three."

"Oh, OK." He picked up the phone. "Good afternoon, Captain Dunn. How are you today?"

"Just fine, Mr. Barron. I need to interview one of your clients. How soon can you get up here?"

"Which client do you want to talk to?"

"Susan O'Dell."

"Suzie?"

"You always call your clients by their nicknames?" the detective asked after a pause.

"Well, I knew her from before—she's from Spokane."

"Is that how you got involved in this case?"

I guess there's no harm answering his question, Peter thought. "Yeah, as a matter of fact, it is. Suzie used to baby-sit my daughter."

"Well, she's the one I want to interview. Tomorrow."

"Tomorrow? That sure isn't much notice."

"Yeah, well, sorry 'bout that."

"What's wrong with next week?"

"Look, I'm following the rules, Barron, so don't push me. Otherwise I'll find ways around them."

"OK, OK, I was just wondering why the rush," Peter said apologetically.

"I'm sure I don't have to tell you that the county prosecutor has a special interest in this case—he wants me to make as much progress as possible before the feds move in."

"But why Suzie? I don't mind telling you that comes as a surprise."

"All I can tell you is we've got some evidence that points to her. Now I'm not saying we're accusing her of anything—we just want to talk to her. That's all I can say. I think you understand."

"Can it be late tomorrow afternoon? I've got a hearing in the morning. I can catch a flight around noon and be in Bellingham by three. How about if I pick up Suzie and meet you at the police station at four?"

"That'll work. Just tell her not to think about running. We've got her under surveillance; if she drives even five miles north of Bellingham, we'll intercept her."

"I'll call her right now."

"Four o'clock. See you then."

Peter rocked backwards in his chair with a hard jerk and emitted a loud groan. Within moments he heard shuffling steps coming toward his office. It was Sally's trademark hurry-up.

"What's wrong?" she blurted out. "I heard you make some weird noise."

"The Bellingham police want to interview Suzie tomorrow. Sounds like they've found something."

"Suzie? Your baby-sitter?"

"Yeah, that's the one. I can't believe she's done anything wrong, but the detective seemed awful sure of himself."

"Should I schedule a flight?"

"Yeah, get me a flight at noon. I'll go right after the motion docket in the morning. Call my afternoon appointments—have the Freeds come in and sign their will with Joe. Postpone the rest, I guess. I'd better call Suzie's parents."

"When do you want your return?"

"Last flight out of Seattle tomorrow night. I think it's at ten."

"You don't want a flight directly into Bellingham?"

"No thanks, I'm not in that big a hurry."

Sally left the room. Peter picked up the telephone receiver, then placed it back on its cradle. He wondered how he would tell Suzie's parents about this, especially after assuring them last Sunday in church that Suzie "would be the last person on earth to be suspected of anything."

Vince Davis received the Federal Express package on Monday as promised and found the papers to be in perfect order. "Thomas Beard," he muttered. "I wish they'd let me pick my own names." Scrambling through the envelope, he found what was most important—a deposit receipt for $75,000 in U.S. funds into the Royal Bank of Canada, under his new assumed name. Over the next couple of months he planned to gradually withdraw it all and redeposit it into other accounts throughout Toronto. He didn't want a trace to be easy.

Vince negotiated a furnished apartment in an exclusive section of the city and took out a six-month lease on a Range Rover. He'd always wanted a macho, four-wheel-drive rig, and spending six months in Canada seemed to be the perfect opportunity to fulfill this particular fantasy. He revitalized his golf game and frequented a local sporting goods store to buy every known piece of fishing paraphernalia. With its many lakes and streams, Canada was perfect fly fishing country.

But as much as he succeeded in occupying his days, the nights were excruciatingly long. Sleep came only with excessive drink, and nightmares of Rhonda often kept him awake for hours on end. He tried to fill the evening hours with female companionship, but even that lacked its usual degree of satisfaction.

One evening, with a woman asleep by his side, Vince, unable to sleep, stumbled into the living room and flipped on the radio on the stereo system. Scanning the stations, he came across a late-night, call-in talk show on a Christian station from nearby Buffalo. They were discussing the abortion/pro-life issue, concentrating on the recent abortion clinic fire in Washington state. Vince listened, half awake, to an hour of dialogue. Same old arguments from both sides, same old conclusions. Regardless of what side the callers were on, everyone agreed the fire was tragic and that whoever was responsible should be "prosecuted to the full extent of the law." He was about to turn the program off when a woman's voice came on the line.

"I feel sorry for the arsonist," she said.

"That's a new approach," the host replied. "Why is that?"

"Well, I think the person who did it must be really hurting right now. Whether or not he meant to harm the doctor, the end result is she's dead. That's a heavy burden for anyone to bear. I'm praying for whoever did this," she concluded.

That set off a whole new round of arguments, none of which Vince paid any attention to. His mind was frozen on the woman's last comment. Someone was praying for him.

Vince's eyes glanced around the room, but his mind traveled far away. Even though he'd not been around to see the explosions at the clinic, he could picture them in his mind. He could picture, too, Rhonda's efforts to try and escape the flames that finally ended her life.

The thoughts overwhelmed him, and his mind rushed back to the caller's words: I'm praying . . . he must be really hurting . . . really hurting . . . really hurting . . . really hurting. He lumbered back to bed and tried to go back to sleep.

"Really hurting—" Vince said aloud, rolling dejectedly onto his side.

The woman beside him moaned. "Huh?"

Vince didn't respond.

13

Suzie grabbed Peter's arm and squeezed hard as he opened the glass door to the Bellingham City Hall that housed the police department. It had been an overcast Friday, but now darker clouds were moving in over the horizon, threatening a rainy weekend. A gust of cold wind blew in the door as it shut behind them.

"I'm scared, Mr. Barron," she said.

Peter could tell she was on the verge of tears. "Suzie, I'm here, and the Lord is with us. Armed with the Lord, the truth, and a so-so lawyer, you've got it made." He smiled, hoping his self-deprecating humor would lighten her mood.

They negotiated a series of turns and found a sign that said "Bellingham Police" above a reception area. A woman in her late forties sat behind a computer terminal with a dictaphone plugged into her ears. Her eyes focused on the screen ahead of her; she did not notice Peter and Suzie until a sneeze broke her concentration.

"Peter Barron and Susan O'Dell to see Captain Dunn," he announced as she looked up.

The receptionist nodded, picked up her telephone and whispered a few words, then resumed her syncopated rhythm. "He'll be right with you," she droned at Peter, who remained standing at the edge of her desk.

A young dark-haired man suddenly appeared in an open doorway. "Mr. Barron, I'm Detective Castille. Follow me, please." Castille reversed his direction, turned a corner, and paused in front of the second door on the right. "Right in here," he said, pointing to a tiny interrogation room.

Inside the room were three chairs surrounding a small table; a fourth chair stood in the corner. Detective Dunn sat in the single chair on one side of the table and motioned to the two chairs opposite him.

"Mr. Barron, Ms. O'Dell, please sit down," Dunn said, squishing a half-smoked cigarette out in an ashtray. "Don't suppose you two smoke, so I'll try to accommodate you."

"Thanks," Peter said.

"I guess we should begin by reading your client her *Miranda* rights. Castille, would you do the honors?"

The dark-haired detective had begun to leave, but turned around and, clearing his throat, addressed Suzie. "You have the right to remain silent. You have the right to counsel before you answer any questions. If you cannot afford an attorney one will be appointed for you. Anything you say can and will be used against you in a court of law," Castille said from memory.

Suzie gripped the table hard when Castille began the litany. Peter had warned her that they might do this, keeping to himself that it was a bad sign if they did.

Peter pulled his chair closer to Suzie. "Remember to wait before answering anything," he whispered. "Give me a chance to stop you. I'll speak up if need be."

Detective Dunn began with some basic questions, similar to those he'd asked Colonel Danners several days before. Finally he said, "All right, Miss O'Dell, let's get down to the meat of this." Peter scooted his chair forward another quarter-inch closer to Suzie. "You are a part of the leadership team of this anti-abortion group, aren't you?"

"We prefer to call it a pro-life group," Peter interjected.

"Whatever," Dunn replied. "Are you one of this group's leaders?"

"Yes, sir," Suzie said weakly.

"Board member, is that your title?"

Suzie nodded affirmatively.

"Do you know a member of your group named Stephen Gray?"

Suzie glanced at Peter. He nodded.

"Yes, sir, I know Mr. Gray. He's not part of the leadership, but he's a member of the group."

"What is the nature of your relationship?"

"I just know him through the group. Nothing more."

"You two ever date?"

"No, sir. He's been dating Lisa Edgar. She's also a member of the group."

"Uh-huh," Dunn said, noting Lisa's name. It was not the first time he'd heard it.

"You ever been out alone with Mr. Gray?"

"Alone? Not that I can recall."

"Are you sure you've never been alone with him—for any reason?"

"No, sir, we never went out," Suzie insisted, her mind still focused on a "dating" scenario.

"Never went shopping with Mr. Gray?"

"Oh, that," Suzie began. Peter grabbed her arm. "What's he talking about?" he whispered in her ear.

"We stopped in a store after one of our meetings," she whispered back. "He was giving me a ride home and wanted to stop in before it closed."

Peter nodded.

"We stopped at Fred Meyer one night. I was thinking about a date," she said matter of factly.

"So tell me about your trip with Mr. Gray to Fred Meyer." Detective Dunn leaned into the table with great interest.

"Sure. He was giving me a ride home after one of our committee meetings. As we approached Fred Meyer, he slowed and asked if he could stop in and get a couple things."

"Did you and Mr. Gray talk about the abortion clinic on the drive home that night?"

Peter looked hard at Suzie. She shrugged with an "I don't know" expression. He gave her permission to continue with a nod.

"I don't remember what we discussed."

"Did he mention to you anything about setting the clinic on fire?"

"No, of course not!" Suzie said. Peter was relieved to see a bit of a fighter's spirit coming out.

"You're sure that topic didn't come up—a joke, perhaps—'Wouldn't it be nice if the clinic accidently burned to the ground?' something of that nature?"

"We did not talk about any such thing!" Suzie said, her voice cracking as though she were on the verge of tears.

"Ever?" Dunn pressed.

"Captain Dunn, I think you've harped on this subject long enough. Suzie's admitted that she and this Gray fellow stopped at Fred Meyer and picked up a few items. I don't see how that translates into a discussion about setting a fire, so can we move on?"

Dunn heard Peter's words, but his glare never shifted from Suzie's face. "Ms. O'Dell, why don't you tell your lawyer here what you and Mr. Gray bought that evening."

At first Suzie's mind drew a blank. Suddenly all the blood drained from her face as she remembered the items Gray had purchased.

"Suzie, what is it?" Peter said.

"Oh my. . . . He bought some gas cans, a roll of wire, and some large batteries," she whispered quietly into Peter's ear, allowing her head to drop into her hands.

Peter tried to hide his shock, but Dunn saw enough to know that Barron was genuinely surprised with what he had just heard. "We've got it all on videotape from the store's security system," Dunn said.

"Suzie and I need to go outside for a minute," Peter said firmly, standing and pushing his chair back with a hard shove.

"Hold on, Barron," Dunn replied. "Detective Castille and I will leave you alone for as long as you need. And don't worry, the room's not bugged."

Peter glanced at the other detective, who'd been sitting quietly in the corner all this time, as he stood and followed Dunn from the room.

"What's going on, Suzie?" Peter said, speaking softly but urgently. "Batteries, gas cans, wire—what in the world?"

"He told me he was buying a few things for some yard work. The items didn't seem that unusual at the time—"

"Not unusual!" Peter's voice was intense, but quiet—a whispered yell. "Suzie," he said with obvious disappointment, repeatedly shaking his head.

Suzie looked at him with eyes filled with bewilderment. "I'm sorry, Mr. Barron, I guess I wasn't thinking. I mean, it's not like, 'You better watch what he buys because he might be putting together a bomb.'" Suzie began sobbing uncontrollably.

"Oh, Suzie," Peter said, walking over to her and holding both of her hands in his. "I know you didn't realize what was happening at the time, but this is a really bad thing you've gotten yourself in the middle of. And I don't think you should answer any more questions. I'll go down the hall and tell the detective we're leaving."

"Can we do that?"

"Yeah," Peter replied, hoping he could actually pull it off.

Castille stuck his head around the corner as soon as he heard the conference room door open.

"OK?" the young detective asked.

"Can I talk to the two of you alone?"

"Sure, the Captain's down in his office," Castille answered.

Dunn's feet were propped up on his desk, his hands clasped behind his head when Peter entered. A smirk was on his face. "Got her, don't I, Mr. Barron?" he said.

"You may or may not have something on Gray, but Suzie's innocent."

"Sure she is," he said mockingly.

"What other evidence do you have?" Peter demanded.

Dunn pulled his feet off his desk, leaned forward, and looked Peter straight in the eyes. "We've got one of the three gas cans she and Gray bought that night—it was in the garbage behind the clinic. There are two sets of prints on it. I think one will be Ms. O'Dell's. And we got the remnants of the other two cans—melted down from the fire. They were found in the burned-out rubble. We really don't have much," he said sarcastically.

Peter stood frozen in thought. "So what do you want?" he said after a moment of awkward silence.

"We would have to get the prosecutor's final OK on this, but we think he'll follow our recommendation to offer Suzie a deal. We'd allow her to plead to second degree murder and arson. She can duck the first degree murder charge—and the death penalty that potentially goes with it—if she helps us with Gray and tells us about the conspiracy involving the rest of her little band of protesters."

"You can't be serious! There's not enough evidence for a first or second degree murder charge!"

Dunn rocked back in his chair and twirled a ballpoint pen in his hands. "Let me assure you that we are dead serious, Mr. Barron."

"But you don't have anything on Suzie that will stick. You've got the tape that shows how her fingerprints got on the gas can, if in fact that's what you find. She's no more implicated than the clerk at Fred Meyer."

"Oh, come now, Mr. Barron," Dunn replied with a smirk. "You're a better lawyer than that. The clerk at Fred Meyer may have his fingerprints on the gas can, but he didn't have a motive to torch this clinic. Little Suzie did."

"I assume you've brought Gray in for questioning?"

"That's one of the reasons we want to offer Suzie a deal," Dunn replied. "It seems that Mr. Gray has disappeared off the face of the earth. We want her to help us find him."

"If he's disappeared, then you know he's the only one responsible for this," Peter replied.

"Save it for the jury, Mr. Barron. Of course he's responsible, but solely responsible? We think not."

Peter leaned back against the wall of the detective's office and rubbed his eyes with his fists. "There's a problem with your deal, Captain. How can we make a deal when you keep alluding to the FBI. If I plead her to something—and it won't be second degree murder—what assurance do I have that she won't be facing federal felony charges right afterwards?"

"You do have a point on that one. You can talk to the prosecutor about that, but he assures me that it can be successfully worked out—now that you're beginning to see reason and realize you're going to have to plead her to . . . to something."

"I have said no such thing. If Suzie's innocent—and I think she is—she ain't pleading to anything more than a parking ticket. I just wanted to get a handle on this federal thing. I need to talk to Suzie again."

"Certainly, Mr. Barron. No problem," Dunn said, rising to his feet. "Right after we take her fingerprints. Then it'll take another little while to get her through booking. You can see her in the lawyer interview area of the jail in forty-five minutes or so."

"Are you crazy? You're booking her in jail?" Peter shouted.

"We certainly are, Mr. Barron. And your yelling isn't going to change that one bit. She's being booked for first degree murder and arson, and we're going to ask that bail be denied. We've already had one suspect hightail it out of town. We don't want another disappearance."

Peter looked frantically at his watch. 5:30 P.M. The judges would all be gone by now, and it was Friday afternoon. "You deliberately did this so she would have to spend the weekend in jail, didn't you? You know I'll get her out on Monday—no judge in his right mind will hold her without bail."

"You set the time for this appointment, Mr. Barron, remember? Don't start accusing me of anything."

His answer took the wind of moral indignation out of Peter's sails. "You're right, I'm sorry," Peter grumbled. "Can you please just give me five minutes with her before taking her down to the booking area?"

"Yeah, since you said you were sorry, we can do that," Dunn replied.

Peter prayed frantically as he walked the few steps down the linoleum-covered hallway, pausing just in front of the door to the interview room. As he reached for the door, he suddenly realized that he was sick to his stomach. He tried smiling as he walked in and sat down beside Suzie, but he knew that it was unlikely to come across as a reassuring look.

"Suzie," he said, looking for a second in her eyes, but then quickly looking down at the table. "Suzie, I'm afraid we're in for some hard times for a while."

"Wha—what do you mean?" she stammered.

"They're going to arrest you, and I'm afraid you're going to have to spend at least the weekend in jail."

"Jail? Me? What did I do?" she cried.

"They are going to charge you with the death of the doctor and the burning of the clinic." Peter couldn't bring himself to say "murder and arson."

"But I didn't do anything!" Her voice was breaking. "Didn't you tell them that?"

"Yeah, Suzie, I did. But they've got this videotape of you and Stephen Gray in Fred Meyer, and they found a gas can with a Fred Meyer sticker on it in a garbage can behind the clinic. They're going to take your fingerprints—they think yours will match one set of prints on the can they found."

"I can't believe this. And you promised everything was going to be OK." Her voice was choked with sobs.

"Suzie, I'm sorry—" Peter thought his apology sounded weak and meaningless, but he could think of nothing else to say. He was interrupted by Castille's tapping on the glass window of the door. The detective pointed at his watch. Peter held up his index finger, asking for just one more minute. Castille nodded.

"Suzie, I believe you. And I'm going to fight this. I can't promise you anything, but I believe with all my heart that God is going to rescue you and vindicate you in the end. You may face a trial—and God doesn't promise us we won't go through trials, right? But He does promise to be with us every step of the way." Peter scooted his chair away from the table. "We've got to go."

Suzie tried to smile bravely as she stood, but she collapsed against Peter's chest and cried bitterly, clinging tightly to his arms until Castille entered the room and gently pulled her away.

Peter walked out of city hall into the spacious open area between the complex of government buildings. The Whatcom County courthouse, with a magnificent modern edifice attached to the front of the considerably older original court house with a three story glass entryway, lay to his right toward the bay. The county jail, Castille had told him, was right behind the courthouse. Bounding up the steps of the court house, he spotted a phone about thirty yards away on the back side of the huge entrance area. He was grateful no one was using any of the phones; he didn't want to have to make these calls in front of anyone else. Peter stood in front of the phone, searching his wallet for his telephone calling card.

"Hello, Barron residence," Casey said.

"Hi, Casey doll, this is Daddy. Is Mommy there"

"Sure," she chirped. "I'll go get her. Mommy, Daddy's on the phone!"

Laughing, Gwen took the phone out of Casey's hand. "Hi honey, I was standing right here the whole time—I'm going to have to talk to Casey about that yell of hers—"

Peter was silent for a moment.

"Peter?"

"I'm here. . . . I've got some really bad news," Peter began.

"Oh, no, what's wrong?"

"Suzie's in jail. She's been arrested for first degree murder and arson."

"What?!"

Peter told Gwen the entire scenario of the videotape taken at Fred Meyer and the fingerprints on the can.

"Do you think she was involved?" Gwen asked.

"No, I don't. I think she was at the wrong place at the wrong time."

"So how long until she can get out of jail? She will be allowed to get out, won't she?"

"I hope so. But I won't know until Monday."

"Are you coming home tonight?"

"I don't think I should. Her parents will probably want to fly out, and I think I should stick around to meet them."

"Have you called them yet?"

"No, you were my first call. You need to pray for that conversation."

"I will. . . ."

"Honey, I'm going to need you to pack some things and give the bag to Bill and Linda. They can bring them over with them when they come."

"Peter?" Gwen said in a tone that indicated a change of subject.

"Yeah?"

"Oh, never mind, it can wait," she replied.

"You can't do that to me. What is it?"

"I'm sorry I said anything. It's not the right time."

"Don't do that to me," Peter cried out. "Now it's going to drive me crazy the whole weekend."

"I'm pregnant," she blurted. "Satisfied?"

Peter stammered for several seconds. "That's great news, isn't it?"

"I think so. But it's scary, too. Especially telling you when you're four hundred miles away. I don't want to have this baby alone. Or lose it alone."

"You aren't going to lose this baby, and you won't have it alone. I promise."

"Peter, sometimes things are out of your control—then even the great 'Peter Barron Guarantee' is worthless."

Her words hit him like a linebacker crushing a quarterback.

Peter said softly. "I know. You can't rely on my promises in this area or anyone else's. But you can rely on God's—nothing gets out of His control."

"You'd better call Suzie's parents," Gwen said swiftly, her voice becoming overrun with tears.

"OK, love. I'll call you back later."

14

Ground fog was starting to gather over the runways as the blue lights at the far end of the field started to play peek-a-boo with those watching from inside Bellingham's modest airline terminal. Standing behind a crowd of people, Peter wished the floor would open up and swallow him whole. Facing Suzie's parents would be the hardest task he'd ever done in his ten years of practicing law.

Finally the United Express twin-engine plane landed silently and rolled to a stop in front of the terminal building. A trio in matching jackets scurried around the plane. Two of them began opening the passenger door and guiding the passengers down the walkway, while the third opened the rear cargo hold and began unloading bags. Bill and Linda O'Dell were the last ones off the plane.

Trim and fit, they were a handsome couple in their late forties. Like Suzie, Linda had rich chestnut brown hair that she wore stylishly at shoulder length. She looked like a shorter and only slightly older version of her eldest daughter. Bill wore his salt-and-pepper hair army-short, showing off his steel blue eyes.

"Hello, Peter," Bill said. "I guess we're a little late."

"Don't worry about *that,*" Peter replied. "Let's go find your bags."

"We checked the bag Gwen gave us for you," Linda said, flashing a polite smile.

Peter, Bill, and Linda quickly made their way to the baggage claim area. Their bags were already rounding the carousel.

"Can we still see Suzie tonight?" Bill said, grabbing all their luggage with a single hand.

"If we hurry," Peter replied, locating his bag. "Because of her age and the nature of the charge, they're being a little more flexible about visiting hours. You'll be allowed to stay with her in the visiting area until eleven. That gives us a little over an hour."

Bill joined Peter in the front seat of the red Tercel he'd rented for the weekend. Linda sat directly behind her husband.

"Peter," Linda began, "Bill told me everything he could remember from your conversation. But I would like to hear it from you directly—how much trouble is Suzie really in?"

"Well, in one way, she's in as much trouble as anyone could be—at least from a lawyer's perspective. She's been arrested for first degree murder and arson, and political forces want a pro-lifer to be blamed."

"Do you think the police are after her for political reasons?" Bill interjected.

"No, I don't think the police have a political motive. They've got some fairly straightforward evidence—did Bill explain that part to you, Linda?"

"Yes, but she is innocent, isn't she?"

"She says she is and I believe her," Peter replied. "The problem is, this other fellow on the tape—Stephen Gray is his name—is almost certainly guilty. He bought the cans and the other stuff, the remnants of which were found at the crime scene. But Suzie was with him when he made the purchase, and that's where she looks bad."

"Has this guy actually accused Suzie of being his accomplice?" Bill asked angrily.

"That's another problem. He's disappeared, and no one has any idea where he's gone."

"Do you think this Gray person had help?" Bill asked, as Peter negotiated the exit off of Interstate 5 and headed through downtown toward the courthouse and jail.

"That's where politics come into play. The police want Suzie to cooperate with them so they can convict the rest of the pro-life leaders with conspiracy. They've already offered us a deal."

"A deal?" Bill said, a bit bewildered. "You mean they'd let her off if she confessed to something?"

"Should she do that?" Linda asked before Peter had a chance to reply.

"Well, it's not much of a deal and it's no deal at all for a person who's not guilty. The police offered to let her plead to second degree murder, which eliminates the possibility of capital punishment, but she would still be facing a life sentence."

Bill threw his head back against the head rest, moaning loudly. "Oh God," he cried, "please no. Please make this go away. Not Suzie. Not our Suzie!"

A few somber moments later, just as they were pulling up in front of the courthouse complex, Linda spoke up. "Tell us straight, Peter. Is there any chance Suzie will actually be sentenced to—to death?" she stammered.

"I want you to listen to me very carefully. I've been accused by my wife of promising things that I can't guarantee, so I won't do that. There is a theoretical possibility—under first degree murder—that she could be sentenced to death, but that's highly unlikely. Even if she had shot someone in cold blood in an armed robbery to support a drug habit, there's no way anyone would sentence a girl her age with no criminal record to capital punishment. But because of the political implications of this case, the mix changes a little. Killing as a politically motivated act is more likely to get someone the death penalty than just a plain old, calloused murder. Both are murder—but the punishment is likely to be harsher in the political case than in the non-political case. So when you balance all that out, I still think Suzie's age and lack of criminal record will prevent a death sentence. Remember, we're here to fight. And despite my wife's cautions about making promises, I think we'll win."

"I hope so," Bill replied grimly. Linda scrambled out of the car and caught her husband's arm as they approached the jail.

A few minutes later the large, orange metal door swung shut behind them as they entered the all-concrete waiting area for the jail. The attendant behind the bullet-proof glass enclosure reached for her speaker button. "I'm sorry folks, no more—oh, you're Susan O'Dell's attorney, aren't you? You've been cleared to visit until eleven."

"Thanks," Peter replied.

"I'll tell the guards to move her down into the attorney visitation area."

"Thanks again," Peter called out as he led Mr. and Mrs. O'Dell to the elevator. They rode up a single flight, where the doors opened to a smaller cement landing. Another orange steel door loomed to their right. A small video camera was attached to the wall near the ceiling on the left. The door buzzed open, and a long, narrow, cement hallway stretched out before them. The trio walked down past a row of small cubicles that jutted off to the left. Inside each cubicle was a single chair, a heavy glass window with a small screened opening, and a shelf just below the window that could be used by attorneys to take notes from the interviews that were so often conducted in the rooms.

Suzie was not yet in any of the cubicles, so they stood waiting. Sounds of heavy metal clanking and banging followed by subdued voices indicated someone's approach. "I think it's Suzie," Peter said.

Linda had firmly resolved to maintain her composure, but as soon as she saw her handcuffed daughter in a bright orange prison jumpsuit, she burst into tears. Suzie forced a smile through taut lips as the guard turned the key that unlocked the final iron gate, allowing the prisoner into the interview room.

"Suzie, honey!" her mother cried in desperation. She placed both hands on the glass barrier, wishing she could hold her daughter tightly in her arms. Linda suddenly pivoted and looked frantically at Peter. "Can't we be in the same room with her?"

Peter shook his head slowly. "You'll be together in the courtroom Monday morning, but for now, this is it," he said, waving his arms around to indicate the surroundings. "I'll leave you alone."

Peter walked far enough down the hallway until he couldn't make out what was being said. Still, he could hear Linda's crying and the low rumble of Bill's voice. He slowly paced down the narrow hall, looking into each of the empty visiting areas. Suddenly he thought, *What if that were Casey down in that cell? How would I feel?* The idea of his child facing the death penalty made him feel even worse for the O'Dells. A wave of guilt hit him hard, as if he had failed Suzie and her parents. Peter silently vowed to do everything he could for Suzie, as though she were his own child.

15

"Justice Department," the switchboard operator whined.

"Deputy Attorney General Mervyn's office, please," a man's voice said.

"I'll ring that for you."

The phone rang twice before a much more professional voice responded, "Good morning, Ms. Mervyn's office."

"Is Wendy, uh, Ms. Mervyn in? This is Max Franklin calling, prosecuting attorney in Whatcom County, Washington."

"May I tell her the nature of your call?"

"Tell her it's about the murder of an abortion doctor here in Bellingham, Washington. The police have already arrested one suspect for murder and arson."

"Oh, yes, Mr. Franklin. I'm familiar with the case. There was an article about the arrest on the front page of the *Washington Post* yesterday morning."

"Really? Sunday morning's *Post?*"

"I'll see if she can talk to you now."

Thirty seconds later another woman's voice came on the line. "Max Franklin—what's a Yale graduate doing in Bellingham, Washington?"

It was the same melodious voice he remembered from law school. He had tried to take her out several times, but she had an iron-clad rule against dating the "competition," as she called her fellow classmates.

"Hey, it's a great place to live and a good place to launch a bid for higher office. And how is the most successful member of the class of '83?"

"I'm having a great time. But the most successful members of our class are making $300,000 a year on Wall Street. I don't fit that description," she said with a laugh.

"Yeah, and they're working 150 hours a week, too. Probably making about nine dollars an hour when you figure it all out. That kind of rat race wasn't for me."

"You were always one of those altruistic types, weren't you, Max? Well, what can I do for you?"

"Wendy, I know you're busy, but I need to ask you a big, big favor."

"Is it ethical?"

"You bet. And legal, too."

"Is it about that abortion doctor who was murdered by some college girl?"

"Yeah, that's the one. I want you to let me prosecute this case first. Then if the jury does something crazy—like lets the girl off the hook— then you can prosecute her for violating federal civil rights. Just like the Rodney King case."

"I'd like to do that, but you know the president's view on abortion murders, and the attorney general's as well. They see this as a high priority."

"A high political priority you mean."

"Well—"

"Let me be straight with you about how the local politics of this matter fits in with your national politics."

"I'm listening," Mervyn replied, pulling out a pen.

"I know your boss, the attorney general, is supporting Hillary Clinton for the democratic nomination in 2000. Right?"

"Yes. Go on."

"Well, if this case were to be tried on the federal side, it would be tried by Al Spillman, the U.S. attorney in Seattle, right?"

"I know Mr. Spillman, a capable lawyer even if he is a Stanford grad."

"Yeah. Anyhow, Spillman is out running for attorney general of Washington State right now, and as you probably know, he's tightly aligned with the forces who are supporting Al Gore for the nomination. Do you really want to give the political spotlight to a Gore supporter, when there is a Rodham-Clinton supporter ready to do the job at the state level?"

"You mean you."

"That's right. I'd also like to run for attorney general in 2000. This case would give me just the visibility I need. And I would commit myself to playing whatever role you all want me to play in the Rodham-Clinton campaign if I'm allowed to simply go first. I've got a bail hearing on our first defendant this afternoon, but expect other arrests as well."

"I don't know," Ms. Mervyn said hesitantly.

"Hey, I don't mind if Spillman tries the case a second time. He can hang these pro-lifers from the highest tree as far as I'm concerned. And you know that all I'm asking you to do is to follow the routine policy of the Department—state prosecutions come first—even though this case involves abortion."

"Well, Max, I'll chat with some folk about your request. I can't make any promises."

"Thanks a lot," he replied.

"Keep your mouth shut about this until I get back to you."

"Hey, whatever it takes."

Peter marveled at the gracefully aging courtroom as soon as he walked through the black walnut swinging doors. Eight rows of dark walnut benches spanned the massive room, while a row of paneled windows ran down the entire left wall. A tiny slice of the bay was visible between a group of buildings two blocks away. Undoubtedly, this part of the original courthouse had been built in a day when the view was completely unobstructed.

"Why don't you sit right here for now," Peter said to the O'Dells, motioning to a bench near the front. "We're about twenty minutes early, and I'm going to go ahead and get set up. They won't bring Suzie in until the hearing begins at 1:30."

Peter walked through the swinging gate at the front of the courtroom and chose the table on the right side of the courtroom, closest to the jury box. There would be no jury today, but Peter had a long habit of always trying to sit next to the jury unless specifically assigned to another table. Another door separated the jury box from the witness stand, which was built to the judge's left. A clerk's perch was located to the judge's right. An opaque glass door at the back of the courtroom led to the judge's chambers.

As Peter began pulling a thin file with some documents out of his briefcase, he saw the door swing open in the back of the courtroom.

Colonel Danners, Shirley Alper, and about a half dozen of the group stepped tentatively into the room. Seeing Peter and the O'Dells alone, they relaxed and approached Peter.

"Nice to see you again, Colonel," Peter said.

"Nothing could keep me away," the colonel said briskly.

"Colonel, let me introduce you to Suzie's parents," Peter said, motioning toward the O'Dells. "Bill and Linda O'Dell, this is Colonel Hank Danners, head of the pro-life group here in Bellingham."

"Thanks for coming to support Suzie," Bill replied with an extended hand.

The colonel took his hand and shook it warmly. "Your daughter's a wonderful young lady. We've been praying fervently about today."

"Thanks so much," Bill replied. Linda smiled, then looked away to avoid any temptation to cry.

"Peter, I'd like to talk with you for a minute. Can I come in there with you?" Danners said.

"Sure. Until court starts, you're allowed to cross the 'magical' bar."

Danners whispered intently in his ear for a minute. Peter nodded at the conclusion of the monologue, then shook the colonel's hand. Danners turned and rejoined the members of his group who were now sitting near the O'Dells.

A short, good-looking man in his thirties came and sat in the front row on the window side of the courtroom. Peter stared at him for a moment, trying to place him. He'd seen him somewhere before. Just as the young man pulled a spiral-bound notepad from the outside pocket of his sports jacket, a group of men and women arrived and took a seat beside him. *Reporters,* Peter thought. *Just what we need.*

A few more college students filtered into the courtroom, followed by more reporters. Soon the room was full, with more people waiting outside the big walnut doors. Suddenly a commotion in the hallway drew several of the reporters to their feet and back out the courtroom door. The attraction was a stocky man with a booming voice—Peter's opponent, he guessed. As several reporters left the room, Peter could see the glare of television lights through the open doorway as they stood filming the impromptu interview. His opponent was apparently happy to feed the ravenous press. A few seconds later, Maxwell T. Franklin III blew into the courtroom with a swarm of reporters still peppering him with questions. He smiled, waved, and simply said, "Later, later," to each request.

Franklin was about Peter's age, but his size and a deep tan made him look considerably older. Peter wondered if he spent a lot of time on a Southern California golf course, or—more likely—if the tan was fabricated in one of Bellingham's many tanning booths. He wasn't far off with either guess. An attractive woman in a business suit with an expensive leather attaché case accompanied him down the aisle and through the swinging gate at the bar. Peter watched them settle into their seats at the opposite council table, then walked over to greet them.

"Good afternoon, Mr. Franklin. I'm Peter Barron from Spokane."

"Yes, Mr. Barron, I've heard a lot about you."

It was true enough, since he'd spent the better part of the morning on the phone with Democrat activist lawyers in eastern Washington asking about his cross-state opponent. He knew about Peter's Supreme Court victory, that he was conservative-leaning but not politically active, and that he had a reputation as an honest lawyer.

Their chit-chat ended when the bailiff and clerk entered the room through the chamber door and took their seats in the packed courtroom.

"All rise," came the bailiff's cry.

Peter noticed Captain Dunn, Detective Castille, and another, younger detective as they appeared and stood at the far edge of the jury box.

"The Superior Court for the State of Washington, in and for the County of Whatcom, is now in session, the honorable Robert Hayden presiding," the bailiff called out in a sing-song delivery.

"Please be seated," the elderly judge said in a quiet tone. Hayden was definitely past the minimum age for retirement, but his eyes were a lively blue that seemed to dance elegantly as he did a thorough visual survey of his courtroom. His hair was only slightly thin and completely white. The daily habit of walking the two miles from his home to the courthouse resulted in a trim appearance and a healthy glow to his skin.

"Could I have counsel stand up," the judge said firmly.

"For the record, Maxwell—"

"I know who you are Mr. Franklin," Hayden said quickly. "I would like to cover a couple of preliminaries before getting to the introductions, if you don't mind."

"Yes, Your Honor," Franklin replied.

"Very well. Normally this type of disclaimer is not necessary, but normally I don't get calls from the *New York Times* and the *Atlanta Constitution,* either." He paused, looking out over his trifocals at the many reporters in the courtroom. "None of you ladies and gentlemen of the media should feel that, in my mentioning these two publications, I talked to these papers or welcomed their calls. On the contrary, I simply instructed my staff to decline any comment and to warn them sternly not to call my chambers for an out-of-court statement again. My long-standing policy is to never talk about any matter except in the courtroom, on the record.

"Now that we've established that this is no ordinary case," he said, pausing to look at some notes on his yellow pad, "I want to tell you lawyers—that's why I asked you to remain standing, and you've been most patient in that regard—a few rules of this particular court, and my own personal biases." He removed his glasses and stared with calm piercing eyes at Mr. Franklin and Mr. Barron. "First, I abhor lawyers who don't pay attention to our local rules. They're not the same as in Seattle, or Spokane for that matter. So if you read our rules and live by them, you'll find me as friendly as if you were my Thursday afternoon golfing partner. If not, we will have a problem. Clear?" he said, staring directly at Peter.

"I understand, Your Honor."

"Good, we've made an excellent start," Hayden said, glancing at his notes again briefly. "My second point is this: I don't like to have important cases tried in the press. I'm aware, Mr. Franklin, that you are an elected official and the duty to the public that that entails. Besides, most lawyers like to see their names in print now and then. But not this time, gentlemen. This time your comments will be limited to explaining the processes of our courts as applied to this case, and nothing more. You will not discuss the evidence. You will not put on any shows for the press, and you will not leak information. If you fail to follow these instructions, you will be penalized with a gag order, and all of the rest of us who observe this matter will have the inner satisfaction of feeling justifiably superior to the offender. Understood?"

"Yes, Your Honor," came the lawyers' chorus.

"OK. Let's bring in the defendant."

The bailiff scrambled to his feet and opened the door near the front of the jury box. A sheriff's deputy was standing immediately in front of the door. Peter could see Suzie behind him and at least one other deputy in the hall behind her. A shift in the front deputy's position revealed handcuffs on Suzie's wrists.

"Please uncuff the young lady and allow her to stand freely beside her attorney," the judge chided the deputy. Instantly the handcuffs came off, and Suzie walked to Peter's side.

"Now, Mr. Franklin, let's begin with those appearances."

"Maxwell T. Franklin, prosecuting attorney for the state, Your Honor. I'm assisted by Shannon Carpenter, our new deputy prosecutor."

Peter spoke next. "Your Honor, I'm Peter Barron from Spokane, representing the defendant."

"Fine, Mr. Barron, welcome. I understand your client is originally from Spokane as well?"

"Yes, Your Honor. She's attending the university here."

"All right. And your name is Susan O'Dell?" the judge asked, addressing Suzie.

"Yes, sir." Her voice was shaky but clear.

The judge asked several preliminary questions of the defendant, then addressed Peter.

"Mr. Barron, I understand that you are seeking bail in this case. You have the right to postpone parts of the procedure if you'd like. What's your pleasure?"

"Your Honor, we're ready to enter a plea," Peter replied.

"Fine. Miss O'Dell, you've been charged by information with one count of first degree murder and one count of arson. These are, of course, very serious charges. Do you understand the nature of the charges that have been filed against you?"

"Yes."

"Has your lawyer explained the nature of the charges?"

"Yes, sir, he has."

"Has he told you that the potential penalty for these crimes could be capital punishment or life imprisonment?"

"Yes," Suzie replied, staring hard at the ground to maintain her composure, "he's told me about that, too."

"It's his job to tell you those things, young lady. And its mine to double check him. But neither of us are trying to unduly frighten you."

Suzie nodded.

"Fine. Susan O'Dell, to the charge of first degree murder, how do you plead?"

"Not guilty, sir."

"And to the charge of arson, how do you plead?"

"Not guilty."

"Fine. You may have a seat, Miss O'Dell."

"Mr. Barron, are you asking to conduct the preliminary hearing today, or are we reserving that for a future court appearance?"

"I'd like to reserve it for later, Your Honor."

"Fine, I had assumed as much. So let's turn to the issue of bail. Mr. Franklin, please advise me as to the state's position on the matter."

"Your Honor, this is a capital crime. The evidence that is fully set forth in the information demonstrates that Ms. O'Dell—along with a Stephen Gray—purchased the gas cans that were the apparent cause of the fire, and that brought about Dr. Rhonda Marsano's death. Unfortunately, Mr. Gray has fled the jurisdiction and perhaps the country as well. The state believes that Ms. O'Dell may attempt to join Mr. Gray if released. Therefore it is the state's position that bail should be denied."

The judge was about to turn to Peter when Franklin, remembering the reporters in the courtroom, continued. "Your Honor, we also need to consider the callous nature of this murder. While Ms. O'Dell might seem like an unlikely candidate for a murder defendant, she nonetheless has been brought here with strong evidence supporting the case against her. One of the issues the court should weigh in considering any bail application is whether or not the defendant is likely to commit another crime. A person who would turn aside from a peaceful, law-abiding life to murder a young doctor to satisfy a political agenda has crossed a line in her thinking, making her a high-risk repeat offender."

Franklin stopped his pacing and stared straight at Suzie as he thundered his closing denunciation. "Every pro-choice doctor in America will potentially live in terror if Susan O'Dell is released into society."

"Very well, Mr. Franklin, I think I understand the essence of your rather loud and elaborate position," the judge replied without looking up from the notes he was making on his yellow pad. "Mr. Barron, please tell me why you think Miss O'Dell is a worthy candidate for bail, and what amount I should set in the event I am inclined to allow bail at all."

Peter stood and straightened his suit coat.

"Your Honor, there is no question about the seriousness of this charge. And there is no question that the prosecutor has an interesting theory of Miss O'Dell's involvement in the crime, based entirely on circumstantial evidence."

Peter began pacing back and forth behind his own counsel table, occasionally stopping in the aisle between the two tables and looking straight up at the judge. "Mr. Franklin has informed the court in his papers that Miss O'Dell was recorded on videotape at the Fred Meyer store, *purchasing* the items used to set the deadly fire. To correct his recitation, Miss O'Dell did not purchase anything. The items were purchased, according to Visa records, by Stephen Gray, not Miss O'Dell. The fact that Miss O'Dell's fingerprints appear on the one can retrieved from the crime scene is easily explained by the video, which shows her holding the gas can in the store."

"Mr. Barron, please tell me how this relates to the issue of bail," Hayden queried.

"Your Honor, Mr. Franklin's argument against bail is predicated on the theory that Miss O'Dell was a co-conspirator with Mr. Gray—since she was in the store with him, she must have been at the clinic with him setting the fire. Thus she will either run to join him or attack the nearest abortion clinic with another fire bomb."

Peter stopped and grasped the back of Suzie's chair. "That argument is based on two giant leaps in logic. The first is from the store to the clinic—there is no evidence supporting that Miss O'Dell had any knowledge of what the items were to be used for, much less that she aided Mr. Gray in setting the fire at the clinic. The second leap is from the clinic to Canada or another abortion clinic. If Mr. Gray and Miss O'Dell were the Bonnie-and-Clyde team Mr. Franklin fancies them to be, they would have run away together. Mr. Gray does, indeed, appear to be gone. But where did Miss O'Dell run to? Her dorm room at Western. Not exactly the kind of behavior that one expects of a conspirator in a murder plot.

"Therefore, I recommend that she be treated in accordance with the record established by the balance of her life. She's an excellent student, has been on the dean's list at Western. Her school and church records prove her to be responsible and civic-minded. She comes from a good home.

"Conceding that the nature of the charges requires something more than her own recognizance, I would suggest a bond in the amount of $35,000, to be paid by the deposit of a property bond granting a lien on the parents' home. In addition, Colonel Hank Danners here in

Bellingham has also offered to place a property bond on his home to support whatever bail amount you might reasonably set."

"Hmmm," the judge said, wiping his glasses with the sleeve of his robe. "I can see that if this matter gets to a full-blown trial, we are going to have what amounts to a litigation clinic for the members of the bar in this jurisdiction. You're both talented advocates, and you have raised many good points.

"Mr. Barron, I am not persuaded by your two leaps of logic. It is no leap at all to jump from the store to the clinic fire. After all, Miss O'Dell came from a meeting planning protests at this clinic; in the store she could plainly see not just gas cans but batteries and wires as well. In my mind, it should have been evident what Mr. Gray was planning.

"However, your second argument is quite compelling. Why didn't Miss O'Dell run away immediately, either with Mr. Gray or to another location for some further mischief? But since I can't read minds, I'm still not totally convinced that she is not a risk. So I am going to set bond at $150,000, and I will allow a property bond rather than cash for the full amount on one condition: if Miss O'Dell remains here at college, Colonel Danners or someone else here in the city have a vested financial interest in keeping a close watch on her. If she chooses to go home to Spokane during the pendency of this case, as well she might, I want a responsible adult there on the line financially to keep a close eye on her whereabouts. So that is my order—$150,000, property bonds on two homes. Anything else, gentlemen?"

"No, Your Honor, and thank you," Peter replied.

"The state has nothing else," Franklin replied.

"Gentlemen, remember my comments as you pass by our friends from the press. This court stands in recess."

Suzie grabbed Peter around the neck. "Thank you, Mr. Barron, thank you!" She said with a quiet intensity. At Peter's beckon, her parents came through the bar and joined the hug.

A deputy sheriff wandered slowly to the scene of jubilation and remained about three feet behind Suzie. After a couple minutes, he said quietly, "Miss O'Dell, we need to go soon."

"But she's been granted bail," her father answered the deputy with a flash of irritation in his voice.

"Yes, sir. But there is a lot of paperwork that needs to be completed before that order becomes effective. Your property bond and the other property bond will have to be notarized and filed. It will all take about three or four hours. So she will get out a lot quicker if you all just proceed with your part of the paperwork while we take care of ours. When it's all done, your daughter can leave with you."

Linda and Bill looked at Peter. "Fine, deputy," Peter said. "Where can I get the property bond forms?"

"Second floor. Clerk's office. You'll need a legal description of the properties, plus the notarized signature of both legal owners."

"Let's get a move on!" Peter sang out.

16

Max Franklin had his back to his office door, pacing as he talked on the phone. Shannon Carpenter sat on the right-hand side of the room, gazing out the window at a beautiful early summer morning.

"Yes!" he exclaimed as he hung up the receiver.

"Good news?" his attractive assistant asked.

He nodded as he punched the phone for the intercom. "Polly, get Captain Dunn over here ASAP." Hanging up the receiver a second time, he sat down in his large burgundy leather chair, leaned back, and spun a half-circle with a contented smile on his face. "The attorney general has signed off on our request to take our case to trial before any federal criminal action is filed."

"So it's final?"

"Not yet. The attorney general's office has to get White House approval for it to be final."

"The president is going to decide about a case here in Bellingham?"

"No, not the president. Hillary. She has long controlled most Justice Department issues. Now that she's openly running for the nomination in 2000, she's even more aggressive about these things."

"How do you find out things like that?" she asked admiringly.

"Friends in high places. Actually, a classmate from Yale."

"Does the attorney general think the White House will agree?"

Franklin paced over to the window and played with the miniblinds absently. "They're worried that our only defendant is an eighteen-year-old college student without a record. She doesn't fit the normal profile of a crazed pro-lifer."

"So what are we supposed to do? We can't exactly change O'Dell's image."

"No, but they've suggested that we broaden the case so we can talk about a group of crazed anti-abortionists. They want us to bring a conspiracy charge against the whole group—the leaders at least. Spin it around this Stephen Gray guy. Since he's missing, we can paint him as crazy as we like."

"Is there enough evidence to do that?"

"We'll find some," Franklin said with a smile. "Maybe the clinic's lawyer can help us."

While he spoke, Franklin whirled his Rolodex around, found the number he was after, and punched the phone again. "Barry Penner please, Maxwell Franklin calling."

In a moment Mr. Penner came on the line. "Good afternoon, Mr. Franklin, what can I do for you today? I'd like to talk at length, but I'm just leaving for a court appointment."

"Sure, I'll be brief. It's my theory that Susan O'Dell and Stephen Gray didn't act alone. Maybe they lit the match, but I believe this was all planned out by Danners and the others. What do you think of such a theory?"

"Oh, I'm certain of it. Colonel Danners comes across as a law-and-order freak, but I think it's just a mask covering a violent and abusive nature. You know the type. He wanted to control the whole situation, and as soon as the federal judge slapped an injunction on him, the cool facade fell off and the violence took over. I think he orchestrated the whole thing."

"You got any evidence to support that?"

"Well, one thing we were working on—in fact we were about to file a contempt of court charge in federal court before the fire—was the fact that there were a number of harassing calls made to Dr. Marsano's home and the clinic owners' offices in Los Angeles."

"That's a start," Franklin said as he paced in front of the windows. "Anything else?"

"Nothing else at the moment. Call me back in a couple days unless I call you with something first."

"Sure. Thanks."

As soon as he hung up, the intercom buzzed. "Captain Dunn is here."

"Thanks, Polly. Send him in."

Dunn walked in, casting a wary eye on Ms. Carpenter as she directed him to sit opposite Franklin. He didn't want a case of this magnitude messed up by an inexperienced prosecutor, even in a supporting role. "Mornin' Max," the detective said.

"Well, John, we're making progress with the feds, but there's one little glitch. The Justice Department wants to bring in the whole leadership if we can. We've gone over this before—got anything new?"

"Not a thing. We were hoping O'Dell would break down and sing a song for us; but she wasn't even close, and now she's out. You know, if we're supposed to nail the whole group, maybe we should call in the feds. At least they would bring us some experienced help." He looked directly at Ms. Carpenter, but the point went over Franklin's head.

"Here's your next assignment, Dunn. The Los Angeles lawyer for the clinic told me that both Dr. Marsano and the clinic owners in L.A. had been receiving harassing phone calls just before the fire. I'll have Ms. Carpenter get you the subpoenas. I want the phone records of all the leaders—both at work and at home—for the three months before the fire."

"No problem. We do have one harassing call on tape. Not sure who the caller was."

"On tape?" Franklin said.

"Yeah. We talked to the clinic owners the other day, and they told us about a call on their answering machine the night before the fire. 'Your Bellingham clinic had better watch its back,' something like that. Whoever called disguised his voice, but it sounded like a man."

"Why didn't they say something about that right away?"

"Evidently they get crazy calls all the time—they just added this one to the list."

"You've got the tape?"

"Yeah, they FedEx'd it, just came in today. It's a copy—I told them to keep the original under lock and key."

"This is great," Franklin said, leaning back in his chair with his arms crossed behind his head. "OK, Shannon, get the captain his subpoenas. John, go find me a conspiracy!"

Detective Dunn turned to leave, then stopped and addressed Franklin, keeping his eyes on Shannon Carpenter. "Let me know if your assistant here has trouble with the subpoenas. I can prepare them myself if I have to."

Carpenter gave him a cold stare. "I can handle it just fine, Mr. Dunn."

"Yeah, well, let me know when the judge has signed 'em." The detective turned and quickly left the room.

"What's that about?" Carpenter demanded when the door was closed.

"Oh, don't worry about him. He does that to all new prosecutors. He thinks they're all incompetent—definitely not good enough to work on *his* cases. Don't take it personally."

"I thought it was because I'm a woman."

"Maybe. Never thought of that," Franklin replied absentmindedly.

"You've never thought about me being a woman?"

"Oh, I've thought about *that* a lot, as you well know," he said coyly.

Casey came running into Peter and Gwen's bedroom at about 5:30 Saturday evening. Two long sashes trailed out behind her on either side. "Tie the bow on my dress, Daddy," she said after she came bouncing to a stop at the bedside.

"Sure, honey. What a pretty dress; where did you get it?"

"Grandma bought it for me."

"When did she do that?"

"That time you and Mommy went on an airplane ride," Casey said as she scampered back down the hall toward her bedroom to get her shoes.

"Your mom has good taste," he said to Gwen, who was leaning over the counter top in their dressing area finishing her eyeliner.

Gwen took another sip of her iced tea—her constant companion these days. "Yeah," she replied, her mind obviously on something else. "You don't think they'll serve real spicy food do you?"

"Never eaten at the O'Dells before. Your guess is as good as mine."

"I hope it's not too spicy. And onions will be a problem, too."

"Has your stomach been bothering you all day?"

"Pretty much, but it seems worse in the evening."

"I don't remember you having any nausea with the other pregnancy."

Gwen looked at him with furrowed brows. "I didn't. I felt great. But I was sick just like this with Casey."

Peter put his hands gently on her shoulders as she continued to put on her makeup. Bending down to kiss her on the back of the neck, he said, "You may feel awful, but you look great."

Gwen got a strong whiff of his aftershave. "Ummm, Peter, you smell good, but it makes me sick to my stomach."

Peter laughed and stepped back out of range. "I sure don't want to do that."

"This feeling is so baffling. I feel awful, but I'm hungry all the time. Can we go by Wendy's on the way and get a burger? I'm really hungry, and I don't think I can wait another minute for some food. And then at least I'll have something in my stomach in case I can't eat what they serve."

"Sure, honey. Whatever you want."

Gwen stood up, ready except for putting on her favorite necklace. "Here, honey, help me with this clasp."

Peter turned her around with her back facing toward the light and hooked the clasp of her necklace. Then he watched as his beautiful wife walked down the hall. "Casey, you ready?" she said, entering Casey's room.

Watching Gwen and Casey interact as they finished preparing for an evening out reminded Peter how much he loved being at home with his two girls. Gwen was right, he wasn't home enough. Suddenly he wished they were spending the night at home rather than going to the

O'Dells, but he knew Suzie's parents wanted to celebrate her home-coming, and he was a big part of that celebration.

Jamie MacMillan hurried down the corridor, glancing at his watch. Dunn would be on his backside since he was five minutes late. He opened the captain's door slowly, expecting a growling diatribe the moment he set foot in the door.

"You're saved by the bell," Castille's voice called out.

MacMillan's partner was leaning back in Detective Dunn's chair with his arms folded across his chest.

"I take it Cap'n isn't here yet?" MacMillan asked.

"Naw, he's over at the prosecutor's office. Seems Franklin's new assistant wanted to know his progress on the case. He wouldn't tell her—said he'd tell Franklin personally. She blew up about it, and Franklin called him over for a meeting."

"Whew, sounds like the captain's ego has some competition for once," MacMillan said, plopping down in the other empty chair.

"She's a lawyer, ain't she?" Castille replied sarcastically.

"You got a point there, old buddy. So when's the captain supposed to be back?"

"Right now," came a gruff voice. Dunn slammed the door, threw his jacket over the coat hook, and pulled a cigarette out of his shirt pocket. Castille jumped out of Dunn's chair and landed himself in one motion adjacent to MacMillan. "And don't you start on me about your allergies, MacMillan. I've already been chewed on enough for one morning."

"No problem, Cap'n," MacMillan replied. "Was Franklin that upset with you?"

"He acted like it. I think it was for show."

"Show?" Castille asked.

"Yeah. I think he's messin' with that little assistant of his and she's reaping the benefits."

"Good theory," MacMillan replied. "This detective stuff comes natural to you, I guess."

"Humph," Dunn grunted. Taking a long drag on his cigarette, he turned his head and blew the smoke away from MacMillan. "Well, MacMillan, let's see if it comes natural to you. What do you have for me from the phone company?"

"Just one call, from Colonel Danners's house to the clinic headquarters in L.A."

"Yeah?" Dunn replied impatiently.

"Tuesday night before the fire, there was a call from the colonel's house to the clinic headquarters in Los Angeles."

"Does the clinic have a recording of that call, too?"

"No, evidently someone picked it up that time. But the clinic does have a phone log notation of the call, something about killing babies in Washington. The time matches almost exactly the time the phone company records show."

"Almost exactly?" Dunn repeated.

"Well—the phone company shows the call from Danners's house to the clinic at 7:56 P.M. The clinic's got it logged in at eight o'clock. Probably someone just rounded the time to the nearest five minutes."

Dunn stared blankly at his two assistants. "Humph," he grunted. "Not bad for a rookie. Sounds like the beginning of conspiracy to me. Good job."

"Thanks, Cap'n," MacMillan replied.

"All right, Castille," Dunn said. "What did you learn from Lisa Edgar?"

"She's really mad at this Gray dude. He was supposed to propose to her the Saturday morning after the fire, but he never showed up. Broke her heart and everything. I think she would tell us his whereabouts if she knew."

"When was the last time she saw Gray?"

"The morning after he and Susan O'Dell went shopping. They met over at Shari's by the mall for breakfast."

"What were they doing at the coffee shop?"

"She was miffed that he hadn't been spending enough time with her, and she wanted to talk to him about it. That's when he told her to expect a proposal on Saturday morning."

"Does she think O'Dell was in with Gray?"

"She doesn't think so, but she's not sure."

"Any other time she knows about Gray and O'Dell being alone together?"

"Only the Tuesday before the fire. He gave her a ride home from a meeting at the colonel's."

"At the colonel's, huh?," Dunn said, sitting on the edge of his chair. "What time was the meeting?"

"It started at 8:00 P.M. But she got there early in hopes of talking to Gray. She said Gray was there, but he kept going in and out of the living room prior to the meeting like he was preoccupied with something."

"Where was O'Dell during this?"

"She was in some kind of preliminary meeting with the colonel and the four others on the leadership team down the hall in the study."

"Who else was at the eight-o'clock meeting?"

"All five in leadership, plus Gray, Lisa, and about a dozen others. She couldn't remember all the names, but she was certain that all five members of the leadership team were there."

"Did she say what they talked about?"

"Just the regular stuff, how to proceed in future protests, that sort of thing."

"Humph," Dunn said again, staring vacantly out the window. "At approximately eight o'clock there's a call from Danners's home to the L.A. clinic. At that very moment, all five leaders are huddled alone in his den. Did you ask Edgar if Danners has a phone in his den?"

"No, Cap'n, it didn't occur to me at the time. But I'm sure he does," Castille replied.

"Well, it occurs to me that Peter Barron will clean our clocks if we're not sure of that little detail. Go call your songbird. Now."

"Sure, Cap'n sure," Castille said, jumping to his feet. Even with his olive complexion, MacMillan could see that his partner was a bit red around the ears, embarrassed about not having asked about the phone.

Dunn twisted in his chair and blew smoke rings while Castille was gone. He was lost in thought, and MacMillan knew better than to interrupt him. Two minutes later, they heard running steps, then the door flew open. "He's got a phone in the den. She's used it herself."

"Bingo, Gray, Suzie, and the other leaders in the Col's den with a phone at the exact time a threatening call was made to the clinic in L.A.," Dunn replied. He ground his cigarette out in the ashtray, stood, and picked up his jacket. "It's time to go report our findings to Franklin and his prima donna assistant. Good work, gentlemen—I think we found our conspiracy."

The following Monday morning, Hank Danners looked up in surprise from his front flower bed to see a police cruiser pull to a stop in front of his driveway. Two uniformed officers emerged, the one on the passenger side holding a piece of paper in his hand.

"Hank Danners?" the paper-carrying officer asked.

"Yes, sir. What can I do for you?"

Just then a white Suburban with a satellite dish on the roof and KING-TV emblems on the side screeched to a halt across the street. A camera man and reporter jumped from the van—camera and microphone in hand.

"What's going on here?" Danners demanded.

Before Danners knew what was happening, the officer spilled out the familiar litany of rights, followed by the charges: "Mr. Danners, you are under arrest on four felony charges—conspiracy to commit murder, conspiracy to commit arson, as well as the substantive crimes of murder and arson. You'll have to come with us."

"What? You're just going to haul me away, just like that? There must be some mistake. Let me call my lawyer."

"You can call him from the jail, sir. You need to come with us immediately."

"I can't believe this," Danners said. "Can't I at least tell my wife what's going on? She's just inside."

The officer who had been doing all the talking looked at his partner. The second officer nodded.

"OK, but walk slowly to the front door, ring the bell, and let her come to the door. You are not to go inside. Understand?"

As he heard his wife's steps nearing the front door, Danners spoke up loud enough for her to hear. "Evie, just open the door a crack. There's a TV crew in our front yard. Don't let them see you."

He could see her bewilderment as the door opened ever so slightly. "Evie, the police are here to arrest me."

"What?!" she exclaimed.

"I have to go with them right now. I want you to call Peter Barron immediately and tell him what's going on. OK?"

"OK," came her quavering reply.

Danners leaned in the door and kissed his wife on the cheek. "I'll be OK, honey. Get Peter."

"Let's get going, Colonel," the first officer said.

"All right, I'm coming." He turned and began walking toward the squad car.

"I'm afraid I'm going to have to cuff you," the second officer said as he neared the vehicle.

"Son, I served this nation for thirty years. I'm a law-abiding citizen and innocent of these charges. The cuffs are unnecessary."

"I'm sure you're right, sir. But I'll lose my job if I don't. Please, turn around."

Danners turned slowly and stood still while the cuffs were flung around his wrists. As he walked to the squad car, the reporter yelled out, "Mr. Danners, do you have any comment on your arrest?"

"Just one." He stopped for a split second with one leg already in the back of the car. "I'm going to find out how in the world you knew to be here, and I will bring that person to justice if it's the last thing I do."

After talking to Evie Danners, Peter groaned, slammed down the receiver, and shoved his wheeled chair back from his desk in frustration. Sally, hearing the noise, came racing into his office with her usual shuffle.

"What was that noise?" Seeing the handset on his desk, she reached over and put it back in the cradle.

"Get Max Franklin on the phone immediately," he groaned, shaking his head in disgust. "He's the prosecutor for Whatcom County."

"Right away." Sally left quickly without another word. A moment later she buzzed Peter's office.

"Franklin on line two."

Peter whipped up the receiver. "Mr. Franklin? Oh, I'm sorry, is he there please? This is Peter Barron."

"He's in a conference right now," came the reply about forty-five seconds later.

"Tell him it's urgent and I must speak to him—now!"

"I'm sorry but I can't disturb him; I'm sure Ms. Carpenter would be happy to speak to you though. I'll transfer you," she said before Peter could argue.

"Yes, Mr. Barron, what seems to be the problem?" Carpenter said a moment or two later.

"You've arrested my client for murder without letting me know, that's the problem. Your office should have called me first and asked to have the colonel surrender himself if it came to this."

"Mr. Barron, it is not our habit to inform murder suspects of pending arrests. We simply get an arrest warrant and then pick them up. I'm sure that's the way it's done over there in Spokane, as well." Her voice dripped with condescension.

"Yes, Ms. Carpenter, that's the way it is normally done out here on the frontiers of Spokane, as well. We even have some paved roads and talking pictures at the movie theater down on Main Street. But you know good and well this is not a typical case, and the colonel is not a typical suspect. But I can see that trying to talk reasonably with your office is like trying to teach a pig to sing. It wastes one's time and annoys the pig."

"I don't have to listen to this," she replied angrily.

"Well you'd better listen to this, Mzzz. Carpenter. You and your boss had better be prepared to explain to Judge Hayden how the TV reporters knew when to show up at the colonel's house, because he ordered us both not to try this case in the press and his office is the next call I'm making."

"We did *not* tell them to go to the colonel's house. We merely told them that there were going to be four arrests this morning in an important case. They must have figured it out themselves."

"Four arrests!" Peter screamed. "How can you—"

Peter stopped himself short of completely losing his temper and disconnected the call by punching the intercom button. "Sally, get Shirley Alper on the phone. Warn her that she's about to be arrested and to stay put until I talk to her. Just put her on hold. I'm calling Pastor Wallace."

"Certainly," she replied.

A pang of guilt shot through Peter's gut as he realized he was probably embarrassing Sally by his intemperate outbursts. He'd have to apologize later. The phone rang twice, then a secretary answered the phone.

"Pastor Wallace, please," Peter said.

"Pastor Wallace is not . . . uh . . . not here right now." The secretary sounded very flustered.

"Ma'am, this is Peter Barron, the pastor's lawyer. I need to talk to him immediately."

"Mr. Barron, I'm afraid you're too late. The police were just here and left with Pastor Randy not more than five minutes ago."

"Were there reporters with them?"

"Yes, sir, an entire crew."

Peter sighed. "OK, thanks anyway. I'll be over to Bellingham as soon as possible. We'll get them out of jail today or tomorrow, Lord willing."

"We'll be praying for that. Goodbye."

"Did you get Shirley?" Peter yelled out the open office door.

"I'm transferring her to you now," She said as his phone began to ring.

"Thanks, get Ginny Kettner next," Peter yelled again. "Tell her the same thing." He picked up the ringing line.

"Shirley? No police at your place yet?" Peter asked.

"Why? What's going on?"

"The police have arrested the colonel and Randy. The assistant prosecutor told me they were making four arrests this morning, I assume the other two are you and Ginny."

"Arrest us for what?"

"I'm not totally sure, but I believe they are going to charge all of you with conspiracy to kill the doctor and burn the clinic. At any rate, I think some reporters are going to show up with the arresting officers."

"What should I do?"

"I want you to write a note and stick it to your front door. Say that you are driving to the police station to turn yourself in. I don't want you arrested in front of your neighbors and on TV."

"Uh . . . Peter, I appreciate your advice, but a squad car and a white van just pulled up in front of my house. What do I do now?"

"Obey them. You have no choice."

"Fine," she replied with an almost chipper tone. "I'll go out looking the part of the poor defenseless grandma being hauled off to jail. That'll play well on the six o'clock news."

"I'll be there as soon as I can. I'm sorry about this, Shirley."

"I know, Peter. See you soon."

Sally was standing in the office doorway when Peter finished. "No one answered at the Kettners."

"Well, either she's already been picked up or they're out," Peter replied. "Sally, can you call the travel agent and see when I can get to Seattle?"

"I've already done that. The next flight is at 1:15 P.M."

"That puts me in Bellingham around 4:30—that's too late to see a judge about bail . . ."

"Even if the prosecutor did agree to such a quick hearing," Sally said, finishing his thought.

Peter sighed. "Not much chance of that after the singing pig line, is there?"

Sally was silent.

"I guess I'm going to have to apologize to her." Peter sighed again and stared at the phone. "Might as well get it over with. But first, I'm sorry I growled at you as well. You didn't deserve that."

"That's OK, Peter, I know you're under a lot of stress. I'll go make that reservation."

Peter punched in the prosecutor's phone number. "Shannon Carpenter, please."

"May I tell her who's calling?"

"Just tell her it's someone who needs to apologize."

In a moment Peter heard Carpenter's icy voice. "Yes?"

"Ms. Carpenter, I guess you know this is Peter Barron calling. I owe you an apology. I was surprised by the arrests, especially the TV reporters, and I lost my temper. But I realize you're just doing your job."

"All right, Mr. Barron . . . and thanks. A lot of lawyers yell. You're the first to call back and apologize."

"Sure. Goodbye."

He put the receiver down more gently. Sally walked back into the room. "I wish I wouldn't lose my temper like that," he said to her.

"Well, you just did the right thing, Peter. I'm proud to work for you."

"Yeah, right. Did you get me that flight? I guess you and Joe will have to take care of tomorrow's schedule again."

That evening Peter rushed through the main doors to the jail and up to the reception window.

"Good afternoon, Mr. Barron."

Peter looked closely through the glass at the woman deputy seated on a metal swivel stool. It was the same woman he'd seen when he came to visit Suzie. "Oh, hi, I'm surprised you remembered me, Sheila." He was grateful for the name tag on her uniform.

Sheila couldn't help smiling, more out of embarrassment than anything else. Even though she had a boyfriend, she had scanned Peter's left hand when she'd seen him before to ascertain his marital status—she thought he was as handsome a man as she'd ever seen in person, and she got a bad case of stomach flutters just looking at him.

"Oh, just remembered your face," she said.

"Is there any way I can see all four of my clients together?"

"No, but we can let you see the two men and two women separately."

"Sure, I understand."

"Who do you want first? The men or the women?"

"I guess ladies first," Peter replied.

"Good luck, Mr. Barron. I'll buzz you inside. You know the routine."

"Yeah, thanks again, uh, Sheila. It's good to see you again."

Sheila smiled. Peter looked at her for a moment, surprised at her friendliness. Sheila turned red, pressed some buttons, and then turned her back to talk to another deputy working further back in the enclosed office.

As the elevator doors closed on Peter, the second deputy burst out laughing. "Down girl," she said. "Just 'cause he's better looking than any attorney in Bellingham doesn't mean you can drool." As Peter exited the upstairs elevator, Sheila, who was monitoring his progress on the video monitor, buzzed him through the secure entrance into the lawyers' visiting area. He sat down in the second booth and waited.

Heavy steel doors opened and closed, revealing Ginny Kettner and Shirley Alper. They both looked extraordinarily out of place in their orange jail jumpsuits and handcuffs. Ginny's eyes were red, but Shirley was grinning almost impishly.

"Afternoon ladies," Peter said rising to his feet.

"Hi, Peter. Like our outfits?" Shirley asked cheerfully.

"Sure. Maybe they'll let you keep them when I get you out tomorrow morning."

"Does that mean we get out for sure, then?" Ginny whimpered.

"No, not for sure. But I've talked with Judge Hayden's clerk, and she has confirmed that we have a 9:00 A.M. bail hearing; so you're almost as good as out. I can't imagine the judge denying you bail in light of his ruling on Suzie. The only question is whether you will have enough property value in your houses for a bond."

"We're just renting," Ginny replied sullenly.

"Well, that won't work," Peter replied. "Shirley, how much do you think your house is worth?"

"Maybe $65,000. It's pretty little. Is that a problem?"

"Well, it depends on how much the judge sets for your bail. If it's much more than $50,000 we may have to find someone who will put his house on the line as well. Do either of you have a friend or relative who would back you up? Isn't there someone in your church, Ginny?"

"Maybe. You'd have to talk with my husband."

"You doin' OK?" Peter asked, noting her slumped posture.

"Not really," she said in a forlorn voice. "Can you tell us what to expect from here on out?"

"Tomorrow you'll be arraigned, just like Suzie was. Then in a couple of weeks there'll be some preliminary motions. I need to find out what they think they have on the four of you. Any clues?"

"Not a thing," Shirley replied. Ginny just shook her head.

"Well, assuming they have next to nothing, we can ask the court to dismiss the charges when we make our preliminary motions."

"What is this conspiracy thing about, anyway?" Shirley asked.

"Well, it means that you all planned the arson and subsequent murder, even though you weren't actually in on the action."

"Why don't they just charge us with murder and arson? Why all this conspiracy mumbo-jumbo?"

"They did that, too. But the conspiracy gives them an easier target in case they can't get you on the main charges."

Ginny got up from the chair and walked to the back of the cell. Peter looked at her, perplexed.

"Ginny is really scared," Shirley said softly. "Personally, this whole thing has struck me as hilarious. I was actually chuckling to myself the whole way over here—those officers must've thought I was loony toons. But Ginny doesn't share my perverse sense of humor. Maybe it's just that I'm so much older."

Ginny came back to her chair and quietly sat down. "I'm sorry," she said between sniffles.

Shirley squeezed Ginny tight to her side. "Everything's going to be all right, Ginny. I can just feel it." The younger woman said nothing.

"Well, I need to talk to the colonel and Randy, so I'd better move on. But first, let's pray and ask the Lord's blessing and protection, OK?"

Ginny nodded her head silently while Shirley put her arm securely around the younger woman's shoulders.

Forty-five minutes later, Peter emerged from the elevator back on the first floor of the jail. His session with the two men had been mixed with more anger—mainly at the TV reporters—than fear.

Peter tapped on the window to get Sheila's attention before leaving. "Don't I need to sign out?" he said when she looked up.

She walked to the window and slid the clipboard into a steel drawer that slid to the other side of the partition.

Peter signed the log and slid it back in the drawer. "Is that it?"

"Yeah, sure. Good night, Mr. Barron." She spoke in a subdued voice, still a little embarrassed from the ribbing she'd received earlier from her partner.

"Night, Sheila . . . and thanks."

Peter lugged his suitcase and briefcase down the hall of the third floor of the Holiday Inn Express. He glanced at the room number on his registration sheet once again and then at his watch. 10:15 P.M. He struggled with the plastic electronic key. On the third try, a green light flashed, and he opened the door. He threw his bags on the bed and unzipped the suitcase, removing the white shirt and grey suit he would wear to court in the morning. He crossed the room, drew the curtain, then opened the window. A cool breeze flapped the curtains ever so slightly. The sky was clear, and dozens of stars shone brightly in the night sky. Peter stared out the window, breathing deeply as he tried to collect his thoughts. He needed to call Gwen before it got too late.

It was at times like this that he didn't like being gone from home any more than Gwen. During the day the action was sufficiently hectic and interesting that he didn't notice he was far from home. But the loneliness of the evenings nullified whatever glamour was associated with travel. He would have to ask his good friend, Aaron Roberts, how he coped with all his travels at their next Bible study together.

He turned from the window and hung his coat in the closet, then sat on the edge of the bed and pulled off his shoes. The bed creaked as he sank into the mattress. *There's no bed like home. . . . There's no bed like home,* Peter thought, remembering Gwen's comment as they watched *The Wizard of Oz* from a terribly uncomfortable hotel bed while on vacation about a year ago. He flopped over on the bed and picked up the phone, pulling it onto his stomach as he dialed.

"Gwen, it's me, honey," he said when she answered on the fourth ring. "Is everything OK?"

"I guess," she sighed. The frustration in her voice was obvious. "Where are you?"

"In my hotel room at the Holiday Inn."

"How long have you been there?"

"About ten minutes, I guess." It was Peter's turn to sigh.

"What's wrong with you?" she asked.

"Oh . . ." he said, sighing again. "I guess I'm just feeling lonely. I don't like coming back to a hotel room alone."

"You'd better come back to your room alone, cowboy." Her voice sparkled with a touch of laughter.

Peter smiled. "You know what I mean. I'd rather have you here with me right now. I guess I'm beginning to understand your loneliness."

"Well, it's more like a feeling of abandonment than loneliness. I'm in my normal surroundings, Casey's here and everything; yet it feels so empty because you're not here. I just—"

Peter hesitated, waiting for her to finish her thought. "What's wrong?"

"I just had a thought that snapped me out of my pity party."

"What's that?" Peter asked.

"There are four people who are going to sleep in a jail cell tonight, who would be thrilled to exchange places with either of us."

"I love you, Gwen," Peter whispered. "You are astonishing."

"Don't be so silly. Tell me what you accomplished today," Gwen said with a smile in her voice.

"Basically I've been trying to get things set up to try to get the four of them out on bail in the morning. We have a hearing at 9:00 A.M. Sally made a bunch of calls and found four people with nice houses who'll put them on the line—assuming the court grants our request."

"Will they lose their houses if they're found guilty?"

"No, not as long as they show up for trial."

"Anything on Stephen Gray yet?"

"Not yet, but I'm hoping a few days of solid research will come up with a few leads—I don't think the police are looking too hard for him right now."

"A few days? Are you telling me you are going to be gone for several days?"

"So we're back to that, are we?"

"Whatever," she replied tersely. "I don't appreciate you making me feel guilty for wanting you here more; there's nothing wrong with that."

"I'm not *making* you feel guilty, you're doing it all by yourself!" he replied a little too sarcastically.

"Oh, listen to us! Look. I won't mention this again if you promise to seriously consider how to find a better balance between work and your family when you get home. Is that a deal?"

"OK, and in the meantime, why don't you ask Lynn Roberts about this. Aaron's been traveling in his work for years; he's never mentioned any struggles with this."

"Shows how blind you men are—Lynn and I have talked about this several times. She doesn't like the situation any more than I do, but she doesn't know how to change it. So she simply accepts it. But that doesn't mean it's not a problem."

"Well, maybe that's something the four of us can discuss sometime soon. Right now I need to go to bed."

"Just get them out of jail and fly home soon, OK?"

"Goodnight, Gwen, I love you."

"Good night, Peter."

Peter hung up the phone and stared at the ceiling for a long time. He didn't feel good about his conversation with Gwen but knew that calling back wouldn't help—he wouldn't know what else to say. He turned the TV on and immediately fell asleep, then awoke around three o'clock to the sound of sirens. In his dreamy state, he wondered who else in the leadership group was being arrested, then remembered that there was no one else left. He lay awake the rest of the night, wondering how to convince the judge that his clients were all worth the risk of bail.

After a couple weeks of continual practice, Vince was starting to get the hang of it. He swung his arm behind him, the line would follow, then flick sharply toward the water again with a smooth twist of his wrist. With precisioned accuracy he landed the fly at his target—a spot just upstream of a promising pool. He would let the fly drift with the current into the pool and sit there for a minute or two, hoping to attract the big brown trout he had seen skirting through the rocks and rapids of this powerful stretch of river.

For the first few days of fishing, he would see Rhonda's face in some shadow or ripple in the water. When he looked closer, the illusion quickly vanished. But hours of self-talk had finally convinced the seared remnants of his conscience that he had no responsibility for Rhonda's death. It was purely an accident. Now he didn't see her face at all.

Today, however, his mind was occupied with a different young woman. He had seen CNN coverage of the bail hearing for Suzie O'Dell and the subsequent arrests of the other four leaders. For days he rolled the scenes over and over again in his mind, virtually memorizing every line of the broadcast. Even at night, after hours of hard drinking, he couldn't force the images and words out of his head. And when he awoke, they were still there.

It was not an accident that Suzie O'Dell had landed in jail; it was exactly what he had intended. He'd thought about bringing Lisa Edgar along to Fred Meyer, but having two people with him might have got them started talking to each other—or to the colonel—about his purchase. So he'd singled Suzie out as the best prospect for his purposes, and it had worked beautifully.

Although he'd had random thoughts about Suzie and the others going to jail, he had not focused on the possibility of them actually spending serious time in prison. Now the reality of that pursued him day and night, even into his dreams. To make matters worse, the anchorwoman on CNN kept talking about the prosecutor seeking the death penalty. That was something Vince had never imagined.

Suddenly his line disappeared, and a strong yank pulled the tip of his rod nearly to the surface of the water. The brown trout burst into the air, with Vince's hook and line firmly planted in its mouth. It was a beautiful, strong fish, and it fought valiantly to regain its freedom.

Vince often released the fish he caught. Others, which he intended to release, were so damaged from the hook and the battle they simply didn't survive, so he would eat them for dinner.

After ten minutes of fighting with the trout, Vince finally reeled it in. He held it tightly, struggling unsuccessfully to release the hook from its mouth. Finally the fish lay still in his hands, still alive for now, but with the hook planted deep inside he knew its eventual fate. Vince stared at it, then threw it, hook and all, back into the stream. "Swim—blast it—get away!" he yelled at the helpless fish. The trout became distorted in his vision as a wave of guilt and nausea hit with a vengeance. Suzie's face seemed to struggle in the stream as he looked on in panic. She tried to swim away, but a hook, line, and swivel dangled ominously from her mouth.

17

"All rise," came the cry of the bailiff.

Peter stood alone, while Franklin rose hastily with Shannon Carpenter by his side.

"Please be seated," Judge Hayden said softly as he adjusted some files in front of him. "Good morning, counsel. I guess we are here to arraign four people."

"That's right Your Honor," Franklin said, popping up and down like a jack-in-the-box.

"Any preliminaries before we bring the defendants in from jail?"

"Your Honor," Peter said standing up. "I'm not sure whether you want the subject of our discussions with the press in these four cases to be dealt with as a preliminary matter or later on. Perhaps I incorrectly assumed that all counsel were under the same restrictions for all matters relating to the fire at the clinic. Apparently Mr. Franklin had a different understanding."

"I suspect that your clients may want to listen to this issue, so let's bring them in first," the judge replied.

The bailiff opened the old, dark wooden door and was met by a sheriff's deputy standing beside Colonel Danners. Randy Wallace, Shirley Alper, and Ginny Kettner marched in single file behind the colonel and took the four seats that had been assembled around Peter at the counsel table.

"Mr. Barron, please proceed," Hayden said.

"Your Honor, yesterday three out of four of my clients were arrested at their homes. At each arrest, the police were accompanied by television reporters—cameras rolling—filming everything from handcuffing my clients to shouting questions at them and their spouses. Then, on the 11:00 P.M. news I saw Mr. Franklin giving a press conference on the steps of the courthouse about these new arrests, going into considerably more detail than this court permitted in the Susan O'Dell case. Your Honor, I'll admit I was quite incensed at this spectacle because of this court's prior order. I ask for clarification of the court's intent."

Peter glanced over at Franklin, who was staring hard at him, and then took his seat.

"Well, Mr. Franklin, you want to tell me your side of this?" The judge stared at the prosecutor, eyebrows raised over the top of his glasses, which had slipped down his nose.

Franklin stood beside his chair. "Your Honor, I guess I really don't have anything to say. I thought this court's previous order was applicable to the case against Miss O'Dell only. This is a new case. I simply followed my normal process of informing the press. After all, I am an elected official with a responsibility to the public." Franklin started to sit back down.

"No, no, Mr. Franklin, please remain standing," the judge began. "I'd like to ask you a question or two. First, are you planning to ask this court to consolidate these four cases with the case against Miss O'Dell?"

"Yes, Your Honor."

"I see. Well, in light of your actions I have no choice but to tell you that all Mr. Barron has to do is object to your motion, and it will be denied. If he thinks it is in his clients' best interest to be tried together, then, of course, I will not punish his clients by denying his request. Is that clear?"

"Yes, Your Honor," Franklin said, staring straight at the judge.

"My second question is, will you be wanting to talk with the press further about this case, in accordance with the guidelines we had established in the case against Miss O'Dell?"

"Yes, Your Honor, I will."

"Well, then in light of your behavior—which, I guess, arguably obeyed the letter of my order but openly defied its spirit—I am going to impose one additional condition. That you record *every* conservation you have with *every* reporter, and you will furnish copies of those tapes to Mr. Barron for his review within forty-eight hours of the interview. There are to be no off-the-record conversations. And if Mr. Barron finds anything in any of the tapes that he believes violates my order, he need only bring it to my attention. Do you understand this?"

"Yes, Your Honor, I understand. It's a little unprecedented, but I will comply."

"Excellent choice, Mr. Franklin. I am so glad that you have graciously consented to obeying an order of this court. Very decent of you."

The prosecutor resumed his seat, smiling sheepishly at his assistant.

Out of the corner of his eye, Peter saw Ginny smile for the first time since she had been arrested.

"All right, Mr. Barron, unless you have any other preliminaries, let's proceed. Would you like me to read the charges in the formal information to your clients or will you waive the reading?"

"We have been furnished with copies of the information, Your Honor. We'll waive the reading at this time," Peter replied.

"All right," Hayden said. "Mr. Franklin, could you briefly summarize the evidence in this case. And no theatrics, please."

"Yes, Your Honor," Franklin said, rising with a sheet of typed notes in his hands. "The court is fully familiar with the events concerning the fire and the death of Dr. Marsano, so I won't repeat them. Our evidence linking these four defendants to the crime and the underlying conspiracy is based on an interview our detectives conducted with a member of the pro-life group. This particular individual informed the police detectives that these four defendants, Miss O'Dell, and Stephen Gray were in a meeting in Colonel Danners's study just before 8:00 P.M. the Tuesday before the fire. The phone log at the clinic's headquarters in Los Angeles reveals that, at 8:00 P.M. that same evening, the clinic received a threatening call from a male concerning the Bellingham clinic. We subpoenaed Colonel Danners's phone records, and on that date, at 7:56 P.M., there was, in fact, a call made from his home to the L.A. clinic that lasted a minute or less. Despite the minor discrepancy in time, it is clear that the threatening call is the one that came from the colonel's home. Besides, what reason would the colonel or his friends have to call the clinic other than for an improper purpose!"

Peter glanced quickly around the council table at each of the defendants, who were looking at each other in wide-eyed disbelief. Ginny, who had been smiling a minute before, quickly reverted to silent tears.

"Moreover, we have a tape recording from the L.A. clinic of a call received at 7:40 P.M. on the Wednesday before the fire. That particular evening the clinic was closed, so the answering machine picked up the call. On that recording, a male voice is clearly heard saying, 'Your Bellingham clinic had better watch its back.' And, of course, we now understand the meaning of that vague threat.

"Again, our informant has told us that on that same day, all five defendants—these four plus Miss O'Dell—were at a public meeting held at Pastor Randy Wallace's church. We subpoenaed Mr. Wallace's phone records, at home and at the church, and sure enough, we found a call to the Los Angeles clinic on the church's phone bill at the exact time the clinic's recorder logged the threatening message.

"These facts and others have caused us to conclude that there was, in fact, a conspiracy between these four defendants, Miss Susan O'Dell, and Mr. Stephen Gray to burn the clinic, which resulted in the death of Dr. Rhonda Marsano."

"Very well. Mr. Danners, Rev. Wallace, Mrs. Alper, and Mrs. Kettner, will all of you please rise."

All four defendants took to their feet. Ginny looked pale and withdrawn, and Shirley was biting her lower lip—whatever had struck her as funny yesterday was no longer on her mind.

"Each of you," the judge continued, "has been charged with four felonies arising from the fire at the Whatcom Women's Center for Choice: murder in the first degree, arson, conspiracy to commit murder, and finally conspiracy to commit arson. If you are found guilty of the conspiracy charges, each of you could be sentenced to up to twenty years in a state penitentiary or a fine of $20,000, or both. If you are found guilty of the charge of arson, you could face a maximum sentence of life imprisonment. And on the count of first degree murder, each of you could face the death penalty, since Mr. Franklin has indicated in the Information that he intends to ask for that penalty. Have you had the opportunity to discuss this matter with your counsel?"

"Yes, Your Honor," the defendants agreed in unison.

"Let the record reflect," the judge said, "that all four defendants joined in the last answer saying that they had discussed this with Mr. Barron.

"I will now ask each of you how you plead to each of these charges. Mrs. Shirley Alper, to the charge of conspiracy to commit arson, how do you plead?"

Shirley glanced over at Peter, who nodded. "Not guilty, sir."

Judge Hayden smiled graciously at the older woman, whose quivering voice betrayed her nervous state. "To the charge of conspiracy to commit murder, how do you plead?"

"Not guilty."

"To the charge of arson, how do you plead?"

"Not guilty."

"And finally, to the capital charge of murder in the first degree, how do you plead?"

"Not guilty, Your Honor."

The judge took each defendant alphabetically, asking them the same questions he'd asked Shirley Alper. In each case, he heard pleas of not guilty.

"Mr. Franklin, regarding the issue of bail—and because you have the propensity to use this occasion to make a little speech for our friends, the reporters—you can save us a lot of time by simply stating any special circumstances about any of these defendants that you feel the court should consider in its decision."

Franklin stood to his feet and began to stammer. "Uh . . . I guess there is nothing about any of them," he said, flipping through pages in a file, "except that Ginny Kettner appears to have lived in Whatcom County for only a few months."

"Fine, Mr. Franklin. Is that it?"

"Yes, Your Honor, it's just that the position of the State of Washington—"

"I know your *position*, Mr. Franklin, and I don't want to hear it again. You may be seated."

The judge glared down at Mr. Franklin until he took his seat.

"Mr. Barron, under the totality of circumstances and my opinion that these defendants present little risk of flight, I am going to grant bail to your clients in the amount of $50,000 each. I will again allow property bonds for each of the defendants—will any of them be unable to meet this amount with a property bond?"

"None of the defendants can meet the bond personally, Your Honor," Peter said, rising to his feet. "The colonel's home has already been pledged in the Suzie O'Dell matter. But we have four people lined up with appropriate real property to meet these amounts."

"Very well, anything else?"

"Just one more thing. I'd like to request that the omnibus hearing be scheduled for late next week sometime."

"Fine, I'll set that hearing for next Friday at 9:00 A.M. Any conflicts for either of you?"

"No, Your Honor," both attorneys agreed.

"This court is in recess until then," the judge declared.

"All rise," the bailiff's voice rang out as the judge exited through his chamber door.

Peter whispered instructions to his somewhat encouraged clients, who quickly filed out of the courtroom to begin the process to be cleared for release.

Jim Kettner appeared at the swinging gate that separated the spectator area from the inner bar. "Peter, can I talk to you for a minute?"

"Sure, Jim, come on inside while I gather my things."

"First, thanks for getting Ginny and the others out of jail. How soon can I see her?"

"Probably an hour and a half or so. By the time we get all the paperwork done she'll be ready."

"Sounds great. The other thing is," Kettner lowered his voice and pulled Peter by the arm about six feet further away from Shannon Carpenter, who was still picking up papers from the prosecution's table. "I think I know who their informant was. She's sitting back there in the second row—Lisa Edgar."

Peter looked out over the now near-empty courtroom and saw a dark-haired woman with her head bowed and her hands covering the greater part of her face.

"She wrote me a note during the hearing saying she had been interviewed by the police. I don't know if you remember us talking about her, but she was in love with Stephen Gray."

"That sounds familiar."

"Anyhow, she said when she talked with the police, she thought she was just helping them find Gray. She's really mad at him and wants him to be caught. She didn't realize what she said might hurt someone else. She's beside herself with guilt."

"Let me go talk with her," Peter replied.

Kettner nodded and stood aside as Peter passed through the bar and sat down beside Lisa Edgar, leaning close to her face. He whispered, "Lisa, you don't need to feel guilty about any of this. It's not your fault."

"But I was the one who told them all those things," she said, pulling her hands away from her face. Peter could see that her face was flushed and her eyes darted with anxiety, but her voice was clear.

"Maybe so, but the police have the ability to get you to tell them what you know, without you even realizing it. Besides, if you hadn't talked with them voluntarily, they would have forced you to eventually. You simply saved them a step."

"But couldn't I have refused to talk to them, like you told Ginny and the others?"

"No, not really. You aren't the object of a criminal investigation. Witnesses are required to tell what they know. Only those who are suspected of crimes have the right to remain silent. So you have nothing to be ashamed of."

Lisa looked up from her dejected pose and looked Peter in the eyes. "Thanks, a lot. That makes me feel a little better."

"No problem," Peter replied. "But let me ask you a question. Did the prosecutor get it all right? And was there anything else that happened that they didn't mention today?"

"Well, there is one thing. I didn't think to say anything to them about it, and it's not something they asked me about, either."

"What's that?"

"I think Stephen Gray made the call from the church they were talking about."

"Why do you think that?"

"During the meeting, he left me for a few minutes, saying he had to go make a call."

"When was that exactly?"

"The meeting started at 7:30, so 7:40 would be about right. It was only a few minutes after the meeting started."

"Lisa, that information is invaluable. You've just helped me take a giant step toward getting these charges dismissed. What about the call from the colonel's house—could Gray have made that one as well?"

"He could have. All I know is that he arrived around 7:40 and was walking in and out of the living room and study while the others were continuously in the colonel's study."

"OK, that's fine, just fine. I guess it's too much to ask for you to have slam-dunk evidence that he made both calls."

A crestfallen look again overtook her countenance. Jim Kettner, who had been standing quietly behind her, gently put his hand on Lisa's shoulder and patted her softly.

"Lisa, I'm sorry for my choice of words," Peter said. "I didn't mean it the way it sounded. You've helped me find one big piece of evidence that helps Ginny and the others tremendously. And remember, you are not to blame for talking to the police."

Kettner looked at Peter with beseeching eyes. "Has Lisa's information helped solve the case against Ginny and the others?"

"I'm afraid we're going to need more evidence," Peter replied. "As long as they have that private planning session going on in the colonel's study at the same time as the threatening call to the L.A. clinic, the prosecutors still have a shot at getting a jury to buy the conspiracy idea. They could say that Gray made the call per Danners's instructions or that he was in the study with the others when the call was made."

"So things still don't look very good," Kettner said ruefully.

"Well, I think it overstates our situation to be either optimistic or pessimistic. We've just got to work harder to produce better evidence of the truth—truth that they can't manipulate."

"It's hard to be objective when your wife is facing the death penalty."

Both Kettner and Peter were talking over Edgar's head, forgetting that she could hear every word.

"You know, I really don't think any of them has to be too concerned about that, even Suzie, although she is arguably more at risk. The death penalty is usually reserved for the one who does the actual killing. Gray, on the other hand, would be dangling by a rope with little question."

"Yeah," Kettner replied. "Suzie's in a tough spot. Stephen Gray really did her dirt."

"He managed to mess me up pretty bad, too," Lisa replied, suddenly standing up and forcing the two men to make room for her. "I need to get some air, or something." She walked quickly down the black-and-white marble aisle and disappeared out the double doors at the rear of the courtroom.

Kettner and Peter looked at each other. "That was probably hard for her to hear—I'd better go check on her," Kettner said. He, too, was gone in a moment, leaving Peter alone in the solemn courtroom.

Later that afternoon, Max Franklin's secretary buzzed him in his office. Shannon Carpenter was sitting on the desk next to the phone and punched the speaker phone button. "Wendy Mervyn on line two," the secretary's voice said.

"Justice Department," Franklin whispered in a boastful tone as he punched at line two. "Wendy, so good to hear from you," he proclaimed as he swiveled his chair away from his assistant and toward the window.

"Good to talk to you, too." Her tone indicated that her salutation was nothing more than a polite obligation. "Look," she said earnestly, "I've gotten a call from Barry Penner in Los Angeles."

"What—"

"Penner is very concerned about the progress of your case. He's putting a lot of pressure on the attorney general to file a federal complaint simultaneous to yours. He thinks you have insulted the trial judge or something. What's going on up there?"

"Oh, nothing, really. The judge was a little miffed that I tipped off the press about our arrests of the four additional defendants and then gave a few interviews myself. It'll blow over. And why does Penner have so much clout anyway? He's just a private L.A. lawyer."

"Maybe so, but he's tightly connected with several major constituency groups of this administration. He represents, as you obviously know, one of the biggest abortion providers in the nation. I need not tell you how strongly this administration feels about the full protection of the legal rights of women's choice. Additionally, he is the past president of the California Trial Lawyer's Association. The members of that group gave us nearly $5 million in the '96 election campaign. Simply put, Barry Penner's phone calls, either to the White House or the Justice Department, get returned."

Franklin squirmed uncomfortably in his chair, looking vacantly out the window at the library across the street. "Well, I assure you, everything is OK, and I'll bring in five convictions in this case."

"Sorry, Max, but your assurances aren't good enough," Mervyn said deliberately. "What do I say to my boss when she asks me why we can't simultaneously prosecute these people in state and federal court?"

Franklin stood up and began to pace as far as the tether of his phone cord would allow. "Two reasons come to mind," he said, suddenly sitting on top of the desk beside Carpenter.

"I'm listening," Mervyn responded tersely.

"First, Peter Barron would move, quite successfully I believe, that one case be stayed until the other jurisdiction had completed its work.

I'm virtually certain that our local fossil of a judge would grant his request—for that matter, so would the federal judge.

"Second, I don't think such a move would play very well in the court of public opinion. Right now we have the press almost uniformly on our side. If you filed federal charges on top of the state charges, it would look like these poor folk are being plowed under by a biased Justice Department.

"All in all, it's not the course of action I would recommend if I were in a position to give advice."

"Not bad, Max. Not bad at all. You do have a good political head on your shoulders. I can plead that to my boss. But let me warn you, if anything else goes wrong in this case, all hell will break loose over here. So don't be the cause of further consternation, OK?"

"Gotcha."

"Good. See ya later. I'm late for a meeting."

"Goodbye, Wendy, and I certainly hope I will see you later; we're overdue for a reunion."

Still holding the receiver, Franklin spun slowly around toward his desk just in time to see Shannon Carpenter scooting out his office door. "Shannon, where are you going?"

"Oh, I'm just *overdue* for some fresh air," she said mocking Franklin's tone. The door slammed shut behind her with a resounding bang.

Peter Barron, Joe Lambert, and Cooper Stone had been locked up in the conference room since before nine o'clock, and there was no sign of a break forthcoming. Sally walked around her work station, through the reception area, and knocked on the glass wall that looked in on the modest meeting area. Peter stood scribbling notes on the markerboard

while his associates sat at the table, throwing out ideas. Sally knocked
again, then opened the conference room door. "You three want me to
bring you some sandwiches from the deli or something?"

"Sure thing!" Joe called out.

"Food. I remember food!" was Cooper's reply.

Peter collapsed onto the swivel chair he had been standing close
behind. "Come on, guys! We're trying to prepare for a trial, and all you
can think about is food."

"Look at your watch, Mr. Litigator," Joe replied with an exhausted
smile. "It's almost two o'clock. If we were in court, the judge would have
taken a break long ago."

"But I feel like we're getting nowhere!"

"Exactly why we need to go eat," Cooper moaned.

"Well, try your problem on me," Sally suggested.

Peter explained to Sally the problem of trying to pin the phone call
made from the Danners' house on Gray without implicating any of the
others and about the discrepancy of time between the phone company
records and when the call was logged in at the L.A. clinic.

"How long was the call?" Sally asked.

"The prosecuting attorney said a minute or less."

"Have you verified that with the colonel?"

"No, I just assumed what he said was accurate."

"Why don't I call the colonel and ask him to look at his phone bill?"
Sally asked. "Never hurts to double check."

Peter sighed. "I guess you're right—go ahead."

Peter paced while Sally walked back to her work station. He could
hear her talking fairly clearly and knew she'd connected with the colonel.
After a minute of conversation, she stood silently for a long time.

Noticing Peter staring at her inquisitively, she said, "Mr. Danners has gone to the study to get the phone bill; he said it will take him a little bit to get it and return to the kitchen," she explained.

Two minutes later, she picked up a pencil and made a couple notes. "Thanks, Colonel," she said, and hung up the phone. "The prosecutor was right—one minute long, Peter."

Deep in thought, Peter didn't respond to Sally's comment. Sally looked at Joe and Cooper. Both men looked at Peter and shrugged.

"Did you hear what I said, Mr. Barron?"

"Yeah . . . I did . . . but . . . did you say the colonel had to find the bill in the study, then return to the phone in the kitchen?"

"Yeah. So?"

"So!" Peter exclaimed. "So it's just that you're brilliant! Get the colonel back on the phone and then all of you, go eat. Steaks at Clinkerdaggers or whatever you want! It's all on me—you too, Sally!"

"Brilliant? Did something go over my head?" Cooper asked, staggering to his feet.

"Whatever," Joe replied. "Let's just get out of here, quick, before his call to the colonel doesn't pan out."

Only Pat, Joe, and Cooper's secretary remained behind to answer the phones while Peter talked excitedly with the colonel.

18

The image of Gwen's pained expression as he kissed her on his way out the door of their home in Spokane remained fixed in Peter's mind as he pulled up in front of Bellingham's courthouse complex. It was an unusually clear and bright June morning—the weatherman promised sun all day, with a possibility that the temperature might crack the 75-degree mark.

In Spokane it would be considerably warmer. Gwen would probably spend the day watching Casey swim in Liberty Lake. Gwen had reminded Peter as he was walking out the door, that last summer he had taken off nearly every other Friday and spent the day with his family, either relaxing by the lake or doing yard work around the house. So far this year, with the urgency of his case in Bellingham, he had not taken off a single Friday.

A car honked at Peter just as he bounded up the steps toward the modern entrance into the courthouse. He stopped and turned in time to see Randy Wallace wave as he drove by, with two women riding in the seat behind him. One of the women was Shirley Alper; the other, although he couldn't see clearly, he assumed was Randy's wife, Kristy. Peter paused on the steps, waiting for his two clients.

"Morning, Peter," Randy called with a wave of his hand.

"Morning," Peter called back. As the trio approached, he watched a number of sea gulls hovering on the incoming breeze and got his first whiff of the pulp mill odor that dominates downtown Bellingham. Every time he smelled it he remembered Gwen. *I'm glad she's not here to smell this; it would definitely make her sick,* he thought.

"So are we going to win this motion today?" Wallace asked earnestly as he neared the bottom step.

"I sure hope so," Peter replied.

"Do you think we have a chance? All four of us?" Shirley asked.

"Well, your chances are greater than Suzie's, since the evidence against her is considerably stronger. But still, getting charges dismissed is never easy. To charge you with a crime, the prosecutor need only show 'probable cause' to believe you may be guilty. That's the stage we're in now—the prosecutor is going to try and convince the judge he has probable cause to believe you committed a crime, and that you should stand trial for that crime. So our battle lies in trying to disprove his probable cause theory."

"Is probable cause the same as 'reasonable doubt'?" Randy asked as the group of four approached the elevators. "I hear these terms thrown around all the time, and they sound so confusing." The elevator door opened and they stepped in. A man in a brown plaid suit was already inside, so Peter delayed answering Randy's question. The elevator stopped at the second floor.

"*So?*" Wallace repeated as the elevator doors opened and the man stepped out.

Peter placed his index finger in front of his lips, making the familiar "ssshhhh" sign. He subtly motioned with his head in the direction of the stranger as the doors closed tightly.

"OK," Peter said. "What I'm going to say is pretty innocuous, but, still, you never can be too careful in places like this. It's kind of a gut-level thing that most judges have a pretty good feel for. It takes only a moderate amount of evidence to reach probable cause. It takes substantially more evidence with almost no room for doubt to be considered beyond a reasonable doubt. There are a lot of technical definitions for both terms, but the gut of a judge works pretty well to weigh the different tests."

The elevator doors opened on the third floor. Colonel and Evie Danners were sitting on a bench immediately outside the elevator. Mrs. Danners looked up and caught Peter's eye, then looked away nervously.

"Morning, everyone," the colonel said. "Peter, Mr. Franklin is already in the courtroom. Some woman lawyer from Washington, D.C. is with him. I heard him introduce her to one of the court clerks in the hall. What's she doing here?"

"Depends on who she's with. Did you hear her name?"

"Not clearly. Maybe attorney general, or something."

"Janet Reno? Did she look like Janet Reno?" Peter exclaimed.

"No, it wasn't Janet Reno. I would have recognized her." The colonel shook his head. "I'm just not sure."

"Well, there's an easy way to find out," he said. "You three wait here." Peter walked into the courtroom with his briefcase and was gone for about three minutes. "You weren't far off, Colonel," Peter said, returning to the hall. "Her name is Wendy Mervyn. She's the assistant attorney general of the United States. I figure that puts her about fourth in the chain of command at the Justice Department. She and Franklin appear to be good friends."

"Does this mean we've been charged with a federal crime?" Shirley asked.

"No, not yet at least. She's just here to monitor the case. 'The administration,' she told me, 'is tracking this case closely.'"

"What's that supposed to mean?" the colonel asked.

"I think her presence is meant to intimidate someone. Maybe us. Maybe Franklin. Or maybe the judge. All I can say is we should all shrug it off. I know Judge Hayden won't care one way or the other. He's been on the bench long enough that tactics like this probably don't bother him in the slightest." Peter reached for the courtroom door.

"Can we pray before we begin?" Wallace asked.

"Oh, of course," Peter said, releasing his grip on the handle. "But where's Ginny?"

"Oh her." The colonel sighed. "She'll be late for her date with the hangman in Walla Walla, if it comes to that."

"Not a bad thing to be late for, if you ask me." Shirley Alper was grinning.

"That's enough of that kind of talk," Randy said. "Let's just pray, OK?"

When Randy finished, Peter looked up and searched the hallway for Ginny one last time before entering the courtroom. "We only have a couple minutes before we begin. Colonel, you, Shirley, and Randy need to come in with me. Mrs. Wallace, will you wait out here and make sure that Ginny comes down to the rest of us the moment she gets here?"

"Sure," she replied.

Peter led the way down the center aisle of the courtroom and through the swinging gate and assigned seating to each of his clients: the colonel, Randy Wallace, and then Shirley Alper. The seat at the end of the table, across from Peter, was reserved for the missing Ginny Kettner.

At one minute until nine, the bailiff approached Peter. "Aren't you supposed to have four clients here this morning, Mr. Barron?"

"Yes, I am. I don't know where Mrs. Kettner is. She apparently has a reputation for being late."

"I just hope she hasn't skipped bail," the bailiff replied.

A shot of alarm surged through Peter's veins. "No, I'm sure she'll be here." He turned to look at the door yet another time. "Oh, here she is now," he said with relief.

Peter stood up from the table and walked to meet Ginny at the bar. "Where were you?" he whispered.

"Flat tire," she replied. "Honest."

"No problem," Peter replied. "Just have a seat over by Shirley."

"All rise," the bailiff cried just seconds after Ginny found her seat.

"Good morning, everyone," Judge Hayden said.

"Good morning, Your Honor," came the attorneys' response.

"Ladies and gentlemen, this is the time set for the omnibus pretrial hearing in the case of the State of Washington versus Henry Danners, Randy Wallace, Virginia Kettner, and Shirley Alper. We have several matters to take up this morning. Why don't we begin with Mr. Barron's motion to dismiss. Mr. Barron, it is your motion, so why don't you begin."

"Thank you, Your Honor. May it please the court, these four defendants are charged with murder, arson, and related conspiracy charges, as the court is well aware. We believe there is insufficient evidence to constitute probable cause—that under *State of Washington v. Knapp*, decided by the Supreme Court of Washington in 1985, this court can consider a motion to dismiss on a pretrial basis when the uncontroverted evidence demonstrates that as a matter of law it is impossible to sustain a conviction. We believe the evidence that will be presented here today will demonstrate that we meet this standard, and that this court should dismiss this case. May I call my first witness Your Honor?"

"Yes, unless Mr. Franklin has anything on a preliminary basis."

"No, Your Honor," Franklin said, rising to his feet. "I am confident that this court will confirm that there is indeed probable cause to bind these four defendants over for trial."

"All right, Mr. Barron, call your first witness."

"I'd like to call Detective John Dunn to the stand. And Your Honor, I have subpoenaed three witnesses to court today. I gave them all written instructions to wait in the witness room down the hall. I am invoking the rule requiring sequestration of witnesses, if the court pleases."

"That is fine, Mr. Barron. And I'll ask my bailiff to go and retrieve Detective Dunn from the witness waiting room and to inform the other witnesses that they must remain outside the courtroom until called."

A minute later, Detective Dunn came through the door at the rear of the courtroom. He wore a clean tie and a starched shirt under his navy blazer, and his tan slacks were pressed with a crisp crease. For a moment, Peter did not recognize him.

"Please swear in the witness," the judge ordered.

Dunn raised his right hand.

"Do you promise to tell the truth, the whole truth, and nothing but the truth so help you God?" the bailiff sang out.

"I do."

"Please be seated and state your name and business address," the judge said.

"Detective John Dunn, Bellingham City Hall, room 326."

"Detective Dunn, you are the chief murder investigator for the Bellingham Police Department, are you not?" Peter began.

"Yes, sir."

"How long have you held this position?"

"This position—about ten years. I've been with the department for just over twenty-one years altogether."

"Have you personally conducted or supervised the investigation of the death of Dr. Rhonda Marsano and the fire that caused her death?"

"Yes, sir, I have."

"And, forgive me for being mundane, but your work has included the investigation that led to the charges that have been filed against Colonel Danners, Pastor Wallace, Mrs. Alper, and Mrs. Kettner, is that right?"

"Yes, that's right."

"You prepared the affidavit that supported the filing of the formal criminal Information against these four defendants?"

"More or less. I did the investigation and prepared the affidavit in draft form. Miss Carpenter, Mr. Franklin's assistant, prepared it in final form, and then I signed it."

"Fine, Captain Dunn," Peter said, walking toward the witness stand. "May I approach the witness, Your Honor?" Peter asked.

"It appears you already have, Mr. Barron," the judge replied tersely.

"I apologize, Your Honor. I'll ask in advance next time."

"Carry on, Mr. Barron," came the judge's reply.

"Detective Dunn, I am handing you what has been premarked as defendants' exhibit 1. Is this the affidavit you just described, and is that your signature on it?"

Dunn took the document out of Peter's hand and examined it for a few seconds. "Yes, sir, it appears to be the same document."

"Fine, Captain. Did you include every fact that you are aware of that leads you to believe there is probable cause to charge these four defendants with these four felonies?"

"Yes, we put in every fact we had at the time. Of course, we expect to have more police work done by the time of trial."

"But you recognize, detective, that probable cause is based on the evidence you have right now. Correct?"

"That's right, Mr. Barron."

"Fine. Are there any other facts you have discovered since you prepared this affidavit that leads you to believe that these defendants are guilty of these four crimes?"

"No, sir," Dunn replied. "It's all right there in the affidavit."

"Captain Dunn, I am not going to ask you any questions that relate to that portion of your investigation concerning the fire or the fact that the fire was the reason Ms. Marsano's death. None of these defendants are going to question those matters—at least not in today's hearing. I would like you to begin with me on page three and look through that portion of your affidavit that specifically relates to these four defendants. We'll deal with Miss O'Dell another day—and someone else will have to deal with Mr. Gray if he is ever apprehended."

"OK, sir, I have page three."

Peter paced back and forth over the black-and-white marble flooring. "All right. It seems to me you have six facts that lead you to believe that these four defendants are guilty of these four felonies. Let me review them.

"First, they were the leaders, along with Ms. O'Dell, of the protests against the abortion clinic on Garden Street.

"Second, they were engaged in a private meeting in the colonel's study, prior to a combined meeting for the entire pro-life group, at the Danners' living room on Tuesday, May 17, less than one week before the fire. During the time of that private meeting, at 7:56 P.M., telephone company phone records indicate that a call was made from the colonel's home to the Los Angeles headquarters of the clinic.

"Third, phone log records from the L.A. clinic headquarters indicate that at approximately eight o'clock that same night, clinic headquarters received a threatening call about the Bellingham clinic.

"Fourth, another call was made to the clinic on Wednesday, May 18, at approximately 7:40 P.M. The caller was a male, again threatening the Bellingham clinic. And you even have that call on tape, do you not?"

"Yes, sir, we have it on tape."

"OK. Fifth, you again obtained records from the phone company, this time showing that a call was placed from Immanuel Bible Church to the L.A. clinic headquarters, also on May 18 at 7:40 P.M.

"And finally, sixth, you know that there was a pro-life meeting going on at Immanuel Bible Church at that time that night, at which the defendants were all in attendance.

"Are these facts that you have listed in your affidavit the essence of your case against these four defendants?"

"Yes. That is, in essence, my affidavit word-for-word," the detective replied.

"Detective Dunn, would it be fair to say that you have inferred these four defendants' participation in the alleged conspiracy, murder, and arson is based on their presence in the buildings when and where these two threatening calls were made?"

"Not just their presence, sir, but control of the buildings from which the calls were made. Both Colonel Danners and Randy Wallace clearly had a plausible motive for harming the clinic and Dr. Marsano. And we have evidence from a witness that Colonel Danners controlled every aspect of the actions taken against the clinic. So I believe a reasonable inference can be made that the colonel and the rest of the leadership were behind the phone calls, the fire, and ultimate death of Dr. Marsano."

"Would you agree that your case against the defendants is entirely circumstantial?"

"We don't have a witness who saw them make the phone calls if that's what you mean. But we aren't required to have such a witness for every step in a crime sequence."

"I'm aware of that, Captain Dunn. My question is this: If there was uncontroverted evidence that demonstrated that Stephen Gray made both of the threatening phone calls, you would lose your strongest evidence tying these four defendants to the conspiracy and crime, wouldn't you?"

"Uncontroverted evidence?"

"Yes, Captain Dunn."

"Well, if you had uncontroverted evidence that none of these defendants had any connection to the phone calls, then—"

"Then you wouldn't have probable cause, would you?"

"Uh . . . that would be for the court to decide, I guess."

"Fine, Captain Dunn. One final question—who was the insider who provided you with this information?"

"Lisa Edgar."

"I have no more questions, Your Honor."

Peter walked back to the table and sat down beside the colonel and whispered briefly in his ear.

"Any questions, Mr. Franklin?" Hayden asked as he glanced up momentarily from his ongoing task of taking notes.

"No, Your Honor. All Mr. Barron did was reiterate the detective's sworn affidavit. There is nothing for me to cross-examine."

"Fine. Mr. Barron, who's next?"

"I'd like to call Lisa Edgar to the stand."

After another pause, a noticeably pale Lisa Edgar came slowly through the door and worked her way toward the front. After being sworn and giving her basic identification, Lisa settled uncomfortably in her seat, shifting from side to side and unwilling to look directly at anyone.

"Miss Edgar," Peter began, "I know you are nervous, but I have only a few questions for you."

"OK."

"Miss Edgar, please describe your relationship with the Whatcom Life Coalition."

"I was an active member and participant."

"Did you participate in the protests and sidewalk counseling at the clinic?"

"Yes, I did—nearly every Saturday."

"How did you first get involved with this group?"

"Ginny Kettner is my best friend, and she heard about the initial meeting and asked me to go. I was there from the very beginning, with Ginny."

"Have you read the affidavit signed by Detective Dunn that was filed to support the formal charges in this case?"

"Yes, you gave me a copy and I read it."

"Fine. Did you supply much of the information that was contained in that probable cause affidavit?"

"Yes. The police came to me and told me that I had to answer their questions, and so I did."

"Lisa, did you know Stephen Gray?"

"Yes, unfortunately I did."

"Why do you say unfortunately? What was the relationship between you and Mr. Gray?"

"He was my boyfriend for about three months before the fire. I thought we were very serious. In fact, we had a date for the Saturday morning after the fire, when he had told me he was going to ask me to marry him. I showed up. But he never did."

"Do you have any idea where Stephen Gray is?"

"None."

"Have you heard from him since the fire?"

"No."

"Did he ask you to become involved in the fire bombing of the clinic?"

"No."

"Do you know whether Mr. Gray was responsible for that fire?"

"No, but it seems to make sense since he disappeared immediately after the fire."

"Just answer his questions, Miss Edgar. He didn't ask for speculation." Judge Hayden looked kindly over his trifocals at the witness.

"Now, Miss Edgar, I'd like to focus your attention on the meeting that was held at the Danners's home on Tuesday, May 17. Were you at that meeting?" Peter continued.

"Yes, I was."

"When was the meeting scheduled to start?"

"At eight o'clock, sharp. The colonel always started everything right on time."

"When did you arrive at the meeting?"

"A little after 7:30."

"And where were the colonel and the other leaders when you arrived?"

"In the colonel's study for a leadership meeting."

"How do you know that?"

"Well, I normally rode to those meetings with Ginny Kettner, but that night she had to go early for a leadership meeting at seven."

"So you drove to the Danners's house alone that evening?"

"Yes, I did."

"And when you arrived, the members of the leadership group—all five of them—were in the colonel's study, is that correct?"

"Yes, at least that's where Mrs. Danners said they were."

"Objection—hearsay," Franklin said, leaping to his feet. "That doesn't prove they were, in fact, in the study."

"Your Honor, I would simply point out that the colonel and the others being in the study is a fact that appears in Detective Dunn's affidavit, and it is obvious that Miss Edgar was the source of that report. If it is hearsay now, it was hearsay then."

The judge looked over his glasses at Max Franklin. "Mr. Barron makes an interesting point, Mr. Franklin. I'm prepared to rule in your favor on this objection, but if I do, we'll probably have to look into the sufficiency of the detective's affidavit. What is your pleasure?"

"I'll withdraw my objection, I guess."

"Fine," the judge said. "Continue, Mr. Barron."

"Where were you from the time you arrived a little after 7:30 until the meeting started at 8?"

"I was in the living room, where the group meetings were held."

"Was Mr. Gray there during that time?"

"Yes, he was."

"When did he arrive, if you know?"

"He came early with Suzie—Susan O'Dell. She needed a ride, so he picked her up."

"So he was already there when you arrived. Where in the house was he when you arrived?"

"He was in the living room, reading."

"Did he stay there in the living room the entire twenty or thirty minutes until the group meeting started at eight o'clock?"

"Well, mostly, but he left the room two or three times."

"Do you mean he would be in the living room, leave for a bit, then come back to the living room again—and he did that two or three times?"

"Yes, that's it."

"How long was he gone each time?"

"For two or three minutes."

"Where did he go?"

"I don't know, exactly. There were snacks in the kitchen, so he may have gone in there."

"Where do you think he went?"

"Objection," Franklin called out. "Calls for speculation."

"Sustained," the judge called out.

"Fine," Peter said, looking briefly at the yellow tablet he held in his right hand as he paced back and forth behind his counsel table. "Miss Edgar, does Colonel Danners have a phone in his den?"

"Yes, he does."

"How do you know?"

"I've used it myself to make a couple of calls over the last several months."

"Does he have other phones in the house?"

"The only other one I have seen is in the kitchen. I haven't been in the bedrooms."

"So you have seen one phone in the study and one phone in the kitchen. Right?"

"That's right."

"Fine," Peter said, smiling. "Now, Miss Edgar, I would like to direct your attention to a meeting on the following night, May 18. This meeting of the Whatcom Life Coalition was open to the press and public, I believe, dealing with the previous week's court injunction regarding behavior at pro-life protests at the clinic. Did you attend that meeting?"

"Yes, I did."

"With whom did you go to the meeting?"

"I rode with Ginny Kettner."

"Did Stephen Gray come to the meeting?"

"Yes, he did."

"Where did he sit?"

"He sat right next to me in an aisle seat near the back."

"Excuse me, Miss Edgar, I guess I forgot ask you where this meeting was held."

Lisa smiled. She had become more relaxed with the easy give and take of Peter's line of questioning. "It was at Immanuel Bible Church at North and Lynn Streets, in Bellingham."

"What time did the meeting start?"

"Seven-thirty."

"Was Mr. Gray already at the church when you and Ginny Kettner arrived?"

"No, in fact, he was almost late."

"So you sat down, he took the seat beside you, then the meeting started, and you both stayed in your seats until it was over?"

"Well, after Pastor Wallace prayed and about five minutes into the colonel's talk, Stephen leaned over to me and said he had to make a phone call and left the room."

"Objection, it's hearsay," Franklin called out. "That doesn't prove Gray actually made a call."

"Mr. Barron, if you're trying to use that statement to prove that Mr. Gray did, in fact, make a call, I will have to sustain Mr. Franklin's objection."

"For now, Your Honor, I am only using it to show what excuse Mr. Gray gave for getting out of his seat."

"Fine," Hayden replied. "The answer will be allowed to stand for that limited purpose."

"Did Mr. Gray, in fact, leave?"

"Yes, he did."

"How long was he gone?"

"About five minutes, not more than ten, for sure."

"Was Colonel Danners speaking the entire time Mr. Gray was gone?"

"Yes."

"Where was Pastor Wallace during this time?"

"He was sitting right behind Colonel Danners, on a little platform."

"So neither Randy Wallace nor Hank Danners ever left the room during the duration of that meeting, is that right?"

"That is correct."

"Now, I'd like for you to pin-point, if you can, the exact time that Mr. Gray left his seat."

"Well, the meeting opened at 7:30. Pastor Wallace welcomed everyone for about three minutes or so, then prayed for another minute. Then he introduced Colonel Danners. So by the time the colonel began speaking, it was probably about 7:35. Stephen left about five minutes into the colonel's speech, so I'd say it was about 7:40 when he left the room."

"The phone records attached to Detective Dunn's affidavit indicate that the call from Immanuel Bible Church to the L.A. clinic headquarters was made at exactly 7:40 P.M. that night. It is your testimony, then, that Stephen Gray was outside of the meeting at 7:40?"

"Yes, I'm sure he was."

"And neither Randy Wallace nor Colonel Danners were out of the room at that time?"

"No, they were both in front of the crowd until the meeting adjourned at 8:30."

"That's all the questions I have for this witness," Peter said, resuming his seat beside the colonel.

Franklin stood and walked toward a lectern stationed on his left-hand side. He picked it up and carried it to the center of the courtroom, just in front of both counsel tables.

"Miss Edgar, I do have a few questions for you.

"You talked with the police at great length about this case didn't you?"

"Yes, sir, I did."

"You did so voluntarily?"

"I guess. They told me I was supposed to talk to them. I cooperated. They didn't serve me with any subpoenas or anything."

"Did you ever tell Detective Dunn about Mr. Gray's departure from the meeting at the church?"

"No, I didn't."

"Kind of left that part out. Right?"

"I don't know what you mean, sir."

Franklin walked around the edge of the lectern and took one step toward Lisa. "Well, Miss Edgar, doesn't it strike you as a little convenient that when you are freely talking to the police, you never mention the fact that Gray left the meeting for five or ten minutes? But now that your friend, Ginny Kettner, is being charged with murder and arson, you suddenly remember Gray leaving the room just at the time the phone call was made. Why didn't you tell the police about that?"

"I guess because they never asked me. They only seemed interested in finding out whether the pastor and the colonel were in the building at the time."

"I see. You didn't feel you had an obligation to tell the police the whole truth?"

"Objection," Peter said, leaping to his feet. "Counsel is arguing with the witness."

"Overruled. This is a cross-examination," Hayden said firmly. "Miss Edgar, you should answer the question."

"Well . . . I thought I was telling the whole truth by answering his questions. He never asked me to give a narrative or anything. He just asked me specific questions, and I gave specific answers. No one told me I had to volunteer things that he never brought up."

"I see," Franklin said, walking back to his lectern. "But you are certain that both Colonel Danners and Randy Wallace were in the colonel's study at 7:56 on Tuesday, May 17?"

"Yes, I am sure of that."

"And you are certain that he had a phone in the den?"

"Yes, like I said, I have used it myself."

"Are you going to tell me now that you saw Stephen Gray making a phone call at exactly 7:56 on that evening as well?"

Peter started to object, but something in his spirit kept him quiet and in his seat.

"No, Mr. Franklin. I do not have a clear memory of when Mr. Gray was in and out of the living room on that occasion, and I have no idea where he was at 7:56."

"OK, Miss Edgar, that's all."

"No further questions, Your Honor," Peter said. "May this witness be excused?"

"I'd like her to wait in the hallway or waiting room, Your Honor," Franklin said.

"Fine," Hayden replied. "Miss Edgar, we may or may not need you to testify again. But the process will be materially aided if you will just wait in the hallway until this portion of the hearing is completed. Thank you, you can get down for now. Counsel, perhaps now would be a good time for a short morning recess. We'll reconvene at 10:30."

Everyone rose as the judge went out of the courtroom. Reporters stood pressed along the bar rail, waiting for Peter or Max Franklin to exit the inner sanctum so they could bombard them with questions. Eager to have the first word, Franklin exited the courtroom, taking over half the press in his wake.

Ginny and Shirley latched onto Peter before he could leave. "Who's the last witness?" Ginny asked.

"It's a surprise," Peter replied.

"You can't tell us?" Shirley asked. "Aren't we your clients?"

"Of course you are, and if you insist I'll tell you. But my strategy has been to keep all of this a secret so that there was no possibility of anything leaking out. With Franklin's knack for twisting the truth, he would surely find some antidote to the evidence I've prepared. You're going to find out in less than ten minutes anyway, can't we just keep it a surprise?"

"Sure," Shirley replied. "It still seems too much to hope for, but Peter, you seem so confident."

Finally alone for a minute, Peter walked over to the wall of windows on the left side of the courtroom, unfastened one of the ancient window clasps, and opened the window. He breathed in deeply the fresh air that rushed into the courtroom. Even the pulp mill aroma invigorated him. He went over his questions for the next witness in his mind, and then his final argument. Suddenly he was roused from his concentration by a strange female voice. Wendy Mervyn was standing in a shaft of light that came skirting through the open window.

"Pardon me, Mr. Barron. I wanted to simply greet you and let you know that our administration is willing to cooperate with you in attempting to locate Mr. Gray."

"Thank you, Ms. Mervyn was it?"

"Yes, Mervyn. That's right."

"Well, we appreciate the offer. If the FBI could locate Gray, I believe you would have your killer. And I genuinely believe he acted alone."

"I understand that's your theory, but of course, our official position is to back the prosecuting attorney. We think these kinds of protests are what cause people to start thinking about killing abortion doctors. Violent words breed violent acts."

"I personally don't believe that Gray was a true pro-lifer," Peter countered. "I think he acted out of his own interests."

"But you've seen the evidence otherwise—Gray went to all the meetings, participated in the songs and prayers. And, apparently, he was the one who killed the doctor. Whether he acted alone is a question you and my former classmate can debate."

"Well, again, I appreciate your offer to help find Gray. I hope he'll make the FBI's ten most wanted list."

"That's not a bad idea—I think that can be arranged," she replied.

Suddenly it occurred to Peter that all of this chit-chat was diverting his thinking from the task at hand. "Ms. Mervyn," he said as he closed and latched the window, "I've got a little preparation I have to do for the next witness. So if you'll excuse me—"

"Oh, I'm sorry if I interrupted."

"No, that's fine," Peter replied. "Maybe we can talk more about finding Gray at the end of the hearing."

"Certainly," she replied, turning to exit the sanctum of the inner bar.

Peter walked back across the courtroom to his table. Colonel Danners was already back in place. "What did she want?" he whispered.

"She assured me that the Justice Department was committed to finding Stephen Gray."

"Hmmm. Well, I'm for that," Danners replied. "Was that it?"

"That's all she said." Peter glanced quickly at his watch. "You'd better go round everyone up, only three minutes before we start again."

"Done," said the colonel.

A few minutes later the bailiff called the courtroom to order, followed by Judge Hayden's order for everyone to resume their seats.

"All right, Mr. Barron, call your last witness, please."

"The defense calls Paul Cavner to the stand."

Within minutes, a fiftyish man in a grey business suit and conservative tie was quickly sworn in and seated in the witness stand.

"Paul Cavner, my business address is 426 Commerce Street, Everett," he said in response to the judge's instruction to identify himself.

Peter stood and walked over to the lectern. "Mr. Cavner, please tell us the name of your employer and your position."

"I'm the supervisor of the billing department for Pacific Northwest Bell."

"How long have you held this position with the phone company?"

"I've been in this position for five years. I've worked for PNB for thirteen years altogether."

"In response to a *subpoena duces tecum*, have you brought with you the phone records for Colonel Hank Danners' home?"

"Yes, I have."

"How many phones are in the Danners's home?"

"We don't keep track of the number of phones as such any more. The homeowner can install as many phones as he likes. We simply keep track of the number of phone lines and the location of phone jacks."

"So how many phone lines are installed in the Danners's home?"

"Two."

"Your Honor, may I approach the witness?"

Judge Hayden nodded.

"Mr. Cavner, I am handing you a copy of a phone bill that shows a call from the Danners's home to a number in Los Angeles. This bill was attached to a probable cause affidavit filed by the prosecution in this case. Does this copy agree with the records that you have with you here today?"

"Let me take a minute or so to compare," Cavner responded. He flipped through the phone bills in a manila folder he'd been holding in his lap. "Oh, yes, here's the month in question. Yes, that bill is consistent with our records."

"Which line was that call made from?"

"It was made from the 555-4903 line."

"What is the number for the other line?"

"It is 555-7563."

"Do your records show which phone jacks service which lines?"

"Yes, they do."

"Where are the jacks located for the 4903 number?"

"In the kitchen, two bedrooms, and the garage."

"Now just to be sure, the 4903 number is the one on which the call to Los Angeles was made?"

"Yes, that's right."

"Where are the phone jacks for the 7563 line?"

"There is only one."

"Where is that one jack?"

"In the den toward the back of the house."

"Is there a jack for the 4903 number in that room?"

"Not according to our records."

"So would you say that it is impossible for that call on the 4903 line to have been made from the den?"

"Correct, that would not be possible."

"So from what room or rooms could the call to Los Angeles have been made?"

"Either the kitchen, one of the two front bedrooms, or the garage. There's no way of knowing which."

"That is all I have at this time."

As Peter sat down, the colonel clapped his back. "Great job," he whispered.

"Mr. Franklin?" the judge said, holding his glasses in one hand.

"Just a couple questions." He walked to the lectern. "Mr. Cavner, is it possible for a person to install a jack in a location that you don't know about?"

"Yes, sir, that's possible. We consider it illegal, but a person with the right know-how and equipment could do it."

"Can you say for certain that there is no illegal jack accessing the 4903 line in the Danners's study?"

"No, all I can say for certain is that our company did not install any 4903 jacks in that room."

"That's all," Franklin said.

Shannon Carpenter nodded and shrugged as he sat down beside her.

"Other witnesses, Mr. Barron?"

"No, Your Honor, that's all we have for our motion to dismiss. We're ready to argue."

"All right. Mr. Franklin, any witnesses you would like to call?"

"No, Mr. Barron has called both of our principal witnesses—Detective Dunn and Miss Edgar."

"Fine. Gentlemen, I'd like you to keep your arguments to about five minutes each. I know this is an extremely important case, but the issues before me are very narrow and by keeping you to five minutes, it is my hope that you will focus just on the pertinent issues and not wander around unnecessarily in other aspects of the case." The judge looked at one lawyer and then the other to make sure his point had been understood. "All right, Mr. Barron it's your motion, you can begin."

"Thank you, Your Honor," Peter began. "We have filed our motion to dismiss and the brief in support of our motion. As I am sure the court is aware, we predicate this motion on *State v. Knapp,* which the Supreme Court of Washington decided in 1985. In that case, the court gave defense counsel an opportunity to ask the superior court to reevaluate the question of probable cause. Defendants can move to dismiss a felony charge if, construing the evidence most favorably to the prosecution, there is simply insufficient evidence to believe that there is probable cause that the defendants committed the crime charged.

"Here we believe this motion should be granted because, based on the testimony you heard this morning, the prosecution has failed to provide sufficient evidence to constitute probable cause that my clients committed capital murder and these other very serious felonies. We do not dispute, of course, that there was a fire and that a terrible tragedy occurred when Dr. Rhonda Marsano died in that fire. It seems clear that there is probable cause to try Stephen Gray for this crime. And for obvious reasons, we will not discuss the charges against Susan O'Dell today."

Peter ran his left hand along the side of his head through his jet black hair as he turned to resume his pattern of pacing—three steps left, turn, three steps right, turn.

"But today's motion focuses on the charges against Colonel Hank Danners, Pastor Randy Wallace, Mrs. Shirley Alper, and Mrs. Ginny Kettner. The question before the court is whether there is sufficient evidence to connect these four defendants to the crimes with which they have been charged.

"The prosecutor's case against these four has been built largely on two threatening calls received by the Los Angeles office of the Bellingham clinic. Detective Dunn indicated that without these calls, probable cause would be—as he put it—a question for the court. Implicit in that statement was an admission of the self-evident fact that the prosecution has made much of the fact that one of the calls came from the home of Colonel Danners, and the other call came from the church pastored by Randy Wallace. In the abstract there may be a reasonable inference that calls made from someone's home or office were made by the owner. But such an inference cannot supply the necessary evidence for probable cause to commit murder—especially when the uncontroverted evidence shows that they could not have personally made the calls.

"That the police relied on Lisa Edgar has been established by both Miss Edgar and Detective Dunn. Her testimony conclusively places all four defendants in the Danners's study when the first call to Los Angeles was made. But Mr. Cavner's testimony makes it absolutely clear that they could not have made the call to Los Angeles while in the study, because the phone in the study is on a completely different line. Therefore the evidence presented clearly absolves these four defendants from any suggestion that they made the call.

"As to the call from Immanuel Bible Church—a threatening call by a male caller apparently disguising his voice—the uncontroverted evidence is that Pastor Randy Wallace and Colonel Hank Danners were either seated or standing in front of a large audience at the time the call was placed—an event that was recorded on the cameras of several television stations.

"Other than those two calls, the case against my client is purely guilt by association. Stephen Gray bought the gasoline cans, batteries, and wires. Stephen Gray disappeared afterwards. Stephen Gray looks guilty; therefore my clients must be guilty, or so the prosecutor contends, because Stephen Gray was a part of their group.

"Guilt by association is rejected in this country as adequate proof of anything, at least standing alone without other evidence. Without these phone calls, there is no other evidence suggesting a direct link between these four defendants and the apparent arson, only speculation. Therefore, we respectfully ask this court to dismiss all charges against these four defendants since the evidence clearly shows that none of these four had any ability to make calls either."

Peter pulled out his chair and sat down slowly. His gut was churning as the moment for decision was rapidly approaching.

Max Franklin strode confidently to the lectern and grasped it firmly with both hands.

"Your Honor, Mr. Barron has given this court an entertaining rendition of the evidence, but has failed to approach this discussion in the very way the case he cites commands. *State of Washington v Knapp* says that there must be uncontroverted evidence and that the evidence must be considered in the light most favorable to the state.

"However, his review of the evidence was conducted only from the perspective of the defendants—not from the state's perspective. Let us consider two areas of evidence. First the phone calls themselves, and second, the other evidence that was supplied earlier by affidavit and corroborated by testimony today. Looking at all the evidence leaves the clear conclusion that we have established probable cause. We do not have to establish final guilt today, just probable cause, so that we can go forward, do more investigative work, and be prepared for the full trial sometime down the road.

"Let's review the evidence now under this correct standard. Regarding the first phone call. Who was in Colonel Danners's study when the call was placed? It was not only these four defendants, but Susan O'Dell as well. And we know that Miss O'Dell was involved in this conspiracy at a very deep level since we have her on videotape helping to purchase the materials for the fire bomb. And we also know, from Lisa Edgar, that Stephen Gray was back and forth from the living room to other parts of the house.

"When this evidence is read in the light most favorable to the state— as it must for the purposes of this motion—it is reasonable to infer that Stephen Gray may well have gone into this meeting in the study for a minute or two and have learned of the plan to set the fire that led to Dr. Marsano's death. One fire bomber was in the meeting, the other was wandering around the house. Even if the call wasn't placed from the study, even if Stephen Gray made the call, there is not conclusive evidence that his actions were not a part of the secret planning going on in that meeting.

"Moreover, there is not conclusive evidence that the call was not made from the study. Mr. Cavner admitted that someone could have installed another jack, and what about a portable phone? Why couldn't the colonel have taken a portable phone from another room and made a call from the main line while physically located in his study?"

Franklin put his hand in his left pants pocket as he took a single step to the right of the lectern. "As to the call from the church, perhaps Stephen Gray did make that call. But again, what uncontroverted evidence is there to prove that the leadership committee didn't instruct him to make the call?

"This brings us to the other general body of evidence that is uncontroverted in our favor. The record clearly reflects that Colonel Danners exercised what may fairly be called an iron-fisted control on the so-called Whatcom Life Coalition. Nothing, absolutely nothing, could be done by any of the participants without his approval. Whatever reason there may be to think of Stephen Gray as a lone wolf, the *evidence* shows that Susan O'Dell—a mild-mannered little college girl—most certainly was following the colonel's direction, and we have seen her on videotape when she entered Fred Meyer to buy bomb supplies. That is how the evidence must be construed in the light most favorable to the state.

"Maybe Mr. Barron can convince a jury to construe the evidence his way; maybe I can convince them to go my way. But this court today has a responsibility to give the state the benefit of the doubt. We have enough evidence to secure a conviction if the jury believes our theory. That is all that is necessary to establish probable cause. We have done our job." Franklin walked back to his table and sat down beside a beaming Shannon Carpenter. He looked over at Wendy Mervyn, who nodded and smiled at her classmate from her seat in the front row of the other side of the bar.

Peter's stomach churned as he stood to his feet, prepared to rebut the prosecution.

"Mr. Barron please be seated. The court is prepared to rule, and I am not interested in a rebuttal at this moment."

Peter sat down and looked at his note pad. He picked up the gold pen he'd been scribbling with throughout Franklin's argument, then placed it slowly back down on the pad, sighing heavily. He looked up at the judge.

"Both sides have acknowledged," Hayden began, "that the court's duty is to construe the evidence most favorably to the state in assessing whether there is probable cause. And I have every intention of doing just that."

Peter's head dropped. Colonel Danners picked up Peter's pen and scrawled, "We lose?" on his yellow pad, looking sharply at Peter. Peter did not acknowledge the question.

"So let's review the evidence briefly. As to the call from the Danners's home on May 17, the evidence is clear and uncontroverted that the call was not made from the study—where these four defendants plus Miss O'Dell were present at 7:56. There could, of course, have been a portable phone. And there could, at least in theory, have been an illegally installed jack in the study. But there is a difference between possibilities based on speculation and possibilities based on evidence. There is no evidence that the colonel owns a portable phone, and there is certainly no evidence that he has illegally installed an extra jack in his study.

"As to the call from the church, it was a male voice, and I am asked to infer that it was the pastor who made the call since he is presumptively in charge of that building. If the call was placed at a time when the pastor was alone in his office, I would have to construe the evidence in a way favorable to the state and say that this is enough to tie the pastor to the conspiracy. But the evidence—the uncontroverted evidence— does not allow this conclusion."

Peter picked up his pen and wrote on his legal pad, then pushed it toward the colonel. "Not yet!!!" it read.

"But Mr. Franklin correctly points out that there are more than these phone calls in evidence. Colonel Danners did exercise tight control over the activities of the coalition, and he did approve everything that was done, as far as we can tell."

Danners shook his head softly, gripped with the apparent injustice that his effort to keep people from breaking the law was now being used to suggest that he was guilty of murder.

"But once again," Hayden said, taking off his glasses and laying them down on the bench. "The totality of the evidence shows that Danners's efforts to control were done for the sole purpose of trying to keep the protests absolutely within the letter of the law. Therefore the prosecution is asking me to infer that the law-abiding control efforts were a front for a man to plot violent crimes. That kind of inference is speculation. The prosecutor gets every inference the evidence allows. But he gets no inferences from speculation.

"I would note that the prosecutor has produced no evidence at all concerning Mrs. Alper or Mrs. Kettner. They have been charged under the apparent theory that the leadership team planned this fire. That is an inference that, as Mr. Barron points out, is guilt by association plus nothing, and as such it is an insufficient basis for probable cause.

"Accordingly, the defendants' motion to dismiss all charges against Henry Danners, Randy Wallace, Shirley Alper, and Virginia Kettner is granted. The court will stand in recess since there is no need to conduct any further of the scheduled proceedings in this case."

"All rise," came the cry of the bailiff.

Feeling unshackled from the judge's order, bedlam broke loose as the reporters began yelling questions as soon as the judge's door closed behind him.

$$\boxed{19}$$

Wendy Mervyn and Max Franklin walked side by side into the jammed hearing room normally used by the Whatcom County commissioners. The mere presence of a high-ranking U.S. Justice Department official would merit some news coverage in Bellingham, but the fact that she was participating in a news conference to respond to Judge Hayden's ruling earlier that morning guaranteed maximum press attendance.

All the TV cameramen switched on their glaring lights the moment the duo walked into the room. Sound technicians scrambled on the floor to position their long boom poles with microphones coated in dense grey foam. Print photographers aimed their foot-long telephoto lenses at the Yale classmates and continuously snapped their motor-driven cameras.

Max Franklin couldn't help but smile at the overflowing of media. It was the best coverage of his career—guaranteed not only to make statewide news but also the four national networks plus CNN. It was coverage of a legal loss, but in the two hours since Hayden's ruling he'd convinced himself that it was nevertheless a political gain to be shown as the leading force behind the pro-choice issue in the Evergreen State.

He strode confidently to the microphone. "Ladies and gentlemen of the press, as I'm sure most of you know, I'm Max Franklin, the prosecuting attorney for Whatcom County. I'm here today with Wendy Mervyn, the assistant attorney general of the United States from Washington, D.C. Ms. Mervyn and I were classmates at Yale Law School a few years back—she's just had a few more lucky breaks than I have."

A few local reporters chuckled—the Seattle reporters just rolled their eyes. "Ms. Mervyn is the highest ranking official in the Justice Department who supervises the department's response to violence against those engaged in the constitutionally protected activity of offering services related to reproductive freedom. Ms. Mervyn will make a statement, then I will add a few comments on today's ruling and our future plans. After that, we will both entertain questions from this fine group."

A ripple of subdued conversation ran through the overwhelmingly sympathetic crowd of some six dozen journalists and technicians as they jockeyed for position as Mervyn and Franklin switched position.

A flurry of flashes accompanied Mervyn's approach to the lectern. "Good afternoon, ladies and gentlemen. On behalf of the United States Department of Justice and the entire Clinton administration, let me express how shocked I am by today's ruling. In the guise of rejecting speculation, the court today actually rejected two hundred years of settled American jurisprudence that allows the use of circumstantial evidence at every stage of a criminal proceeding.

"Normally, the Justice Department does not comment or participate in state court prosecutions. But this is not a normal case, as it represents a frightening pattern of escalating violence against women in this nation—violence that is aimed at a woman's constitutional right to reproductive freedom. I need not remind you that this freedom is a constitutional right that has been recognized since 1973 in the seminal case of *Roe v. Wade.*

"My friend and classmate, Max Franklin, is doing an admirable job of seeking justice in this case. The United States Justice Department will endeavor to employ all of its resources to aid Mr. Franklin in the prosecution of these cowardly acts of violence that have resulted in the senseless death of Dr. Rhonda Marsano.

"But our efforts to seek justice in this case will not consist merely of supporting and assisting Mr. Franklin. In the event that the courts of Washington State see fit to let the people who are responsible for this act of terror and violence walk free, I can assure you that the United States will not hesitate to bring federal criminal charges to bring those responsible to justice."

Mervyn paused and looked slowly across the room to let her last statement sink in. "Let me be clear. We hope and expect that the state courts will clearly follow the controlling principles of law. And, again, Mr. Franklin can expect the full resources of the United States to back his efforts. Thank you."

Another flurry of flashes exploded as the two lawyers again exchanged places. Max Franklin was beaming with self-importance as he resumed center stage.

"Today the Superior Court for Whatcom County dismissed four capital murder charges and related felonies against the leaders of the so-called Whatcom Life Coalition. Tomorrow morning I will file an appeal of this unprecedented decision in the Court of Appeals in Seattle. We believe that today's decision is contrary to the facts and contrary to the law.

"We are confident that when the court of appeals judges review our briefs and the records, they will reverse this decision; and we will again be on track to secure justice in our state court system.

"The law clearly allows us to begin our prosecution with less evidence than required for a final conviction. There are investigations to be conducted, and we are making every effort to find Stephen Gray. This missing member of the pro-life coalition can provide us with the necessary evidence to get to the full and complete evidence we need for a final conviction.

"If anyone knows the whereabouts of Stephen Gray, we call on you to come forward with that knowledge. My assistant has a copy of a photo taken of Mr. Gray during a meeting held at Immanuel Bible Church. This is the church that held the last rally of the anti-abortion forces before members of that group we believe set fire to the women's clinic, brutally murdering Dr. Rhonda Marsano. And this is the church from which the second phone threat against the clinic was made. Churches that become sanctuaries for violence have crossed the line of respect that our religious institutions deserve. We will not tolerate such extremist churches in our community. I, for one, am at a loss in trying to understand how supposed Christianity can condone, support, and advocate extremism, violence, arson, and murder."

Franklin's attack on Immanuel Bible Church had not been a part of the strategy on which he and Mervyn had agreed. But his political and rhetorical juices got flowing, and he thought it was an opportune time to demonstrate that he was a staunch opponent of the religious right. Such a reputation would serve him well in his desire to become the Democrat nominee for Washington's attorney general.

Franklin paused and nodded at Jessica Angell, an anchor for CNN whose hand was waving madly in the air. "Ms. Angell, why don't you begin the questioning, if I can ask Ms. Mervyn to rejoin me."

"Yes, Mr. Franklin, I have a two part question—the first part for you and the second for Ms. Mervyn. How long do you think this appeal will take? And will the Justice Department file federal charges immediately, or will it await the final outcome of the state litigation?"

Franklin leaned over to the cluster of microphones leaning helter-skelter over the edges of the lectern. "The appeal will take from three to five months. We will do everything we can to seek expedited consideration."

"It is our current intention to wait for the final conclusion of the Washington state court system before taking action in the federal courts," Mervyn said, bending toward the microphones. "I spoke with the attorney general about this moments ago, and she confirmed our current intentions."

"Peter Laker, *Seattle Times,*" sang out a young reporter seated in the second row. "Ms. Mervyn, what is the Justice Department doing to aid the capture of Stephen Gray?"

"We have engaged in substantial efforts thus far, which cannot be fully disclosed for obvious reasons. But you can expect renewed efforts from the FBI to catch this fugitive. Within a few days, Mr. Gray will be on the FBI's Ten Most Wanted list."

Every print journalist in the room scribbled furiously.

"Mr. Franklin, Mr. Franklin," came a persistent cry from a middle-aged male reporter on the left side of the room.

"Yes, sir," Franklin replied.

"Tim English, KIRO News Radio, Seattle. How does your appeal affect these defendants' right against double jeopardy? Can they be tried a second time even if you win on appeal? And for that matter, can they be tried a second time in the federal system if you don't like the result in the state courts? Isn't that also a double jeopardy issue?"

"Excellent questions. Let me assure you there is no double jeopardy problem either way. Perhaps I will answer the state part of your question, and let Ms. Mervyn answer the federal issue.

"A person's right not to be tried twice for the same offense does not mean he cannot be put through the preliminary stages of a legal proceeding twice. It means that he cannot face a trial twice. So a defendant's right to avoid double jeopardy does not begin until a jury has been chosen and sworn. If he is found not guilty after that point, he cannot be tried again. That does not apply to a pretrial hearing such as we had today. Judge Hayden dismissed the charges at the preliminary stage. If we win on appeal, *then* there will be a trial."

Franklin stepped back from the microphones, allowing Ms. Mervyn to come forward.

"Mr. Franklin is absolutely right. The state's right to appeal these preliminary rulings cannot be debated. As to the federal system, we would not be trying any of these defendants for murder. Murder is a state charge. We would be charging and seeking convictions for violating the civil rights of Dr. Rhonda Marsano. Most of you remember the Rodney King case, I'm sure. The state court jury brought in a 'not guilty' verdict against the white police officers who were filmed beating Rodney King. Then the Justice Department charged these officers with a different crime—violating Rodney King's civil rights—and were successful in securing a conviction. That demonstrates how the Justice Department would approach this case, as well."

"Does that mean that every state case could also be a federal case if the Justice Department doesn't like the state courts' results?"

"Not at all, Mr. English," she replied. "There must be additional elements involved beyond the normal state law crime. Not every murder is a proper subject for a federal case. Two appropriate examples would be a killing that was motivated by racial prejudice and a victim who was exercising a federally protected, constitutionally protected right. And we can bring those charges no matter what the result of the state court system. Whether a person was found guilty or innocent, we can make an independent charge, so long as the additional federal elements are present."

"Mr. Franklin, Laurie Pierson, KING-TV. Will the trial of Susan O'Dell be delayed as a result of this appeal?"

Franklin paused for a moment before answering. "I'm sure all of you can appreciate that I am under a gag order in the O'Dell matter. With that in mind, I would just simply say that the case of the State of Washington versus O'Dell is a different case both factually and procedurally from the case against the four defendants who were dismissed today. They were filed on a different track. I expect that they will remain on a different track."

"Stacey Sorenson, *Portland Oregonian,*" came the shout from the back of the room. "Mr. Franklin, are you seriously pursuing the death penalty in each of these cases, or is this simply a bargaining chip?"

"Ms. Sorenson, the death penalty is not something to be taken lightly. I do not file papers seeking the death penalty except when I sincerely believe the murder case at hand warrants that penalty. If the charges are reinstated against the four defendants, I will again be in serious pursuit of the death penalty."

"And against Susan O'Dell as well?" came a follow-up question from a different part of the room.

"Yes, I am seeking the death penalty in that case as well."

Mervyn tapped Franklin inconspicuously on his side. "That's it," she whispered. "Let's quit while we're ahead."

Franklin nodded. "Thank you, ladies and gentlemen. Ms. Mervyn has just reminded me of her tight schedule. So that will have to be the last question. Again, thank you."

Vince Davis watched the entire press conference with increasing alarm as it was carried live on CNN.

He hurried to his bank the following morning and made arrangements to wire the entire balance of his Austin Hall account to the main branch of Credit Suisse in Zurich. Wearing a baseball hat and sunglasses, he boarded a Swiss Air flight bound for Zurich at five o'clock that evening.

"Suzie O'Dell and her parents are here," Sally's voice said over the intercom.

"Tell them I'll be right out," Peter replied.

Peter tapped out the last two sentences for a motion in another case he was preparing on his personal computer, saved the file, and sent an e-mail to Sally telling her to put the final touches on the document so he could sign it right after his meeting with the O'Dells. Then he got up from his desk and opened the door. All three O'Dells looked up. "Good morning, Suzie. Hi, Bill and Linda. Come in!" The trio entered Peter's office and took seats along a long leather couch opposite his mahogany desk. "How's your summer going, Suzie?" Peter asked, taking his seat behind the desk.

"OK, I guess. You know . . ." came her labored reply.

Peter caught Bill O'Dell's eyes, seeking an explanation.

"Suzie's having some trouble relaxing this summer," her father said, hugging his daughter with one arm.

"That's understandable," Peter replied, his voice considerably toned down from his salutation. "Suzie, I understand you have a job—how's that working out?"

"It's good," she replied. "I like waitressing, and working at night is better than I expected. The tips are pretty good."

"And," Linda said, looking at her daughter before continuing, "working at night helps her keep her mind off the case. She comes home exhausted and falls right to sleep."

"Frankly, Peter, this has been real hard on all of us. Especially when we see this character Franklin on TV talking about seeking the death penalty. That's not an easy thing to just listen to and shrug off."

"I apologize for Mr. Franklin," Peter said, exhaling loudly. "Lawyers rarely realize the emotions their clients are feeling. We see a case like a giant chess game where we push pieces here and there, then our opponent counters by pushing a piece into another spot. We don't seem to realize that our chess men are real people with real feelings about where they're being pushed."

Linda nodded knowingly.

"Well, the reason I wanted you folks to come in today was to go over the latest developments with you and get your consent on the next steps in Suzie's case. As you know, a couple of weeks ago Judge Hayden dismissed the charges against the colonel, Pastor Wallace, Shirley, and Ginny."

"We're happy for them," Linda replied, "especially for Colonel Danners. He and his wife have been so kind to Suzie. I was really glad that he was able to put this behind him."

Peter picked his gold pen up off his desk and began to fiddle with the cap. It was a nervous habit that made Gwen frown whenever he did it in her presence. "Well, it's not quite behind him. We got the formal notice in the mail this morning that the prosecutor indeed took the case to the court of appeals in Seattle. If we lose that appeal, he and the others will be back in court just like Suzie."

"Is that likely?" Linda asked.

"It's hard to say. I'd say it's fifty-fifty either way. The judges in this state are mostly pro-abortion, and whether they admit it or not, abortion cases get treated differently than almost any other subject matter. Even groups like the ACLU get off their high horse when abortion is the subject. People can protest almost anything and the ACLU will back them, but protest abortion and suddenly free speech has limits. I think some in the ACLU are aware of the obvious hypocrisy, but the feminists in their ranks carry the day. Judges are the same way. Abortion distortion, that's what most pro-life litigators call it."

"What will happen to Suzie's trial date with this appeal going on? It's scheduled for September now, isn't it?" her father asked.

"Yeah," Peter replied. "And that's exactly what I want to talk about. We have some choice in this matter. We can simply go forward with the trial in September, and Suzie will be tried alone while the appeal is going on, or we can ask Judge Hayden to delay the trial until the appeal is settled for the others. If we do that, we'll have to tell the court that we want the case consolidated with the others."

"Is there any chance the judge would grant a motion to dismiss the charges against Suzie, like he did with the others?" Linda asked with a hopeful expression.

Peter shook his head slowly. "No, I don't think there's any chance of that. If they didn't have Suzie on video at Fred Meyer's and didn't have her fingerprints all over the one gas can they found at the scene, then she would have been in the exact same position as the other four. But there is much stronger circumstantial evidence against Suzie . . ." Peter's voice trailed off as he shook his head.

"So what do you recommend?" Bill asked.

"It's a hard question from the perspective of legal strategy," Peter replied. "If she is tried alone, she seems a little more of a sympathetic character—just an innocent young girl who has been singled out for mistreatment. If she is tried in the group, there may be some tendency to see Suzie as a point of compromise. The jurors might say, 'Well, there's not enough evidence here to convict everyone, so let's convict Suzie. After all, she was caught on videotape.'

"But on the other hand," Peter continued, "jurors might say this whole case is so flimsy, even the videotape is being blown out of proportion. It's just really hard to say which way they might go."

"How long will this appeal take?" Bill asked.

"I can only make an estimate," Peter answered. "They have forty-five days to file their brief; we have thirty days after that to file ours, then they have twenty days to file their reply. That's about three months just for briefing, which would take us into mid-October or so. Then it would be scheduled for oral argument in another month or two after that. Decisions take anywhere from one to four months. I think that, because of the nature and seriousness of this case, the court will try to expedite these time frames, but I wouldn't expect an answer until around the first of the year."

"If we tried it in September, we would get this behind us sooner," Linda suggested.

"Yeah, but if we wait, there's a greater chance the FBI might find that creep, Stephen Gray," her father said. "Wouldn't that help her out?"

"Oh, very much." Peter replied. "Suzie, what do you think about this?"

Suzie looked up and smiled a scared little smile that invigorated all of Peter's protective instincts. "I like the idea of more time to catch Stephen Gray. But I was thinking of waiting for another reason."

"What's that?" Peter asked.

"I was just thinking that if the colonel and the others are going to go through this too, I would like to go through it together. At least I wouldn't feel quite so alone."

"Chess pieces," Peter mused aloud.

"What?" her mother asked.

"I've been giving you advice as if we were playing chess, like I mentioned earlier. Suzie has just given us a perfectly good reason to wait. Chess players never seem to think of those things; those being pushed around the board, do."

"Sounds good to me," Suzie's father replied.

Mother and daughter nodded their approval.

"OK, I'll prepare the motion right away," Peter replied.

"When will we know if the judge approves it?"

"In a couple weeks," Peter answered.

"Let's pray that we made the right decision," Bill said, standing and taking his daughter by the hand.

"Not a bad idea," Peter said.

It took Vince Davis about ten days of touring Switzerland by train to choose a new place to live under the name Austin Hall. The remote village of Wengen, in the Jungfrau district of the central Alps, seemed as safe a place as he could find with the kind of comfort and beauty that he desired.

Wengen was a carless village that allowed only a few small vehicles, not much bigger than golf carts, to carry luggage from the train station to the dozen or so small hotels and guest houses. Everyone walked or rode bikes to their destinations.

Vince arrived in Wengen midday on a Saturday. Using the passport of Austin Hall for identification, he checked into the Hotel Eiger. The registration clerk looked at the passport, then up at Vince, whose ten-day-old beard made him look considerably older than his picture. "Will you be staying with us long, Mr. Hall?" the clerk asked.

"Long enough to find a rental," Vince replied. "I'll be in the area for several months."

Wearing his light-sensitive prescription sunglasses and a baseball cap, Vince felt comfortable enough with his appearance to tour the city and surrounding countryside for a place to rent. A quiet little village on the edge of the Alps, Wengen's narrow cobblestone streets were comfortably filled with hundreds of tourists making a brief stop on their way from Lauterbrunnen through the picturesque valley to the "Top of Europe." Americans were a common sight in Wengen, Vince reasoned, and no one would pay any attention to a single American male hiking the Alpine trails and gazing at the spectacular scenery.

The balcony of his room at the Eiger looked out the left onto the treeless slopes that ran up gently above the timberline until the sudden thrust of the mountains jutted out in jagged glacial peaks of extraordinary beauty. To the right, Vince could see a different valley from the one where he had begun his ascent. It was a narrow little valley hedged in by the Jungfraulich on the near side and another sheer wall on the far side rising to an impressive but slightly smaller group of peaks. At night he could see the lights of the village of Grindlewald twinkling some three thousand feet below on the valley floor. During the day he could see the thin ribbons of five or six waterfalls that evidenced the trek of melting snow and glacial ice. Vince, who had traveled extensively, had never seen a more majestic and spectacular view.

Sometimes, when he saw the full moon rise and illuminate the valley and cast shadows on the mighty steeps, his mind wandered back to his childhood and the many times he sat in his father's church singing of the magnificence of God and His creation. These were thoughts that he had learned to suppress for more than a decade and a half, but the sheer beauty of his surroundings and the aching loneliness that began to settle into his soul made his thoughts of God a little more difficult to put aside. To counter his contemplative mood, he would walk back inside his room and flip on the TV, allowing the raunchiness of European broadcasting to dominate his already seared conscience.

It was not cheap at all to live in Wengen—even after finding a very nice room in a boarding house two weeks after his arrival. The house lay a half mile up a walking trail from the Hotel Eiger. One day, in early August, he boarded the train to Lauterbrunnen, caught the main train to Geneva, and changed yet again to his final destination in France, to the city of Nancy. In less than an hour he'd found the Western Union office, where he anonymously completed the paperwork to send a message to Jane and Karen at their home in North Hollywood.

Top Ten hit put me in the mood for overseas jaunt. Ran a little shy of living expenses. $250,000 by wire to Swiss Bankcorp, Geneva with 72 hours. Account 5827563. Otherwise, Top Ten DJ in Reno will learn the secret identity of my songwriting duet.

The diamond and ruby matching necklace and earrings glistened in the cloudless sky on Shannon Carpenter's skin as Max Franklin escorted her from his car to the front door of the Chart House Restaurant. Franklin had promised Carpenter a night without discussion of the office; his preoccupation with the hearing and Wendy Mervyn's extended visit warranted some reparations in their relatively new relationship. Although he had vehemently defended his sexual fidelity when Carpenter finally confronted him, it was not without an inward struggle to do so. That "absolutely nothing happened" was true—but not because of any lack of effort on Franklin's part. A nice dinner out would make amends, he thought.

The hostess seated them at a corner table with an unobstructed view of the bay. It was a quiet scene. A single Japanese freighter lay silently anchored a quarter mile offshore. The lights of the pulp mill, a mile away on the south side of the downtown core, illuminated a plume of ever-billowing smoke. Situated on the edge of the hill that was home to the university, the Chart House rarely fell victim to the mill's aroma because of a favorable wind pattern.

"Shannon," Franklin said, looking over the top of his menu. "I know I promised you no discussions about work, but can I ask for just one exception?"

She rolled her eyes, then set her menu down on the table with a quiet thud. Crossing her arms, she leaned back and sighed, "Oh, go ahead."

"Well, it's really partly about work, and partly about my personal future."

"That sounds a little better."

"We got this motion in today from Barron in Spokane. He's asking the court to delay Susan O'Dell's trial pending the appeal. He wants the cases consolidated if the appeal is reversed."

"Gee, I'm a little surprised—not at the delay but that he wants the trials consolidated. I'd think he'd want to keep the others away from the evidence we have against O'Dell."

"Yeah, that's what I've always thought, too. But anyhow, I need to decide whether I'm going to agree to his motion or fight it, and I'd like your opinion."

"OK," she said as she leaned forward and picked up her water glass. "But this sounds like all work and no personal future. Mind explaining?"

"Fine," he replied shaking his head. "First off, I'm simply not prepared to let Peter Barron get anything easily. Whatever he wants, I am inclined to oppose, especially after he yelled at you that day."

"Thanks," she replied coyly.

"But the main reason I am thinking about agreeing to his motion really involves my desire to run for attorney general. September is a prime time for elections and fund raisers and fairs. If I am going to be the statewide candidate for attorney general in two years, I think I had better get out and around the entire state. A September trial would hinder that."

"That sounds like a good idea. If you decide to wait and try the case later, your political appearances will more likely be the consistent front-page, above-the-fold kind of story you want, without nearly so much competition."

"You know, you've got a pretty good political head on your shoulders."

"Thanks for noticing," she replied, smiling demurely.

She really is considerably better looking than Wendy Mervyn, Franklin thought. But concerning his greater infatuation with power, she couldn't hope to compete. For now, though, he would make do.

Smiling, Franklin reached out and took her hand. "You really are beautiful, you know that?"

20

The fall passed quickly for Peter and Gwen. Peter's case load was routine, and he spent as much time as possible with his wife and daughter. Gwen continued her habit of going for a two-mile walk every day—although as she progressed to the middle stage of her pregnancy, it took about ten minutes longer to complete her loop. With each passing day, Gwen became less nervous about losing her pregnancy and more content with the amount of time Peter was spending with her and Casey. But every time the subject of Bellingham would come up on their walks, Gwen's insides flared with a fear even she began to label as irrational.

In the last week of September, Peter received notice that oral arguments had been scheduled in the appeal for his four clients on Monday, November 1, at 9 A.M. Peter talked Gwen into driving over with him on the Friday evening before and spending the weekend with him as he prepared for oral argument.

She wanted to bring Casey along, but the issues and briefs were far too complex to easily accommodate the constant interruptions of a seven-year-old, so Casey stayed with Grandma and Grandpa in Spokane. On Sunday evening, Colonel Danners, Randy Wallace, Ginny Kettner, and all their spouses, together with the widowed Shirley Alper, joined Peter and Gwen for a quiet dinner in the hotel restaurant of the downtown Marriott.

In the early part of the evening, Shirley was in rare form and even had Ginny laughing. After dinner, Peter again briefed them on the expected procedure the following day; and by the time he had finished, Ginny was crying openly and bitterly. Even Evie Danners, who was usually stoic and distant, displayed a show of emotion. They had reason to be afraid—Peter had told them honestly that he could make no guarantees. At the end of the evening, they prayed.

21

"Mrs. Alper! Mrs. Alper! Do you expect to be facing murder charges after today's hearing?"

"Good morning," Shirley replied cheerily as she walked briskly toward the courthouse. "It's a beautiful Seattle morning, don't you think? I can't remember a more beautiful first of November in several years." She was nearly laughing as she taunted the reporters with a series of fluffy non-responses.

After about three attempts, the pack of media wolves withdrew to get in position for the next arrival. Peter had briefed his clients appropriately. All were to be pleasant and say nothing of substance. Ginny Kettner simply called many of her former colleagues by name and shouted her personalized hellos. She would not, under any circumstances, let the members of her former profession see any evidence of the paralyzing fear that had kept her up most of the night.

Peter and Gwen walked through with little difficulty after Peter called out to the vanguard, "My only statement will be in the courtroom in a little while. Thanks so much."

Franklin paused and pontificated for about three minutes upon his arrival with Shannon Carpenter and John Dunn.

The courtroom was no bigger than Judge Hayden's trial chamber. A short bench of modern blond oak was centered with a clerk's station just off to its left. Three matching brown leather chair backs peered out from behind the bench.

A small crowd of lawyers for the three other cases to be argued that morning sat crowded together on the first two rows on the right side. The Bellingham defendants and their immediate families occupied the first two rows of the opposite half of the spectator area. About twenty of their friends and supporters sat immediately behind them.

The press had been assigned to three of the six rows on the right-hand side of the courtroom. No cameras were allowed, yet every allocated seat was taken by the print media and TV journalists. Nearly a dozen other reporters stood in the back of the courtroom with their pads ready, hoping that the bailiff who was controlling the seating would release one of the remaining rows.

Jane Hayward and a woman whom Shirley Alper recognized as the Bellingham clinic's bookkeeper slipped into the back row at about five minutes before nine. The clerk had wisely scheduled the case of *State of Washington v. Danners, et al.,* first on the docket. The sheer intensity of the audience and media would, he surmised, have swallowed the concentration of the participants for any other case.

Peter took his seat at the left counsel table, alone. Franklin and Shannon busied themselves with files and copies of red and blue appellate briefs.

A short buzz was audible in the courtroom as the bailiff lumbered to attention. "All rise. The Court of Appeals for the State of Washington, Division One is now in session."

Three judges entered the room—Wilson, Haynesworth, and Rogers—and took their seats front and center. Bob Haynesworth, as the chief judge, occupied the center seat. He was a former Democratic state senator, having served on this bench since 1982. He had hoped to be appointed to the federal bench, but twelve straight years of Republican presidents had made that impossible. By the time Clinton had taken control of the White House, Haynesworth's political contacts had grown cold, and he had been told by a twenty-two-year-old aide that he was too old to be actively considered for a federal appointment.

Wilson and Rogers had been big-firm lawyers with little political experience. Michael Wilson was a nominal Republican who grew tired of practice and simply lobbied the bar to get support in a popular election to fill an open seat. Carol Rogers had been the local bar association president and had steered clear of non-judicial politics. She was assumed by many to be somewhat of a feminist.

"Case number one," Haynesworth said, "State against Danners and others. Mr. Franklin, if you are ready, you may begin."

Franklin walked confidently and sat his notes and copies of five cases carefully on the lectern. "May it please the court. My name is Max Franklin and I represent the State of Washington in this important appeal. It is the state's contention that the trial court erroneously dismissed capital murder charges, plus three other related felonies, against each of these four defendants, under the false belief that circumstantial evidence could not be used to supply the elements for probable cause—"

"Counsel," Judge Wilson interrupted, "is that precisely what Judge Hayden ruled? Didn't he rule that what you believed to be circumstantial evidence was mere suspicion?"

"Perhaps that's what he believed he was doing. It's our position that he wrongfully rejected circumstantial evidence."

"Yes, but that's a slightly different argument, isn't it? Do you believe that a suspicion is the same as circumstantial evidence?"

"No, Your Honor. I certainly do not."

"That's good," Wilson replied. "Then why don't you focus on your evidence and tell us why you think it falls into the category of circumstantial evidence rather than suspicion."

"Fine, Your Honor. There are three main points of evidence that we believe were misconstrued by the trial court as speculation when in fact, each of these points were proper inferences drawn from the undisputed demonstrative evidence.

"First, there was the evidence of the totality of control—exercised by Colonel Danners. The defense does not really dispute this evidence. Danners and the committee dominated all activity by the Whatcom Life Coalition.

"We ask this court to draw an inference from that evidence—an inference that supports a finding of probable cause. If Danners controlled everything, it is permissible to infer that he controlled the activity of Stephen Gray, who clearly appears to have set the fire that killed Dr. Rhonda Marsano."

"But counsel," Rogers interjected, "can we infer an illegal activity when Danners's control was always exercised to make sure the group behaved itself? Calling it control is a bit general, isn't it?"

"Not at all, Judge Rogers," Franklin countered. "One person may interpret his action as control, another as insisting on lawfulness. These are the kinds of questions settled by juries, not by motions to dismiss. It is a matter of interpretation, which is not the kind of dispute that should result in the dismissal of a murder charge.

"The same thing is true for our second point of circumstantial evidence. It is true that the only evidence concerning the threatening call made from the church is that it was done at a time when Danners and Wallace were on the stage in front of a group of people. And further, that Gray was out of the room at the same time. But, once again, it is reasonable to infer that Gray was under the control of Danners.

"Second, there are at least three ways that one of these four defendants could have made the call from Danners' home, consistent with the evidence. First, they could have had a portable phone. Second, they could have used a phone plugged into an extra extension that Danners could have wired into his den. Why would he want a study without any connection to his main phone line? That doesn't make sense, and Danners probably saw his mistake and remedied it by simply installing his own line.

"Third, any member of the leadership committee could have slipped out of the study and made that call from one of the other bedrooms without being noticed by the group congregating in the living room. If someone on the leadership committee made the call threatening the Bellingham clinic, then there is strong circumstantial evidence that the members of the leadership committee were part and parcel of Gray's action in burning the clinic."

"Counsel, your time has expired," Haynesworth said. "Mr. Barron, you may begin."

Peter walked to the podium with a single 4 x 6 index card containing some key points, plus copies of all three briefs in case they demanded an explanation of any particular page.

"May it please the court. The defendants respectfully suggest that the state is still asking this court to engage in wild speculation. The evidence strongly suggests the involvement of Stephen Gray in the fire and subsequent murder. But, the evidence against him is purely circumstantial and based on inferences. Gray spoke publicly about wanting to go farther than mere protests. Gray is on videotape purchasing the materials that appear to have been used to make the firebomb. And Gray disappeared simultaneously with the discovery of the fire.

"To infer that Gray is responsible for the fire is a permissible inference of probable cause based on circumstantial evidence. It is not wild speculation to believe that he is responsible. That is the kind and quality of evidence necessary to sustain a holding that there is probable cause to try a person for murder.

"I ask this court to compare that appropriate use of circumstantial evidence that points to the guilt and inferences of Stephen Gray as compared to the inferences based on speculation made by the state against these four defendants."

Judge Wilson spoke first. "But doesn't the state make a reasonable point about its three pieces of evidence that point toward the involvement of these defendants? We may or may not agree with these theories if we were jurors, but aren't we required to give the state the benefit of the doubt?"

"Yes, the state is entitled to certain presumptions, Your Honor. But, there is a marked difference between believing one version of evidence that simply asks the jurors to make an interpretation as opposed to having the jurors make up whole new pieces of physical evidence in order to make an inference.

"They have to make up a portable phone, which is pure speculation. They have to make up an illegal jack—again speculation. I would suggest that when they are having to make up physical items for which no proof exists, then we have gone beyond circumstantial evidence and jumped to a naked suspicion."

"Counsel, a medical doctor died," Rogers began, "because she wanted to offer choices to women. These defendants had targeted her clinic for protests. A federal judge found at least some of their protests to be unprotected activity and had enjoined further such behavior. Can't we find that there is probable cause to believe they were acting in malice towards this clinic based on those federal court findings against your clients?"

"I don't think that the technicalities the federal court mentioned in its order support a finding of the kind of malice necessary to sustain a conviction for murder or arson."

"Technicalities, Counsel? You call trespassing and loud chanting that interferes with a woman's constitutional rights a 'technicality'?"

"That evidence was disputed, Your Honor; and the court simply said, 'If you protesters claim you do not wish to pursue certain lines of behavior, then I will enjoin against those practices since you say you don't want to do them anyway.'"

Rogers persisted. "That's an interesting explanation; but we don't have the full federal court record in front of us, nor do we have the ability to overturn the federal court's ruling. We can only read the order and apply it exactly as it is written. Isn't that right, Mr. Barron?"

"Yes, it is, Your Honor. But conceding your point for a moment, the most one can infer from the federal court order is that the defendants had a motive. Probable cause for a murder charge requires more than a motive. In some murders many people may have motives to kill the victim. Proof of motive alone is not enough to demonstrate probable cause. There's got to be at least some evidence that these defendants acted in accord with that motive and that their actions were connected to the fire and the death. That kind of connective evidence is simply missing."

"But don't you think we should be very careful about dismissing capital murder cases?" Rogers asked.

"Yes, Your Honor. But this court should also be very careful about upholding the constitutional requirements here. Probable cause is no mere legal test created by some obscure court decision. The Constitution of the United States demands that its citizens be protected from frivolous criminal charges. And the standard that our forefathers chose was probable cause. They understood that standard to require real evidence before real people would have to go through the misery and heartache of being tried for a serious crime. Americans shouldn't have to stand trial for murder if the best a government prosecutor can do is to stand before the court and say, 'Well maybe the defendant owned a portable phone.' That is not the kind of justice our forefathers had in mind."

"Thank you, Mr. Barron, your time has expired," Haynesworth said. "Mr. Franklin, you have less than a minute for rebuttal."

"Your Honor, I would just say one thing. It seems strange that Mr. Barron can stand before this court and plead the constitutional rights of his clients. But these are people who are organized for the very purpose of denying the constitutional rights of women. Why should they—"

"Counsel, are you suggesting that these four defendants do not have the ordinary constitutional rights of every person who is accused of a crime in this country?" Rogers asked. "Can we dispense with a jury and simply hang people once the charges have been filed if the facts suggest that they were conducting anti-abortion activity?"

"No, Your Honor, they certainly have *some* procedural rights," Franklin replied.

"Which procedural rights do they lose because they are pro-life, Counsel?" Rogers asked again.

A red light flashed on the lectern. "Uh . . . I see that my time is up," Franklin said. "Thank you very much."

"The matter will be taken under submission. A decision will be issued in due course," Haynesworth announced. "We're going to take a five-minute recess before the next case to allow the courtroom to be cleared promptly and quietly."

The wind blew thin wisps off the top of the new-fallen snow. Vince had seen a few white Christmases, but this was his first white Thanksgiving. Of course, it was not a holiday in the Swiss Alps, just a Thursday like any other Thursday. After rolling out of bed and taking in the view from his balcony for several minutes, Vince started a fire and ate a light breakfast of bread and jam. Soon the kindling burned brightly, inflaming the larger pieces of wood.

The warmth of the blaze reminded him of the many evenings he and Rhonda had snuggled up together before her fireplace in Bellingham. One memory led to another, and soon Vince was plunged deep in thought about his baby that Rhonda had been carrying—a thought he had long suppressed with an iron will. Suddenly, he felt compelled to get out of there—away from the fire. The image of Rhonda and his baby in a blaze was more than even he could bear.

Brushing away a few bitter tears, Vince threw on his parka and headed down the wanderweg toward the village. Christmas decorations were beginning to appear here and there in the village and made the day seem a bit more traditional. He was hoping that perhaps he would meet another lonely American or two in the Gasthaus Krone, where he intended to spend the afternoon.

If he had taken the train into Zurich or Lucerne, he could have found a restaurant or two featuring turkey dinners for traveling Americans, but broiled chicken was the closest he could come amidst the mountains in Wengen. Gerhard Stuckelburg, the proprietor of the Gasthaus, had taken a liking to Vince—or Austin Hall, as he knew him. Frequently Stuckelburg would take Vince into his kitchen to teach him the art of European cooking. It wasn't fancy fare like he would have learned if he had settled in the French-speaking portion of Switzerland. But the sausages and potatoes, veal, vegetables, and beef suited Vince's personal tastes much better anyway. And lately, he relished the sheer purposefulness of any sort of work. Today, however, he would simply eat, drink French wine, sit, and stare at the mountains and swirling snow.

Around four in the afternoon, he got up abruptly from his seat in the corner and walked deliberately—so as not to stumble—out the front door of the restaurant and down the stairs. His near-intoxication caused him to look both ways for traffic, even though cars never graced the town's streets. He staggered slightly as he mounted the curb and went directly into the lobby of the Hotel Eiger. He ascended about a half dozen stairs and began to turn to his left away from the front desk, then stopped and nodded at the middle-aged woman behind the desk.

Krista had worked the registration desk since the first day Vince checked into the hotel ten weeks earlier, and he had been unfailingly polite to her ever since. She liked his friendliness but would never have dared to ask him why he stayed so long in Wengen. Like all Swiss, she placed considerable value on privacy.

Vince continued down the hall past the restaurant and plopped down hard on a wooden bench in front of the hotel's sole pay phone.

He picked up the receiver, put in a Swiss Franc, and punched the access code for AT&T Direct. He heard the familiar bong and punched another series of numbers followed by the credit card number that Jane and Karen had given him to use to bill calls from Bellingham. The card still worked.

"Hello?" a female voice said. Vince could hear the sounds of other people in the background.

"Mom, this is Vince."

"Vince? Vince! Is it really you?"

"Yeah, it's me."

She heard enough to know that he was drunk. "Son, where are you?"

"I'm in Europe, I can't say exactly where."

"What are you doing in Europe?"

"Oh, I jus' needed some time to get away and think. . . . oh, you know . . ."

"How long have you been there?"

"A little—a long while, Mom. I really can't say . . . uh . . . exactly."

The line was silent for about twenty seconds.

"Are you still there, Mom?"

"Yes Vince, honey. I'm sorry, it's just been so long since I've heard from you."

"Yeah, four years is a long time, I've been real busy. . . ."

"We were trying to find you about a month ago—tracked you to California and talked to some woman named Karen, who we thought was your boss. At least that's what your neighbor told us. But Karen said you didn't work there anymore and she had no idea where you were."

"Why were you trying to find me?"

"Oh, Vince, we wanted you to come. . ." Her calm voice rapidly changed to tears. ". . . to your father's funeral."

"What? Dad?" Vince jumped to his feet, hitting his head on the phone. "What happened?"

"He was just sitting in the church study and had a massive heart attack right there at his desk. He lived for about four hours, then just slipped away."

"Ah, Mom, I'm sorry." Vince began sobbing again. He was drunk enough that his usual tightly-reigned emotions flowed freely through his voice.

"You know, Vince," his mother said through sniffles, "you were your father's deepest disappointment. His last prayer was not for himself, but for you. He prayed that you would find the Lord. Then he cried and asked God to forgive him for being a bad father to you."

"That's . . . that's . . . ." Vince couldn't complete the thought.

"Vincent, why don't you come home? Come home and see your sister and me. In fact, Christy is here today with her husband and a little niece you've never even heard of. She's about two and looks just like Christy did when you used to call her 'Tee-Tee.'"

"Mom, I—I need ta go . . . this is all just too hard."

"Vince, I know it's hard, but give—"

"Mom, I love you. I really really do. Bye." He hung the receiver up quickly before he changed his mind.

Several hours later, the phone rang at Karen and Jane's Los Angeles home. "Karen, would you get that?" Jane called from the kitchen.

"Hello," Karen said mutely.

"Hello, Jane?"

"No. Karen. Who's calling?" she said.

"Oh, hi Karen, this is Vince."

"What do you want?" Her tone changed to disdain. "Another little advance on your expense account?"

"You wanna know what I want? I want out. I am sick and tired of hiding. You two have got to fix this thing so I am off the hook. I never bargained for the kind of heat you two have generated."

"I have no idea what you are talking about," Karen said. Jane looked into the living room. "It's Vince," Karen mouthed the words silently to her roommate.

"Get off it," Vince replied. "The two of you like to brag about your connections in Washington and how you can control this deal in Bellingham. I want it controlled. I want this fixed. I want off the FBI list. I want out."

Jane picked up the extension and listened in silence.

"I'm afraid things are a little more complicated than you seem to believe—assuming I have any idea what you are talking about, which I don't," Karen replied.

"What's wrong? FBI got your phone bugged? Lose the innocence, it's not becoming," Vince snarled.

"I don't believe I know who you are," Karen said with a sarcastic tone in her voice.

"That's what you told my mom, apparently. And by the way, thanks for trying to find me and tell me about my dad."

"How are we supposed to find you? You're in hiding, remember?"

"Did you try or didn't you? I want to know—it's important to me."

"Yeah, we tried."

"You're lying, I can tell it in your voice. I think someone important needs to hear a few details about this little fire of yours."

"Get lost, you—" She slammed down the phone.

Jane walked into the living room and plopped down in the arm chair. "So what are we going to do with him?"

"He's all talk," Karen said disgustedly.

"But what if—"

"He'll regret it. Badly."

Gwen smiled as Peter headed their Explorer down Interstate 90 toward Spokane.

"What are you smiling about?" Peter inquired.

"You. You surprised me today, helping with the Christmas shopping, and it's not even Christmas Eve yet."

"Hey, I know my priorities—" The car phone rang and diverted his attention.

"Peter's car, Peter doin' the talkin'," he said, doing his best Lum and Abner imitation.

"It's Sally. I'm sorry for calling, but our answering service called me as soon as I got in. You've received three calls from Seattle reporters in the last fifteen minutes. Looks like the court of appeals has issued a ruling."

"Oh, boy," Peter said, sighing loudly. "Any indication which way?"

"None. Do you want me to call and let you know?"

"No, I'm dying of curiosity. Just give me the first name and number and I'll find out myself." Peter punched the numbers into the phone's memory as Sally called them out. "Great, Sally, I'll call you back." He hit several buttons to reset the dial tone, then the memory button.

"Tim English, please," Peter said.

"Speaking."

"Tim, Peter Barron. I'm returning your call."

"Barron? Oh, yeah, the lawyer from Spokane. I was just calling to get your reaction to the court of appeals ruling this morning. OK, if I roll tape?"

"Uh, yeah, I guess. But I don't know how the judges ruled yet, you're my first indication."

"Oh, well, I guess they affirmed the trial court. It was a two-to-one vote. Haynesworth dissented."

"Yahooooo!" Peter yelled in delight. Turning to Gwen, he whispered, "We won, can you believe it? The charges are dismissed!"

"That'll make a good sound bite. First time I've ever gotten a reaction like that out of a lawyer," the reporter said, chuckling. "I just talked to the prosecutor. He indicates that he's going to study an appeal to the state Supreme Court. What do you think of your chances?"

"Two courts have confirmed that there is not enough evidence to even take my clients to trial. These people are innocent—I am very confident that will be the final result as well."

"Let me check my tape," he said, pausing for a few seconds. "That came out fine. Thanks Mr. Barron, and congratulations."

Peter turned on his turn signal, looked over his right shoulder, crossed over into the right lane of travel, and then continued until he could stop safely on the shoulder of the interstate.

"You gonna call Sally?"

"First things first," he said, leaning over and kissing his wife energetically.

"What was that for?"

"That was for your sacrifices so I could do this case," he said seriously. "Yessss!" he squealed suddenly in unrestrained delight.

Gwen shook her head with a bewildered smile. "I'm just glad you won. That's going to be a great Christmas present for everyone concerned."

"It sure is," Peter said exuberantly. "I need to call my clients right away. I'll get the numbers from Sally."

"Does this mean you have to go to work when we get to town?"

"Not a chance. Twenty minutes on the phone is all I need—and I can get that all done in the car."

Gwen smiled in amazement. Maybe he was a changed man after all, just like he'd been assuring her so often in recent days.

22

Vince set his luggage down in a heap in front of the distinctive red phone booth. Sounds of heavy traffic were still audible even after he shut the door.

He fumbled for change. He had grown used to the feel of Swiss Francs—British coins were a new challenge. Hearing the dial tone, he punched in a long series of numbers, glancing at a card he held in his hand.

"Whatcom County prosecuting attorney," the receptionist said.

"Mr. Franklin, please, I'm calling from Europe."

"Oh, I'm terribly sorry, Mr. Franklin is not available."

"Tell him it's Stephen Gray. I think he'll take my call."

"I'm sure he would, Mr. Gray, but he's in court. Can someone else help you?"

"Isn't he the one trying the Rhonda Marsano case?"

"Yes he is. But Shannon Carpenter is assisting him. She can take your call, if you'd like."

"OK, I guess."

Shannon Carpenter nearly dropped the receiver when the receptionist told her that someone named Stephen Gray was calling from Europe. "Yes, of course I'll take his call," she replied to the receptionist's inquiry.

"Hello," she said, her voice trembling. "Mr. Gray?"

"So you know who I am?"

"Yes, I do. . . . uh . . . Where are you calling from, Mr. Gray?"

"Let's just say Europe. That's close enough."

It suddenly occurred to Carpenter that she should try to have the call traced, but she had no idea how to go about it. She sat silently for a moment, trying to think of what to say next.

"Listen, I'm not volunteering to come back there to be railroaded for something I didn't do."

"We'd give you a fair shake, Mr. Gray, if your story checked out. As long as you stay on the run you're going to be our prime suspect."

"Well, that's a chance I'll have to take, for now. But I am going to tell you who's really responsible for the fire and Dr. Marsano's death."

"Colonel Danners?"

"No . . . He and I never got along, but it's not him. The owners of the clinic hired me to burn it and make it look like the pro-lifers did it."

Carpenter, who had been standing when the phone rang, sat, dumbfounded, on the edge of her desk.

"It's no story. Subpoena their records, you'll find a money trail to prove it. The way I figure it, I'm not guilty of much more than burning a building at the request of its owner. Still, I'm going to hold out here a little longer until you've had a chance to check the facts."

"Murder for hire isn't excusable under any circumstances, Mr. Gray."

"I didn't murder Rhonda, no way. In fact . . . oh never mind, I'm saying too much. Rhonda was an accident. She was supposed to get out. Maybe Karen did something to her—knocked her out or something. But I had no idea Rhonda was going to be in that fire."

"OK, we'll listen to you. Maybe we can make a deal, but I can't offer immunity without my boss. You've gotta call back."

"The only thing I gotta do right now is get off this phone before you complete some kind of trace. Follow the money. You'll find your real killer."

Vince hung up the phone and looked rapidly in both directions. Months of running had instilled in him a paranoia he never knew he was capable of, and he didn't like it. He checked his inside jacket pocket once more and felt his new passport safely inside. It was as good or better than any forgery Jane and Karen had ever furnished him.

Dave Cummings, with newly red hair and a four-month-old beard, was about to go home for Christmas.

Shannon Carpenter slipped into the last row of Judge Patrick Garvis's courtroom. Franklin was just finishing a sentencing on a rape case. The public defender asked for probation; Franklin asked for twenty years. He got fifteen.

Walking triumphantly down the center aisle of the courtroom after the trial, Franklin caught sight of his assistant. He approached her, smiling.

"Now that's how to argue a sentence. Did you hear all that?" he said.

"Most of it. We gotta talk. Now!"

"What is it?"

Her voice dropped to a faint whisper. "Stephen Gray called."

Without a word, Franklin grabbed her by the hand and led her into the jury room adjacent to the courtroom. He closed the door behind them.

"Stephen Gray—are you sure it was him?"

"Yeah. About twenty minutes ago. He was calling from somewhere in Europe."

"What'd he say?"

"He said that the owners of the clinic hired him to burn the clinic down. He said that Rhonda—that's what he called her—was either an accident or one of the owners knocked her out. She was supposed to be out of the building, according to him."

"That's crazy."

"I know it sounds crazy, but I think he *might* be telling the truth."

"So is he coming in so we can check out his story?"

"I don't think so, not yet, anyway."

"You don't think so!" Franklin screamed in a burst of anger. "Didn't you think to ask him?"

"Of course I asked him! I told him you might offer him some kind of deal if his story checked out, but that he had to call again for that to happen."

"So what did he say to that?"

"'No thanks,' and then he hung up."

"You think he was in Europe?"

"I don't know. All I know is I could hear a bunch of traffic. Maybe some airplane noise, too. I can't be sure of that."

"Did he say anything else?"

"Yeah, he said to subpoena the financial records of the clinic owners. He said we'd find a money trail leading us to the real killers if we did that."

"Humph," Franklin snorted, thinking things over. "What'd ya know. Stephen Gray called."

"So are we going to subpoena the records?"

"I think so."

"Think so?" Carpenter asked incredulously.

"Yeah. Gotta check with the Justice Department first. They can get California business records in a snap."

Ten minutes later Franklin got Wendy Mervyn on the phone. She promised to review the matter "up the chain of command" and with the FBI and get back to him in a couple hours.

Jane and Karen waited patiently in the small conference room just two doors down from Barry Penner's office. Two cups of latté steamed untouched in front of them. *Get there immediately,* they had been told. His urgent manner was so unlike Penner, they complied without question.

"Morning ladies," Penner said flatly as he entered quickly into the room.

"What's this all about?" Jane demanded.

"Don't get too huffy with your savior, Jane," he replied.

"What are you talking about?"

"I got a call from my source at the Justice Department. The Whatcom County prosecutor's office just made a request to subpoena the clinic's financial records—*your* financial records. A person claiming to be Stephen Gray called there this morning, saying that you two hired him to set fire to the clinic. You get the drift."

"What did you say?"

"I told her that you two wouldn't set fire to an incense stick without checking with me first and that Gray was just trying to create a diversion from his partner, Susan O'Dell's, trial and the potential appeal for the others."

"What did she say to that?"

"She said I was probably right, but that she would check it out just to be safe."

Karen's face turned white. *"So, savior,* what did you do then?"

"Let me finish, OK?" he said with restrained coolness. "I told her that this would be a bad idea because in the unlikely event they found something that would require further investigation, it would create a big political stink. Pro-choice factions all over the country would come unglued, accusing the Clinton administration of selling out to the fundamentalist conspiracy theorists. When she doubted my prediction, I told her it wasn't a prediction—but a promise. Wisely, she took my meaning and opined that it probably wasn't Gray at all, just some crank. And the Justice Department wouldn't add insult to your injury by snooping through your records for a fantasy."

"Well done, Barry," Karen said smiling.

"My bill for this will reflect your sentiments," he replied, standing to leave.

"Wait a second," Jane said. "What about the yokels in Bellingham? Can't they subpoena the records?"

"My source said that Ms. Mervyn, Franklin's colleague, would instruct him to lay off. They're confident he will. It seems he is planning to run for Washington State attorney general—that he fully shares our political sympathies and understands this case in its larger context. They think he'll work with us."

"He'd better," Karen replied.

"Wonder what got into Vince?" Jane said menacingly. "After all these years . . ."

"We've got to take care of him properly," Karen said, scowling.

"If you two have private matters to discuss, I'll return to my office," Penner said, standing to leave. Jane and Karen waved him away, then turned toward each other across the conference table for further discussion.

"What do you have in mind for Vince?" Jane asked.

"McDougal can take care of him."

"Dan McDougal? Really?"

"Really," Karen replied in a low, gravely growl.

Franklin had his feet propped up on his desk talking politics with the Yakima County chair of the Democratic Party when he heard a quiet tap on the door. Shannon Carpenter opened it and stuck her head inside.

"Wendy Mervyn on line four," she whispered. She slipped quietly into one of his visitor chairs.

Franklin scrunched his eyebrows in surprise. "Ernie, I'll have to get back to you—I've got a call coming in from Washington, D.C. Yeah, fourth from the top in the Justice Department—good friend of mine," he bragged. "OK . . . see ya later. And thanks again for your endorsement."

He punched the button for line four. "Wendy, you're calling late for D.C."

"Can't be helped," she replied.

"Are you all ready for Christmas?"

"Not really," she said tersely. "Max, sorry to be so abrupt, but I'm trying to get out of here. I just wanted to get back to you about your request to subpoena the records of the clinic's main office."

"Yeah?"

"We've run the idea up the chain here and the conclusion is that we aren't going to be able to accommodate your request."

"Why not?"

"All of our experts believe the call to be a hoax."

"But what if it's not a hoax? It might be real, right?"

"Theoretically. But we have to weigh that slim chance against the other ramifications of the decision to go digging through their files."

"What kind of ramifications?"

"You know . . . public interest kinds of concerns. Are we really acting in the public good to raise any suggestion that it is the clinic operators themselves who are really responsible for these crimes? We all know that this is exactly what the anti-choice forces want people to believe. This administration has cooperated with you fully, but we cannot let our authority be used to antagonize our friends and promote the extremists' wild theories just because of one crank call."

"I understand. That makes sense to me. I guess we can go through the state courts in California and get the subpoena ourselves."

"Certainly you can, but I am *asking* you not to do that."

"Why not?"

"I guess for three reasons. One is that even if you do it and not us, it will reflect the same policy concerns that we have just discussed. Second, with your own long-range political future, I don't think it would serve your personal interests either; you need the vigorous backing of pro-choicers in your future ventures. And those forces both inside the administration and nationally—especially in Los Angeles—will be eager to help you . . . but only if you relinquish this risky course of action. And finally, I'd ask you not to as a personal favor to me. I've taken some heat about the dismissal of the action against Danners and the others.

Some people are second-guessing my recommendation to let you go first with your prosecution. It would just compound my personal difficulties if you—you know."

"Sure, Wendy, and I appreciate everything you've done for me. You can count on me to return the favor. One crank call won't divert my attention from the real objective."

"Thanks, Max. I appreciate it. I think you'll see that you've made the right decision."

"Good night, Wendy. And have a Merry Christmas."

"You too, Max. And thanks again."

Carpenter leaned forward in her chair. "You're gonna have to explain all that to me. I can't believe what I think I heard, listening to your half of the conversation."

"The powers that be have decided not to take any action on a single crank call—that's all."

"Yeah, but it sounds like they twisted your arm to get you to back off."

"I wouldn't call it arm twisting. They asked nicely, and I have chosen to accept their experience and wisdom. It was a crank caller, that's all."

"That's what you keep saying, but you forget that I was the one who took the call. I say it was really Gray, not some hoax."

"I know, and perhaps you're right. But even if it was Gray, he was probably lying through his teeth. The bottom line is the same. He's just trying to throw us off the trail of his fellow pro-lifers."

"Now I know why they don't let appellate courts judge the credibility of witnesses," she replied angrily.

"What are you talking about?"

"You know the rule. 'Trial judges see and hear the witnesses and they have the ability to evaluate whether or not the witness is telling the truth.'

Truthfulness can be sensed sometimes. I think it was Gray and that he was telling the truth. And I want to subpoena their records and check out his story!"

"I'm sorry, Shannon. We can't do that. I've given my word to Wendy."

"Wendy, Wendy! I would think you'd at least try to camouflage the fact that you've got the hots for her when you're around me."

"That's crazy. What are you talking about?"

"I've seen your kind before, *Mr. Franklin*. It's like that old song—*when you're not with the one you love, you love the one you're with.*"

"Shannon, honey, that's just not right. I do not have the hots for Wendy. I'm just thinking about the political implications of what I'm doing. When I run for attorney general, I don't want to get on the wrong side of the pro-choicers. They can be real helpful to me."

"So that's it—politics first, truth second, and me last."

"That's not what I said!"

She stood up, red in the face. "But it *is* what you meant. I think I have a Christmas present or two to return. Good night, Mr. Franklin."

The door slammed behind her. Max Franklin turned slowly and stared out his darkening window. A few Christmas lights could be seen on the apartment building to the left; the sky to the right glowed as the lights of the pulp mill bounced off the low clouds.

Suzie O'Dell lay in front of the fireplace, cuddled in an old quilt her grandmother had made. She glanced up at the clock in the kitchen. 11:23 P.M. December 23 would soon give way to Christmas Eve. *My last Christmas Eve,* she thought.

That sour thought waded through her sludge-like mind until she was over-wrought with fear—fear that thoughts of the death penalty seemed to generate almost every night. No matter how many times Peter tried to reassure her that capital punishment was a highly unlikely possibility, all she could think of was spending her last Christmas Eve with the family. Her fear-controlled mind simply wouldn't allow her to see her future in any other light.

Suzie had initially been thrilled that the case against the colonel and the others had been thrown out. It gave her hope that her case could be, too. But soon the thought that she would be tried alone blossomed in her conscious mind, and it unnerved her. Her friends would go on with their lives and forget her, she reasoned. Now, going to school and working were both emotionally challenging. Even sleeping at night was difficult.

About two in the morning, Suzie jumped when she heard a noise from behind.

"It's just me, honey," her mom said. "I'm sorry I scared you."

"Oh, that's OK." She laid back down and wrapped the quilt back around her.

Her mom sat down beside her on the carpet and patted her gently on the side. "Having trouble sleeping again?"

"Yeah, sort of."

"Have you prayed about it?"

"Yeah, constantly. But I can't seem to shake the fear."

"I know how hard it is. I feel the same way sometimes when I think about all of this."

"I just wish it was all over. Sometimes I feel like just pleading guilty, just so I can be done with all of this."

Mrs. O'Dell shook her head sadly. "Suzie, the Bible says, 'God has not given you a spirit of fear, but of power, love, and a sound mind.' You know that thought is straight out of the pit of hell."

"I know, Mom, but I just can't figure out why God is making me go through all this. Why me? Why only me? I know I didn't do anything wrong criminally, but maybe God is letting me be tried because of some sin in my life or something.

"Has He pointed out some sin to you when you think these things?"

"No, nothing that makes sense."

"Well, then that's probably not what God is trying to tell you. God always wants to take our difficulties and use them to make our character more like that of Christ."

"My character must need a lot of improvement to face all this. Nobody else faces this kind of trial."

"Well, Jesus did face the death penalty, and He certainly wasn't guilty of anything."

"I never thought about it that way before," Suzie said quietly. "That's really something."

They both fell silent for a long time.

"Why don't you go to bed, honey?"

"OK, I think I might be able to sleep." Suzie raised up on one elbow. "Thanks, Mom, what you said about Jesus really helps. I don't know why exactly, but the fact that He has gone through this exact same thing makes me feel better."

"I love you, honey."

"Good night."

It was a frigid Christmas Eve in Dayton, Ohio. Each time a visitor would enter the large double doors at the rear of the church, gusts of snow would blow in, dusting the mat on the foyer with a layer of melting powder. The church was brimming with excited children and exhausted parents. Angel costumes seemed to outnumber shepherds in bathrobes by about two to one.

Vince was dressed in a stylish black and white houndstooth sports jacket with a black collarless shirt. He carried a small gift in his left hand. Many people spoke to him, but no one recognized the handsome, red-headed, bearded stranger. It had been so many years since Vince had attended his father's church, it was doubtful that anyone would have known who he was even without his disguise. He settled into the fifth row back, on the far left side of the sanctuary. Nonchalantly scanning the crowd every minute or two, he didn't see her until just before the service began—a striking woman of sixty with silver and brown hair coming down the center and settling in the aisle seat in the second row. It was the same seat that she had always occupied during Vince's childhood.

He tried to watch the children in the Christmas pageant, but his eyes kept straying toward his mother. A strange battle raged inside. A very small voice inside him yearned for true reconciliation, but mostly he simply felt nostalgic and homesick.

The brief remarks of the associate pastor slipped past Vince without notice. He sang *Silent Night* and *O Come All Ye Faithful* by rote. And then it was time for the service to conclude. He slipped quietly through the crowd and found his mother talking to a young woman. Vince smiled as he watched her flashing green eyes twinkle at the proud mother of an angel; her typical enthusiasm had not changed.

"Merry Christmas," he said.

She turned with her practiced greet-a-stranger smile. But in a flash the smile was replaced with a look of genuine astonishment. She started to speak.

"Please don't say my name," he said just above a whisper.

"But son, it's—it's been so long." Her voice was choking with emotion, but her practiced stage presence returned her usual smile to her face.

"Too long, Mom. But you look great. You look as young as the day I left."

"What is going on? Your hair, the beard—all this whispering."

"I'm afraid I'm in a bit of trouble."

"Let's go home and you can tell me about it there."

"I can't go home with you. I'm afraid someone will track me there to you."

"Who? What have you done?" She began to look nervously from side to side as if FBI agents were watching him at that very moment.

"I didn't do what they think, but it's real complicated. My best bet is to just keep moving until I'm sure my old identity has been left completely behind."

"Does that mean you are going to disappear from my life again?"

"Probably for a while, until things get straightened out. I've taken a few steps to try to get things moving in the right direction. But I'm going to have to depend on others to get to the bottom of the real mess—if they do, I'll be pretty much exonerated."

Her smile suddenly returned. "Son, I am probably just imagining things, but there is a man in the first row of the balcony who's not moving. He's just standing there watching us."

"OK," Vince replied without moving. "I'm going to give you this present, and then I want you to take a step toward the back, then turn around and give me a hug. I'll look over your shoulder while you're hugging me."

"Well, thanks very much for the present, Warren," she said somewhat loudly. "And be sure to hug those children for me and send your wife my love."

"McDougal!" he said in whispered astonishment.

"You know him?" she replied.

"Mom, is the basement exit still there through the furnace room?"

"Yeah, son. Is he the police?"

"No, I wish he were. Merry Christmas, Mom. Grab a deacon or somebody and call the cops if he comes anywhere near you."

Vince turned and headed toward the stage, mounted the platform, and ducked quickly through a choir door exit. He saw McDougal racing to the stairs.

He went quickly down an internal set of stairs, through a Sunday school area, and found the door to the furnace room. His dad used to take him there for necessary spankings between services. If only he was there to protect him now. He went quickly out the side door and ran down the block into the residential neighborhood where he had parked his rental car.

Although he repeatedly looked over his shoulder while unlocking the car door, he failed to see anyone giving chase. He got the engine running and squealed the tires as he took off. He was about halfway down the block going in the opposite direction when McDougal rounded a corner. There was too much traffic in the area and too little chance of a successful shot, so McDougal left his chrome-and-steel pistol in his pocket. But his chase had not been completely in vain—he pulled out a pen and scrap of paper and jotted down the license number of the white car racing out of sight.

23

It was nearly eleven o'clock on Christmas Eve. A young woman in her early twenties shuffled papers along a counter in the small Hertz Rent-a-Car office at the Dayton Airport, wishing she were anywhere but there.

"Oh brother, what now?" she muttered to herself as she saw a dark-haired man of forty accompanied by a Dayton police officer walking deliberately in her direction.

"Good evening, ma'am," the officer began.

"Yes, sir," she replied, "is something wrong?"

"This gentleman says that one of your cars hit him, then took off about an hour ago. I've inspected the side of his vehicle, and he has certainly been in a collision with a white car. We ran the plates on the tag he gave us and it checks out to a white Taurus registered to Hertz at this location."

Oh no, she thought, shaking her head. *This is going to take forever.* A heavy sigh betrayed her thoughts.

"Officer, we don't have to do a complete report now," the man offered. "Why don't we just get the driver's information, and I'll come by your station day after tomorrow and finish up?"

"OK with you, officer?" she said, begging.

"Sure, I guess," he resigned.

She hit some key strokes on her computer after the stranger gave her the plate number. "That car was rented just this morning to David Cummings. I'll write his address and phone number down for you."

"Can you give each of us his information and be sure to include his license number?" the officer said.

"Why don't I just give you a photocopy of his full rental agreement? That will have everything you need," she said.

"That'd be great," the man replied.

"When is Mr. Cummings due to return the car?" the man asked as she ran the copy.

"On December 27th by noon," she replied. "It's on the copy I'm giving you."

"Thanks so much—both of you," the man said. He stuck the rental copy with Cummings's driver's license and Visa number in his overcoat pocket and started for the door, then turned and called back, "Oh, and Merry Christmas."

"Merry Christmas to you too, Mr. McDougal," the officer replied. He turned to the clerk. "Nice fella. Took this whole thing very graciously."

On the third of January, Peter arrived at his office promptly at 8:00 A.M. Judge Hayden had scheduled a conference call for a status report on the case at 8:15.

He barely had time to start the coffee maker and grab the file when the phone rang. After a couple minutes on hold, the operator came back on the line.

"OK, Max Franklin?" she asked.

"I'm here."

"Peter Barron?"

"Yes, ma'am."

"Well, Judge Hayden, your call is ready to go."

"Thank you, young lady," the judge said. "Morning, gentlemen, I trust you both had an enjoyable holiday?"

Both attorneys gave a short, positive response.

"Well, this morning I wanted to come to closure on a trial date for Susan O'Dell and make sure there are no more pretrial motions that we need to schedule. Mr. Franklin, what is the status of your intention to appeal the decision of the court of appeals?"

"Your Honor, we have decided not to appeal that matter further. The court of appeals made it clear that we could refile the charges if we developed further evidence that implicated those four defendants. So we intend to go ahead and try Miss O'Dell. We are certain that the additional evidence coming out during that proceeding will enable us to satisfy even the most strict interpretation of probable cause."

"All right," the judge replied. "We could have been through with O'Dell two months ago if you would have taken that same position after my ruling, but what's done is done. In any event, are you both ready to try the O'Dell matter?"

"I am," Franklin replied.

"I need about a month to be ready, Your Honor," Peter said.

"OK, I believe this is scheduled for a two-week trial," Hayden said. "Uh . . . looking at my calendar, and giving Mr. Barron his month, means we will not be able to begin until February 20. Is that date OK with both of you?"

"Sure," Franklin replied.

"That will be fine," Peter said. "Any later and I might have a problem. My wife is due to have a baby on March 22."

"All right," Hayden said. "We'll keep firmly to that date then. I'll want your trial briefs, any motions *in limine,* and your proposed jury instructions seven days before trial. I want to begin picking a jury bright and early on the morning of the twentieth. Anything else, gentlemen?"

"No, Your Honor," Franklin replied.

"I have nothing," Peter said.

"I'll see you both at 8:30 A.M. on the twentieth. Goodbye, gentlemen."

McDougal logged in on his computer from his hotel room in Colorado Springs. For nearly two weeks he had been on a circuit chasing Vince via his Visa card usage, but the trail ran cold after a charge three days earlier at the Steak & Ale Restaurant down the street. Since then, nothing.

After fifteen minutes of frustrating searches through a series of supposedly secure files, McDougal snapped off his laptop in disgust without even properly going through the logout sequence. He would have to call Karen.

"Might as well get it over with," he muttered to himself as he disconnected the modem cord and punched the requisite numbers.

"Karen, please," he said when the receptionist answered.

"Hello," came her voice a couple minutes later.

"McDougal here."

"Yeah, McDougal? Anything to report?"

"The trail seems to have run cold in Colorado Springs. He seems to have stopped using that Visa card."

"Why do you think he did that? He doesn't have any reason to know that we've penetrated his new identity, does he?"

"Vince is smart. He's lived a double existence a long time. This will just take a while."

"Yeah, right," she replied sarcastically. "And in the meantime, he'll continue making random phone calls trying to implicate us."

"Have you thought of trying to control your problem from the other side?" McDougal asked.

"What do you mean?"

"Do you have any idea who he might call next?"

"We can make some pretty good guesses."

"Then why don't you just get someone to tap the lines of the people he's likely to call and see if he makes contact?"

"Don't *you* do that sort of thing?"

"Well, I can have it done. I've got some contacts. But if you want round-the-clock listening posts, the costs are going to be sky high. It'd be cheaper to run a tap and tape operation. Then we can screen the calls until we know who he's contacted, then go live if we need to."

"I say go for it."

"So who might he contact?"

"Well . . . first, his mother in Ohio. Then Shannon Carpenter in the Whatcom County prosecutor's office. Those are the two we know that he's called before. Possibly that Lisa Edgar woman he was romancing from inside the pro-life group. And I guess I ought to include Peter Barron. Better do office and home phone."

"Done," McDougal replied.

Peter stuck his head in the office door of his associate, Cooper Stone. "Morning, Coop. How was your little journey to Bellingham? I really appreciate you going over for me," he said, sipping his first cup of coffee of the morning.

"I bet you're glad. It was miserable weather."

"Yeah, that's another reason I'm glad you went," Peter said, plopping down into one of Stone's leather side chairs. "But I meant that it allowed me to pamper Gwen—she's getting real anxious about me leaving with her pregnancy getting toward the end."

"Well, that's why partners hire associates," Stone said, laughing.

"Yeah—especially single associates like you. We can work you twenty hours a day and there's no family to complain," Peter said, continuing the jovial banter.

"Peter, in all seriousness," Stone began, "I am real glad that you and Joe hired me out of law school. If I had to go with that big firm in Seattle, I would be working twenty hours a day and still be ten years away from any real trial experience. You guys are great to work for. So if I get a little cold rain in January in Bellingham, it's a small price to pay to have escaped the big firm salt mines."

Peter smiled and nodded. "Well, did our grateful associate find out anything we didn't know?"

"Well, I subpoenaed the phone records you wanted," Stone said, twisting around to grab his briefcase off of his credenza. "Stephen Gray didn't make a lot of long distance calls."

"Yeah, but did he make any interesting calls?"

"From home he made a couple real interesting calls—and about a dozen that need further checking. I found out he had a cell phone, too. An interesting expense for a part-time assistant manager at a pizza parlor in Ferndale, Washington."

"Yeah it is. I don't know how it helps us, but it is interesting," Peter replied, setting his coffee mug on the floor beside him.

"Well, from home he made two calls to Dr. Marsano's residence—from Ferndale to South Lake Sammish is a toll call. One time he was on the line two minutes, the other seven minutes."

"Why would a threatening call last seven minutes?" Peter asked.

"Good point," Stone replied. "I asked myself the same question."

"What were the other dozen calls you mentioned?"

"I don't understand them exactly. All of them were to Southern California, most to private residences. None of the people I was able to get a hold of had ever heard of Stephen Gray. One was to a restaurant, a couple others I can't track down."

"That's strange. What do you make of it?"

Cooper shook his head, his reddish-blond hair flopping from side to side. "Can't say for sure. And his cell calls are more of the same."

"Who was he calling?"

"Well, since cellular phones record every call, I found three short calls to the Bellingham clinic itself—all of them after five o'clock, for about five minutes each. Here, look at these," he said, tossing photocopies of phone bills onto Peter's side of the desk. "There was one call to the L.A. clinic headquarters—the same number that was called from the pastor's study that was so central to your motion to dismiss. And then there were a couple calls to another Bellingham-based cell phone. See there," he said pointing. "But when I called it, it was disconnected."

"Did you ask the cellular company who the number belonged to?"

"Yeah, they said we would have to get a separate subpoena for that phone number. Our subpoena was only good for Stephen Gray's account. They did tell me that the phone had been disconnected on June 7."

"You got a theory about that?" Peter asked.

"Yeah, I do. I think it was Rhonda Marsano's cell phone. It was cancelled about two weeks after she was killed. It would take people that long to clean up those kinds of odds and ends."

"It sounds like there's more to your theory, Coop."

"Yeah, I guess I do have more, but proving it would be difficult," Stone said, biting at the nail on his index finger. "I think Gray was obsessed with Rhonda Marsano. I saw some pictures of her . . . she was a good lookin' lady. I guess I think he was stalking her, like a spurned suitor. That puts a whole new spin on things if none of this was about a pro-life protest."

"I dunno," Peter replied. "Lisa Edgar was supposed to be Gray's love interest."

"Yeah, I went by to see her, too. Cute girl. But I wasn't convinced that she was in love with Gray. That whole deal seemed strange."

"Why do you say that?" Peter asked.

"Oh I don't know. Just the way she talked about him, and uh—"

"Quit stammering and just say it," Peter said impatiently.

"Oh, it's just that she seemed all ga-ga eyed and everything while I was talkin' to her."

"So what?" Peter said sarcastically. "Half the legal secretaries in Spokane do that to you, Mr. GQ."

"Whatever, but this was different. In any event, I'm convinced this Gray fellow was a strange bird—maybe crazy enough to become infatuated with the beautiful woman he's supposed to be protesting. Kind of a love-hate thing."

"Was your undergrad major in psychology or something?" Peter asked with a wry smile.

"No. . ."

"I thought not," Peter replied. "This is crazy."

"Maybe it is crazy, but I'd like to go back to Bellingham and subpoena Marsano's home phone records and this unknown cell phone as well. It's kinda fun playing detective."

"Sure. Maybe you can find some real evidence, not just a bunch of theories. Anyway, Gwen'll be glad it's you and not me."

"Kennewick comes from an Indian word meaning 'warm winter,'" the in-room *Travel Host* magazine declared. Indeed, it was fifty-five degrees in this southeastern corner of Washington, on the dry side of the state. Not bad for February 5. Vince decided that it would have to do.

He wanted to be close enough to Bellingham to monitor the trial but far enough away to avoid any chance of running into one of the clinic's people. Two hundred ninety miles seemed safe enough. He still had plenty of money left from his last payment from Jane and Karen; but he felt that if he didn't find some kind of work to keep his mind occupied, he would have real trouble maintaining his sanity. He talked his way into a men's clothing position at Penney's in the Columbia Center Mall. He really enjoyed interacting with people every day without the need to form any kind of ongoing relationships that would lead to questions.

By mid-February, the story of the upcoming trial was on the front page of every paper in the state. Vince flinched when he opened up the *Tri-City Herald* one morning and saw his picture in living color on the front page. He left the paper sitting on his dining room table and walked to the bathroom mirror. He looked at his appearance carefully for a minute, then went back to the kitchen and fetched the phone book from a cabinet. His hair was convincingly red and long, and the beard had so dramatically altered his appearance that he felt sure no one would recognize him. Still, the color photo convinced him to add a final touch.

He would go that day to the optometrist at Wal-Mart and get contact lens to change his eye color to green. Getting ready for St. Patrick's Day, he would say.

He returned to the paper to read the full story. Two law professors from the University of Washington and University of Puget Sound confidently asserted opinions that Suzie O'Dell would be convicted. "A case based entirely on circumstantial evidence can certainly bring in a conviction; but here, they've got her fingerprints on the gas can and a videotape of her buying the materials for a bomb. No one can expect them to produce an actual videotape of the fire itself."

The editorial debate in every paper Vince read went beyond the question of Suzie's guilt. The only debate left was whether she should get the death penalty once convicted.

He wanted to save Suzie, but he wanted to save himself more. He would simply have to wait and see what happened.

24

Peter stared at the clock when Gwen got up and staggered toward the bathroom for the third time that night. *Eight months pregnant and she looks like she's going to burst,* he thought as the earliest rays of morning illumined her outline. He rolled over when she came back to bed and snuggled up close behind his wife. "I am so sorry to leave you like this today. You look so uncomfortable."

Gwen said nothing.

"It'll all be over in a couple weeks, and then I'll be home for good."

"Yeah, until the appeal," she replied bitterly.

"Honey, you know an appeal only takes me away for one night. That's all."

"OK, until the next really important case comes along. With all the press you've been getting—not just in Washington, but across the country— you're going to be getting more and more calls to go who knows where."

"Not if I lose this one," he replied somberly.

Gwen looked at him with astonishment. "Peter Barron, you listen to me." In the years Peter had known Gwen, he'd never seen this fierce look in her eye. "Don't you dare lose this case. If my worries and pity cause you to do anything less than you and I know you are capable of, I simply couldn't live with myself."

Gwen smiled in a way that normally made Peter's heart sing, but even that couldn't alter his recent pessimistic outlook as the trial date approached. He fell back on his pillow and thought out loud.

"If only she hadn't been such a diligent student. That Friday night when the clinic was torched, she was in the library studying for finals and didn't go to her room until after eleven. If only we could find somebody who had seen her in the library. Cooper's been over there trying, but nobody remembers her being there."

"Maybe you need to go over there yourself and snoop around."

"No, it wouldn't make any difference, honey. And besides, those coeds think Coop's a Greek god or something. If anyone can squeeze information out of them, he can."

"Then I'm glad you had him go. Coop's cute, but you're the heart throb, Peter Barron."

Peter pulled Gwen toward him with her head on his chest and hugged her tight, saying nothing for a long time.

"I'm going to miss you more than you know," he finally said. "And I'm going to be so worried about you."

"My parents will take good care of me, you know that. What time are you and Coop and Sally leaving, anyway?"

"Around ten. I figure we'll get there around dinner time. Then we'll go over to Pastor Wallace's church and set up Sally's temporary office. It's a good thing computers are so portable these days. I can't imagine pulling a case like this off without a real secretary and equipment. Then, on Saturday, we'll go over the witness lists and Coop and I will practice my cross-examination of Franklin's witnesses. And on Sunday—"

"You'd better be in church and pray."

"Yeah, for sure. Suzie needs a miracle. Her lawyer sure hasn't found her an alibi."

"Why is it that real crooks always have an alibi?"

"Suzie could have had one. A guy who has a crush on her told Coop that he and Suzie had a date that night, and that they were out until nearly one. Suzie said he was lying. If we wanted to cheat and lie, she could have an alibi, and we could have coached the kid to sound real convincing. Some lawyers would have done that. Maybe Suzie should have gotten one of those lawyers instead of me. She would probably not be so worried about the death penalty right now."

"Boy, you are down," Gwen said, stroking her fingers through his hair. "You know better than that—her hope is in God, not in phony alibis, or even good lawyers."

Finally Peter smiled. Gwen moaned and rolled onto her back.

"Sorry, I can't stay in that position any longer," she said. Rubbing her round stomach, she continued, "Peter."

"Yeah, honey."

"You will pray for me and Casey and little 'Edgar' in here, won't you?"

"Sure, lover. But on one condition."

"What's that?"

"That if our baby comes while I'm gone, and it turns out to be a boy, you will not name him Edgar under any circumstances."

Gwen laughed and sidled up close to Peter's side.

"In fact, let's pray right now. O Lord God," he began. "I ask you to protect my wonderful wife, and Casey, and our new little baby. Keep them all safe until I get back in a couple weeks. And I ask you to give us a healthy little baby, to raise to become a godly young man or woman. Comfort Gwen. Bless her parents, and I thank you for them. Keep us all safe as we drive today.

"And God, I pray for Suzie. Please help us to win. Help truth to come out. Help us find that break we've looked for in vain. Oh, please God, she's so young and innocent. Thank you for hearing our prayer, in Jesus' name, amen."

Noise pervaded the streets in front of the courthouse as people dashed around heading for work. Sally glanced at her watch—7:55 A.M., February 20. "It must open at eight o'clock," she thought aloud as she paced the atrium in front of the courthouse coffee shop. She turned to look once more out the numerous windows in the front of the court-house. Peter and Cooper were coming up the stairs with the last set of boxes. It was overcast and cool, but fortunately no rain yet.

A Jeep Wagoneer suddenly honked its horn, and the two lawyers twisted around to see Bill, Linda, and Suzie O'Dell exiting the colonel's Jeep. Bill rushed to open the courthouse door for his daughter's lawyers.

"So how were your accommodations?" Peter asked as they shuffled through the courthouse door into the atrium.

"The colonel and Evie took magnificent care of us," Bill responded.

"But I don't think any of us got much sleep," Linda added with a nervous little smile. "This is all so scary."

Peter set his box down on the first table in the eating area and hugged Suzie around the shoulders. "Suzie, the Lord is going to keep you strong. The only thing you need to do is try to get some sleep while we're here.

I'm going to need you to be at your best when I put you on the stand to testify."

"When do you think that will be?" Linda asked.

"Sometime early next week," Peter replied. "It'll take a couple days to pick the jury. Then the prosecutor will probably take about three days to put on his case. Then we'll begin our testimony."

"How long will that take?" Bill asked.

"That'll take a day or two, then we'll argue it to the jury next Wednesday or Thursday. But I could be off a day or so on any of these guesses. It's impossible to say exactly."

"Why don't the three of you just sit at one of those tables over there with Sally while Cooper and I go up to the courtroom and get all our stuff organized? At around 8:25 come on up and I'll show you to a witness waiting area. The colonel knows where it is as well. The media knows jury selection begins at 9:30, but I think you'll be safe until around 8:30. Remember, if any reporter asks any of you anything, you are to say—"

"Good morning, we're very optimistic about the outcome of the trial and have no further comment," Bill O'Dell said in a sing-song fashion.

"Excellent," Peter replied with a broad smile. "Next week we'll change a word or two to give you some variety."

Cooper joined his boss as they started down the hallway toward the elevator. Peter suddenly stopped and turned back to the O'Dells. "Oh . . . one more thing. Sometime this morning there will be several dozen potential jurors wandering around this courthouse. At some point they will be given juror badges, but until then you won't know who's who. Don't talk to anyone at all anytime this week. Not even good morning or hello. Just smile and nod if you feel you need to acknowledge someone. It could really mess things up if any one of our team talks to a juror.

"For that matter, you shouldn't have any conversations of substance around anyone who can hear you. Talk about the weather or the coffee. OK?"

"I think they've got it, chief," Sally said saluting. "Great coffee, beautiful weather, never seen it better."

Peter waved her off with a smile as the elevator doors opened and he and Cooper stepped inside.

At 8:30 the judge's secretary stuck her head in the courtroom. "Counsel, Judge Hayden would like to see all of you in chambers."

Franklin and Carpenter had just been in the courtroom for a few minutes. It was not nearly as complicated for the prosecutor to get ready with an office just on the next floor. Peter and Cooper followed the prosecuting attorneys through the door to the left of the judge's bench, back through the secretary's office and into the judge's private chambers.

Hayden stood erect behind his chair as the four lawyers filed in silently. They stood awkwardly in front of four overstuffed burgundy leather chairs that looked like they had been in use for most of the twenty-five years Hayden had been on the bench.

"Please, be seated all of you," Hayden announced as he did the same. "You must be Cooper Stone—I've seen your name on the trial brief and other pleadings. Nice to meet you."

"Thank you, Your Honor."

"Has everyone met Ms. Shannon Carpenter?"

"No, Your Honor, I haven't had the pleasure," Cooper replied. He stood to shake her hand. She remained seated, but smiled warmly at his friendly gesture.

"This is going to be a long and difficult trial," Hayden said when Cooper had resumed his seat. "And it is not mere tradition that causes me to urge all of you to continue this professional atmosphere. My forty years as a lawyer and judge has led me to a firm conviction that we get better justice when the lawyers treat each other with respect. This case is far too important to let any one of you develop a case of clouded judgment because you are trying to seek revenge against the other side for some personal affront."

Peter and Franklin both nodded.

"Fine, then. I've read your briefs and your proposed jury instructions. Both of you have done excellent work, and we are indeed ready to try this case. Mr. Barron, I understand that you intend to call your client to the witness stand."

"That's right, Your Honor."

"That's fine. Any chance you'll change your mind?"

"No—not unless you grant the motion to dismiss this case at the close of the prosecution's evidence."

"Understood. I just like to confirm these things because if a defendant is not going to testify, I like to warn jurors up front that they shouldn't weigh that against the defendant in any way. But that will be unnecessary here."

Hayden reached to the right-hand side of his desk and picked up a large black notebook and handed it to Franklin. Then he picked up its twin and offered it to Peter. The third copy he placed directly in the middle of his desk.

"We have worked with the jury administrator to bring in a hundred of Whatcom County's finest citizens as jurors. You'll find each potential juror's questionnaire in alphabetical order in your binders. My bailiff and I drew lots earlier this morning and placed each juror in one of four panels of twenty-five. I will call in the first twenty-five, and you both can question them as to their qualifications. Then we can begin to use your peremptory challenges—unless, of course, I have allowed you to strike any of the jurors for admitted prejudice. When we run out of jurors from the first panel, I will bring in the second group of twenty-five, and so on. I hope it will not take more than two panels to seat twelve jurors and two alternates. But in case we find a lot of preconceived notions because of pretrial publicity," Hayden paused and stared hard at Franklin, "it may take more than that, so I thought we'd call a hundred just in case. Any questions?"

"No, Your Honor, we're ready to begin," Franklin replied.

"Same here," Peter said smiling outwardly, but inside the butterflies in his stomach felt more like small, angry birds.

"I'll be on the bench at 9:30 sharp. Oh, Mr. Barron, your client has appeared, hasn't she? I wouldn't want any problems there."

"She's here, Your Honor. Quite nervous, but present."

"I don't mind telling you, I'm nervous too. I still get that way after all these years on the bench—at least when important cases are about to begin. I hope you're all suitably nervous about what we are about to do. After all, this is a nineteen-year-old girl charged with capital murder," Hayden said somberly, staring blankly out the window. He picked his glasses and put them back on. "See you in a few minutes."

Suzie was seated in the far right chair of the counsel table, closest to the empty jury box, Cooper was in the middle, and Peter sat on the left-hand side of the table. To their left, Detective Dunn sat in the far left-hand chair, Shannon Carpenter was placed in the middle, and Max Franklin sat eyeing Peter carefully as the bailiff entered the courtroom.

"All rise," came the familiar cry.

"Good morning, everyone. Please be seated," Hayden said. "This is the time and place set for the trial in the matter of the State of Washington versus Susan O'Dell. I have conferred with counsel in chambers, and we have completed all our preliminary matters. Is everyone ready for me to call in the jury panel?"

"Yes, Your Honor," came the response from both sides of the courtroom.

"All right, I'll ask the bailiff to show them in."

The double doors in the back right-hand side of the courtroom swung open, and an irregular line of people came slowly into the courtroom. The bailiff herded the first twelve into the jury box and directed the remaining thirteen to be seated in the first two rows on the left side of the courtroom.

Suzie felt a dozen pair of eyes scan across her slowly as the potential jurors seated in the box scanned the courtroom, trying to figure out who was who.

"Ladies and gentlemen, we have selected twenty-five of you to be in this panel of potential jurors," the judge began. "The first procedure we will go through is to select a group of twelve jurors and two alternates to serve in this case.

"This is a very serious and important case between the State of Washington, the plaintiff in this case, and Susan O'Dell, the defendant. This is a criminal case. Miss O'Dell is charged with four felonies. She is charged with conspiracy to commit arson, conspiracy to commit murder, arson, and first degree murder. The maximum penalty for any of these charges is death by hanging."

Cooper put his hand reassuringly on Suzie's forearm.

"I am going to read you a brief summary of the charges that have been filed in this case," Hayden continued. "Nothing in this summary should be considered as evidence. In fact, nothing you hear in any of these preliminary matters is evidence. The evidence begins only after the jury is completely selected and witnesses are sworn to testify. But we read you this preliminary summary so that the court and the attorneys for both sides can ask you more intelligent questions.

"Susan O'Dell is charged with these four felonies in connection with the death of Dr. Rhonda Marsano, who died on May 20 of last year in a fire at the Whatcom Women's Center for Choice here in Bellingham. I now want to ask you all some preliminary questions. Please raise your hand if your answer would be yes to any of the following questions."

Peter nudged Cooper to turn and watch the jurors seated in the audience. Peter would keep track of any raised hands among the jury box and had assigned his associate to do the same for the remainder.

"How many of you have heard about this case in any way—through television or radio or have seen stories about this in the newspaper?"

Every juror, save one lady who appeared to be about seventy seated in the first row in the jury box, raised a hand.

"How many of you feel that what you have read or seen has given you an opinion about whether or not Miss O'Dell is guilty of these charges?"

Cooper noted a young man in his late twenties in the second row who raised his hand.

"Do any of you know Miss O'Dell personally?"

Suzie again felt every eye in the courtroom focused on her with penetrating stares. No one raised a hand.

"The State of Washington is represented by the Whatcom County prosecuting attorney, Maxwell Franklin. Mr. Franklin, of course, is an elected official, and so I'm sure that most all of you have heard of him before, but do any of you know Mr. Franklin in a personal way, more than simply reading his name in the newspaper?"

Three hands went up.

"The defendant is represented by Peter Barron, who is seated there at the table on my left and your right. Do any of you know Mr. Barron in a personal way?"

A woman in her late forties surprised Peter by raising her hand.

"All right, Mr. Franklin, you may begin."

Franklin flipped the page to the jury questionnaire for the juror seated in the first position in the jury box. "Is your name Michael Storino?"

"Yes," said the fiftyish, slightly overweight man in a sports jacket and an open-collared shirt.

"I see from your questionnaire that you are a professor at Western. What subject do you teach?"

"History. Mainly European history," came the reply.

"Now, the evidence is going to show that Miss O'Dell here was a college student at Western at the time of the incident in question. Have you ever had Miss O'Dell in one of your classes?"

"Not that I recall. The name doesn't sound familiar. She may have been in one of my large survey courses where there are two or three hundred students. But I have no memory of that."

"Would you have any difficulty in fairly deciding this case based on the fact that Miss O'Dell was once a student at Western?"

"No, I can't imagine any difficulty for that reason," he said, shaking his head slowly.

"Professor Storino, since you are the first juror to be called, I want to explain to all of the jurors why I am about to ask you a certain question. This case involves the murder of a doctor who worked at an abortion clinic. The defendant was—and there is no dispute about this point—a protester at this clinic, so you can see that the difficult issue of abortion is a central factual matter in this case. My question is this: Do you have strong feelings about the subject of abortion one way or the other? Would you consider yourself strongly pro-choice or strongly pro-life?"

"I am pro-choice, sir, but probably not *strongly* pro-choice, as you put it."

"Fine, Professor Storino," Franklin said smiling. "I'll pass juror number one for cause."

Peter motioned for Suzie to lean over so he could whisper to her. "Did you ever have this guy?"

She shook her head sideways.

"Have you heard of him?"

"Some," she whispered.

"What's his reputation?"

"He's real liberal—some of my friends in the Christian group think he's a socialist or something."

"OK," Peter replied, resuming his normal position in his chair. "Your Honor, no questions for Professor Storino." Across Storino's name in the jury chart, Peter wrote "PREEMPT" in large letters. Storino would be among his list of jurors to strike.

Kathi Kling, a thirty-five-year-old secretary for an insurance company in the north county town of Blaine was next. Franklin eventually asked her what became his standard abortion question.

"I think abortion is generally a bad idea, but some women might feel differently. I dunno, I don't think about it much," she replied.

When it was his turn, Peter remained in his chair, leaned back, and smiled at the juror. "Mrs. Kling, I believe you—like almost everybody else—raised your hand when the judge asked whether you had read or heard any news accounts about this case. How many such news accounts have you heard or read?"

"Quite a few," she said.

"Do you think you have read most or all of the articles about the clinic fire and this case that were printed in the *Bellingham Herald?*"

"Well, I read the paper every day, so I probably read most of them, maybe all of them."

"That's fine," Peter replied, still smiling. "Did you hear about this case on the radio or TV?"

"Both."

"Many times?" he asked.

"Yeah, I would say so."

"Do you read any papers from Seattle?"

"I read the *Seattle Times* on Sundays."

"Did you read articles about this case there?"

"Yeah, I'm sure I did. They don't report much about Whatcom County, so I was always interested to read what they did say about our local case."

"Mrs. Kling, do you understand how important it is to both sides to find jurors who will decide this case based solely on the evidence presented in the trial, and not on any preconceived ideas you've gleaned from the media?"

"Yes, sir."

"One more question, and I want you to understand that I intend no disrespect—I think it's good for citizens to pay close attention to the news. But it does cause a little concern when one who has paid very close attention to a highly publicized case is a potential juror. When it came time to deliberate in this case, do you think you would be able to distinguish between what you've heard solely in this courtroom and what you've seen or read in the media? Or is there a chance you might innocently mix things up?"

"I would try to concentrate on the evidence, but it's possible I could get mixed up."

"Your Honor," Peter said, taking to his feet, "I would ask that Mrs. Kling be honorably excused at this time. I think that this is the path we are going to have to take because of the heavy publicity."

"Mr. Franklin?" Hayden said, inviting a response.

"Your Honor, Mrs. Kling has said she would do her best to decide this case on the evidence. That's all we can ask of a juror. I think the challenge should be denied."

"Well," the judge said, sighing out loud, "I think I have little choice in the matter. I'd hoped to avoid this with the pretrial orders, but I guess a certain amount of publicity is unavoidable. The motion will be granted. Mrs. Kling you are excused. Please check with the jury administrator's office on your way out for your proper payment for today."

The juror nodded and made her way out of the courtroom.

In total, thirty-one potential jurors admitted that they had followed every article in the local papers, as well as other news reports regarding the clinic fire. Judge Hayden had excused each one of them "for cause," and neither side had to use any of its allocated twelve challenges for those individuals. By noon on Wednesday, however, each side had used all twelve peremptory challenges for one reason or another. Franklin systematically eliminated all Catholics and any person from a conservative evangelical church. He also eliminated all jurors from the north part of the county with names like Vandermeiden, Vandenhauk, and Vander Vort. The communities around Lynden were populated with people with a conservative Dutch Reformed background, whose staunch social and political views were ardently pro-life.

For his part, Peter struck every juror even remotely associated with the university, except one secretary who professed to being a serious Catholic. Franklin took her out. When Peter had four challenges left, he began to strike older single men and tried his best to protect women with children or grandchildren.

In the end, seven women and five men were selected for the jury itself late the following morning. Ten of the jurors claimed mixed or no opinions on the question of abortion. One was mildly pro-life, while another claimed to be pro-choice with exceptions. Six of the women were mothers. It was an all-white jury, which was not surprising given the racial composition of the county. "It's as neutral a jury as we could have expected," Peter told Suzie and her family over a quick lunch. "But I had hoped to do a little better than neutral."

25

After lunch, twelve eager jurors and two alternates began to study Suzie O'Dell. It was easy for them to conclude that she didn't look much like a murderer and arsonist; but then again, she didn't look like a girl who would brandish a picket sign, either.

At the judge's invitation, Max Franklin rose to address the jury. He buttoned the jacket of his gray flannel suit, adjusted his blue and red striped tie, and walked to the lectern stationed squarely in front of the jury box. "Good afternoon, ladies and gentlemen of the jury. Again, my name is Max Franklin. As the prosecuting attorney for Whatcom County, I have the solemn responsibility of representing the people of the State of Washington in this incredibly important case.

"At this time I have the opportunity of outlining the evidence I expect to bring to you during the next few days. You will shortly hear from the Whatcom County coroner, Dr. Hugh Weber, who will tell you that Dr. Rhonda Marsano died from smoke inhalation on the evening of May 20 of last year. Then you will hear from an arson investigator from the Washington State Police who will testify that the fire that killed Dr. Rhonda Marsano and destroyed the Whatcom Women's Center for Choice was deliberately set—ignited by a simple yet deadly device. In fact, two such devices were strategically placed within and outside the clinic. When the timers went off, the gasoline ignited and the clinic was caught up in flames—those flames of course produced the smoke that killed Dr. Marsano."

Franklin paused and looked for the first time at his single sheet of notes on a yellow tablet lying in front of him on the lectern. "Then, ladies and gentlemen, you will hear from Detective John Dunn, who will testify that an identical gasoline can was found in a dumpster behind the clinic. He will testify that he took fingerprints off this can and that he later obtained the fingerprints of the defendant, Susan O'Dell." Franklin paused and looked back and forth to made sure every juror was looking straight at him. "The prints were a perfect match." He turned and stared hard at Suzie, who lowered her eyes to escape his stare.

"Another detective, Jamie MacMillan, will testify that he went to the Seattle headquarters of the Fred Meyer chain looking for evidence, because the gas can found in the dumpster still had a Fred Meyer sticker on the bottom. There he identified Susan O'Dell on videotape, purchasing items that were later found at the crime scene. The video came from the Bellingham Fred Myer store. On the video, a man and Susan O'Dell went to the cash register carrying three gas cans, some copper wire, and two large dry-cell batteries. The man's name was Stephen Gray. We know that because he paid for the purchase with a Visa card bearing his name.

"There can be little doubt that Mr. Gray was involved in this crime. However, he has disappeared. I am certain that counsel for Miss O'Dell will do his best to convince you that Stephen Gray acted alone. We will introduce other evidence that will show that Susan O'Dell had been more than a peaceful protester exercising her First Amendment rights. We will show that Miss O'Dell listened as Mr. Gray spun radical and dangerous tales . . . and that she responded with her own radical and dangerous statements.

"You will probably hear evidence about what a nice girl Susan O'Dell has been. We won't be presenting any evidence to the contrary, but that does not alter the fact that we have good reason to charge her with four felonies—felonies that are sometimes committed by nice people who are capable of expressing their passion in dangerous ways.

"Ladies and gentlemen, we are not responsible to produce evidence about her psychological journey. We simply have to link the evidence together. It is true that Miss O'Dell was with Stephen Gray when he purchased the bomb materials. Her fingerprints were found at the scene of the crime. She had the motive. She had the passion. And now Dr. Rhonda Marsano is dead. These kinds of crimes rarely have eye-witnesses to every detail. But the evidence you will hear puts all the links together. And so, we hope you will do your duty to return a just verdict."

Franklin nodded with a firm, solemn expression on his face, and with strong steps he returned to his seat.

Peter had intended to reserve any opening statement until after the prosecution rested. But he felt uneasy doing so in light of the impression the prosecutor had obviously made on the jury. Peter whispered briefly to Cooper, then rose nervously from his chair.

"Ladies and gentlemen of the jury. My client and I are both from Spokane. I know that you are men and women of character and will not hold that fact against either of us, and especially not against Susan O'Dell, or Suzie as you will get to know her in the course of the next several days.

"In fact, ladies and gentlemen of the jury, when the prosecutor finishes calling all of his witnesses—and I'm sure you realize that he gets to call all of his witnesses before we get to call even one witness to the stand, so please keep an open mind until the very end—then you will have a chance to meet Suzie personally and hear her side of the story. She will tell you that she is a college student at Western. Previous to that, she will tell you that among her other jobs, she babysat my darling daughter, Casey."

Cooper noted that three of the women jurors were subtly smiling as Peter exuded personal charm.

"You will also hear from a number of people who know Suzie O'Dell and who will describe her as an innocent, earnest nineteen-year-old girl, not the kind of girl who would engage in deadly conspiracies." Peter paused and let the word sink in. "And certainly not the kind of girl who would commit arson and first degree murder, the penalty for which is death by hanging."

Every eye in the courtroom was riveted on Peter as he paced back and forth directly in front of the jury box.

"In fact, Suzie O'Dell is so innocent and naive that she went inside Fred Meyer on the way home from a pro-life meeting believing that she was helping a friend shop for some lawn equipment. Ladies and gentlemen, Suzie is majoring in English literature at Western, not science—she had no clue that the equipment Stephen Gray was purchasing was to be used for any purpose other than what he told her. Yes, her fingerprints were on the can—she helped carry Gray's purchases to the check stand. I believe the evidence you will hear will demonstrate that Suzie

O'Dell is just the kind of girl who can be easily tricked into holding a can at Fred Meyer. But she is not, I repeat, not the kind of girl who would sneak up to a clinic at night, place gas cans around, start a fire, and kill a young woman doctor in cold blood."

Suzie picked up her pen and wrote on the pad Peter had given her. *He's good.*

Cooper nodded discreetly.

"No matter what the prosecutor has said about supposed links of evidence, he is relying on convincing you of a warped character in order to supply the missing links in his story. He has told you there will be evidence about some supposed radical statements made by Suzie O'Dell. From those alleged statements he is suggesting that Suzie is somehow capable of creating bombs and killing innocent people. Whatever that evidence turns out to be, it will pale into insignificance in comparison to the greater weight of evidence you will receive about a girl who loves people and was simply caught in a slippery trap made by a man elusive enough to disappear."

Peter paused and solemnly paced three steps toward the audience, then turned, placing both hands on the jury rail. "Death by hanging," he said, looking slowly at each member of the jury. "Please keep your minds open and don't let the prosecutor's suggestions and imagination fool you into sending an innocent girl to her death."

Peter smiled, swiped at his hair to put a few stray strands in place, then sat down.

"Good job," Cooper whispered encouragingly. Peter frowned.

"We'll stand in recess for twenty minutes," Hayden pronounced with a bang of his gavel.

Peter stepped outside for a fresh air. When he returned, he was surprised to see Cooper seated in his spot with Shannon Carpenter leaning on the counsel table, engaged in animated conversation. As Peter came closer, Shannon caught him in her peripheral vision and quickly departed for her own side of the courtroom.

Peter said nothing at first and simply thumbed through a large black notebook where he had some typed notes concerning each potential witness under separate tabs.

"What was that all about?" he finally whispered to Cooper.

"I really don't know," his associate responded. "She was just telling me about good restaurants and things like that, kind of playing tour guide for the out-of-town lawyer."

"I'd say she was flirting with you; just don't get too friendly. The O'Dells and everybody else would begin to wonder whose side you are on. Try to keep her away."

"No problem with me," Cooper replied.

The bailiff made his preliminary rounds through the courtroom to get everyone in place, and shortly the court was back in session, with Dr. Hugh Weber called as the first witness.

The county coroner dutifully marched through the details of finding a dead body and performing the necessary exams to conclude that Rhonda Marsano had died from smoke inhalation between 10 and 11 P.M. on Friday, May 20.

Peter rose for his chance to cross-examine the coroner. "Dr. Weber, did you find any other injuries to Dr. Marsano—anything else that might have contributed to her death?"

"Of course, there were severe burns on her body, but as best as I can tell she was already dead from the smoke by the time the fire got to her."

"Anything else?"

"I did note a small hematoma on the back of her head."

"Would you explain that in layman's terms?"

"It's an area of under-the-surface bleeding, a bruise if you will. To put it even more simply, Dr. Marsano had sustained a moderate bump on the head that evening."

Peter began pacing, trying to decipher this unexpected bit of evidence. "Were you able to determine what caused this bump on the head?"

"No, not specifically," the coroner replied.

Peter paused, pulling out his gold pen and twirling it in his fingers as he thought. "Well, what could have caused it?"

"Objection. Calls for speculation," Franklin cried out.

"Sustained," said Hayden.

"All right, Dr. Weber, what kind of blow would be likely to cause such an injury—confining your answer to possibilities that would occur with reasonable medical probability?"

"Same objection," Franklin said.

"Overruled," the judge replied, turning again to watch the witness.

"Well, it *could* have been that someone hit her with some kind of a blunt instrument, but that seems a bit unlikely since there are no other signs of a physical confrontation. But a blow with an instrument certainly could have caused that injury. It is more likely that Dr. Marsano simply fainted from the smoke and bumped her head on something."

"Could this blow *have caused* Dr. Marsano to pass out, assuming she was still conscious at the time the blow occurred?"

"Hmm . . . Yes, I guess it is predictable that she could have been knocked out from a blow of that magnitude, at least for a little while."

"Thank you, doctor. No further questions." Peter returned to his seat, snapping the cap back onto his pen.

"Where were you going with that?" Cooper whispered.

"I don't know. Just fishing. Seemed interesting."

Franklin was on his feet headed toward the lectern that had been repositioned back in the center of the courtroom.

"Dr. Weber, have you changed your mind as to the cause of Dr. Marsano's death as a result of any of the questions Mr. Barron asked you just now?"

"Oh no, not at all. The cause of death was definitely smoke inhalation."

"Did the bruise on the back of her head contribute to her death in any way?"

"Certainly not in any direct way," Weber replied. "Indirectly, if she was laying there knocked out cold, she would have been unable to get up and break out some windows to prevent the smoke from getting her so soon. But in a direct sense, the bruise was absolutely unrelated to her death."

Franklin decided he had better shut up. A careless question might cause the coroner to open a bigger hole for the defense than Peter had accomplished. "Thank you, Dr. Weber."

Franklin walked back to his table and took a new pad with questions from Shannon Carpenter. "The State calls Reyn Ward to the stand."

"It's almost four o'clock," Hayden said. "How long will you be with this witness?"

"Only about thirty minutes, Your Honor," Franklin replied.

"Fine, let's see if we can finish with him even if we have to go a few minutes past five," the judge said, leaning back in this chair, waiting for the bailiff to bring Ward into the courtroom.

Two minutes later a six-foot-two-inch police investigator came in through the back door, wearing the trademark blue blazer and grey slacks.

Ward appeared to be about fifty, but had only a few patches of grey mixed in with his dark brown hair.

Franklin asked for his name and occupation.

"Reyn Ward, chief arson investigator for the Washington State Patrol."

"Where are you headquartered?"

"I'm in the Seattle district office."

"How long have you been an arson investigator?"

"Seventeen years."

"And how long in the State Patrol altogether?"

"Twenty years. I went into arson after three years of regular road patrol. Before that I was a city police officer for the City of Bellevue for six years."

"How many arson investigations have you conducted?"

"Something around 250."

Franklin stood firmly planted at the lectern, looking again at his sheet of typed notes. "Did you have occasion to conduct an arson investigation at the Whatcom Women's Center for Choice?"

"Yes, sir," he said crisply.

"When did you begin your investigation?"

"I arrived at the scene around 10 on the morning of May 21, the day after the fire."

"How long did your investigation take?"

"Well, there were two phases. First, there was the on-the-scene search for evidence, and then we conducted certain tests in our laboratory to try to verify our field evaluation."

"How long were you on the scene doing the first phase of the investigation?"

"Three days. Saturday, Sunday, and Monday."

"Did you do the investigation by yourself?"

"Oh, no, sir. I had a team of two associates from our office who were with me the whole time."

"Were you in charge of their work, and did you review and supervise the entire operation?"

"Yes, sir."

"Were you able to find the cause of the fire?"

"Yes, we were."

"Where did the fire start?"

"It started on the outside of the building on a porch. I guess you would call it the back porch from pictures I have seen while the building was still intact."

"Had the building collapsed?"

"No, the fire department was able to stop the blaze before the walls actually gave way, but the damage was so substantial that the building has subsequently been razed."

"What caused the fire to start on the outside of the building?"

"There was an incendiary device made of a gas can, some wire, a large square battery—the kind used on what we would call an old camping flashlight—and a windup alarm clock."

"How do you know that these were the components of the device?"

"We found the melted pieces."

Franklin walked forward with a neat white cardboard box. "May I approach the witness, Your Honor?"

"Yes, Mr. Franklin."

"Mr. Ward, I'm handing you what has been marked as plaintiff's exhibit 5 for identification. And there are four sealed plastic bags in this box, labeled 5A, 5B, 5C, and 5D. Can you please identify each of these items?"

"Well, 5A here," Ward said, holding up a large plastic bag with a mass of scorched sheet metal, "is the remains of the gas can. It exploded, and then the paint melted off pretty much in the fire. There is no doubt that it was a gas can."

"What is 5B?"

"This," he said, holding up a much smaller bag with a barely visible blob inside, "is a bit of copper wire that was found inside the top of the remains of the gas can."

"And 5C?"

"A melted and scorched flashlight battery."

"And finally, 5D?"

"That's a melted alarm clock," he said holding up a bag with a blob of white plastic goo with metal flecks apparent here and there.

"In what proximity were these four items found?"

"They were all within about eighteen inches of each other."

"How did the device work?"

"The gas can had to have a little space in the top for air to get in. Then the wire ran through the can—probably a loop of wire was just stuck through the big hole and out the vent hole. The battery supplied the necessary power to heat the wire and create enough heat to ignite the gas."

"What role did the alarm clock play?"

"It was used as a simple timing device. When the alarm went off, the circuit was completed, and a minute or two later, a small spark would have been followed by a fire."

"Did you see any indications of other gasoline being used to feed the fire?"

"Yes, we found significant residue in two areas. First, there was clear evidence of gas having been poured around the perimeter of most of the

back of the building. And then there was a high concentration of gasoline inside on an area not too far from the stairs in the first floor of the
building."

"Did you determine what caused the high concentration of gasoline
near the stairs?"

"Yes, there appeared to be another of the same kind of device in this
area. The gas came from the gas can."

"But this second device did not cause the fire?"

"No, the fire was well underway before the gas in this can ignited.
It appears that this device failed, or perhaps someone had dismantled
the device. At any rate, the pattern of burning absolutely rules out any
role this device may have had in starting the fire."

Franklin double-checked his list and then looked at the judge. "No
further questions, Your Honor."

"Mr. Barron, you may inquire, provided that you intend to conclude by five fifteen. That gives you forty-five minutes."

"That will be more than enough time," Peter replied, already on his
feet.

"Mr. Ward. I am very interested in this second device," Peter began.
"Can you tell why, exactly, it didn't work?"

"It's impossible to say for sure. It sustained considerable damage in
the fire."

"Did you find the same four component parts for this gas can inside
the building, as you found in exhibit 5?"

"Yes, we did."

"Including the wire?"

"We found wire in the gas can, but no wire was found on the remains
of the battery."

"Do you have an explanation for that?"

"There were fire fighters racing through the building; it could have been kicked. It might have been knocked off in the fire itself. The force of a fire hose could have done something to it. Many things could have happened."

"What was the proximity of the four components you found inside?"

"Again, within about eighteen inches."

"If the battery had been kicked or hit hard by a blast of a fire hose, would it have remained in that eighteen-inch circumference?"

"No, that would not be likely."

"Could the wire have been deliberately taken off?"

"Yes, of course."

"It would have to have been taken off by someone in the building before the fire, wouldn't it?"

"Yes, that is assuming the device had been completely wired in the first place."

"Did you find any evidence that anyone other than Dr. Marsano was in the building after the fire began?"

"There was no evidence of that. But, of course, the only evidence that Dr. Marsano was in the building at the time of the fire was her dead body. We found no other bodies if that is what you are asking."

"No further questions," Peter announced triumphantly.

Cooper waited anxiously for him to return to the table. "You got a theory?" the associate asked.

"Not a one. I'm just throwing dust in the air, hoping for a miracle or the ability to create a diversion," Peter whispered in reply.

The judge admonished the jury not to watch any television news, and not to listen to the radio at all. "This case is going to be on every single newscast, so simply avoid all papers and news programs. And do not talk about this case to anyone—even your spouses when you call them from the hotel. You are to contact the bailiff at once if any member of the media or any person associated with this case tries to talk with you. Enjoy your dinner, and the bailiff will give you further instructions."

After the judge and jury had filed out for the evening, Suzie sat back down hard into her seat, her head in her hands.

Peter walked over and laid a hand on her shoulder. "The first day of testimony is always the hardest, Suzie. We're going to come out of this. Remember, Franklin gets to call all his people first."

She just shook her head and sat silently for a long time.

Nothing prevented Vince Davis from watching two versions of the story on local TV stations, as well as additional stories on CBS, ABC, and CNN. The reports uniformly carried expert commentators who gave the prosecution good marks for the first day of testimony.

Vince emptied a six-pack to show his disgust for the prosecutor, who apparently chose to ignore Vince's call.

26

Detective Dunn's direct examination took most of Thursday morning as Franklin methodically laid out the details of the discovery of Dr. Marsano's body, the finding of the gas can in the dumpster behind the clinic, the discovery of the Fred Meyer videotape, and the department's efforts to locate Stephen Gray. Right after lunch Dunn was ready to be cross-examined.

"Detective Dunn," Peter said, smiling as he rose to his feet, "I would like you to focus on the Fred Meyer videotape—plaintiffs' exhibit 12."

"All right," Dunn replied, shifting his weight to his left hip to try to give some relief to his back. Three hours on the witness stand that morning had created a moderate level of discomfort.

"We all watched that tape twice this morning and there is no doubt that Suzie O'Dell is in that picture holding a gas can as plain as day. Sir, what part of her anatomy did Suzie use to hold the gas can?"

"What part of her anatomy?" Dunn asked, scrunching up his eyebrows, thinking there had to be something more to the question than it appeared.

"Yes," Peter replied, pausing his pacing for a moment.

"Her hands. Is that what you mean?"

"Yes, that's it exactly. And, Detective, I am sorry if these seem like silly questions, but please bear with me. Did she appear to be using her fingers while she was holding the gas can in her hands there at Fred Meyer?"

"Yes, Mr. Barron, indeed she was using her fingers." His voice wavered between amusement and contempt.

"Was she wearing gloves or can you see her naked hands there in the video?"

"Her naked hands are visible in the video. She was not wearing gloves."

"OK, is there any reason her fingers would not have left fingerprints on that can while she was holding it there in the Fred Meyer store?"

"No reason."

"So her fingerprints would have been placed on the can on Wednesday May 18, two days before the fire. Isn't that correct?"

"Yes, that is correct."

"Do fingerprints last that long if no one wipes them off?"

"It depends on the surface on which the fingerprints appear," came Dunn's reply, shifting his weight uncomfortably to the other hip.

"Well," Peter said smiling, "how about—for instance—metal gas cans? Would fingerprints last for two days on a gas can?"

"Yes, they would."

"Fine. Now, do you know where these three gas cans were between the time they were purchased on Wednesday, May 18 and Friday, May 20?"

"No, sir, I don't."

"Your investigation proved, did it not, that the purchase at Fred Meyer was paid for by Stephen Gray's Visa card?"

"That's correct."

"So when Mr. Franklin here," Peter said, gesturing toward the prosecutor, "says that Suzie O'Dell purchased the gas cans and other items, he is not being precisely accurate is he?"

"No, he is not being precisely accurate, but—"

"Just answer the question; no exposition is necessary, Detective," the judge interrupted.

"So your evidence simply demonstrates that Suzie O'Dell was present during the purchase of the gas cans and other items. It demonstrates nothing more than that, does it?"

"You're correct, I guess."

Peter stopped his pacing and crossed his arms, staring at the witness for a moment. Detective Dunn returned the stare, then looked away. Peter continued. "The sole physical evidence you have is that Suzie had her hands on the gas can two days before the fire, nothing more. Isn't that right?"

"Yeah, that's one way to look at it."

Peter began to return to his seat, then froze in mid-step, unwilling to let Dunn get away with that wimpy answer. Turning to the detective, he fixed an icy stare on the witness. "Does your last answer mean yes? Or does it mean something different?"

"It's means yes," Dunn growled.

"Thank you, Detective," Peter said, completing his descent into his chair. "No further questions, Your Honor."

Franklin was on his feet in a flash. "I have no need to ask any further questions," he said disdainfully. "I'd like to call Rachel Grove to the stand."

Suzie jerked her head to the left and looked at Peter with her mouth agape. "Rachel?" she whispered.

"Who is she?" Peter whispered back.

"She's a friend from college. She was in the pro-life group for a time, then dropped out."

Peter rolled his eyes and scooted his chair back into place. Every juror had watched their interchange.

A young, brown-haired coed in a blue jumper walked into the courtroom. She froze just inside the door when she saw the room was packed.

"Come forward, young lady," the judge said in a kind voice.

Franklin got up and held open the swinging gate to let her inside the bar of the courtroom. "Right over there," he said, pointing to the witness stand.

She sat down, and the bailiff stood directly in front her with his right hand raised. "Do you promise to tell the whole truth so help you God?"

"Yes, sir," she said in a voice that was barely audible.

"Young lady," the judge said softly, "I understand that you are nervous and that's fine. But I would ask you to speak as loudly as possible so that everyone, particularly our jurors there on your left, can hear you clearly. OK?"

"Yes, sir," she said just a bit louder.

"Please state your name and address."

"I'm Rachel Grove, and my home address is Route 2, Roy, Washington. Did you want my address at college?"

"No, home is fine," Franklin said. "But you are a student at Western?"

"Yes, sir, I'm a sophomore."

"Ms. Grove, do you know the defendant, Susan O'Dell?"

Suzie stared hard at Rachel, still puzzled as to why she had been called as a witness.

"Yes, she's a member of the Campus Christian Fellowship, and so am I," Rachel said.

"What are some of the activities you have done together?"

"Both of us sing most mornings on Red Square by the big fountain. And there are meetings some evenings. A few parties. Things like that."

"Are you and Miss O'Dell personal friends—I mean, do you do things together, one on one, or are you usually just a part of this larger group together?"

"We're friends, but I guess you would say we're mostly just a part of the same Christian group."

"OK," Franklin said, smiling. "Ms. Grove, were you a part of the pro-life group that was protesting the abortion clinic here in Bellingham?"

"I did a few things."

"Can you please describe what you did?"

"Uh . . . well, I went to two, no, I guess three protests at the clinic on different Saturdays. And I went to one meeting at a home over on Lake Whatcom."

"Colonel Danners's house?"

"Yes, that's right."

"When did this meeting take place?"

"I don't remember exactly, last spring sometime."

"Was it before the fire at the clinic?"

"Oh yes."

"How long before?"

"A few weeks before, I don't really remember."

"All right. Ms. Grove, how did you get to the meeting at Colonel Danners's home?"

"I got a ride from Stephen Gray."

"Who else was in the car?"

"His girlfriend, Lisa Edgar, was in the front seat. In the back seat there was me, my other friend Kim Batey, and Susan O'Dell."

"How did you come to ride with Mr. Gray?"

"Suzie arranged it. She asked me to go to the meeting and said this guy could give Kim and me a ride with her."

"Do you remember anything unusual happening at the meeting at the colonel's house?"

"Sort of. I guess you're talking about the thing Stephen Gray said, is that right?"

Franklin smiled. "Ms. Grove, I'm not allowed to prompt you, I would just like you to tell the jury if you heard or saw anything unusual at the meeting."

"Well, I thought Stephen Gray's talk at the meeting was a little strange."

"What did he say?"

"He read a couple passages from the Bible and then started talking about us needing to do more to stand up for the unborn, to rescue them and stuff."

"What did you find unusual about that?"

"Well, it's just that the passages seemed to be twisted around to fit his message; they didn't necessarily have anything to do with unborn babies. And too, he was sort of suggesting illegal activities at the clinic—which was in direct contradiction to what the colonel had been saying all along."

"How did the other people feel about his little talk; for instance, what did the colonel say?"

"The colonel was visibly upset at the time; but he didn't say much except that if we started engaging in illegal behavior, we'd eventually have to stop the protests altogether. But after the meeting, the colonel took him aside while Suzie, Kim, Lisa, and I waited. We could hear the colonel talking to him. He wasn't exactly yelling, but you could tell he was mad at Mr. Gray."

"Fine, Ms. Grove," Franklin said, glancing at his notes. "Now I'd like to have you focus on the ride home. First, were the same people in the car going home?"

"Yes, we were all there."

"Did anything happen on the ride home that you found to be strange or unusual?"

"I was a little surprised at some things Suzie said."

Peter turned quickly to look at Suzie. She was still staring straight at Rachel.

"What did she say?"

Peter was on his feet in a flash. "Objection, hearsay, Your Honor."

"It's an admission against interest," Franklin replied.

"Objection overruled," Hayden said, looking intently at Rachel.

"Ms. Grove, you can answer my question," Franklin said. "What did Miss O'Dell say that surprised you?"

"Well, she started talking about what Mr. Gray had said, and that she didn't understand why the Colonel got mad. And then she said she thought that we ought to do more—join God's army, whatever it took to save the babies."

"Are you sure of that?"

Rachel paused. Peter noticed a red glow creeping up Suzie's neck. He hoped the jury wouldn't notice.

"Well, I doubt I got it right word for word. But that's pretty close to what she said—I definitely remember the part about God's army."

"Did you understand what she meant by the phrase God's army?"

"I didn't know for sure. I meant to ask Kim what she thought, but I just forgot about it after we got back to the dorms."

"When did you next remember that conversation?"

"The morning after the fire at the clinic. As soon as I heard the news, it was the first thing that came to mind."

"Ms. Grove, you didn't want to come here today to testify against your friend, did you?"

"That's right."

"The only reason you're here is because I had a subpoena served on you and you were forced to be here, isn't that right?"

"Yes," she said, lowering her eyes.

"Thank you, Ms. Grove, I have no further questions."

Peter asked for and received a fifteen-minute recess. He took Suzie, Cooper, and Suzie's parents into the witness conference room.

"Suzie," Peter said plaintively, "did you really say those things?"

"I—I don't remember," she stammered looking at her parents and then down at her feet.

"Come on Suzie, it's important," Peter said, a little impatiently. "Try your best to remember."

"I guess I did," she replied, her eyes starting to fill with tears. "I guess I got a little carried away with what Stephen had said. Later on, though, I thought more about it, and it didn't seem so right anymore. Then I just kind of forgot all about it."

"That's OK," Peter said. "It really doesn't prove anything."

Suzie's father slipped up beside her and put his arm firmly around his daughter.

"But it looks bad, doesn't it?" Suzie asked.

Peter smiled and said nothing, trying to think of a way to give her a non-answer. Finally, his smile faded and he shook his a head. "It looks kind of bad, but it's still not enough in my opinion."

"It'll be fine," Cooper said, trying to sound reassuring. "Peter is great at this kind of thing. He'll be able to turn it around."

"Yeah, it'll be fine," Peter said.

Linda O'Dell thought that Peter's last assurance sounded hollow but said nothing.

"I guess we'd better be getting back in," Cooper said.

"Yeah, let's go," Peter replied.

As they started to file out of the witness room, Peter grabbed Cooper's arm and held him back. "Double check me on this, Coop," he said softly. "I think maybe I should just let her step down without any cross-examination. Suzie says she got it right, and anything I ask her is just likely to reinforce the jury's suspicions. What do you think?"

"You're probably right," Cooper said. "But you're the seasoned litigator. I'm the rookie. Remember?"

"Yeah, I remember," Peter said smiling. "But even a rookie has a good idea once in a while. Let's go."

"Your Honor," Peter said after the court had resumed, "I have no questions for Miss Grove."

Hayden raised his eyebrows, registering the kind of subdued surprise a judge learns after several years of service. "All right. Mr. Franklin, you can call your next witness."

"The state rests, Your Honor," Franklin said, popping up on his feet briefly.

"Your Honor—" Peter said, taking his feet as soon as Franklin sat down.

"You have a motion, Mr. Barron?"

Peter nodded.

"Fine, let's take care of the jury first." Hayden turned in his swivel chair to once again face the jury. "Ladies and gentlemen of the jury, we've come to the point of the case where the state has rested. Our normal rules of procedure require us to deal with some intermediate matters right now that will consume the balance of the hour or hour-and-a-half that we have left in the day. So I'm going to excuse you early today. Then we'll be back tomorrow morning at nine."

Peter argued for dismissal for about half an hour. Franklin stood up ready to begin his rebuttal.

"Please keep your seat, Mr. Franklin," Hayden said. "There's no need. Mr. Barron's motion was argued as well as I have ever heard. Miss O'Dell, you indeed have an excellent lawyer. But I'm going to deny the motion. There is clearly a *prima facie* case, here. It's going to be up to this jury to decide. I'm not going to take the case away from them. All right, gentlemen, anything else?" Hayden asked.

Peter shook his head, and Franklin answered no.

"Fine. We'll reconvene tomorrow morning at nine."

The surprise witness who told of Susan O'Dell's advocacy to "join God's army" was the lead story on all the Seattle stations that night. Expert commentators uniformly called it a "serious blow to the defense." Many of the law professors who hadn't seen the inside of a courtroom in twenty years openly criticized Peter's decision to forego any cross-examination of Rachel Grove.

Shannon Carpenter was in her flannel pajamas sitting on the couch in her living room watching the eleven o'clock news when her phone rang.

"Hello."

"Shannon Carpenter?" a male voice asked.

"Who is this?"

"Stephen Gray," Vince Davis said.

"How did you get my number?"

"Directory assistance," he replied. "S. Carpenter wasn't that difficult to figure out."

"Where are you?"

"You know I'm not going to answer that question."

"Why are you calling me?" she asked.

"I want to know why you guys aren't following up on the owners of the clinic. I told you they hired me to torch their clinic. Suzie O'Dell is innocent."

"We talked about it a lot," she replied dejectedly. "My boss and the people in Washington, D.C. think you're a crank and not really Stephen Gray. And even if you are, they think you're lying to protect your pro-life friends."

"What do you think?" Gray asked.

There was a long silence on the line.

"Are you still there?" Gray asked.

"Yeah . . . I guess it doesn't matter much what I think. There's nothing I can do. My hands are tied."

"So what do I do?"

"I'm not sure. Come here and testify. That'd get everybody's attention."

"No way. You got any other suggestions?"

"I guess you'll have to call Peter Barron and tell him your story. I can't do anything with it."

"You know what hotel he's in?"

"No, I don't. Why don't you call his house? I know he's married and his wife's at home. She can tell you."

Now it was Vince's turn to be silent. Finally he said, "I dunno. Maybe I should wait until after the trial's over and see what happens. I could still save Suzie afterwards if things turned out bad for her, couldn't I?"

"I've already said way too much," Carpenter replied. "But for some crazy reason I think I believe you. So all I can say is whatever you decide to do, you'd better do it right away. Unless you come in person and tell the whole story, after the trial it'll be too late for Suzie."

"When's it going to be over?"

"I'd guess next Tuesday or Wednesday it'll go to the jury."

"I'll think about it."

The line went dead.

Suzie O'Dell crept out of bed at the Danners's house around 1:30. She took some logs out of the bin in the living room and expertly started a blaze.

With a blanket wrapped tightly around her, she watched the flames in the fireplace, while flames of recrimination burned in her mind throughout the night. *Why did I ever say those things?* she asked herself repeatedly. She dozed only sporadically until just before dawn. At the first sign of light, she tiptoed back into her room and lay back on the bed, trying to gain the inner peace to face another day.

McDougal was awakened by the phone at his home in Chicago at six.

"Yeah?" he said in the dark.

"Someone claiming to be Gray called Shannon Carpenter at home last night," the voice said.

"You got the tape?"

"Yeah."

"Play it for me," McDougal commanded.

He listened intently to the seven-minute conversation.

"OK, I want live taps on Barron's home and office phones. The moment he calls, I want it traced. You page me immediately when you've got him on line. I'll get a chartered jet ready. If he's on this continent, I'll get him today."

27

Just after one o'clock Friday afternoon, Gwen heard their kitchen phone ringing. She struggled to her feet from the kitchen table where she was drinking a cup of hot tea. The weight of the baby seemed to be in an uncomfortable position right then, and it took her until the third ring to cover the twelve feet between the table and the phone.

"Hello?"

"Mrs. Barron?" asked Vince.

"Yes."

"This is Stephen Gray."

Gwen thought the name sounded vaguely familiar, and then it clicked. "Stephen Gray from Bellingham?"

"You got it," he replied.

"A lot of people have been looking for you."

"Yeah, I know. I don't want to talk about that. I just want you to get a message to your husband."

"OK," she replied.

"Tell him that the owners of the clinic, Jane Hayward and Karen Ballentine, hired me to torch the clinic. Karen and Dr. Marsano were both in the clinic when I left. I think Karen must have hit her on the head or something, and that would explain the bump. I didn't mean to hurt Rhonda; I loved her." He paused for several seconds.

"Anyhow . . . if your husband subpoenas their financial records, they'll find proof that the owners paid me to do all this."

"Oh my," Gwen said. "Can you say that all again so I can take some notes?"

"No, you got the drift—just pass it along to your husband. I want him to find the records so he can nail those two. When they're exposed, things will be OK for me, too. Until then I'm not safe. I just want to do what I can to save Suzie."

Something in Gwen's spirit told her to speak boldly. "Mr. Gray, I think the person that needs to be saved is you."

"I appreciate the sentiment," he replied.

"I don't mean saved from the owners of the clinic—I'm talking about saved from your sins."

"Yeah, I know, I messed this deal up and I'm trying to make amends by helping Suzie."

"It's good to try to do whatever you can for Suzie, but I'm talking about you personally now. You can't ever make amends for all of your sins."

Rhonda's face flashed into Gray's mind, then thoughts of their unborn child. "You got that right," he replied dejectedly.

"There's only one way to truly deal with all of your sins, and that is to accept Jesus as your Savior and ask Him to forgive you for all the wrong things you've ever done. Do you understand what I'm talking about?"

"Yeah, I do. My dad was a pastor—Assembly of God. He told me this stuff all the time. I just didn't buy it."

"Then you should know exactly what I'm talking about. What's stopping you from accepting Jesus right now? You know that's the only way to be truly saved from the eternal mess you're in."

"Well, at this point, I have a hard time believing that God would forgive me. I've done a lot of really bad stuff."

"That doesn't matter to God. King David committed adultery and murder, yet God forgave him. Paul was an accessory to the murder of Christians. He called himself the chief of sinners, and God saved him. You can't have sinned too much for God to be able to forgive."

Something in her voice sounded so warm and tender; Vince found himself wanting to please this woman. But a wave of coldness overtook his mind from years of practice shutting out his father and his own conscience. "I gotta go," he said. "Just tell your husband to get the financial records."

"Please, Mr. Gray . . . Mr. Gray!"

The line went dead.

"Yeah?" McDougal growled into his phone.

"Got him. He called Peter Barron's home number from Kennewick, Washington. The phone is registered in the name of Dave Cummings at an apartment on Canal Drive in Kennewick."

"That's him. He's used that cover before," McDougal responded. "I'll be there in about four hours."

At about 1:20 P.M., Peter's beeper began to vibrate under his suit coat. *Call Sally at the church ASAP. It's not the baby,* the digital message read.

He dashed out of the witness room—where he had been preparing the lineup of character witnesses he had called for that afternoon—into the hall, down two flights of stairs, and into the phone booth just outside the eating area for the coffee shop.

"Sally? What's up?"

"You'll never believe this—Stephen Gray called Gwen at home!"

"What?" Peter exclaimed.

"Yeah. She started going into the details, but I told her to save them for you. I didn't want you to get third-hand information."

"OK, bye," he said as he disconnected the call and dialed his home number furiously.

"Gwen?" he said as soon as she answered.

"Peter, I'm glad it's you. I'm OK; it's not the baby."

"Yeah, I know. Sally told me that Stephen Gray called you. Tell me quick. I have to be in court in less than five minutes."

"Well, he told me that the two clinic owners, two women—I'm sorry I can't remember their names—oh well . . . they hired him to set fire to the clinic. One of them, I think he said her first name was Karen, was in the clinic with Gray and the doctor just before the fire. Gray left, and he thinks that Karen hit Rhonda on the head and then left. He said to subpoena their financial records and that you would find the evidence."

"Won't he come forward and testify?"

"No. I tried to ask him."

"Is that it?"

"Uh . . . one more thing. He said he loved Rhonda."

"He did?"

"Yeah."

"What's that supposed to mean?" Peter asked.

"I don't know. He just said he loved her."

"OK," Peter said, trying to assimilate it all. "I gotta go. Thanks, honey."

At Peter's request, the bailiff ushered the four lawyers back into the judge's chambers before the afternoon session began.

"Mr. Barron, my secretary said you wanted to make a quick request before we began," the judge said.

"Yes, Judge Hayden," Peter said, "It's a little unusual, and I think we had better put it on the record."

"All right, Mr. Barron," Hayden replied. He picked up his phone. "Clarice, can you have Nancy come in here with her machine?"

A minute or two later, the court reporter was in position with her shorthand machine in front of her.

"Your Honor, I would like to ask for an order with a couple of components to it. I want ask this court to issue a *subpoena duces tecum* to the owners of the clinic and to bring all of their financial records. I want them to testify here on Monday or Tuesday."

"And your reason for this last-minute request?" the judge asked.

"Well, as strange as it may sound, my wife got a call about forty minutes ago from the missing Stephen Gray. He claimed that the owners of the clinic hired him to burn the clinic down. And he says that if we subpoena their financial records, we'll find evidence of this."

"Is Mr. Gray going to come back to Bellingham and testify to any of this?" Hayden asked.

"No, Your Honor, he told my wife he isn't coming back."

"Mr. Franklin, you haven't heard anything from Mr. Gray have you?"

"No, Your—ooh!" Franklin felt a sharp kick on his right leg from the point of a high heel. "Sorry, Your Honor, I had sudden stomach pain. Shouldn't have eaten onions at lunch. Anyway, nothing directly from Mr. Gray. One of our staffers received a call from a person claiming to be Gray some time ago. We thought it was a crank call. Since I didn't take the call myself, I can't say precisely what was said. We've had several strange calls about this case. I don't know what else I can say."

"Hmmm," Hayden said. "This is an interesting request, and an even more interesting reason. Here's what I am going to do. Mr. Barron, if you can fly to Los Angeles tonight or in the morning, I will order the clinic owners to produce their records in front of a court reporter tomorrow at noon. Perhaps you could do this in the law office of the firm that represented them in the federal action. You can look through their records in a deposition format. I will not permit you to bog this trial down with a fishing expedition conducted on the stand. I will, however, issue the *subpoena duces tecum* requiring them to come testify. Even though they are in California, they are the complaining witnesses in the arson matter and, I believe, are sitting in my courtroom; and you are entitled to call them as a matter of right. If they refuse to come, I will indicate in the order that I will seriously consider a motion to dismiss the arson charge. That ought to get their cooperation.

"If you come back with some focused evidence, so be it. If not, I do not want a general parade of their finances put forth in front of this jury.

"Any objections, Mr. Franklin?"

"Uh . . . I guess not, Your Honor. I don't see the point that Mr. Barron is making, but I guess the only thing I would request is that we be allowed to attend the deposition."

"Well, of course. You can certainly be in attendance and raise the normal objections and so forth."

"The only problem is that I am scheduled to speak at a political event in Wenatchee tomorrow—the duties of an elected official, you know. I guess I'll have to send Ms. Carpenter to represent our office."

"I'm sure she'll do a good job," Hayden replied.

"Yeah, she's fast on her feet," Franklin said, rubbing the back of his leg with his opposite foot.

"All right. Are we ready to resume the trial?"

"Yes, Judge," Peter replied.

"More character witnesses?" Hayden asked.

"Yes, I am going to call both of her parents."

"OK. Let's go."

McDougal's chartered jet landed at the Tri-City Airport in Pasco, just across the Columbia River from Kennewick, about an hour before dusk. A man identified only as Eddie was waiting in a silver Lincoln Continental. McDougal placed a call to some underworld friends in Seattle and found a "discrete driver."

"You got the address?" McDougal asked as he snapped the seat belt closed.

Eddie nodded and pressed down the accelerator.

Two miles later they hit Highway 395 and headed south across the long blue bridge that spans the Columbia River. Eddie stayed left when they approached a series of cloverleaf ramps immediately after crossing the bridge. A mile later they turned right at a stop light, and in a moment were on Canal Drive looking for the apartment number.

Two miles later, Eddie slowed the Continental and pulled right into the parking lot of Vince's apartment complex.

"Come with me," McDougal said.

Again, Eddie just nodded.

They headed for a set of exterior stairs looking for the correct unit when suddenly McDougal spotted Vince, dressed in a suit and tie and descending an identical set of stairs twenty yards to their right.

"That's him," the Chicago hit man growled.

Both men pulled their pistols from underneath their jackets.

"I want the first shot," McDougal whispered as they turned to go back to the parking lot.

The clamor of their running feet caught Vince's attention. An involuntary guttural cry emerged from his lips as he recognized McDougal scampering down the stairs.

Vince dashed to his left. McDougal took aim and fired. Vince ducked and ran hard to his left and rounded the corner of the building.

Both men ran rapidly across the parking lot, but McDougal, trim and about forty, was much faster than his overweight companion of about fifty. They cautiously rounded the corner where they had last seen Vince. He was fifty yards down a steep slope ahead of them, just disappearing over a fence and headed downhill in the direction of the Columbia River.

Eddie took aim.

"Save it," McDougal said. "He's gone and it'll attract even more attention than the first shot." Pulling a portable cellular phone from his pocket, he tossed it to Eddie. "You keep an eye on him and call me in the car. He's headed for that park, if you ask me."

"Yeah," Eddie muttered.

McDougal ran back to the car and started the engine. Ninety seconds later the car phone rang. "Where is he?" McDougal demanded.

"He crossed that big stretch of sage brush and has gone across the railroad tracks and the irrigation canal. Right now he's climbing the chain link fence beside the freeway. Where are you headed?"

"I'm going back down Canal Street. Isn't there a road straight down this hill?"

"No, you'll have to go back the way we came. Just before the blue bridge there's a cloverleaf going to Richland and Yakima. Take that and then take the first exit on your right. You'll be at the entrance into the park at that point."

"Got it," McDougal replied.

"OK, he's crossed the first side of the freeway and is in the median strip. He runs pretty fast. . . . Now he's going over the second fence and is in that little golf course. You'll see it on your left as soon as you take the exit. Where are you?"

"I'm on the cloverleaf right now. How far to this exit?"

"About two minutes," Eddie replied. "You should be going up an overpass with a pretty good view of the park pretty soon. Maybe you can see him. He's cutting across the course at a pretty good pace."

"Just a second, I'm starting up the overpass right now; yeah, I see him! This'll be easy. And I like this deserted park."

"Not many people there in February," Eddie said with a sarcastic chuckle. "Can you see him? He's crossing the road that goes the whole length of the park. I can see you now as well. Just pull off the road for a second right after the exit. If he turns left, head down that road he just ran across. If he goes right, you'll want to take that right turn about fifty yards ahead of you."

"I've lost him behind some trees," McDougal said. "Can you still see him?"

"Yeah . . . this hill is a perfect vantage point. He's just about to the river. OK, he's turning right. He's headed toward the blue bridge. If you hurry, you can catch him before you run out of road."

McDougal pushed the accelerator to the floor. The Continental flew around the slow curves of the empty park roads.

"Man, he's fast. He's about to pass the spot where that road you're on dead ends. You won't catch him in time going that way. Flip a U-turn and head back, I'll send you a different way."

The Continental squealed and threw gravel from the edge of the road as McDougal forced a 180-degree turn.

"Stay straight and go south around that muddy lagoon area right in front of you. That road will take you right under the blue bridge. You should get to the bridge just about the same time he does. He's got a definite advantage of being able to go straight across those fields."

"I can't see him anymore," McDougal yelled into the phone. "You still got him?"

"Yeah . . . he's definitely going for the bridge. He's scrambling up the dike. It's getting dark, and it's hard for me to see him now. He's gotten pretty far away."

"I got him," McDougal said with a smile. "A hundred yards from now and he's mine." He hung up the cellular phone and pressed just a little harder on the accelerator.

McDougal screeched to a stop just under the bridge and jumped out of the car as he saw Vince disappear behind a large cement bridge piling.

McDougal walked slowly up the rocky slope of the dike, taking care to keep the piling right in front of him so he could see Vince if he darted out in either direction. He reached the top of the dike. It would be impossible for Vince to escape in either direction without being seen. McDougal waited for about fifteen seconds and decided to round the piling to his right. The dike was all rocks, and Vince would certainly make a lot of noise if he decided to run in the other direction.

McDougal inched his way around the right edge of the piling, reaching the edge in about fifteen seconds. He dashed quickly to his right, expecting to see Vince either hiding or taking off in the opposite direction. He froze as he saw and heard nothing.

Suddenly a cry from overhead was heard as Vince dropped ten feet from the undergirding of the bridge right onto McDougal's right shoulder. McDougal's large chrome pistol fell into the rocks. McDougal dove for the gun, ignoring the sharpness of the jagged rocks that made up the dike, but Vince lunged after it and kicked it into the dark waters of the Columbia.

Vince immediately scrambled back up the piling, pulling himself up to the edge of the bridge with a loud groan. He knew better than to engage in hand-to-hand combat with a man of McDougal's reputation.

The hit man was up the bridge in a flash. When he pulled himself up to the bridge deck, he could see Vince running desperately down the pedestrian sidewalk that went the length of the bridge. McDougal closed the gap quickly on his prey, who had been running for nearly two miles by now.

Hearing rapidly closing footsteps behind him, Vince suddenly stopped and turned to face his pursuer. Vince's eyes burned with hatred and fear.

"Come on McDougal, let's go for it," Vince said, taunting his foe.

The hit man slowed to a cautious walk, slipped his right hand into the jacket of his suit, and pulled out a switchblade that he quickly flicked into the ready position.

Vince knew he had only once chance. He screamed wildly and charged with his head down, ignoring the knife that flashed menacingly in the hit man's hand. Vince planted his head squarely into McDougal's chest in an NFL-style tackle. He felt the knife go deep just under his rib cage. Vince screamed again in pain; and then a split second later, both men screamed in absolute terror as Vince's momentum carried them both over the railing a hundred feet into the deep, swift waters of the Columbia River.

The violent current carried them down among the giant boulders, where they disappeared into the swift water. After a week of searching, authorities—alerted to the fight by passing motorists—found both bodies along the river—Vince's near Wallula Junction, fifteen miles downstream of the park. Two days after that, McDougal's was found ten miles even further downstream, caught on a small island about three miles before McNary Dam.

28

Cooper Stone pulled Peter's Explorer up in front of Lisa Edgar's house at eleven o'clock Saturday morning, as planned. Sally stayed in the back seat while Cooper went to the door.

Within five minutes they were on their way north on I-5 toward Ferndale. Lisa directed Cooper toward their first stop—the pizza parlor that had employed Stephen Gray.

The trio walked inside into the just-opened restaurant. There were no customers.

"Is Stan Wilcox in?" Cooper said to the dark-haired teenage girl who was putting place mats on the tables.

"Yeah, he's in the back," she replied, continuing her job unabated.

"Can we talk to him?" Cooper said after it became apparent she had no intention of calling Mr. Wilcox to the front.

"Sure, go ahead. I said he was in the back," she replied with a tone that was more surprised than indignant.

Cooper turned to the two women, shrugged his shoulders, and led the trio toward the swinging door. A short, blond man in his late forties, wearing a wrinkled white shirt, tan slacks, and a bright purple tie, was assembling pizza boxes and stacking them on a shelf.

"May I help you?" he said, as he wiped his hands on his pants leg.

"Yeah," Cooper began, "I assume you are Stan Wilcox."

"Yeah, that's right," he replied. "You must be that lawyer who called me."

"Yes, I'm Cooper Stone from Spokane," he said, extending his hand, "and this is Sally Finley, our legal secretary, and this is Lisa Edgar from Bellingham."

"OK. So what can I do for you?"

"We wanted to ask you some questions about Stephen Gray," Cooper said.

"You're not the first ones to tell me that one," Wilcox replied. "There's been cops and a woman lawyer and who knows who askin' about him. I can tell you I don't know nothin' about abortions or fires or bombs or nothin'. Been there, done that with all those questions. So if you all will excuse me, I've got real work to do here."

"Well, we probably would have ended up asking you those questions, too, so you've saved us some time. But what we really wanted to ask you about—and this won't take a lot of your time—was if Gray had any girlfriends. Did you see him in here with anyone who you'd consider a girlfriend?"

"Well, now that you mention it, this lady here looks kinda familiar," he said gesturing at Lisa. "Wasn't you in here with him once or twice?"

"Yes, I was," Lisa said, turning a little red.

"Was she the only woman he was with here?" Cooper asked. "We think he may have been seeing someone else, too."

"Hey, I ain't gettin' involved in no paternity suit or nothin'. You can forget me if you're trying to gather evidence about that sort of thing."

"No, Mr. Wilcox, I assure you that's not our intent. Our office is defending a young girl who is being tried for murder. We think Stephen Gray may have had another girlfriend besides Lisa. If there was, then it may help us save our client."

"Murder, huh? Is that the case I heard about on the TV the other night?"

"Yeah," Cooper replied, "I'm sure it's the same one."

"Well, yeah, murder. That's pretty serious, huh?" Wilcox muttered.

Sally rolled her eyes, and Lisa nodded back in the unspoken recognition that they were not in the presence of a genius.

"Uh . . . I wasn't goin' to say nothin' 'cause it isn't none of my business, but I did see him leave the restaurant two or three times with a couple of women."

"A couple of women?" Cooper asked.

"That's right, like he was pickin' them up or somethin'. They were customers . . . pretty young . . . eighteen, nineteen years old. Girls like that."

Lisa felt her stomach churning in anger.

"Well, let me give it one more try," Cooper said. He drew a white envelope out of his sports jacket pocket and pulled out a four-by-six-inch photograph. "Did you ever see this woman here? Her name was Rhonda Marsano."

"No, I never seen her here. I don't remember too many women that good lookin' who ever came in here. I can tell you that those eighteen-year-olds Gray was leavin' here with weren't near as cute as the lady in that picture."

"Do you ever remember Gray talking on the phone to anyone named Rhonda, or perhaps Dr. Marsano?"

"Dr. Marsano? Now that name does sound familiar."

"It does?" Cooper said hopefully.

"Yeah. Isn't that the name of the lady doctor who died in that abortion deal? I think I heard that name on the TV the other night."

"Yeah, that's her all right," Cooper replied.

"So she's the one who died in the fire?"

"Yeah," Cooper said, losing hope.

"Boy, that's a shame to lose a good lookin' one like that," Wilcox said. "Not that anybody should get killed or nothin'. But still it's a shame."

"Yeah, we think it was very, very sad for her to die," Cooper said. "So other than on the TV, did you ever hear the name Rhonda Marsano used by Gray at all?"

"No, I wish I could help you. You seem like nice people and everything, but . . . hey . . . I can't make up stuff if I don't know it."

"Yeah, that's right," Cooper said, nodding. "Well, Mr. Wilcox, thanks for your time. It's been a real pleasure."

"Hey, glad to do my civic duty and all that," he replied, wiping his hands again on his pants as he shook hands with Cooper once again. "Come back and eat here sometime. I'll give you guys a supreme for the price of a cheese pizza. Ya can't beat a deal like that."

"I'm sure we can't," Cooper replied.

Jane Hayward and Karen Ballentine waited impatiently in the small conference room outside of Barry Penner's office. Even on Saturday morning, the huge law firm was far from vacant. The only difference seemed to be the wardrobe, with blazers and collarless shirts replacing suits and ties.

They heard a tap on the door as Penner entered the room. "Morning, Jane, Karen," he said nodding to each of them and quickly taking a seat. "Peter Barron again, huh?"

"Yeah," Jane growled. "So what do we do?"

"Did you bring your financial records that the subpoena requires?" Penner asked.

"Are you crazy?" Karen responded.

"Let me ask you again, more slowly this time. Did you bring your financial records that the subpoena requires?"

"I don't know why you insist on these charades, Barry. You play your games, we'll do it our way," Karen said disgustedly. "We brought the clinic's official books. We never paid Vince out of our main accounts. And as far as we know, Barron thinks we wrote checks to Stephen Gray. Even if we brought the right account, he wouldn't necessarily figure it out—he doesn't appear to know Vince's real name, and since the subpoena tells us to bring all records concerning Stephen Gray. . . ."

"What are you going to do if Vince calls them again and tells them to look for his real name?"

"I don't think Vince is likely to call anybody," Jane snickered.

"And neither will McDougal from what we hear," Karen added.

"I don't even want to know what you are talking about," Penner said, as pleasant as can be. "Let's go down the hall and you answer Barron's questions however you see fit."

Door-to-door interviews of the four houses on the narrow little lane where Stephen Gray lived near the intersection of Smith Road and Northwest Boulevard produced nothing. One neighbor remembered seeing Lisa. No one else remembered seeing anyone. The trio got back into Peter's Explorer and eased slowly down the lane, pausing at the stop sign.

"Where now?" Cooper asked. "I'm out of ideas."

"Why don't we stop at that little convenience store over there at the corner?" Sally asked.

"Might as well," Cooper replied. "Not a spot I would take a date, but hey . . . we can't go to every restaurant in Bellingham."

Thirty seconds later the trio was heading across the parking lot toward the side of the store. Metal bells clanked against the door as it was opened, and a heavyset clerk looked up and then back at the magazine he was reading.

"Want something to drink?" Cooper asked.

"Sure," Lisa said.

They walked to the cooler and drew out three bottles of pop and walked to the counter.

"That it?" the clerk said, barely looking at them as he hoisted his weight off of the stool and started punching numbers in the cash register.

"We want to ask you a couple questions, if it's OK," Cooper said.

"'Bout what?"

"About a guy named Stephen Gray, who used to live about a block from here," Cooper responded.

"Who's askin'?" the clerk asked.

"I'm Cooper Stone, a lawyer from Spokane. Our office represents

Suzie O'Dell, the college girl who is being tried for murder right now. You've probably seen it in the paper."

"You don't say? Hmmmph," the clerk grunted. I've been wonderin' about that case. I assumed when Gray stopped comin' in here, he was the same Gray bein' talked about in the papers. But I wasn't sure."

"So you do know him?" Cooper asked.

"Yeah, well, sort of. He was a regular customer here for a few months. Seemed like a real nice guy, didn't bother anybody."

"Did you ever see him in here with a woman?"

The clerk sat down thoughtfully on the stool. In a moment his face lit up. "Yeah—one time. He came in here early one morning, asking for a toothbrush. He was by himself at first, but then this woman stepped inside for just a second and asked him to get something else, some mouthwash or something. A real good lookin' woman as I recall."

"Any chance you would recognize her if you saw a photograph?"

"You can try me. Who knows?"

The clerk stared hard at the photo Cooper handed him. "This is strange," he responded after about fifteen seconds.

"Why is that?" Cooper asked.

"This is that abortion doctor who got killed in the fire, isn't it?" the clerk asked. "This picture of her has been in the newspaper, hasn't it?"

"Yeah, you're right," Cooper responded.

"Hmmmph," he grunted. "When I saw that picture in the paper I thought she looked kind of familiar, but until you asked me about it just now, I never put two and two together. There's no question—she's the one I saw in here that morning with Gray."

"You're sure?" Cooper said excitedly.

"Positive."

"Is there anything else you can remember about her?"

"Well, I remember kind of teasing Gray about her a few weeks later. He claimed that she was his cousin. But that morning she was in here, I assumed that they had spent the night together."

Cooper, Sally, and Lisa were all smiles as Cooper took back the photograph of Dr. Marsano.

"From the looks of you guys, I guess you think this helps somehow?"

"Oh, man. That is the understatement of the year," Cooper said beaming.

"Can I have some more coffee?" Peter asked without looking up from his reading as a young woman hovered over him in the aisle of the United Airlines 727.

"Uh—" came the female voice.

Peter looked up, surprised to see Shannon Carpenter standing next to his seat. "Oh, Miss Carpenter, I thought you were a flight attendant."

"Sorry to disappoint you," she replied. "Mr. Barron, can I talk to you for a minute?"

"Well, I guess so, but we can't make a habit of this. What can I do for you?"

"Can you scoot over? I don't want to broadcast this all over the plane."

Peter slid over to the window seat in the empty row he occupied. Shannon sat down in Peter's former seat on the aisle.

"Interesting depositions today," she began. "You did a good job with those two."

"Thanks," he said guardedly.

"I know I could get in real trouble for telling you this, so I hope you will keep what I have to say in confidence."

"Yeah?" Peter replied.

"I just wanted you to know that I was the staffer that Max mentioned, who took the call from Steven Gray. I wanted us to look into this matter ourselves. But Max and the Justice Department in Washington didn't want to. They thought it would offend the pro-choice political forces if our side looked into it. I pushed really hard, and it has cost me big time."

"Oh my," Peter replied. "That's really something. Well, eventually Gray decided to call my wife at home, so I guess it all worked out."

"Yeah, I know about that, too."

"Really?"

"Yeah. He called me last Thursday night demanding to know why we hadn't followed up on his tip. I told him that I had tried. When he asked me what else he could do, I suggested he call you. I didn't know what hotel you were staying at in Bellingham; so I told him to try your wife at home, and she could get in touch with you."

"So that's how that happened," Peter said. "Miss Carpenter, can I ask you why you're telling me all this?"

"That's a fair question," she said, looking the other way for a long pause. "I'm not totally sure. But that first time we talked on the phone and you got so mad, and then you had the courage to call me back and apologize, something about that impressed me; and I felt like you deserved to know the whole truth about this Stephen Gray thing, rather than the partial truth Max told the judge."

"I appreciate you telling me that; it really means a lot to me," Peter said softly. "But I guess it looks like your boss was right about one thing."

"What's that?"

"We sure didn't find anything in their financial records today to corroborate Stephen Gray's story."

"Do you believe them?" Shannon asked.

"No, do you?" he replied.

"I think I've said enough for one day," she answered.

29

On Monday morning, Peter requested another conference in Judge Hayden's chambers prior to the start of the trial. The four lawyers waited in the secretary's office, files and note pads in hand. Shannon caught Peter's eye, smiled, but said nothing. Peter nodded subtly in reply. A moment later the four were seated in Hayden's chambers.

"Well, did you have a productive trip to Los Angeles, Mr. Barron?" Hayden asked.

"Not as productive as I had hoped. But I certainly intend to call one of the clinic owners as a witness first thing this morning."

"OK. As long as you are not going to be rummaging around in their financial records on the stand. Do you have some narrow inquiries ready?"

"Actually, I won't be asking them any specific questions from their financial records. Everything they actually showed us was irrelevant to what we were looking for. Whether they had another set of records or other accounts they weren't telling us about, we don't know."

"All right," Hayden replied. "As long as you keep your inquiries to relevant matters."

"I'll do my best," Peter replied. "There's another thing I wanted to bring up and get a ruling on if I can today. It concerns a potential witness for tomorrow—my wife."

"Your wife?" Hayden said with raised eyebrows.

"Yes, Your Honor. As you will recall she is the one who received the call from Stephen Gray. I'd like her to testify to the conversation and to use it to impeach the owners of the clinic. The reason I bring it up now is that she is about three weeks from delivering a baby, and I don't want to fly her over here to testify if the court is going to rule her testimony about this conversation to be inadmissible."

"I certainly appreciate the sense of seeking an advance ruling on the point, Mr. Barron," Hayden said. "Mr. Franklin, do you have an opinion on this question?"

"Yes, Your Honor. If Mrs. Barron had a face-to-face conversation with Mr. Gray and she could identify him, we might have a closer question about the obvious hearsay this issue raises. Or, if Mrs. Barron could testify that she had met Mr. Gray in the past and could positively identify his voice over the phone, then, again, maybe the question would be closer. What we have here is not just hearsay, but we have an unidentified source—basically an anonymous tip that he intends to use as the truth in court.

"And by the way, I read the U.S. Supreme Court case that Mr. Barron argued on behalf of his wife concerning anonymous tips. It would seem that if anyone in this country should be sensitive to the unreliability of anonymous phone calls, it would be Mr. and Mrs. Barron."

"Mr. Barron?" Hayden said inviting another reply.

"I think I had better withdraw my request. Unfortunately, he's probably right."

"That makes my job a lot easier. I was about to rule the same way. You saved me the trouble," Hayden replied. "All right, let's get the jury in and keep this trial moving along."

"Your Honor, the defense calls Karen Ballentine to the stand," Peter announced as soon as the court reconvened.

The back door opened and the owner walked in. Ballentine was dressed in a dark grey pantsuit with a large necklace with chrome and black accents. Her hair was cropped close. The numerous flecks of gray revealed her to be in her mid- to late-forties.

"She gives me the—" Suzie started to whisper.

Cooper shushed her with a sign.

Karen raised her hand and promised to tell the truth.

"Please state your name."

"Karen Ballentine."

"Are you one of the co-owners of the Whatcom Women's Center for Choice?"

"Yes."

"And you live in Los Angeles, is that correct?"

"Yes."

"Do you know a man named Stephen Gray?"

"I don't know him. I believe I saw him once at a federal court hearing in Seattle when he was there in attendance with other anti-choice protesters. I didn't know who he was at the time, but I remembered seeing him there after his picture appeared in the newspaper telling the story of how he disappeared immediately after the fire that destroyed our clinic and killed Dr. Marsano. I also saw him on videotape. Our staff saw this guy leading the college students in their chants. It turned out to be Gray. We had nicknamed him 'the ringleader.'"

"Other than that, you don't know Stephen Gray?"

"That is correct."

"You've never talked to him."

"No."

"Did Dr. Marsano know Mr. Gray?"

"No."

"How do you know?"

"Dr. Marsano watched the videotape with me once. When we saw Gray on the tape, I asked her if she knew his name. She said she didn't."

"Any reason to believe that she had a romantic relationship with Stephen Gray?"

Ballentine laughed. "No, Mr. Barron, no reason whatsoever."

"Fine," Peter replied. He walked over to the edge of the jury box and leaned his right arm on the railing. "Ms. Ballentine, did you hire Stephen Gray to burn down your clinic?"

"No, Mr. Barron . . . I did not!" she said, fiercely emphasizing every word.

"Do you know how Dr. Marsano got a bump on her head the night she died?"

"No, Mr. Barron, and I resent these questions."

Peter turned, walked back to his chair, and sat down.

"Are you finished?" Judge Hayden queried.

"Just one more question, Your Honor. Ms. Ballentine, what is your home phone number?"

"It's unlisted, and I don't want to tell it here in front of everyone—especially with all these reporters here."

"Mr. Barron," Hayden said, "I'm not sure I see the relevance of asking her to reveal her home number. Can you tell me the relevance?"

"Your Honor, let me offer a compromise. What if I take a blank piece of paper, we have the clerk mark it as an exhibit, and let Ms. Ballentine write the number on this piece of paper? Then she can give it to you, and no one else can see it. If, later on, I wish to try to establish its relevance, then you can rule on it, and then the number can be revealed to the jury."

"Is that all right with you, Ms. Ballentine?" Hayden asked.

"I'd rather not give it at all, Judge, but if I am going to have to reveal it, I would prefer to give it just to you."

"Fine, then," Hayden replied. "Let's get this paper marked quickly."

The court reporter marked the paper as defendants' exhibit 11.

With a yellow sheet from a legal pad in his hand, Hayden said, "OK, Mr. Barron, that's done. Is there anything else?"

"No further questions," Peter said rocking back in his chair.

Franklin rose and buttoned his dark jacket. "I have no questions for Ms. Ballentine."

Cooper saw many of the jurors giving each other confused looks.

Peter stood while searching his table for his notes on the next witness. "Fine, Your Honor. I would like to call David Marquette to the stand."

A man in his fifties walked into the courtroom carrying a file folder.

After he had been properly sworn, Peter asked his name and position.

"I'm David Marquette, I work in the billing office for Pacific Northwest Bell in the Seattle division."

"Have you brought billing records with you today in response to our subpoena?"

"Yes, I have."

"Can you tell us the owners of these accounts?"

"I have brought cellular bills and home bills for Stephen Gray. And I have also brought cellular and home bills for Rhonda Marsano."

"May I approach the witness, Your Honor?" Peter asked.

"Certainly," Hayden replied.

Peter took the file folder from Marquette and walked over to the clerk who placed a series of stickers on the documents. He took the phone records to the witness and handed them back.

"Mr. Marquette, can you identify exhibit number 12?"

"That is the home bill for Stephen Gray. And the number for this phone is (360) 505-1259."

"All right; exhibit 13 is what?"

"These are billing records for Stephen Gray's cellular phone."

"And that number is what?"

"(360) 303-4991"

"And please identify exhibit 14."

"That is Rhonda Marsano's home phone record. "Her home number is (360) 909-1952."

"And finally, exhibit 15."

"That is Rhonda Marsano's cellular phone billing record."

"Once again, her car phone number is what?"

"That one is (360) 303-5596."

"OK, Mr. Marquette, can you tell from the prefixes whether or not it is a long distance call from one phone to another?"

"In our billing area, yes, I can."

"Is it long distance from the 505 prefix, which was Stephen Gray's home phone, to the 909 prefix, where Dr. Marsano lived?"

"Yes, Gray's phone is a Ferndale exchange; the doctor's number is a South Lake Sammish area exchange. It is long distance from one phone to the other."

"Do your billing records show long distance calls from Gray's home phone to Dr. Marsano's home phone?"

"Yes, there are two. One in April of last year, the other in May."

"How long were each of these calls?"

"The call in April lasted two minutes. The call in May was seven minutes."

"Fine," Peter said. "How about Gray's cellular bill?"

"There are two calls to Dr. Marsano's home phone on Stephen Gray's cellular bill."

"When and how long were those calls?"

"They were both in late April, the first call lasted just one minute. The second was fifteen minutes long."

"OK, Mr. Marquette, we have established that Stephen Gray called Dr. Marsano four times. Do these exhibits reflect whether or not Dr. Marsano ever called Mr. Gray?"

"Yes, they do. There is one call from her home to his home. It was on May 15 and lasted for ten minutes. And from her cellular phone she called his home once for two minutes and his cell phone once for three minutes."

"When were those cell calls?"

"One in March, the other in May."

"OK, and finally, Mr. Marquette, can you please place a check mark beside every phone call from Mr. Gray's home and cell phones to the Los Angeles area?"

"It will take a minute. There are a couple dozen."

"Take your time," Peter replied.

About two minutes later, the witness looked up at Peter.

"Are you finished?"

"Yes," he replied.

"Your Honor, I would ask if you could examine the numbers that Mr. Marquette has checked off and see if any of these calls match exhibit 11, which is the unlisted phone number of Ms. Ballentine."

"Mr. Barron, do you know the answer to your question, to save me the time of searching through these pages?" Hayden asked.

"No, Your Honor. I have not been able to discover her home phone number. It's just a hunch."

Suzie noticed two jurors whispering to each other and several leaning forward in their seats. "Please God, give me a break," she prayed silently.

Hayden deliberately took one page and then another of the phone bill and turned them over. He set one page aside and then kept looking at the others.

"Well, Mr. Barron, there appears to be one call that does match. I will now admit her phone number into evidence. Mr. Marquette, let me do this. I will hand you the exhibit containing her phone number and these exhibits back. I think you will find the match right here on this page," he said, pointing as he reached over the bench and handed the witness the exhibits. "Please don't say the number out loud because of all of the reporters in court today. But just tell the jury if you can confirm that Mr. Gray called this unlisted number."

Marquette looked at the yellow sheet and his records a couple of times to be sure. "Yes, Judge, on March 12, there was a call from Mr. Gray's home phone for four minutes to the home phone number of Miss Ballentine."

"That's all the questions I have for Mr. Marquette, Your Honor."

Franklin sprang to his feet. "Mr. Marquette," he said before he reached his spot at the lectern, "can your records tell you the nature of the conversations?"

"No, of course not."

"So you cannot tell whether they were having friendly conversations or arguments or delivering threats?"

"No."

"Your Honor, I would like to ask Mr. Barron if he will stipulate that there were threatening calls that were made by Mr. Gray to the clinic office in Los Angeles."

"Normally, I would think such a request should be made outside the presence of the jury," Peter replied, "but I would be happy to stipulate to that fact. That was my position in a related case, as this court well knows."

Franklin turned back toward the witness. "Mr. Marquette, the number that received the harassing calls, the clinic's L.A. office, was (213) 555-6413. Do you see calls to that number on Mr. Gray's phone bill?"

"Yes, there are two from his home phone, both in April," the phone official said after thirty seconds. "One was for two minutes, the other for three minutes."

"You have no way of knowing whether these calls you have identified today are not harassing calls, just like the two you've just identified, do you?"

"Objection," Peter called out. "There has been no proof, and I certainly have not stipulated that these particular calls to the clinic office were harassing calls. I have only stipulated that Mr. Gray made some harassing calls to that number. I cannot stipulate about these particular calls. The ones I had in mind were made from Colonel Danners's home and from Immanuel Bible Church. I've always contended that Gray made those harassing calls. But, I would be happy to stipulate that there is no way that Mr. Marquette can tell the nature of any of Mr. Gray's calls from his records. I have already stipulated that Mr. Gray made some harassing calls to the clinic headquarters. I don't think he can prove anything more from this witness."

"Mr. Franklin, are you satisfied with these stipulations?"

"Yes, Your Honor. I think Mr. Barron has made my point for the jury quite adequately. Thank you."

"Can Mr. Marquette be excused?" Hayden inquired.

"Yes, Your Honor," Peter answered.

"Mr. Barron, who will you be calling to testify next?" Hayden asked.

"Larry Bedell, Your Honor."

"Fine, we'll stand in recess for lunch until 1:30 this afternoon.

The courtroom was abuzz when Peter walked back into the chamber shortly before 1:30. No one in the press or public had yet figured out who Larry Bedell was, although a few reporters had cornered Colonel Danners to query him about the witness's identity. At 1:30 sharp, both the judge and the jury filed in, and the courtroom came back to order.

"Mr. Barron, please call your witness," Hayden declared.

"The defense calls Larry Bedell," Peter said, rising.

A titter of laughter was heard in the back corner of the courtroom as an enormous man in a golf shirt and black slacks sauntered through the dark wooden door. His hair was combed straight back, and it appeared to Cooper that the scraggly beard he had seen on Saturday had been trimmed.

Bedell had a bit of difficulty fitting into the witness box that was bound by a railing with a solid panel on three sides. With a final grunt, he successfully mounted the chair, turned toward the defense counsel, and ran his hand back through his hair.

Peter stood beside the counsel table. "Your Honor, if it please the court, my associate, Cooper Stone, will question this witness."

"Fine. You may proceed, Mr. Stone," Hayden said.

Cooper stood and walked to the lectern with a prepared sheet of questions.

"Please state your name and address."

"Larry Bedell, PO Box 212, Ferndale."

"Where are you employed?" Cooper asked, his voice shaking just a bit.

"I help manage a convenience store for Northwest Retail, Inc. We've got a little store on the corner of Northwest Boulevard and Smith Road, north of Bellingham about six miles."

"Mr. Bedell," Cooper said, staring at his notes, "do you know a man named Stephen Gray?"

"Yes, sir, he was a regular customer of mine."

"When was he a customer of your store?"

"Well, he stopped being a customer last May. I'd say he shopped there for about three or four months."

"Did you know where Mr. Gray lived?"

"I didn't know the exact address, but I knew the location. It was a little trailer about a block or so from the store. It's been rented out for years, and the tenants usually end up as customers."

"Did you have any dealings with Mr. Gray outside the store?"

"No, sir, I did not," he replied with perfect crisp diction.

"You saw Mr. Gray in the store with a young woman one time, didn't you?"

"Objection," Franklin called out. "Mr. Stone is leading the witness."

"Sustained," Hayden declared. "Please rephrase the question."

"Did you ever see Mr. Gray in your store with a young woman?"

"Yes, I did."

"When was that, if you can remember?"

"It was in about March of this past year. I can't say exactly, but it was approximately two months before he stopped coming in the store."

"Mr. Bedell, please tell the jury what you observed."

Mr. Bedell turned and faced the jury, making eye contact with several of its members. "What happened was this," he began. "Stephen Gray came in early one morning and picked up a couple things. Just as he was coming to the counter, a very beautiful young woman—at least in my opinion she was both beautiful and young, I'd say she was in her late twenties. In any event, this young woman stuck her head in the door and called out to Gray and told him to be sure and get some mouthwash. Gray already had a toothbrush he had laid on my counter."

"What did you think when you heard the young woman's request?" Cooper said, glancing again at his notes.

"Frankly, I thought they had spent the night together. It's been my experience when a man who looks like Gray and a woman who looks like that one come into my store in the morning and buy a toothbrush, someone has been an overnight guest with the other one."

"Did you ever talk to Gray about this woman?"

"Yeah, some time later I teasingly asked him when he was going to bring her back again. He claimed she was his cousin from Ohio."

"What did you think at the time?"

"I thought he was lying—but I didn't blame him or anything since basically I was sticking my nose into his business."

"Did you ever learn for sure that she wasn't his cousin from Ohio?"

"Yes, I did."

"When was that?"

"Two days ago—on Saturday when you came into my store and showed me a picture."

"Your Honor, may I have the clerk mark this photograph as an exhibit?"

"Yes, Mr. Stone. If you will simply walk over to my clerk here and hand her the photo, she'll be happy to mark it for you."

"Thank you, Your Honor," Cooper replied."

"You're doing fine, Mr. Stone," Hayden replied kindly.

Suzie shot a worried look at Peter.

"It'll be OK," he leaned over and whispered in his client's ear.

"May I approach the witness with this exhibit, Your Honor?" Cooper asked.

"Yes, that will be fine," the judge said.

"Mr. Bedell, I am handing you a photograph marked as defendants' exhibit 16. Is this the photo to which you referred?"

"Yes, it is."

"Is this the young woman you saw with Mr. Gray in your store that morning?"

"Yes, it is."

"Are you sure?"

"Yes, positive."

"Do you know who it is?"

"Yes, I do. It's Dr. Rhonda Marsano."

"How do you know it's Dr. Marsano?"

"This is the same photograph that I have seen run in the newspaper countless times in connection with this case. In fact, after you showed me that photo on Saturday, the same photo ran again in both the *Bellingham Herald* and the *Seattle Times* on Sunday when they did stories about this trial. I think they called the picture a 'file photo' in the caption."

"Your are certain that you saw Dr. Marsano in your store with Stephen Gray in about March of last year?"

"Yes, I am."

"No further questions, Your Honor." Cooper returned to his seat. Beads of sweat were visible on his forehead.

"Excellent," Peter whispered. "You did fine."

Suzie took her yellow tablet and wrote, "Thanks, Cooper. It sounded good to me."

Franklin leaned over and whispered with Shannon Carpenter for a few seconds. He rose and scribbled a couple words on his legal pad as he walked to his usual spot at the lectern in the center of the courtroom.

"Mr. Bedell, let me see if I understand your testimony correctly. You said you have seen this picture of Dr. Marsano countless numbers of times in the newspaper. Is that right?"

"Yes, sir," he replied.

"And every one of those times was in connection with substantive stories about this case?"

"Yes, sir, that is also correct."

"And, would it be fair to assume that you saw a caption giving her name in most, if not all, of these occasions where you saw her picture?"

"Yes, that would be fair."

"And would it be correct to assume that you had read the many articles that mention the presumed role of Stephen Gray in this whole crime?"

"Yes, I have read several that mention Stephen Gray."

"And yet it wasn't until last Saturday when Mr. Cooper showed you a picture that you were able to remember that, 'Hey these two characters that I have read about so many times were in my store together'?"

"You may not believe that, as your tone of voice implies, sir, but that's exactly what happened," Bedell said maintaining his calm.

"What exactly did Mr. Stone say to you that caused you to see the connection?"

"He just asked me if I had ever seen Mr. Gray with any women. So I started thinking about Gray in that vein. And then he asked me if I would recognize the woman if he showed me a picture. I said I might. Then he showed me this picture, and bingo, the whole thing jumped together in my head."

"So it was Mr. Stone's suggestion that got you to believe that Dr. Marsano was the woman you had seen in your store?"

"No, he just asked me if I would recognize the woman and then showed me the picture. I was the one who volunteered the fact that this was Dr. Marsano."

"You don't find your story a bit convenient?"

Peter poked Cooper.

"Objection, he's arguing with the witness," Cooper called out.

"Overruled," Hayden sang out.

"You may call it that if you like, I'm just telling you what happened," Bedell said, glaring at the prosecutor.

"But you can say for sure that you did not remember seeing Dr. Marsano in your store until your conversation with Mr. Stone?"

"It was not something that had crossed my mind in so many words before then."

Franklin turned from the podium. "No further questions, Your Honor."

"Just a couple questions on redirect," Peter said, standing.

"Objection, Your Honor," Franklin said, springing back to his feet. "Mr. Stone did the direct examination; I'm afraid he'll have to do the redirect as well."

Peter's face flushed and nodded at Cooper. "Sorry, we tried," he whispered.

Suzie stared at Peter with a distraught look.

Peter nodded knowingly. "It'll be OK," he mouthed.

"Mr. Bedell," Cooper said, standing. "Who first brought up the name of Dr. Rhonda Marsano in our conversation on Saturday?" he asked gripping the sides of the lectern.

"I did, Mr. Cooper. It wasn't you."

"All right, can you explain to the jury why you had seen Dr. Marsano's picture in the paper so many times and had read many articles that implicated Stephen Gray and still not remembered that they had been in your store together until last Saturday?"

"It's a bit of self-analysis, but I believe I know the answer to your question," Bedell began.

"Objection, Your Honor," Franklin called out. "The witness is about to speculate."

"Overruled. He sounds like he's going to explain his own thinking. That's not speculation," Hayden ruled.

"The reason I didn't think of it before is that I knew Gray was an abortion protester. It just didn't occur to me that an abortion protester was sleeping with the doctor who ran the clinic. And I had seen them together a couple months before the doctor's picture ever ran in the paper. So, I just never went back and ran that early morning encounter over again in my mind until you asked me to do so."

"Do you have any doubt that the woman you saw in your store with Stephen Gray was Dr. Marsano?"

"None whatsoever."

"Thank you, Mr. Bedell. No further questions."

Cooper returned to his seat.

Peter was on his feet immediately. "Your Honor, can we take our afternoon recess now? We may be a bit early, but I have only one remaining witness, Suzie O'Dell, and I'd like to have a short break before we begin with her."

"All right, Mr. Barron. We'll be in recess until three o'clock."

"Let's go into the witness room," Peter said to Suzie and Cooper. "Suzie, ask your parents to come with us while I grab my notes."

Peter followed the O'Dell trio into the witness room, where Cooper was waiting.

"Suzie, why don't you and your parents sit over on that side of the table?" Peter said.

Peter turned a chair around backwards and leaned on the top edge of the chair back. "Well, it's the moment we've been preparing for. Are you ready, Suzie?"

"No," she said, shaking her head and looking down. "Do I have to really do this? Don't we have enough without me?"

"Suzie," Peter said earnestly, "it's my job to tell you the truth as best I can. We have certainly kicked some dirt in their eye by this last witness and by proving the phone calls. But all that proves is that Stephen Gray and Rhonda Marsano may have had a relationship. It doesn't prove that he killed her on his own without your help.

"The worst thing they have produced against you is your army of God comment to Rachel. Jurors can relate to a girl who just happens to go to Fred Meyer and just happens to get her fingerprints on a gas can that was used in a murder. But they cannot relate to a girl who talks about joining the army of God. We have got to let them see you as the sweet, innocent, and yes, even naive girl that you are."

Suzie frowned as tears welled up in her eyes.

"All of those traits are OK, really. But radicalism is something we are going to have to disprove. Does that make sense?"

"I guess," she said, wiping her eyes.

"Honey," Linda said, "it makes a lot of sense to me. You know I love you and would gladly take your place in this trial. But to tell you the truth, when I heard Rachel testifying, I said to myself, 'Is that my Suzie?' I can imagine the jurors are asking themselves the same kind of questions. You are the only one who can break that image in their minds."

"OK, Mom, I'll do it," she said, holding her head up.

"Can I pray for you, honey?" Bill asked.

"Yeah, Dad, I would really like that."

"Dear God," he began, "give Suzie the power and strength she needs to tell the truth convincingly. Help the jurors believe the truth and not believe any lies or innuendos. In Christ's name, amen."

"Everyone ready?" Peter asked, looking around the room. "OK, let's go win this case."

Peter had to brush through a clump of reporters who were inadvertently blocking the door. It was all they could do to contain themselves from shouting questions at the group as they went by. But Judge Hayden's stern warnings had turned them all into a compliant group.

The jury filed in on command. A few snatches of conversation could be observed here and there in the jury box.

"All rise," the bailiff called.

"Please be seated," Hayden announced a moment later.

"Your Honor," Peter, said calmly, "the defense calls Suzie O'Dell to the stand." Peter stood erect and walked crisply to the lectern as Suzie made her way to the witness stand.

She was dressed in an off-white, tea-length dress that buttoned down the front. Sally had suggested the white dress for this day when they had reviewed her wardrobe about ten days before trial. She thought that white conveyed a subtle message of innocence. Suzie's parents and lawyers both liked the suggestion. Her chestnut hair fell over her shoulders with just enough style and curl to seem neither radical nor overly chic.

Suzie raised her right hand.

"Do you promise to tell the whole truth so help you God?" came the bailiff's line. Even he took a bit more time to enunciate the words. It was the first time in his twenty-year career that a young woman ever took his oath when facing the death penalty.

"Yes, sir, I do," she replied.

Suzie straightened her dress and smiled. The nervous reluctance she had expressed just ten minutes earlier was gone.

"Your name, please," Peter said, stationed firmly at the lectern. Cooper had suggested that Peter's habit of pacing would divide the jury's attention. They both wanted every eye on Suzie.

"Susan O'Dell."

"Is it OK if I call you Suzie?"

"Oh, yes, Mr. Barron."

"Where do you live?"

"In Spokane, with my parents."

"Suzie, how old are you?"

"I'm nineteen."

"When is your birthday?"

"It's on June 28. I'll be twenty then."

"Suzie, tell the jury about your educational history."

"I graduated from Central Valley High School in Spokane and then attended my freshmen year here in Bellingham at Western. I haven't attended school this year because of this trial."

"What kind of student were you?"

"I graduated from high school with a 3.6 grade point average—I was on the dean's list every quarter at Western."

"Suzie, please tell the jury what kind of jobs you have had over the years."

"Well, I have been a waitress pretty much since starting at Western. In the summer between high school and my first year in college, I was a camp counselor at Riverview Bible Camp, north of Spokane. And, during high school, I did a lot of baby-sitting." Her words were smooth and confident, and there was a pleasant, girl-next-door lilt in her voice.

"You mentioned church camp. Suzie, are you a member of a church?"

"Yes, sir, I belong to Valley Fourth Memorial Church. It's a church of about a thousand in the Spokane valley. The camp I worked at is owned by the downtown church called Fourth Memorial Church. It has maybe two thousand people in attendance. It's a non-denominational Protestant church."

"Did you attend church here in Bellingham while you were a student here?"

"Yes, I attended Immanuel Bible Church, on the north side of town. It's a lot like my church back home. A lot of college students go there."

"Suzie, can you explain your role in the Whatcom Life Coalition?"

"Yes, the Whatcom Life Coalition was the group that was started in response to the opening of the abortion clinic here in Bellingham. I went to the second meeting of the group and was chosen to be on the leadership committee."

"Do you know why you were chosen?"

"Well, there was a lot of talk at that meeting about the fact that college girls were the main target of the abortion clinic. Colonel Danners thought that the group needed to have at least one college girl on the board. I was the only college girl at the meeting, so I was chosen."

"Had you ever engaged in any abortion protests before?"

"Sort of. Every year on the anniversary of *Roe versus Wade,* there was a candlelight vigil in front of the federal courthouse in Spokane. I attended that twice while I was in high school."

"Had you ever protested in front of an abortion clinic before Bellingham?"

"No, sir. Never."

"Why did you choose to get involved here?"

"Well, partly it was in response to an assignment in one of my political science classes at Western. We were told that we were required to participate in some kind of community activism. I asked if we could do the assignment for a cause that we believed in. The professor said that would be the best alternative. When I heard the pro-life meeting announced at church, it seemed like the perfect opportunity."

"When you went to the clinic, what did you do?"

"Well, we prayed silently a lot as we walked along the sidewalk. We carried signs encouraging girls to not abort their little babies. And when we got the chance, we tried to talk to some girls directly to encourage them to seek alternatives."

"Did you ever talk to such girls?"

"Yes, about three times."

"What happened?"

"Objection," Franklin called out. "I've let this homey history lesson go on pretty far. I don't see the relevance of this question."

"Your Honor," Peter said, "Mr. Franklin has put on evidence that he believes suggests that Suzie had the motive to kill and commit arson. I am entitled to establish her true motives for her true actions."

"Objection overruled," Hayden said matter-of-factly.

"Suzie, let me restate the question. What happened on the three occasions when you were personally able to talk with a young woman who had come to the abortion clinic?"

"On two occasions they changed their minds. The other time, the girl went on in the clinic, and I assume she aborted her baby."

"Suzie, I'd like to focus on the one time where the girl went on into the clinic. What did you do when she went inside?"

It was not a question Peter and Suzie had discussed in advance. She paused for a moment, wondering how much to tell. "Well, Mr. Barron, to tell you the truth, what I did was to walk away from the clinic for a little while because I was crying. I prayed for the girl and her baby. That's pretty much it."

"Did you yell at the girl?"

"No, I didn't."

"Did you cross the property line and try to follow her in to keep trying to convince her to change her mind?"

"Oh no, sir, I wouldn't do that. We were strictly required to stay on the sidewalk."

"Who required that of you?"

"Colonel Danners. He had very strict rules of proper behavior."

"Did you follow his rules at all times?"

"Yes, sir, I did."

"Suzie, I would like to shift gears for a minute and ask you about your father. Did he have very strict rules when you were growing up as well?"

"Well, some of my friends from high school thought he had very strict rules, but those were the rules I was used to."

"Did you ever talk with your friends about the necessity of all of his rules?"

· "Yes, I did," Suzie said, seeming just a little embarrassed.

"Did you ever break any of his rules?"

Suzie sighed. "Yes, Mr. Barron, I did. A couple times."

"What rules did you break?"

"Sometimes I went over the speed limit when I drove. And sometimes I came home later than my curfew. He wasn't home most of those times, and I knew my mom would be more lenient."

"Suzie, most parents wish they had only those kinds of troubles with their teenagers. But, let me ask you about some of the more serious rules. Did your father have rules against drinking?"

"Yes, sir."

"Did you ever break that rule?"

"No, sir. I was called square a lot for obeying that, but I always obeyed that rule."

"Did your father have rules against drugs?"

"Yes—and I never broke that rule either."

"Suzie . . . you had a boyfriend in high school, didn't you?"

"Yes, sir, I did."

"Did your father have a rule against sex before marriage?"

"Yes, he did."

"Suzie, tell this jury the truth. Did you ever break that rule of your father's?"

"No, sir, I never did."

"Suzie, please listen to me carefully, and I want your candid answer to this next question even though your parents are in the courtroom today.

"Did you and your boyfriend ever talk about breaking your father's rule on sex?"

Suzie turned very red. She stared at the floor. Finally, she shook her hair back away from her face and looked Peter squarely in the eye. "Yes, we did talk about it a few times."

"But you never violated your father's rule despite your talk. Is that what you are telling this jury?"

"Yes, Mr. Barron, that's right."

"OK, Suzie, now I want to ask you one final series of questions.

"Why did you go to Fred Meyer with Stephen Gray?"

"I didn't have a car. He offered to give me a ride to Colonel Danners's, who lives over on Lake Whatcom. That's all there was to it. On our way back to my dorm, he told me he needed to buy something for some yard work he was doing and asked me if I wanted to come inside. Unfortunately, I went inside with him."

"Did you handle the gas cans inside the store?"

"Yes, sir, I did."

"What happened to the gas cans after you left the store?"

"Mr. Gray put them in his trunk."

"Did you ever see those gas cans again?"

"No, sir, I didn't."

"Did you know what the gas cans were going to be used for?"

"Well, I did ask Mr. Gray, because I thought it was strange to be buying three smaller cans when there were larger containers that would hold the same amount. He told me he had three different mixes of gasoline for three different pieces of lawn equipment. It made sense at the time," she said, looking down again.

"So you did not know the cans would be used to make a bomb?"

"Oh, no, sir. Absolutely not."

"Where were you on the evening of May 20 of last year—the evening of the fire?"

"I went to dinner in the dorm cafeteria. Around seven I went to the library to study for finals and to finish a paper. I stayed at the library until around eleven, then I went back to my dorm room."

"Were you with anyone at the library?"

"No, I was alone the whole time. I mean, there were other people around, but I wasn't with anybody."

"Did you conspire with Stephen Gray to set fire to the clinic?"

"No, sir, I did not."

"Did you conspire with Stephen Gray to kill Dr. Marsano?"

"No, sir, I did not."

"Did you set fire to the clinic either on your own or in conjunction with any other person?"

"No, absolutely not."

"Did you kill Dr. Rhonda Marsano either on your own or in conjunction with any other person?"

"No! I would never do such an awful thing."

Peter paused for nearly thirty seconds before speaking again. "Suzie, you were obviously here when Rachel Grove testified about the conversation you had with Stephen Gray when you and three others were in the car coming home with him from the Danners's house one night. Do you remember that testimony?"

"Yes, sir, I do."

"Did you say the things that Rachel testified to?"

Suzie turned mildly red. "Yes . . . I did."

"Why did you talk about those things? Why did you talk about being part of God's army?"

"I don't know exactly, Mr. Barron. All I can say is that I kind of got caught up in the discussion that Mr. Gray had started at the meeting. It was an interesting analogy, and I wanted to talk about it a little bit."

"Did you ever take any action based on that conversation?"

"No, I didn't."

"Why not?"

"Because, even though the idea sounded a little intriguing at the time, when I thought about it a little more later on, everything I learned from church, everything I learned from my parents, and everything I had heard the colonel say about obeying the law and being morally upright came back to me. And all of what I had learned made more sense than that one conversation with Stephen Gray."

Peter picked up his notebook and smiled. "I have no further questions, Your Honor."

Franklin took to his feet slowly. "I will, of course, have some questions, Your Honor," he said, as he made his way to the lectern.

"Miss O'Dell, you don't deny that you were photographed in Fred Myer, holding a gas can for Mr. Gray who purchased not one, but three cans, a couple of large batteries, and a coil of copper wire, do you?"

"No, I don't deny it, sir. That is true."

"And do you expect this jury to believe that you thought that these things were for yard work?" he said, with just a touch of sarcasm in his voice.

"That's what Mr. Gray told me. I can only apologize for my ignorance."

"What kind of yard work does a person do with copper wire and flashlight batteries?"

"I have no idea. I didn't really think about it."

"You didn't think about it, you say. Didn't it occur to you that you were buying the ingredients for a firebomb, not for yard work?"

"Mr. Franklin, all I can say is that I never thought about it. I wish I would have thought about it because then I could have called the police or told the colonel or something. And then maybe this fire wouldn't have happened. But I am a stupid nineteen-year-old girl who has a hard time doing anything mechanical, much less putting a bomb together in my head. It just didn't cross my mind!"

"You don't deny that your fingerprints made it to the scene of this arson and murder, do you?"

"No, my fingerprints were there. I don't doubt the testimony of Detective Dunn."

"Isn't it true that you helped Gray, and that he committed arson and murder with your assistance?"

"Mr. Franklin, I don't know for sure if Gray set the fire and killed Dr. Marsano. I think he did. But I don't have personal knowledge of that fact. And it is true that I helped Gray by carrying those items to the cash register at the store and then out to his car. And even that little bit of helping has cost me more sleepless nights than you can imagine. But I have been told, and I believe, that a person is not guilty of murder or arson if all you do is just naively carry some items through a store. You have to intend to commit those crimes."

Suzie's eyes began to fill with angry tears. "You have charged me with murder and held press conferences announcing that you wanted to see me hanged. And what have I done? Carry some stupid gas cans in a store. That's it! I don't know why you've done this to me, but it makes me—" The tears took over.

"Miss O'Dell," Franklin said, coolly. "You have just gotten angry with me because you believe I have been involved in an injustice. You have testified about your feelings about abortion, and it is clear that you think that abortion is an injustice against unborn babies, as you call them. Isn't it possible that you got angry one night in May at the injustices being committed by Dr. Rhonda Marsano at the clinic, and you let your temper flair up again? and you helped set a fire? and you helped kill a doctor? Isn't that what happened?"

"No, it isn't Mr. Franklin." Her voice was smooth and calm.

"I have no further questions," he said with a smile.

Peter stood by his chair as Franklin marched back to his seat. "Your Honor, the defense rests."

"Very well, Mr. Barron. No redirect of this witness?"

"I see no need, Your Honor."

"OK, as you will," Hayden replied. "Mr. Franklin," he said, shifting his gaze to the other counsel table, "do you have any rebuttal witnesses?"

"No, Your Honor."

The judge took off his glasses and laid them on the bench. "Ladies and gentlemen of the jury, we are nearly at the end of this trial. I am going to adjourn the court for the day. It's only four o'clock, and I know we have normally gone until five, but I have given each lawyer one hour to give his final argument. Those will take place tomorrow morning. But first, I will give you your instructions on the law, and by lunchtime tomorrow you will begin your deliberations.

"It is extremely important that you continue to honor my admonitions not to discuss this case even among yourselves, even though the testimony is complete. You need not only the testimony, you need my instructions on the law before you can properly have those discussions. And, of course, the final arguments of counsel will likely be of great aid to you in applying the facts as you have heard them to the law.

"With these important reminders in mind, the court will stand in recess until nine o'clock tomorrow morning."

Suzie spent another restless night in front of Colonel Danners's fireplace. In her mind she watched countless "replays" of her angry outburst on the witness stand. Her mother joined her around two in the morning. They prayed, cried, and sang hymns to each other until it was nearly dawn.

30

Energy, fear, and excitement passed through the crowd as the spectators gathered for the final arguments.

Witnesses were now permitted in the courtroom for the first time, since all the testimony had now been completed. There was substantial grumbling among the members of the media, since many of their customary seats were now taken by new faces that had shown up that morning. Ten members of Campus Christian Fellowship were the first in line at the courtroom door. They sang and prayed quietly from 7:30 until the bailiff arrived at 8 A.M. and told them to hush.

The Danners were seated in the front row on the left of Suzie's parents. To the right of Bill and Linda, the pastor of their home church from Spokane had joined them.

Shirley Alper, Bob and Ginny Kettner, and Lisa Edgar sat on the far right edge of the second row on the right. Randy Wallace and his wife were in the fourth row, surrounded by Suzie's friends from Campus Christian Fellowship.

At about 8:50, Jane Hayward and Karen Ballentine came in accompanied by two former members of the clinic staff. Another staff member had saved them half the front row on the left hand side.

About twenty people who had no direct relation to the case had simply shown up to see the excitement. Another fifty were turned away at the door when the capacity had been reached and exceeded as far as the bailiff would permit.

Peter, Cooper, and Suzie made their way in about three minutes before the hour. Suzie was dressed in a navy dress with plain white trim. Peter had saved his navy blue pinstripe, with his "lucky" yellow tie for the final argument.

Franklin arrived just a single stroke before nine, with Shannon Carpenter grim-faced at his heels.

"All rise," came the cry. Even the bailiff was far more tense than earlier in the week.

"Good morning, please be seated," Hayden said. His voice seemed flatter and drier than it had been any other day during the trial.

"Ladies and gentlemen of the jury, as I told you yesterday, the first item on our agenda this morning is for me to instruct you in the law that will govern this case."

Every person at the counsel table, including Suzie, had a copy of the instructions that the judge was about to read.

"Your first duty when you retire is to elect a foreman. The term 'foreman' should not be understood to say that either a man or a woman should be chosen. Please select the person you believe will best be able to guide and organize your deliberations."

Another half-dozen housekeeping instructions followed. Suzie desperately wanted a drink from the pewter pitcher that had clinked with ice just a few minutes before when Peter had moved it across the table to make room for his files. But she didn't want to create any sort of distraction.

Then came the instructions on the elements of each crime. "Murder in the first degree requires proof of the taking of the life of another with malice, aforethought, and premeditation," Hayden read solemnly. "Malice does not necessarily mean ill-will," the judge continued, "but requires proof of an act intentionally done with an understanding that the act will result in harm to another."

The next instruction had Peter particularly worried. Judge Hayden instructed the jurors that if they found insufficient evidence to convict of murder in the first degree, murder in the second degree was a lesser included offense. He didn't want Suzie to serve life imprisonment any more than he wanted her to face the death penalty.

For thirty minutes, the judge read page after page of elements of crime, rules on circumstantial evidence, rules on credibility of witnesses, and the definition of beyond a reasonable doubt.

"Okay, ladies and gentlemen, that is all I have. Shall we begin? Mr. Franklin," he said. "You may begin your final argument. I understand you have reserved five minutes for rebuttal."

"Ladies and gentlemen of the jury, at the beginning of this case everyone in this courtroom asked you to promise that you would decide this case on the evidence. Not on passion. Not on prejudice. Not on sympathy."

Franklin was stationed firmly at the lectern. But his vision kept moving back and forth to keep constant eye contact with juror after juror. His delivery was smooth and polished.

"I want to review for you the evidence that I believe will lead you to convict the defendant if you follow it without passion, without prejudice, and without sympathy.

"Suzie O'Dell is on videotape participating in the purchase of the murder weapons. Her fingerprints were found at the scene on those murder weapons. She claims she was an innocent little girl who just happened to go shopping. Let's see how that claim adds up in light of the other evidence. She testified that she was an honor student in high school. She was on the dean's list at Western for three quarters in a row. She was taking political science courses. And when asked to volunteer for some form of community service that she believes in, she volunteered to help an anti-abortion protest group.

"Now, if Miss O'Dell had been given a quiz in her political science class about some of the challenges faced by the anti-abortion forces, I believe this honor student would have correctly listed the problems of violence on her examination. Honor student. Political science student. Prolife activist. Dean's list. But now all of a sudden, when she and her fellow pro-life protester are buying materials for a firebomb, she claims to be a ditzy, know-nothing, incompetent idiot. Give me a break. I think she knew what she was buying. The evidence shows she is smart. She is far too smart for anyone to believe she didn't know that she was buying a bomb."

Franklin paused, looked at each side of the jury box, and then glanced quickly at his notes.

"Suzie O'Dell was a protester. She wanted this clinic closed. And she told her friend, Rachel Grove—and three others besides Stephen Gray—that she felt they should do more than merely protest. She said they should join God's army. Let's think about that for a minute. God's army. Does a sweet, innocent young thing talk about such theocratic militancy? Soldiers hunt down and use ultimate force to wipe out their enemies. Which is she? An innocent young thing, or a radical militant?"

"Most of you are old enough to remember a woman named Patty Hearst. Miss Hearst was an ordinary girl from a wealthy newspaper family in California. She was kidnapped by the so-called Symbionese Liberation Army. And what did she do? She ended up joining the radicals and robbing banks and committing crimes that seemed so out of place for the sweet, innocent girl she'd been in the past.

"I do not doubt that Suzie O'Dell had a sweet, innocent upbringing. And I do not doubt that Stephen Gray had a bad influence on her. And in the end, she was the one who was talking about joining—not the Symbionese Liberation Army—but God's army. Radical or naive little girl? Which is it? The evidence shows that Stephen Gray knew who would be sympathetic to his cause when he went to buy the bomb materials. Of all the people he could have taken along with him, he chose the one person who had expressed sympathy with his radicalism. Coincidence? That theory doesn't make any more sense than her 'I'm so stupid' theory. No, she's a smart radical, for sure, and she knew what she was doing all along.

"Finally, you got to see one additional proof of her radicalism in action. You saw her lash out at me and say some pretty strong things because she believed I was committing an injustice in this courtroom. Sweet? Innocent? Stupid? You heard her on the witness stand. She was angry, not sweet. Vindictive, not innocent. And stupid? Why, she was one of the smartest witnesses I have ever cross-examined."

Four jurors nodded in agreement.

"Her own evidence, her own testimony, her own behavior shows that she was an angry young woman, capable of radical statements and

dangerous actions. You should not believe her protests of sweet innocence, because the evidence is simply to the contrary."

Franklin again paused. The jurors were paying attention to every
word and nuance.

"Finally, let me say something about Mr. Barron's very, shall we say,
interesting theory that Dr. Marsano was dating Stephen Gray. There are
three problems with this theory.

"First, even if it is true, what does that have to do with the guilt or
innocence of Suzie O'Dell? If Gray was crazy enough to be a protester
and date the doctor he was protesting, all that proves is that he was a
really bizarre character. Someone that bizarre could set fire to a clinic to
kill his girlfriend, while convincing his accomplice that she was acting
as part of God's army. I know it's a bit convoluted. But, that's Mr. Barron's
problem, not mine.

"Second, Mr. Barron will undoubtedly get up here and make a big
deal about these phone records. I say it is much ado about nothing. Mr.
Barron stipulated that Stephen Gray made harassing calls to the clinic.
Where's the big surprise that he made harassing calls to Dr. Marsano at
her home and even in her car? And where's the surprise that she would
call him back to ask him to stop the harassment? So essentially, the phone
calls prove nothing.

"And that goes for my third point as well—the testimony of Larry
Bedell. Now I'm sure that Mr. Bedell means well. But there he is at his
convenience store, reading newspapers every day, seeing Dr. Marsano's
picture on the cover of the newspaper every day. And never, not once,
does it occur to him that he should call the police and report a very
strange coincidence, at least not until Susan O'Dell's lawyer walks into
his store. The lawyer asks some questions, makes a few suggestions, and
suddenly a memory pops into his brain. Maybe, just maybe, it's not a

memory at all, but an idea—an idea of how Larry Bedell can be the one who gets his picture in the newspaper. The evidence shows that this killer-dates-victim theory is just short of preposterous. It is certainly not reasonable.

"You promised to decide based on the evidence. Not prejudice. Not sympathy. On behalf of the people of the State of Washington and the public who needs to be protected from radicals who burn and kill, I ask you to keep your promise. Thank you very much."

Hayden struck his gavel the moment Franklin finished. "We'll take our morning recess until eleven," the judge announced. "Mr. Barron, my bailiff has just slipped me a note that you have a phone call in my secretary's office. The court will stand in recess."

"What could that be?" Peter said, with a puzzled expression. He shrugged and walked back through the door where the judge had just exited.

"Hello," Peter said, leaning against the secretary's desk.

"Peter? Oh good, this is Lynn. Gwen has gone into labor. She wants you here immediately. When can you come?"

"You've got to be kidding. She's not due for three weeks, and I have to start my final argument in Suzie O'Dell's murder trial in ten minutes. I can't leave right now. . . . oh, what am I going to do?"

"All I know is that she wants you here just as fast as you can get here," Lynn replied.

"Where is she?"

"She left for the hospital with her dad about ten minutes ago. I've been waiting on hold for you for the last five minutes."

"Is she close? What's going on?"

"Well, she told me her water broke about an hour ago. She started having mild, irregular contractions right after that."

Peter moaned into the phone. "What am I supposed to do, God?" he said. To that question, Lynn had no response.

"Maybe Cooper could give the final argument. . . . Lynn, let me get off the phone. I need to talk to some people here. Someone will call you back in about five minutes. You're at our house, right?"

"That's right. Hurry, Peter. Gwen seems almost irrationally desperate to know that you will make it in time. Bye."

Peter dashed out the judge's door back into the courtroom. Sally and Cooper were huddled in a tense conversation by the bar railing.

"Cooper, get Suzie and her parents, and meet me in the witness room immediately. Sally, come here," Peter commanded.

They met at the counsel table. "Listen," Peter said softly, lest the dozen reporters hovering by the bar hear their conversation, "Gwen's gone into labor. Go call the airlines. Find out the quickest way to get me to Spokane, and then come to the witness room immediately."

"Are you going to give the final argument?"

"I don't know. I've got to talk to Cooper and the O'Dells. Maybe Coop could do it. This is just awful. I can't believe it. Why now?" He shook his head.

Sally led the way down the aisle, with Peter right behind, legal pad in hand. He jogged ten quick steps to the witness room while Sally headed out the back door.

"What was that call, Peter?" Cooper asked with a perplexed expression.

"It was about Gwen. She's gone into labor."

"Oh no!" Linda exclaimed. "What are you going to do? Will the judge let the trial stop until tomorrow or something?"

"I don't think so. And it would be a horrible thing in terms of legal strategy. We cannot let the jury have Franklin's final argument as the last thing they hear for twenty-four hours. I didn't really want this morning recess. I was planning to jump right up and start the process of unraveling what he had just done to us."

"He was pretty good, wasn't he?" Bill asked, with a glum voice.

Peter sighed loudly. "Real good," he said, shaking his head.

"What are our options?" Cooper asked.

"Well, there are really only two. Either I stay and make the argument and then leave after that, or, Cooper, you argue it to the jury after we explain to them why I had to leave."

"Do you think I could?" Cooper asked. "I've only argued a final jury argument once, and that was for a real estate case worth $30,000."

A panicked expression hit all three O'Dells at once. Suddenly the door opened, and Sally burst in the room. "Peter, I don't think you're going to like your options."

"Tell me," he commanded.

"The next flight from Seattle is in thirty minutes. That's impossible. The next flight after that isn't until 2:30 P.M. That gets you to the Spokane airport at 3:30. It'll be four before you could be at the hospital."

Peter sighed. "That'll be too late. What's the alternative."

"Well, you can charter a twin engine plane out of the Bellingham airport. The minimum lead time for departure is ninety minutes. If you left at 12:15, you'd be in Spokane at about 1:30. So what do you want me to do?"

Peter shrugged and threw up his hands. "Charter the plane. I can make the final argument, then leave after that."

Sally dashed out of the room.

"Cooper," Peter said, continuing in command mode, "all you will have to do is to say yes, Your Honor, and so on if the jury comes back today or tonight. Oh, if they convict her—listen I'm sorry I have to say this in front of you all—but Cooper, if they convict her, you'll need to ask the judge for permission to make the post-trial motions within the time allowed for in the rules rather than doing it immediately. You'll also have to ask the judge to continue her bail pending an appeal. Got that? Two things. Continue the post-trial motions. Ask to continue her bail. OK?"

"Yeah, I can do that," Cooper said, scribbling some notes.

"Suzie, I'm so sorry about all this. I was supposed to spend this time revising my notes to do a better job of presenting your final argument. There are only three minutes left," he said, glancing at his watch. "I want to at least look at the outline once. You all pray. I'll go back in the courtroom and prepare as best I can in three minutes."

Five minutes later, Peter rose to address the jury. Not a word had been said about his phone call or his wife. The lectern had been moved out of the way, giving Peter full range to roam.

He buttoned his suit jacket and smiled. He left his notes readily accessible on the table, but took nothing in his hands as he walked toward the edge of the jury box.

"Ladies and gentlemen of the jury, Mr. Franklin has put together an argument that I am sure sounds very good to many of you right now. But I would like to remind you of something Judge Hayden has said to you many, many times. Do not let yourself start deciding the case until everything is complete."

Peter held both hands lightly on the jury railing, trying not to look as stressed as he felt.

"In fact, this rule of waiting until the end to even begin deciding is a very ancient rule of American-English law. But its source can be found in an even more ancient source. In the Book of Proverbs, Solomon, the wisest man who ever lived, said, 'The first to present his case seems right, until another comes forward and questions him.' Let's do that now. Let's ask some reasonable and honest questions about Mr. Franklin's theories and evidence.

  "Mr. Franklin seems to believe that any witness that supports Suzie O'Dell is a conniving manipulator. But any witness that supports his position should be accepted at face value. I don't think we ought to quickly conclude that anybody from either side of this case is lying or conniving. Common sense and experience tell us that most people who have no direct interest in a case will tell the truth when they come to court. And that is the way we have tried this case. Both Suzie O'Dell and I have approached the case this way.

  "You obviously remember the testimony of Rachel Grove, who testified about Suzie talking about God's army. Mr. Franklin makes much of her testimony. But do you remember what Suzie O'Dell said when I asked her about Rachel's statement? Do you remember?" Peter stopped in front of the jury box and looked each juror in the eye. "Suzie said that Rachel was telling the truth. This shows a major difference between our approach compared to Mr. Franklin's approach to the evidence. Mr. Franklin claims that everybody who disagrees with him is lying. We have faced the person who delivered the most damaging testimony of all and said, 'Yes, she's telling the truth.' Mr. Franklin is quick to find conspiracies and liars and cheats and manipulators among ordinary citizens who are much like each of you. Remember what he said about Larry Bedell? Most people tell the truth and are not liars or cheats or conspirators like Mr. Franklin so quickly asserts."

  Peter took two steps toward the right end of the jury box and stopped again. "Suzie's admission about Rachel also shows you that she is honest—not a liar or conspirator or murderer like Mr. Franklin claims. It would have been easy for Suzie to say, 'Oh no, Rachel remembers it wrong. I didn't say those words. Stephen Gray did.' Suzie could have lied—but she didn't. Mr. Franklin says she lies about everything else and she's a manipulator and a radical. Ladies and gentlemen, I would suggest to you that a smart, manipulating, radical liar would have found a way to manipulate and lie about the conversation with Rachel.

"What evidence has Mr. Franklin really produced? He has a videotape of Suzie holding a gas can at Fred Meyer. And yes, Suzie's fingerprints are on this gas can, and the can was found at the scene of the crime. But Mr. Franklin has no evidence, I repeat, *no evidence whatsoever* that brings Suzie any closer to the crime scene than the Fred Meyer store. And there are a good couple of miles between the two. I would suggest to you, ladies and gentlemen of the jury, that this two-mile gap is the gap that precludes you all from returning a guilty verdict in this case.

"Where are any witnesses who saw Suzie being picked up by Stephen Gray on Friday evening? There are no witnesses because it never happened. Where are any witnesses who saw Suzie at the scene? There are no witnesses because Suzie was never there. And if Suzie O'Dell is a radical like Patty Hearst, why didn't she run off with her fellow radical, Stephen Gray, when he disappeared? When you join a radical army, you don't go back to your dorm room and sleep late the next morning, then go to class and take finals and turn in reports. No, like Patty Hearst, you disappear. You issue manifestoes. You fall in love with your fellow radicals.

"You've heard the evidence. Stephen Gray was a very good-looking fellow who was quite the ladies' man. If he had succeeded in getting Suzie to help him commit murder and arson, do you think for a minute he would have failed to take her with him when he disappeared? Talk about wild speculation! Mr. Franklin's Patty Hearst theory is truly wild speculation. There is not one shred of evidence that supports it. The best insight we can get about that statement is to look at the pattern of Suzie O'Dell's life. She is a good student. An obedient—not a rebellious—teenager, as her parents both told you. She never gave them a moment of real worry. Yeah, she sped a few times. Got home late a few times. But drugs? alcohol? premarital sex? No. Suzie didn't do any of these things because she'd been taught they were wrong. I think you saw in Suzie's face and countenance that she was genuinely embarrassed when I made her confess for the first time in front of her parents that she had discussed the idea of premarital sex with her boyfriend. However, all she did was talk. Her Christian conviction and her father's instruction were stronger than an isolated discussion. She stuck by her convictions and her upbringing when it came to the big things.

"She did the same thing in this one conversation witnessed by Rachel. It was an intriguing idea to explore. To have a three-or four-sentence discussion. But that was it. It never went beyond three or four sentences. She thought about it. And she went back to her bedrock convictions.

"Now ask yourself a common sense question. Do we have more problems in this country with teenagers committing murder and arson for political reasons? Or do we have more problems with teenage sexuality? I would submit to you that it makes little sense to believe that a girl with the moral conviction to resist premarital sex with her boyfriend would suddenly fall prey to a three- or four-sentence discussion and subsequently commit murder and arson. It just doesn't add up. Yet upon that one conversation Mr. Franklin has tried to build a bridge between the checkout counter of Fred Meyer and the ashes of the clinic. That evidence cannot be stretched that far."

Peter turned his back on the jury and returned to stand behind his chair for just a moment. He picked up his legal pad, read for ten seconds, and sat it back down. Still gripping his chair, he said, "When you analyze Mr. Franklin's evidence, he is asking you to believe a charade orchestrated by Stephen Gray. Let's talk about that charade for a moment. Why would Stephen Gray charge a purchase of bomb materials with a Visa card? Why would he throw a gas can away, knowing full well that it carried Suzie O'Dell's fingerprints? I'll tell you the reason I think Stephen Gray paid for the purchase with the Visa card—I think he wanted the purchase to be discovered. I think he wanted to get this fire blamed on the pro-lifers with whom he was *publicly* associated.

"Privately, Stephen Gray was associated with a different group of people. He had a romantic relationship with Dr. Rhonda Marsano. He called her at home. She called him at home. Conversations that lasted several minutes. Threatening calls don't last longer than a minute or two. And whoever heard of a person calling the car phone of a person who has been harassing her and pleading with him for several minutes to stop the harassment?

"Car phone numbers are not easily obtained. How did Rhonda Marsano get Gray's number, and how did she get his? If they had a relationship, as Larry Bedell—an honest citizen in this community—testified, it makes a lot of sense that they would have each other's unlisted car phone and home phone numbers.

"But I believe that the secret relationships Gray carried on go beyond his romance with Dr. Marsano. I believe that he was employed by the owners of this clinic. I may not have enough evidence today to convict them of conspiracy with Gray, but I believe I have at least as much evidence on the subject as Mr. Franklin has to prove that Suzie O'Dell was involved in a conspiracy.

"First of all, you all saw for yourselves how protective of her unlisted home phone number Karen Ballentine was. Now, ask yourself, if Stephen Gray is a religious nut and part-time pizza manager from Ferndale, how is he going to have the ability to find her secret unlisted number in Los Angeles—and, by the way, how does a part-time pizza manager afford a car phone to begin with?"

Peter briefly rubbed the back of his neck as he picked up the speed of his pacing.

"Stephen Gray was the one who urged the pro-life group to be more aggressive than Colonel Danners and the other leaders wanted. Whose interest would aggression have served? As you heard Colonel Danners testify, Gray's aggressive approach only strengthened the hand of the clinic owners in federal court. Whose interest would have been served if the pro-lifers were blamed for this fire by the actions of a person so careless as to buy firebomb supplies with a Visa card in a store that has clearly marked and clearly announced video cameras? It was the owners of this clinic who now have their political opponents as a scapegoat. So whose interest was served? I suggest it was the same people who gave Stephen Gray their unlisted home phone number. I suggest that they were the ones who made it possible for Gray to afford things like a cellular phone, while living on the salary of a part-time pizza parlor manager.

"Karen Ballentine denied any knowledge of Stephen Gray when I put her on the witness stand. She denied that Gray knew Rhonda Marsano. She even told you that she had a convenient conversation with the doctor about Stephen Gray—remember what she said about watching the videotape together? This made it possible for her to say with certainty that Doctor Marsano didn't know Gray. And yet, we now know that she did."

Peter walked back as close to Franklin's table as he dared. "Now Mr. Franklin here," he said, gesturing, "suggested that Larry Bedell was lying about seeing Rhonda Marsano in his store because he wanted to get his name in the newspaper. Again, like I told you at the beginning, most people who are not personally involved tell the truth in court. I am suggesting that Larry Bedell told the truth and Karen Ballentine is the one who was lying. Remember that she told you she had never talked to Stephen Gray on the phone or otherwise? And again, we know from the phone records that her statement was not true.

"When you get back into the jury deliberation room, I would ask you to read carefully instruction number 14, which tells that if a person is found to be untruthful in one part of testimony, you should feel free to disbelieve testimony in other areas. We have proven that Karen Ballentine lied about never talking to Stephen Gray. She lied when she said Dr. Marsano did not know Stephen Gray. Therefore, instruction 14 says you can discount her when she says that she did not hire Stephen Gray to burn down her clinic. You can disbelieve her when she says she had no idea how Dr. Marsano got the bump on her head the night she died.

"No one has attempted to explain what the true victim—Dr. Marsano—was doing there late at night. Why couldn't she escape from the clinic when it caught on fire? I think the bump on her head has something to do with an explanation."

Peter walked back over to the jury box and held onto the railing. "The next thing I am about to tell you may surprise you. Even though I believe the theory I have described for you, that Ms. Ballentine hired Stephen Gray and that she and her partner are the real coconspirators, because of the quantity and quality of the evidence, I could not in good conscience tell you that you could convict them on this evidence. Why?

Because to convict someone of a crime, proof beyond a reasonable doubt is required.

"Likewise, the evidence against Suzie O'Dell falls far, far short of proving beyond a reasonable doubt that she conspired, that she set fire to the clinic, and that she killed Dr. Marsano."

Peter turned, slowly walked over to Suzie O'Dell, and stood directly behind her. He put his hands on her shoulders and looked one by one at each of the jurors. "Do you have any reason to doubt that Suzie O'Dell is guilty of these horrible crimes? Well, if you do, it is your solemn and sacred responsibility to return a verdict of not guilty on all four charges. May God grant you wisdom as you deliberate."

As Peter turned to sit down, he looked desperately around the courtroom to see if he could spot Sally. Finally he saw her in a far corner. She gave him a thumbs-up sign and then pointed at her watch. Peter had taken his whole hour, and it was time to leave.

He had thoughts of asking the judge for permission to leave before Franklin completed his rebuttal, but decided against it.

The prosecutor rose and walked not to the lectern, but to the jury railing where Peter had spent so much of his time.

"Ladies and gentlemen of the jury, you have just witnessed the work of a master. A master storyteller, that is. Mr. Barron has woven the most imaginative story I have ever heard.

"He takes a phone record and an admittedly faulty memory of a store clerk and weaves it not just into a tale of supposed romance, but now the story is embellished into a phantasmagorical mystery.

"Let me wrap this up with just a couple of questions. Who is on the video buying fire bomb materials, Suzie O'Dell or Karen Ballentine? Whose fingerprints are at the scene of the fire, Suzie O'Dell or Karen Ballentine? Who talked about joining God's army, Suzie O'Dell or Karen

Ballentine? Who would burn down the clinic and murder a doctor providing needed services to young women? A radical-talking protester named Suzie O'Dell or a woman whose life work has been to provide services to women who need help, named Karen Ballentine?"

Franklin shook his head. "Reasonable doubt is not doubt based on fantasies. Reasonable doubt must be based on evidence. What evidence is there that is the equivalent of the videotape of the purchase of the murder weapon?

"Ladies and gentlemen, you should reject unreasonable doubts and return a verdict of guilty on all charges." Franklin glared at Peter as he passed by on his way back to his seat.

"Well, ladies and gentlemen. You have heard from two of our state's finest lawyers," Hayden said. "Now, I am confident that you will follow my instructions and apply the evidence you have heard in the courtroom and render a just verdict in due course. Please rise and take your oaths."

The jury stood and raised their hands.

"Do each of you promise to well and truly try this case in accordance with the evidence and the law as I have instructed you?"

Seven women and five men said, "I do."

"The bailiff will now escort you to the jury room and give you your copy of the instructions. You are dismissed."

As soon as the door closed behind the last juror, Peter popped immediately to his feet. "Your Honor, I have had a bit of a personal emergency arise. The call I took at the last recess informed me that my wife has gone into labor. I have chartered a small plane to get back to Spokane as soon as possible. I would like to leave Mr. Cooper in charge in my stead to receive the verdict and to conduct any further proceedings that the court would direct."

"That's fine, Mr. Barron, and we all wish you and your wife well. You are dismissed now if you'd like."

"Thank you, Your Honor."

There was light drizzle on the windshield of the twin-engine Cessna that buzzed down the Bellingham runway. "Moderate chop until we get over the Cascades" had been the prediction of pilot Chuck Edwards. The plane was less than half the size of the commuter airline planes that scared Peter so badly before. But today his mind was so occupied with concern for his wife and anxiety for the progress of the jury that he only thought about his fear of little planes when there was a severe jolt. Unfortunately, that seemed to happen about every twenty or thirty seconds.

Strapped into the copilot's seat, Peter played the final argument over and over again in his mind. Every time he revisited his performance, he thought of things he had left out and things he should have said instead. *If only I hadn't been so distracted with thoughts of Gwen and the baby,* he thought over and over again, followed by guilt for thinking negative things about the impending birth of his child. The vicious cycles of self-recrimination were punctuated by flashes of fear whenever the little plane was jostled by an air pocket. No matter whether he thought about the trial, the baby and Gwen, or the flight, Peter simply couldn't shake the ominous feeling that something bad was going to happen.

Fifty miles past the Cascades, the clouds and intermittent rain showers dissipated and were replaced with strong gusty headwinds that slowed the ground speed of the plane by fifteen to twenty miles an hour. Although the winds made the ride even more bumpy, Peter felt marginally more comfortable because he could see the ground.

"What time do you think we're going to land?" Peter asked about forty-five minutes into the flight.

"The flight plan called for a 1:25 P.M. landing. I think its gonna be more like 1:35 with this headwind. It's just too strong for this little plane."

"Oh no," Peter sighed. The sense of impending doom welled up again with his own words.

"I'm sure everything will turn out OK," the pilot replied hastily. "I've flown in this kind of wind before."

"I hope so," Peter said in a voice that sounded far less hopeful.

Within twenty minutes, the scab lands and sage brush gave way to lakes and the first few Ponderosa pines. A few minutes later, an FAA air traffic controller was guiding the Cessna into Spokane. Peter sprang out the door as soon as the pilot had it opened. It felt funny to navigate his way down the narrow staircase off the plane with both hands free—he had left his briefcase with Cooper, and his suitcase and all his clothes were still spread all over his room at the Bellingham Holiday Inn Express. As he hit the pavement, he suddenly realized that he was not in the main commercial terminal, where he had planned to grab a taxi straight to the hospital. "How am I supposed to catch a taxi from this terminal?" he shouted, more to himself than anyone else, as he stood frozen on the tarmac looking madly around him.

"You aren't supposed to, buddy-boy."

Peter whirled around to find the source of the familiar voice. Aaron Roberts, Lynn's husband, was waiting on the other side of a chain link fence.

"Aaron! Oh, wonderful! How do I get to you?" Peter cried out happily.

"Just run through that little building and out the front door. No baby yet, but hurry!"

Within half a minute, Aaron's BMW squealed out the driveway of the commuter terminal.

"So what's her status?" Peter asked, breathing hard more out of excitement than exertion.

"It won't be long now, according to Lynn. I just talked to her on the car phone."

"Are they worried about the baby—I mean, she is three weeks early?"

"If they are, they aren't saying anything to Lynn," Aaron answered.

"Oh, man," Peter moaned, rubbing his forehead. "It wasn't supposed to happen like this. I just have this sinking feeling that something's gonna go wrong. It's an awful feeling. I can't discern whether it's the trial or the baby. And until just a minute or two ago, I was worried it might be the airplane. I just can't shake this heavy, dark sensation."

"Yeah, I know what you're talking about, Peter. I have the same kind of feeling from time to time. It's really awful. But you know what? Ninety-nine percent of the time, nothing bad ever happens when I feel that way. I think it's a temptation to worry when we should pray and trust God. I don't think such feelings are worth much of anything in terms of their reliability."

A weight fell off Peter's spirit with those words. Instead of feeling heavy and down, he just felt spent—the kind of feeling he would have when a really bad headache finally went away. "Oh, Aaron, I hope you're right. I couldn't stand it if something went wrong with either Gwen and the baby or with Suzie's trial."

Soon Aaron pulled under the overhang protecting the entry to Sacred Heart Hospital and dropped Peter off. Peter ran through the automatic doors, dashed to the elevator, and repeatedly hit the button for the ninth floor until the door began to close. He tapped impatiently on the polished chrome-colored door as the numbers slowly went by on the display overhead. Peter was out the door before it was fully opened. Two nurses, friends of Gwen's when she had worked at Sacred Heart, were standing by to help Peter discard his suit jacket and jump into the required hospital green coveralls.

Gwen's face was contorted in the pain of a contraction when Peter finally dashed into the birthing room. "Gwen, honey—"

A nurse grabbed his arm and signaled for him to hush. "Tell her when the contraction's over. It'll just be a few seconds now."

Her face began to change back to a more normal look. The nurse released her grip on Peter's arm, and he walked slowly over to his wife. "Gwen, I'm here, honey."

"Finally," she said between huffs and sighs as she tried to recover from her last contraction.

"How far along are you?" he asked.

Her breathing was still hard. Gwen looked at the nurse, "Tell him," she panted.

"She was dilated to nine when we last checked about ten minutes ago."

"Vickie," Gwen panted, "get the doctor. I think I feel an urge to push."

Vickie disappeared in an instant, and Peter felt a flash of panic. He and Gwen had gone through all the classes and he knew what to do, yet he felt totally helpless and unprepared.

Fortunately, the nurse was back in the room in just under a minute with Gwen's obstetrician hot on her heels.

"Well, Gwen," he said in a warm, matter-of-fact voice, "Vickie here says you are having an urge to push. Let's check and see how we're doing."

"Nooo," Gwen groaned in protest of the idea of an examination just as a contraction overtook her.

Peter's heart beat faster and faster during the next ten minutes as the contractions and the pushing and the yelling seemed to come in ever faster waves.

"Mr. Barron has an urgent call from Bellingham," a new nurse suddenly said loudly from the door way.

Vickie was the only one capable right then of responding. "Nothing's more urgent than what's going on in this room. Put the call on hold and tell the caller to wait!" she yelled.

Peter felt close to fainting as his mind swirled.

The intensity of the doctor and nurse increased even more, and in a few seconds, a cry was heard, followed by a matter-of-fact declaration by the doctor, "It's a boy." Peter's heart beat wildly as he heard these words. They continued to work steadily for another minute or so as the cord was cut and the baby was wrapped in a bundle of warm blankets.

"Peter! Congratulations, Peter!" Vickie said moments later. "You have a beautiful son. He's just a little small, but he looks perfect. Here, why don't you hold him while we finish up with Gwen?" Vickie held out a tiny bundle for Peter, who took him gently in his arms. Slowly he eased into a rocking chair, with a dazed glow on his face and looked into his son's face. "I can't believe it," he said, with quiet amazement. "A son." He turned and looked at his wife. "Gwen, you did it. It's a son! He's gorgeous."

"Uh-huh," she sighed happily.

"Mr. Barron," the nurse said from the doorway again, "do you want to take this call? The people say you really need to come to the phone."

Vickie took charge of the helpless attorney. "OK, Peter," she said, "hand me your son and go take that stupid call. We can handle it for a minute."

"Hello?" Peter said, still dazed.

"It's Cooper, Peter. Sorry to interrupt. The jury has come back with a verdict. I thought you should know."

"You're kidding," Peter said with a heavy sigh. The feeling of doom he'd had on the plane welled up once again into his mind. He'd already convinced himself that if the verdict came back quickly, then it was a bad sign.

"Yeah, Judge Hayden said it was the fastest not guilty he'd ever seen in a first degree murder case—isn't that great?!"

"You're kidding!" Peter exclaimed. "But what about the other counts?"

"Not guilty. Everything. You won a total acquittal! Here, Suzie wants to talk to you."

"Mr. Barron, thank you so much. But please, tell us about your baby."

"He just arrived about ten minutes ago. He's a beautiful little boy."

Suzie was crying. "That's so wonderful. You must be even happier than I am. You have a new son, and I feel like I have a new life. And I'll tell you something . . . if God ever gives me a son, I'm going to name him Peter."

It was late July when a pair of men dressed in polyester slacks and blue blazers appeared in the reception area of the Los Angeles head-quarters of the chain of women's choice clinics.

"Morning, ma'am," said the older member of the duo. "Are Jane Hayward and Karen Ballentine in?"

The receptionist paused from her typing and carefully eyed the visitors. "I'm sorry, gentlemen," she said smoothly. "I don't believe I have you on the appointment book."

"No, ma'am, I'm sure you don't," the leader replied. "But it is vital that we speak with both Ms. Hayward and Ms. Ballentine."

"May I have your names and see if they are available?"

"Certainly. I'm Marty Riveria and my partner here is Dan Roberts—Kennewick Police Department."

"OK, let me see," the receptionist replied, fumbling with the buttons on the phone. "Jane, this is Jenna. Marty Riveria and Dan Roberts are here to see you. . . . No, they're not on the appointment book, but they're from the Kennewick Police Department."

Less than two minutes later, the officers were seated across from Hayward and Ballentine in their plush conference room. "What can we do for you gentlemen?" Jane asked in her low voice.

"Well, we're here to talk with you about the death of two men who happened to tumble off a bridge in our town. One was named Vince Davis and the other was Daniel McDougal."

"Never heard of either of them," Karen replied curtly.

"Well, they had both heard of you, or so it would seem. We found some extensive notes and papers in Mr. Davis's apartment that would indicate an interesting business arrangement with your operation. And, it took some cooperation from the Attorney General of Illinois, but we were eventually able to get a note or two from Mr. McDougal's files that made us believe you had hired him as well."

Jane's face turned white, while Karen appeared red hot. It was Karen who spoke next. "We have nothing to say to you other than we want our lawyer."

"Funny you should mention that," Riveria replied. "We were just about to advise you both that you had the right to a lawyer before you answered any of our questions. Ladies, we have to wait for the arrival of our deputy prosecutor who is at the courthouse getting an extradition order to make it official, but you might as well start getting your things together, because you are both under arrest for murder."